A Lady of Expectations

STEPHANIE LAURENS

MIRA

First published 1995. This edition 2008.
MIRA Books, Eton House, 18-24 Paradise Road,
Richmond, Surrey, TW9 1SR

© Stephanie Laurens 1995

ISBN 978 0 7783 0228 5

011-0408

Printed in Great Britain
by Clays Ltd, St Ives plc

Set against a Regency backdrop, in *A Lady of Expectations*, Stephanie Laurens introduces the Lester family. The Lesters were the first family Stephanie created where different books dealt with the romances of siblings, and as such were the precursors of many of Stephanie's subsequent books.

In *A Lady of Expectations*, Lenore's oldest brother Jack discovers that wooing the lady of his choice requires far more effort than he's imagined!

Stephanie lives in a suburb of Melbourne, Australia, with her husband and two daughters. To learn more about Stephanie's books visit her website at www.stephanielaurens.com.

7 0 0 0 0 0 0 0 3 3 5 8 8

Also by **Stephanie Laurens**

THE REASONS FOR MARRIAGE
AN UNWILLING CONQUEST
A COMFORTABLE WIFE

A Lady of
Expectations

CHAPTER ONE

"LADY ASFORDBY, OF ASFORDBY GRANGE, requests the pleasure of the company of Mr. Jack Lester, of Rawling's Cottage, and guests, at a ball."

Ensconced in an armchair by the fireplace, a glass of brandy in one long-fingered hand, the white card of Lady Asfordby's invitation in the other, Jack Lester made the pronouncement with ill-disguised gloom.

"She's the *grand dame* of these parts, ain't she?" Lord Percy Almsworthy was the second of the three gentlemen taking their ease in the parlour of Jack's hunting box. Outside, the wind howled about the eaves and tugged at the shutters. All three had ridden to hounds that day, taking the field with the Quorn. But while both Jack and his brother Harry, presently sprawled on the chaise, were clipping riders, up with the best of them, Percy had long ago taken Brummel's lead, indefatigable in turning out precise to a pin but rarely venturing beyond the first field. Which explained why he was now idly pacing the room, restless, while the brothers lounged, pleasantly exhausted, with the look about them of men not willing to stir. Pausing by the fireplace, Percy looked down on his host. "Lend a bit of colour to your stay, what? Besides," he added, turning to amble once more, "You never know—might see a golden head that takes your eye."

"In this backwater?" Jack snorted. "If I couldn't find any golden head worth the attention last Season—nor during the Little Season—I don't give much for my chances here."

"Oh, I don't know." Unconsciously elegant, Harry Lester lounged on the chaise, one broad shoulder propped against a cushion, his thick golden locks rakishly dishevelled. His sharply intelligent green eyes wickedly quizzed his elder brother. "You seem remarkably set on this start of yours. As finding a wife has become so important to you, I should think it behoves you to turn every stone. Who knows which one hides a gem?"

Blue eyes met green. Jack grunted and looked down. Absent-mindedly, he studied the gilt-edged card. Firelight glinted over the smooth waves of his dark hair and shadowed his lean cheeks. His brow furrowed.

He had to marry. He had inwardly acknowledged that fact more than twenty months ago, even before his sister, Lenore, had married the Duke of Eversleigh, leaving the burden of the family squarely on his shoulders.

"Perseverance—that's what you need." Percy nodded to no one in particular. "Can't let another Season go by without making your choice—waste your life away if you're too finicky."

"I hate to say it, old son," Harry said. "But Percy's right. You can't seriously go for years looking over the field, turning your nose up at all the offerings." Taking a sip of his brandy, he eyed his brother over the rim of his glass. His green eyes lit with an unholy gleam. "Not," he added, his voice soft, "unless you allow your good fortune to become known."

"Heaven forbid!" Eyes narrowing, Jack turned to Harry. "And just in case you have any ideas along that track, perhaps I should remind you that it's our good fortune—yours and mine and Gerald's, too?" Features relaxing, Jack sank back in his chair, a smile erasing the severe line of his lips. "Indeed, the chance of seeing *you* playing catch-me-who-can with all the enamoured damsels is sorely tempting, brother mine."

Harry grinned and raised his glass. "Fear not—that thought has already occurred. If the *ton* stumbles onto our secret, it won't be through me. And I'll make a point of dropping a quiet word in our baby brother's ear, what's more. Neither you nor I need him queering our pitch."

"Too true." Jack shuddered artistically. "The prospect does not bear thinking of."

Percy was frowning. "I can't see it. Why not let it out that you're all as rich as bedammed? God knows, you Lesters have been regarded as nothing more than barely well-to-do for generations. Now that's changed, why not reap the rewards?" His guileless expression was matched by his next words. "The debs would be yours for the asking—you could take your pick."

Both Lester men bent looks of transparent sympathy upon their hapless friend.

Bewildered, Percy blinked and patiently waited to be set aright.

Unable to hold a candle to his long-time companions in the matter of manly attributes, he had long since become reconciled to his much slighter figure, his sloping shoulders and spindly shanks. More than reconciled—he had found his vocation as a Pink of the *Ton*. Dressing to disguise his shortcomings and polishing his address to overcome his innate shyness had led to yet another discovery; his newfound status spared him from the trial of chasing women. Both Jack and Harry thrived on the sport, but Percy's inclinations were of a less robust nature. He adored the ladies—from a distance. In his estimation, his present style of life was infinitely preferable to the racy existence enjoyed by his companions.

However, as both Jack and Harry were well aware, his present lifestyle left him woefully adrift when it came to matters of strategy in handling the female of the species, particularly those dragons who menaced all rakes—the matrons of the *ton*.

And, naturally, with his mild manners and retiring ways, he was hardly the sort of gentleman who inhabited the debutantes' dreams. All the Lester men—Jack, at thirty-six, with his dark good looks and powerful athlete's physique, and Harry, younger by two years, his lithe figure forever graceful and ineffably elegant—and even twenty-four-year-old Gerald, with his boyish charm—were definitely the stuff of which females' dreams were made.

"Actually, Percy, old man," Harry said. "I rather suspect Jack thinks he can have his pick regardless."

Jack shot a supercilious glance at his sibling. "As a matter of fact, I've not previously considered the point."

Harry's lips lifted; gracefully, he inclined his head. "I have infinite confidence, oh brother mine, that if and when you find your particular golden head, you won't need the aid of our disgusting wealth in persuading her to your cause."

"Yes—but *why* the secrecy?" Percy demanded.

"Because," Jack explained, "while the matrons have considered my fortune, as you so succinctly put it, as barely well-to-do, they've been content to let me stroll among their gilded flowers, letting me look my fill without undue interference."

With three profligate sons in the family and an income little more than a competence, it was commonly understood that the scions of Lester Hall would require wealthy brides. However, given the family connections and the fact that Jack, as eldest, would inherit the Hall and principal estates, no one had been surprised when, once he had let it be known he was seriously contemplating matrimony, the invitations had rolled in.

"Naturally," Harry suavely put in. "With all Jack's years of…worldly experience, no one expects him to fall victim to any simple snares and, given the lack of a Lester fortune, there's insufficient incentive for the dragons to waste effort mounting any of their more convoluted schemes."

"So I've been free to view the field." Jack took back the conversational reins. "However, should any whiff of our changed circumstances begin circulating through the *ton,* my life of unfettered ease will be over. The harpies will descend with a vengeance."

"Nothing they like better than the fall of a rake," Harry confided to Percy. "Brings out their best efforts—never more hellishly inventive than when they've a rich rake with a declared interest in matrimony firmly in their sights. They relish the prospect of the hunter being the hunted."

Jack threw him a quelling glance. "Sufficient to say that my life will no longer be at all comfortable. I won't be able to set foot outside my door without guarding against the unimaginable. Debs at every turn, hanging on a fellow's arm, forever batting their silly lashes. It's easy to put one off women for life."

Harry shut his eyes and shuddered.

The light of understanding dawned on Percy's cherubic countenance. "Oh," he said. Then, "In that case, you'd better accept Lady Asfordby's invitation."

Jack waved a languid hand. "I've all the Season to go yet. No need to get in a pother."

"Ah, yes. But will you? Have all the Season, I mean?" When both Jack and Harry looked lost, Percy explained, "This fortune of yours was made on 'Change, wasn't it?"

Jack nodded. "Lenore took the advice of one of the pater's acquaintances and staked a fleet of merchantmen to the Indies. The company was formed through the usual channels and is listed in London."

"Precisely!" Percy came to a flourishing halt by the fireplace. "So any number of men with an interest at the

Exchange know the company was wildly successful. And lots of them must know that the Lesters were one of the major backers. That sort of thing's not secret, y'know. M'father, for one, would be sure to know."

Jack and Harry exchanged looks of dawning dismay.

"There's no way to silence all those who know," Percy continued. "So you've only got until one of those men happens to mention to his wife that the Lesters' fortunes have changed and the whole world will know."

A groan escaped Harry.

"No—wait." Jack straightened. "It's not that simple, thank God." The last was said with all due reverence. "Lenore organized it, but naturally she could hardly act for herself in the matter. She used our broker, old Charters, a terribly stuffy old soul. *He* has never approved of females being involved in business—the old man had to lean on him to accept instructions from Lenore years ago. Charters only agreed on the understanding of secrecy all round—he didn't want it known that he took orders from a woman. Which probably means he won't admit it was us he was working for, as it's fairly well known Lenore was in charge of our finances. If Charters doesn't talk, there's no reason to imagine our windfall will become common knowledge overnight."

Percy frowned and pursed his lips. "Not overnight, maybe. But dashed if I think it'll be all that long. These things filter through the cracks in the mortar, so my old man says."

A sober silence descended on the room as the occupants weighed the situation.

"Percy's right." Harry's expression was grim.

Glumly resigned, Jack held up Lady Asfordby's invitation. "In more ways than one. I'll send round to Lady Asfordby to expect us."

"Not me." Harry shook his head decisively.

Jack's brows rose. "You'll get caught in the storm, too."

Stubbornly, Harry shook his head again. He drained his glass and placed it on a nearby table. "*I* haven't let it be known I'm in the market for a wife, for the simple reason that I'm not." He stood, stretching his long, lean frame. Then he grinned. "Besides, I like living dangerously."

Jack returned the grin with a smile.

"Anyway, I'm promised at Belvoir tomorrow. Gerald's there— I'll tip him the wink over our desire for silence on the subject of our communal fortune. So you can proffer my regrets to her ladyship with a clear conscience." Harry's grin broadened. "Don't forget to do so, incidentally. You might recall she was an old friend of our late lamented aunt and can be a positive dragon—she'll doubtless be in town for the Season, and I'd rather not find myself facing her fire."

With a nod to Percy, Harry made for the door, dropping a hand on Jack's shoulder in passing. "I should inspect Prince's fetlock—see if that poultice has done any good. I'll be off early tomorrow, so I'll wish you good hunting." With a commiserating grin, he left.

As the door closed behind his brother, Jack's gaze returned to Lady Asfordby's invitation. With a sigh, he put it in his pocket, then took a long sip of his brandy.

"So, are we going?" Percy asked around a yawn.

Grimly, Jack nodded. "We're going."

While Percy went up to bed and the house settled to slumber around him, Jack remained in his chair by the fire, blue eyes intent on the flames. He was still there when, an hour later, Harry re-entered the room.

"What? Still here?"

Jack sipped his brandy. "As you see."

Harry hesitated for a moment, then crossed to the sideboard. "Musing on the delights of matrimony?"

Head back, Jack let his eyes track his brother's movements. "On the inevitability of matrimony, if you really want to know."

Sinking onto the chaise, Harry lifted a brow. "Doesn't have to be you, you know."

Jack's eyes opened wide. "Is that an offer—the ultimate sacrifice?"

Harry grinned. "I was thinking of Gerald."

"Ah." Jack let his head fall back and stared at the ceiling. "I have to admit I've thought of him, too. But it won't do."

"Why not?"

"He'll never marry in time for the pater."

Harry grimaced but made no answer. Like Jack, he was aware of their sire's wish to see his line continue unbroken, as it had for generations past. It was the one last nagging worry clouding a mind otherwise prepared for death.

"But it's not only that," Jack admitted, his gaze distant. "If I'm to manage the Hall as it should be managed, I'll need a chatelaine—someone to take on the role Lenore filled. Not the business side, but all the rest of it. All the duties of a well-bred wife." His lips twisted wryly. "Since Lenore left, I've learned to appreciate her talents as never before. But the reins are in my hands now, and I'll be damned if I don't get my team running in good order."

Harry grinned. "Your fervour has raised a good few brows. I don't think anyone expected such a transformation—profligate rakehell to responsible landowner in a matter of months."

Jack grunted. "You'd have changed, too, if the responsibility had fallen to you. But there's no question about it, I need a wife. One like Lenore."

"There aren't many like Lenore."

"Don't I know it." Jack let his disgruntlement show. "I'm seriously wondering if what I seek exists—a gentlewoman with charm and grace, efficient and firm enough to manage the reins."

"Blond, well-endowed and of sunny disposition?"

Jack shot his brother an irritated glance. "It certainly wouldn't hurt, given the rest of her duties."

Harry chuckled. "No likely prospects in sight?"

"Nary a one." Jack's disgust was back. "After a year of looking, I can truthfully inform you that not one candidate made me look twice. They're all so alike—young, sweet and innocent—and quite helpless. I need a woman with backbone and all I can find are clinging vines."

Silence filled the room as they both considered his words.

"Sure Lenore can't help?" Harry eventually asked.

Jack shook his head. "Eversleigh, damn his hide, was emphatic. His duchess will not be gracing the *ton's* ballrooms this Season. Instead," Jack continued, his eyes gently twinkling, "she'll be at home at Eversleigh, tending to her firstborn and his father, while increasing under Jason's watchful eye. Meanwhile, to use his words, the *ton* can go hang."

Harry laughed. "So she's really indisposed? I thought that business about morning sickness was an excuse Jason drummed up to whisk her out of the crowd."

Grimacing, Jack shook his head. "All too true, I fear. Which means that, having ploughed through last Season without her aid, while she was busy presenting Eversleigh with his heir, and frittered away the Little Season, too, I'm doomed to struggle on alone through the shoals of the upcoming Season, with a storm lowering on the horizon and no safe harbour in sight."

"A grim prospect," Harry acknowledged.

Jack grunted, his mind engrossed once more with marriage. For years, the very word had made him shudder. Now, with the ordeal before him, having spent hours contemplating the state, he was no longer so dismissive, so uninterested. It was his sister's marriage that had altered his view. Hardly the conventional image, for while Jason had married Lenore for a host of eminently conventional reasons, the depth of their love was apparent to all. The fond light that glowed in Jason's grey eyes whenever he looked at his wife had assured Jack that all was well with his sister—even more than Lenore's transparent joy. Any notion that his brother-in-law, ex-rake, for years the bane of the dragons, was anything other than besotted with his wife was simply not sustainable in the face of his rampant protectiveness.

Grimacing at the dying fire, Jack reached for the poker. He was not at all sure he wanted to be held in thrall as Jason, apparently without a qualm, was, yet he was very sure he wanted what his brother-in-law had found. A woman who loved him. And whom he loved in return.

Harry sighed, then stood and stretched. "Time to go up. You'd best come, too—no sense in not looking your best for Lady Asfordby's young ladies."

With a look of pained resignation, Jack rose. As they crossed to the sideboard to set down their glasses, he shook his head. "I'm tempted to foist the whole business back in Lady Luck's lap. She handed us this fortune—it's only fair she provide the solution to the problem she's created."

"Ah, but Lady Luck is a fickle female." Harry turned as he opened the door. "Are you sure you want to gamble the rest of your life on her whim?"

Jack's expression was grim. "I'm already gambling with the rest of my life. This damned business is no different from the turn of a card or the toss of a die."

"Except that if you don't like the stake, you can decline to wager."

"True, but finding the right stake is my problem."

As they emerged into the dark hall and took possession of the candles left waiting, Jack continued, "My one, particular golden head—it's the least Lady Luck can do, to find her and send her my way."

Harry shot him an amused glance. "Tempting Fate, brother mine?"

"Challenging Fate," Jack replied.

WITH A SATISFYING SWIRL of her silk skirts, Sophia Winterton completed the last turn of the Roger de Coverley and sank gracefully into a smiling curtsy. About her, the ballroom of Asfordby Grange was full to the seams with a rainbow-hued throng. Perfume wafted on the errant breezes admitted through the main doors propped wide in the middle of the long room. Candlelight flickered, sheening over artful curls and glittering in the jewels displayed by the dowagers lining the wall. "A positive pleasure, my dear Miss Winterton." Puffing slightly, Mr. Bantcombe bowed over her hand. "A most invigorating measure."

Rising, Sophie smiled. "Indeed, sir." A quick glance around located her young cousin, Clarissa, ingenuously thanking a youthful swain some yards away. With soft blue eyes and alabaster skin, her pale blond ringlets framing a heart-shaped face, Clarissa was a hauntingly lovely vision. Just now, all but quivering with excitement, she forcibly reminded Sophie of a highly strung filly being paraded for the very first time.

With an inward smile, Sophie gave her hand and her attention to Mr. Bantcombe. "Lady Asfordby's balls may not be as large as the assemblies in Melton, but to my mind, they're infinitely superior."

"Naturally, naturally." Mr. Bantcombe was still short of breath. "Her ladyship is of first consequence hereabouts— and she always takes great pains to exclude the *hoi polloi*. None of the park-saunterers and half-pay officers who follow the pack will be here tonight."

Sophie squelched a wayward thought to the effect that she would not really mind one or two half-pay officers, just to lend colour to the ranks of the gentlemen she had come to know suffocatingly well over the last six months. She pinned a bright smile to her lips. "Shall we return to my aunt, sir?"

She had joined her aunt and uncle's Leicestershire household last September, after waving her father, Sir Humphrey Winterton, eminent paleontologist, a fond farewell. Departing on an expedition of unknown duration, to Syria, so she believed, her father had entrusted her to the care of her late mother's only sister, Lucilla Webb, an arrangement that met with Sophie's unqualified approval. The large and happy household inhabiting Webb Park, a huge rambling mansion some miles from Asfordby Grange, was a far cry from the quiet, studious existence she had endured at the side of her grieving and taciturn sire ever since her mother's death four years ago.

Her aunt, a slender, ethereal figure draped in cerulean-blue silk, hair that still retained much of its silvery blond glory piled high on her elegant head, was gracefully adorning one of the chaises lining the wall, in earnest conversation with Mrs. Haverbuck, another of the local ladies.

"Ah, there you are, Sophie." Lucilla Webb turned as, with a smile and a nod for Sophie, Mrs. Haverbuck departed. "I'm positively in awe of your energy, my dear." Pale blue eyes took in Mr. Bantcombe's florid face. "Dear Mr. Bantcombe, perhaps you could fetch me a cool drink?"

Mr. Bantcombe readily agreed. Bowing to Sophie, he departed.

"Poor man," Lucilla said as he disappeared into the crowd. "Obviously not up to your standard, Sophie dear."

Sophie's lips twitched.

"Still," Lucilla mused in her gentle airy voice, "I'm truly glad to see you so enjoying yourself, my dear. You look very well, even if 'tis I who say so. The *ton* will take to you—and you to it, I make no doubt."

"Indeed the *ton* will, if your aunt and I and all your mother's old friends have anything to say about it!"

Both Sophie and Lucilla turned as, with much rustling to stiff bombazine, Lady Entwhistle took Mrs. Haverbuck's place.

"Just stopped in to tell you, Lucilla, that Henry's agreed—we're to go up to town tomorrow." Lifting a pair of lorgnettes from where they hung about her neck, Lady Entwhistle embarked on a detailed scrutiny of Sophie with all the assurance of an old family friend. Sophie knew that no facet of her appearance—the style in which her golden curls had been piled upon her head, the simple but undeniably elegant cut of her rose-magenta silk gown, her long ivory gloves, even her tiny satin dancing slippers—would escape inspection.

"Humph." Her ladyship concluded her examination. "Just as I thought. You'll set the *ton*'s bachelors back on their heels, m'dear. Which," she added, turning to Lucilla, a conspiratorial gleam in her eye, "is precisely to my point. I'm giving a ball on Monday. To introduce Henry's cousin's boy to our acquaintance. Can I hope you'll be there?"

Lucilla pursed her lips, eyes narrowing. "We're to leave at the end of the week, so I should imagine we'll reach London by Sunday." Her face cleared. "I can see no reason not to accept your invitation, Mary."

"Good!" With her habitual bustle, Lady Entwhistle stood, improbable golden ringlets bouncing. Catching sight of Clarissa through the crowd, she added, "It'll be an informal affair, and it's so early in the Season I see no harm in Clarissa joining us, do you?"

Lucilla smiled. "I know she'll be delighted."

Lady Entwhistle chuckled. "All wound tight with excitement, is she? Ah, well—just remember when we were like that, Lucy—you and I and Maria." Her ladyship's eyes strayed to Sophie, a certain anticipation in their depths. Then, with determined briskness, she gathered her reticule. "But I must away—I'll see you in London."

Sophie exchanged a quiet smile with her aunt, then, lips curving irrepressibly, looked out over the crowded room. If she were asked, she would have to admit that it was not only Clarissa, barely seventeen and keyed up to make her come-out, who was prey to a certain excitement. Beneath her composure, that of an experienced young lady of twenty-two years, Sophie was conscious of a lifting of her heart. She was looking forward to her first full Season.

She would have to find a husband, of course. Her mother's friends, not to speak of her aunt, would accept nothing less. Strangely, the prospect did not alarm her, as it certainly had years ago. She was more than up to snuff—she fully intended to look carefully and choose wisely.

"Do my eyes deceive me, or has Ned finally made his move?"

Lucilla's question had Sophie following her aunt's gaze to where Edward Ascombe, Ned to all, the son of a neighbour, was bowing perfunctorily over her cousin's hand. Sophie saw Clarissa stiffen.

A little above average height, Ned was a relatively serious young man, his father's pride and joy, at twenty-one already absorbed in caring for the acres that would, one day, be his. He was also determined to have Clarissa Webb to wife. Unfortunately, at the present moment, with Clarissa full of nervy excitement at the prospect of meeting unknown gentlemen up from London for the hunting, Ned was severely handicapped, suffering as he did from the twin disadvantages of being a blameless and worthy suitor and having known Clarissa all her life. Worse, he had already made it plain that his heart was at Clarissa's tiny feet.

Her sympathy at the ready, Sophie watched as he straightened and, all unwitting, addressed Clarissa.

"A cotillion, if you have one left, Clary." Ned smiled

confidently, no premonition of the shaky ground on which he stood showing in his open countenance.

Eyes kindling, Clarissa hissed, "Don't call me that!"

Ned's gentle smile faded. "What the d-deuce *am* I to call you? *Miss Webb?*"

"Exactly!" Clarissa further elevated her already alarmingly tilted chin. Another young gentleman hovered on her horizon; she promptly held out her hand, smiling prettily at the newcomer.

Ned scowled in the same direction. Before the slightly shaken young man could assemble his wits, Ned prompted, "My dance, *Miss Webb?*" His voice held quite enough scorn to sting.

"I'm afraid I'm not available for the cotillion, *Mr. Ascombe.*" Through the crowd, Clarissa caught her mother's eyes. "Perhaps the next country dance?"

For a moment, Sophie, watching, wondered if she and Lucilla would be called upon to intervene. Then Ned drew himself up stiffly. He spoke briefly, clearly accepting whatever Clarissa had offered, then bowed and abruptly turned on his heel.

Clarissa stood, her lovely face blank, watching his back until he was swallowed up by the crowd. For an instant, her lower lip softened. Then, chin firming, she straightened and beamed a brilliant smile at the young gentleman still awaiting an audience.

"Ah." Lucilla smiled knowingly. "How life does go on. She'll marry Ned in the end, of course. I'm sure the Season will be more than enough to demonstrate the wisdom of her heart."

Sophie could only hope so, for Clarissa's sake as well as Ned's.

"Miss Winterton?"

Sophie turned to find Mr. Marston bowing before her. A reserved but eminently eligible gentleman of independent means, he was the target of more than a few of the local matchmaking mamas. As she dipped in a smooth curtsy, Sophie inwardly cursed her guilty blush. Mr. Marston was enamoured—and she felt nothing at all in response.

Predictably interpreting her blush as a sign of maidenly awareness, Mr. Marston's thin smile surfaced. "Our quadrille, my dear." With a punctilious bow to Lucilla, who regally inclined her head, he accepted the hand Sophie gave him and escorted her to the floor.

Her smile charming, her expression serene, Sophie dipped and swayed through the complicated figures, conscious of treading a very fine line. She refused to retreat in confusion before Mr. Marston's attentions, yet she had no wish to encourage him.

"Indeed, sir," she replied to one of his sallies. "I'm enjoying the ball immensely. However, I feel no qualms about meeting those gentlemen up from London—after all, my cousin and I will shortly be in London ballrooms. Acquaintances made tonight could prove most comforting."

From her partner's disapproving expression, Sophie

deduced that the thought of her gaining comfort from acquaintance with any other gentleman, from London or elsewhere, was less than pleasing. Inwardly, she sighed. Depressing pretensions gently was an art she had yet to master.

About them, Lady Asfordby's guests swirled and twirled, a colourful crowd, drawn primarily from the local families, with here and there the elegant coats of those London swells of whom her ladyship approved. This distinction did not extend to all that many of the small army of *ton*-ish males who, during the hunting season, descended on the nearby town of Melton Mowbray, lured by the attraction of the Quorn, the Cottesmore and the Belvoir packs.

Jack realized as much as, with Percy hovering in his shadow, he paused on the threshold of her ladyship's ballroom. As he waited for his hostess, whom he could see forging her way through the crowd to greet him, he was conscious of the flutter his appearance had provoked. Like a ripple, it passed down the dark line of dowagers seated around the room, then spread in ever widening circles to ruffle the feathers of their charges, presently engaged in a quadrille.

With a cynical smile, he bowed elegantly over her ladyship's beringed fingers.

"So glad you decided to come, Lester."

Having smoothly introduced Percy, whom Lady Asfordby greeted with gratified aplomb, Jack scanned the dancers.

And saw her.

She was immediately in front of him, in the set nearest

the door. His gaze had been drawn to her, her rich golden curls shining like a beacon. Even as realization hit, his eyes met hers. They were blue, paler than his own, the blue of cloudless summer skies. As he watched, her eyes widened, her lips parted. Then she twirled and turned away.

Beside him, Percy was filling Lady Asfordby's ears with an account of his father's latest illness. Jack inhaled deeply, his eyes on the slim figure before him, the rest of the company a dull haze about her.

Her hair was true gold, rich and bountiful, clustered atop her neat head, artfully errant curls trailing over her small ears and down the back of her slender neck. The rest of her was slender, too, yet, he was pleased to note, distinctly well-rounded. Her delectable curves were elegantly gowned in a delicate hue that was too dark for a debutante; her arms, gracefully arching in the movements of the dance, displayed an attractive roundness not in keeping with a very young girl.

Was she married?

Suavely, Jack turned to Lady Asfordby. "As it happens, I have not met many of my neighbours. Could I impose on your ladyship to introduce me?"

There was, of course, nothing Lady Asfordby would have liked better. Her sharp eyes gleamed with fanatical zeal. "Such a loss, your dear aunt. How's your father getting on?"

While replying to these and similar queries on Lenore and his brothers, all of whom her ladyship knew of old, Jack kept his golden head in sight. Perfectly happy to disguise his intent by stopping to chat with whomever Lady Asfordby thought to introduce, he steered his hostess by inexorable degrees to the chaise beside which his goal stood.

A small knot of gentlemen, none of them mere youths, had gathered about her to pass the time between the dances. Two other young ladies joined the circle; she welcomed them graciously, her confidence as plain as the smile on her lips.

Twice he caught her glancing at him. On both occasions, she quickly looked away. Jack suppressed his smile and patiently endured yet another round of introductions to some local squire's lady.

Finally, Lady Asfordby turned towards the crucial chaise. "And, of course, you must meet Mrs. Webb. I dare say you're acquainted with her husband, Horatio Webb of Webb Park. A financier, you know."

The name rang a bell in Jack's mind—something to do with horses and hunting. But they were rapidly approaching the chaise on which an elegant matron sat, benignly watching over a very young girl, unquestionably her daughter, as well as his golden head. Mrs. Webb turned as they approached. Lady Asfordby made the introduction; Jack found himself bowing over a delicate hand, his eyes trapped in a searching, ice-blue stare.

"Good evening, Mr. Lester. Are you here for the hunting?"

"Indeed yes, ma'am." Jack blinked, then smiled, careful not to overdo the gesture. To him, Mrs. Webb was instantly recognizable; his golden head was protected by a very shrewd dragon.

A lifted finger drew the younger girl forward.

"Allow me to present my daughter, Clarissa." Lucilla looked on as Clarissa, blushing furiously, performed the regulation curtsy with her customary grace. Speech, however, seemed beyond her. Lifting one sceptical brow, Lucilla spared a glance for the magnificence before her, then slanted a quick look at Sophie. Her niece was studiously absorbed with her friends.

An imperious gesture, however, succeeded in attracting her attention.

Her smile restrained, Lucilla beckoned Sophie forward. "And, of course," she continued, rescuing Jack from Clarissa's tongue-tied stare, "you must let me introduce my niece, Miss Sophia Winterton." Lucilla halted, then raised her fine brows. "But perhaps you've met before—in London? Sophie was presented some years ago, but her Season was cut short by the untimely death of her mother." Switching her regal regard to Sophie, Lucilla continued, "Mr. Jack Lester, my dear."

Conscious of her aunt's sharply perceptive gaze, Sophie kept her expression serene. Dipping politely, she coolly extended her fingers, carefully avoiding Mr. Lester's eye.

She had first seen him as he stood at the door, darkly, starkly handsome. In his midnight-blue coat, which fitted his large lean frame as if it had been moulded to him, his thick dark hair falling in fashionable dishevelment over his broad brow, his gaze intent as he scanned the room, he had appeared as some predator—a wolf, perhaps—come to select his prey. Her feet had missed a step when his gaze had fallen on her. Quickly looking away, she had been surprised to find her heart racing, her breath tangled in her throat.

Now, with his gaze, an unnervingly intense dark blue, full upon her, she lifted her chin, calmly stating, "Mr. Lester and I have not previously met, Aunt."

Jack's gaze trapped hers as he took her hand. His lips curved. "An accident of fate which has surely been my loss."

Sophie sternly quelled an instinctive tremor. His voice was impossibly deep. As the undercurrent beneath his tones washed over her, tightening the vice about her chest, she watched him straighten from an ineffably elegant bow.

He caught her glance—and smiled.

Sophie stiffened. Tilting her chin, she met his gaze. "Have you hunted much hereabouts, sir?"

His smile reached his eyes. A small shift in position brought him closer. "Indeed, Miss Winterton."

He looked down at her; Sophie froze.

"I rode with the Quorn only yesterday."

Breathless, Sophie ignored the twinkle in his eye. "My uncle, Mr. Webb, is a keen adherent of the sport." A quick glance about showed her aunt in deep conversation with Lady Asfordby; her court was hidden by Mr. Lester's broad shoulders. He had, most effectively, cut her out from the crowd.

"Really?" Jack lifted a polite brow. His gaze fell to her hands, clasped before her, then rose, definite warmth in the deep blue. "But your aunt mentioned you had been in London before?"

Sophie resisted the urge to narrow her eyes. "I was presented four years ago, but my mother contracted a chill shortly thereafter."

"And you never returned to grace the ballrooms of the *ton*? Fie, my dear—how cruel."

The last words were uttered very softly. Any doubts Sophie had harboured that Mr. Lester was not as he appeared vanished. She shot him a very straight glance, irrelevantly noting how the hard line of his lips softened when he smiled. "My father was much cut up by my mother's death. I remained with him, at home in Northamptonshire, helping with the household and the estate."

His response to that depressing statement was not what she had expected. A gleam of what could only be intrigued interest flared in his dark eyes.

"Your loyalty to your father does you credit, Miss Winterton." Jack made the statement with flat sincerity. His companion inclined her head slightly, then glanced away. The perfect oval of her face was a delicate setting for her regular features: wide blue eyes fringed with long, thick lashes, golden brown as were her arched brows, a straight little nose and full bowed lips the colour of crushed strawberries. Her chin was definite, yet gently rounded; her complexion was like thick cream, rich and luscious, without flaw. Jack cleared his throat. "But did you not yearn to return to the *ton*'s ballrooms?"

The question took Sophie by surprise. She considered, then answered, "No. Indeed, the thought never arose. I had more than enough to occupy myself. And I frequently visited with my father's sisters at Bath and Tonbridge Wells." She glanced up—and laughed at the comical grimace that contorted her companion's face.

"Tonbridge Wells?" he uttered, dramatically faint. "My dear Miss Winterton, you would be *wasted* there, smothered beneath the weight of ageing propriety."

Sophie sternly suppressed a giggle. "Indeed, it wasn't very lively," she conceded. "Luckily, my mother had many friends who invited me to their house parties. However, at home, I must admit I oftimes pined for younger company. My father lived very much retired through that time."

"And now?"

"My aunt—" she nodded at Lucilla on the chaise which by some magic was now a step away "—persuaded Papa to take an interest in an expedition. He's a paleontologist, you see."

From beneath her lashes, she glanced up, waiting.

Jack met her innocent gaze, his own inscrutable. Despite her best efforts, Sophie's lips twitched. With a resigned air, Jack raised a languidly interrogatory brow.

This time, Sophie did giggle. "Old bones," she informed him, her voice confidingly low. Despite the fact he had just sidestepped a trap guaranteed to depress the pretensions of any overly confident rake, Sophie could not stop her smile.

As her eyes met his, warmly appreciative, the suspicion that while Mr. Lester might be demonstrably confident, he was not overly so, broke over her. Her breath became tangled again.

His gaze sharpened. Before she could react, and retreat, he lifted his head, then glanced down at her, his brows lightly lifting.

"Unless my ears are at fault, that's a waltz starting up. Will you do me the honour, Miss Winterton?"

The invitation was delivered with a calm smile, while his eyes stated, very clearly, that no feeble excuse would suffice to deflect him.

Nerves aquiver, Sophie surrendered to the inevitable with a suffocatingly gracious inclination of her head.

Her determinedly calm composure very nearly cracked when he swept her onto the floor. His arm about her felt like iron; there was such strength in him it would be frightening if it was not so deliberately contained. He whirled her down the floor; she felt like thistledown, lighter than air, anchored to reality only by his solidity and the warm clasp of his hand.

She had never waltzed like this before, precessing without conscious thought, her feet naturally following his lead, barely touching the floor. As her senses, stirred by his touch, gradually settled, she glanced up. "You dance very well, Mr. Lester."

His eyes glinted down at her from under heavy lids. "I've had lots of practice, my dear."

His meaning was very clear; she should have blushed and looked away. Instead, Sophie found enough courage to smile serenely before letting her gaze slide from his. Aware of the dangerous currents about her, she made no further attempt to converse.

For his part, Jack was content to remain silent; he had learned all he needed to know. Freed of the burden of polite conversation, his mind could dwell on the pleasure of having her, at long last, in his arms. She fitted perfectly, neither too tall nor, thankfully, too short. If she were closer, her curls would tickle his nose, her forehead level with his chin. She was not completely relaxed—he could not expect that—yet she was content enough in his arms. The temptation to tighten his hold, to draw her closer, was very real, yet he resisted. Too many eyes were upon them, and she did not yet know she was his.

The last chord sounded; he whirled them to a flourishing halt. He looked down, smiling as he drew her hand through his arm. "I will return you to your aunt, Miss Winterton."

Sophie blinked up at him. Could he hear her heart thudding? "Thank you, sir." Retreating behind a mask of cool formality, she allowed him to lead her back to the chaise. However, instead of leaving her by her aunt's side, her partner merely nodded at Lucilla, then led her to where her circle of acquaintances was once again forming. Larger than life, he stood beside her, acknowledging her introductions with a coolly superior air which, she suspected, was innate. Feeling her nerves stretch and flicker, Sophie glanced up as the musicians once more laid bow to string.

His eyes met hers. Suddenly breathless, Sophie looked away. Her gaze fell on Lady Asfordby, bustling up.

"Glad to see, Lester, that you're not one of those London dandies who think they're above dancing in country ballrooms."

Stifling a resigned sigh, Jack turned to his hostess, an amiable smile on his lips.

Her ladyship's gimlet gaze swept the assembled company, fixing on a bright-faced young lady. "Dare say Miss Elderbridge will be pleased to do you the honour."

Thus adjured, Jack bent a practiced smile on Miss Elderbridge, who assured him, somewhat breathlessly, that she would be delighted to partner him in the country dance about to begin. Hearing a murmur to his left, Jack glanced back to see Sophie place her hand on another gentleman's sleeve. They were both poised to move away, their partners by their sides. Jack grasped the moment, trapping Sophie's gaze in his, lowering his voice to say, "Until next we meet, Miss Winterton."

Sophie felt her eyes widen. Lowering her lashes, she inclined her head. As she moved to her place in the set, she felt his words reverberate deep within her. Her heart thudded; it was an effort to concentrate on Mr. Simpkins's conversation.

There had been a wealth of meaning hidden in Jack Lester's subtle farewell—and she had no idea whether he meant it or not.

CHAPTER TWO

HE DID MEAN IT.

That was the only logical conclusion left to Sophie when, poised to alight from the Webb family carriage in the shadow of the lych-gate the next morning, she caught sight of a pair of powerful shoulders, stylishly encased in the best Bath superfine, and then their owner, wending his way aimlessly through the gravestones. As if sensing her regard, he looked around and saw her. White teeth flashed as he smiled. Recalled to her surroundings by Clarissa's finger in her ribs, Sophie abruptly gathered her wits and descended.

In the protective confines of the lych-gate, she fussed with her reticule and the skirts of her cherry-red pelisse while her cousins, Jeremy, George and Amy, as well as Clarissa—at just six years old, the twins, Henry and Hermione, were too young to be trusted in church—descended and straightened their attire under their mother's eagle eye. Finally satisfied, Lucilla nodded and they fell into line, Amy beside her mother in the lead, Sophie and Clarissa immediately behind, followed by the two boys, their boots on the paving stones.

As they ascended the steps leading up from the gate,

Sophie carefully avoided glancing at the graveyard to their left, looking up, instead, at the sharp spire that rose into the wintry sky. March had arrived, unexpectedly mild. The chill blue of the heavens was dotted with puffs of white cloud, scudding along before the brisk breeze.

"Good morning, Mrs. Webb."

The cavalcade stopped. Although she could only see her aunt's back, Sophie had the distinct impression that even that redoubtable matron was taken aback by the sight of Jack Lester bowing elegantly before her just yards from the church door. His ambling peregrination had, most conveniently, converged with their route at that spot.

Regardless of her surprise, there was no doubt of her aunt's pleasure. Her "Mr. Lester, how fortunate. We had not looked to see you thus soon" positively purred with satisfaction. "Would you care to join us in our pew, sir?"

"I'd be delighted, ma'am." Until then, Jack had not looked Sophie's way. Now, smiling, he turned to her. "Good morning, Miss Winterton." He briefly nodded at Clarissa. "Miss Webb."

Sophie dipped and gave him her hand.

"Sophie dear, perhaps you would show Mr. Lester the way while I take care of this brood." Her aunt waved an airy hand at her offspring, who, of course, could very well have found their way unaided to the pew they occupied every Sunday.

"Of course, Aunt." Sophie knew better than to argue.

As Lucilla swept her children into the church, Sophie

risked a glance upwards, only to meet a pair of dark blue eyes that held a very large measure of amused understanding. Her own eyes narrowed.

"Miss Winterton?" With a gallant gesture, Jack offered his arm. When she hesitated, his brows rose slightly.

Head high, Sophie placed her fingers on his sleeve and allowed him to lead her to the door. As they entered the dim nave, she noted the smothered stir as their neighbours noticed her escort. It was close to eleven and the church was full. Hiding her consciousness behind a calm mask, she indicated the pair of pews, close to the front on the left, where her cousins were already settling. Glancing down as they passed the pew two rows behind, she encountered a malevolent stare from Mrs. Marston and a sternly disapproving one from her son, seated supportively beside her.

Suppressing a sudden grin, Sophie reflected that, as this was God's house, perhaps Mr. Lester was the Almighty's way of assisting her in the difficult task of rejecting Mr. Marston. She had no time to dwell on that unlikely prospect, however, for, gaining the second of the Webb pews, she found herself seated between Lucilla and Mr. Lester. Luckily, the vicar, Mr. Snodgrass, entered almost immediately.

To her relief, Mr. Lester behaved impeccably, as if going to church on Sunday were his normal habit.

Beside her, Jack bided his time.

When the congregation rose for the first hymn, he reached out and touched Sophie's gloved wrist. Leaning closer, he whispered, "I'm afraid, Miss Winterton, that I did not anticipate attending church during my stay in Leicestershire."

She blinked up at him, then glanced down at the slim volume covered in tooled blue leather that she had extracted from her reticule.

"Oh." With an effort, Sophie dragged her mind from the disturbing thought of what, exactly, *had* brought him to the tiny church of Allingham Downs. Her fingers busy flicking through the pages, she glanced up at him and hoped her distrust was evident. "Perhaps, sir, if I hold it between us, we could share my book?"

He smiled, so very sweetly that, if she had not known better, she would have thought his predicament an innocent oversight. Raising her chin, she held her hymnal between them, up and slightly to her right.

The organ swelled into the introduction. Even as she drew breath for the first note of the first verse, Sophie experienced an inner quake. He had moved closer, an action excused by the fine print of the hymnal. His shoulder was behind her, her shoulder close to his chest. She could sense the warmth of his large body, now so near—and feel the dagger glances of the Marstons, mother and son, on her back.

Her hand shook; his came up to steady the hymnal. She quelled the impulse to glance sideways—he was so close, his head bent, his eyes would be very near, his lips a potent distraction. With an effort, she concentrated on the music, only to be thoroughly distracted by the sound of his warm baritone, rich and strong, effortlessly supporting her soprano.

The hymn was one of praise—and an unexpected joy.

At its conclusion, Sophie felt slightly dizzy. She forced herself to breathe deeply.

Her companion hesitated; she knew his gaze was on her. Then he lifted the hymnal from her hand, gently closed it and presented it to her.

"Thank you, Miss Winterton."

It was impossible; she had to glance up. His eyes, darkly blue, warm and gently smiling, were every bit as close as she had imagined; his lips, softened by his smile, drew her gaze.

For a moment, time stood still.

With an enormous effort, Sophie dragged in a breath and inclined her head.

They were the last to sit down.

The sermon brought her no peace; indeed, Mr. Snodgrass would have needed to be inspired to compete with her thoughts, and the subtle tug of the presence beside her. She survived the second hymn only because she now understood the danger; she kept her mind totally focused on the lyrics and melody, ignoring her companion's harmony as best she could. Ignoring *him* proved even more difficult.

It was something of a relief to stroll slowly up the aisle, her hand on his sleeve. They were among the last to quit the church. Lucilla and her children preceded them; her aunt stopped on the porch steps to exchange her usual few words with the vicar.

"Sophia you know, of course." Lucilla paused as the vicar nodded, beamed and shook Sophie's hand. "But I'm not

sure if you've met Mr. Lester. From Rawling's Cottage."
Lucilla gestured at Jack, immediately behind Sophie.

"Indeed?" Mr. Snodgrass was an absent-minded old soul.
"I don't recall ever having met anyone from there." He
blinked owlishly up at Jack.

Sophie looked up in time to catch the reproachful glance
that Jack bent on her aunt, before, with ready courtesy, he
greeted the vicar.

"I'm rarely to be found in these parts, I'm afraid."

"Ah." The vicar nodded his head in complete understanding. "Up for the hunting."

Jack caught Sophie's eye. "Just so."

Sternly quelling a shiver, Sophie turned away. Her aunt
had stopped to chat with Mrs. Marston farther along the
path. Clarissa stood slightly to one side, cloaked in fashionable boredom. This last was attributable to Ned
Ascombe, standing some yards away, his expression similarly abstracted. Noting the quick, surreptitious glances
each threw the other, Sophie struggled not to smile. Feeling
immeasurably older than the youthful pair, she stepped off
the church steps and strolled slowly in her aunt's wake.

Jack made to follow but was detained by the vicar.

"I often used to ride with the Cottesmore, you know. Excellent pack, excellent. Major Coffin was the Master, then."
Launched on reminiscence, the old man rambled on.

From the corner of his eye, Jack watched Sophie join her
aunt, who was deep in discussion with a country matron, a
large figure, swathed in knitted scarves.

"And then there was Mr. Dunbar, of course…"

Jack stiffened as a dark-coated gentleman stepped around the country dame to accost Sophie. Abruptly, he turned to the vicar, smoothly breaking into his monologue. "Indeed, sir. The Cottesmore has always been a most highly qualified pack. I do hope you'll excuse me—I believe Miss Winterton has need of me."

With a nod, Jack turned and strode briskly down the path. He reached Sophie's side just in time to hear the unknown gentleman remark, in a tone that, to Jack, sounded a great deal too familiar, "Your aunt mentioned that she expected to remove to London at the end of the week. Dare I hope I may call on you before you depart?"

Inwardly, Sophie grimaced. "I'm sure, Mr. Marston, that my aunt will be delighted, as always, to entertain Mrs. Marston and yourself. However, I'm not certain of her plans for this week. It's so very complicated, transferring the whole family up to town."

Sensing a presence by her side, she turned and, with inexplicable relief, beheld her late companion. He was not looking at her, however, but at Mr. Marston, with a frown in his eyes if not on his face.

"I believe I introduced you to Mr. Marston last evening, Mr. Lester."

The dark blue gaze momentarily flicked her way. "Indeed, Miss Winterton." Apparently a distant nod was all the recognition Mr. Marston rated.

For his part, Phillip Marston had drawn himself up, his

thin lips pinched, his long nose elevated, nostrils slightly flaring. He returned Jack's nod with one equally curt. "Lester." He then pointedly turned back to Sophie. "I have to say, Miss Winterton, that I cannot help but feel that Mrs. Webb is being far too soft-hearted in allowing the younger children to accompany the party." His gaze grew stern as it rested on Jeremy and George, engaged in an impromptu game of tag about the gravestones. "They would be better employed at their lessons."

"Oh, no, Mr. Marston—just think how educational the trip will be." Sophie did not add that 'soft-hearted' was a singularly inappropriate adjective when used in conjunction with her aunt. Lucilla might appear as fragile as glass, but her backbone was pure steel. Sophie knew the combination well; her own mother had been just the same. "The children have been so looking forward to it."

"I should think, Marston, that Mr. and Mrs. Webb are well able to decide the right of such matters."

Sophie blinked. The coldly superior edge of Mr. Lester's deep voice was distinctly dismissive. She turned, only to find an elegant sleeve cloaking an arm she already knew to be steel before her.

"If I may, I'll escort you to your carriage, Miss Winterton. Your aunt has moved on."

Sophie looked up; his expression was not what she had expected. Superficially assured, fashionably urbane, there was an underlying tension, a hint of hardness in the patriarchal features; she was at a loss to account for it. However, she was not about to decline an opportunity to escape Mr. Marston, particularly in his present, officiously disapproving mood. Nevertheless, she kept her answering smile restrained. Mr. Lester, regardless of his mood, needed no encouragement. "Thank you, sir." Placing her hand on his sleeve, she looked back—and surprised a look of distinct chagrin on Phillip Marston's face. "Good day, Mr. Marston."

With a nod, she turned away, and found herself very close to Jack Lester at the top of the steps above the lychgate. Sophie's heart hiccoughed. She glanced up.

His dark eyes met hers, his expression mellow. "Helping you down the steps is the least I can do to repay you for your…company this morning, my dear."

Sophie did not need to look to know Phillip Marston and his mother were close behind; all the confirmation she needed was contained in Jack Lester's smooth, deep and thoroughly reprehensible tone. Incensed, unable to contradict his subtle suggestion, she glared at him. "Indeed, Mr. Lester, you are *certainly* in my debt."

His slow smile softened his lips. "I'll look forward to repaying your kindness, Miss Winterton—when I see you in London."

He made it sound like a promise—one her aunt made certain of as he handed her into the carriage.

"I would invite you to call, Mr. Lester," Lucilla declared. "Yet with our departure imminent, I fear it would be unwise. Perhaps you might call on us when you return to the capital?"

"Indeed, Mrs. Webb, nothing would give me greater pleasure." The carriage door was shut; he bowed, a gesture compounded of strength and grace. "I shall look forward to seeing you in London, Mrs. Webb. Miss Webb." His blue eyes caught Sophie's. "Miss Winterton."

Outwardly calm, Sophie nodded in farewell. The carriage jolted forward, then the horses found their stride. The last view she had was of an elegant figure in pale grey morning coat, tightly fitting inexpressibles and highly polished Hessians, his dark hair slightly ruffled by the breeze. He dominated her vision; in contrast, in his severe, if correct, garb, Mr. Marston seemed to fade into the shadows of the lych-gate. Sophie laid her head back against the squabs, her thoughts in an unaccustomed whirl.

Her aunt, she noticed, smiled all the way home.

SUNDAY AFTERNOON was a quiet time in the Webb household. Sophie habitually spent it in the back parlour. In a household that included five boisterous children, there was always a pile of garments awaiting mending and darning. Although the worst was done by her aunt's seamstress, Lucilla had always encouraged both Clarissa and herself to help with the more delicate work.

Her needle flashing in the weak sunshine slanting through the large mullioned windows, Sophie sat curled in one corner of the comfortable old chaise. While a small part of her mind concentrated on the work in her hands, her thoughts were far away.

The click of the latch brought her head up.

"Melly's here." Clarissa came through the door, followed by her bosom bow, Mellicent Hawthorne, commonly known as Melly.

Sophie smiled a ready welcome at Melly, a short, plump figure, still slightly roly-poly in the manner of a young puppy, an impression enhanced by her long, floppy, brown ringlets and huge, spaniel-like eyes. These were presently twinkling.

"Mama's talking to Mrs. Webb, so I'm here for at least an hour. Plenty of time for a comfortable cose." Melly curled up in the armchair while Clarissa settled on the other end of the chaise. Seeing Clarissa reach for a needle and thread, Melly offered, "Would you like me to help?"

Sophie exchanged a quick glance with Clarissa. "No need," she assured Melly. "There's really not that much to do." She blithely ignored the huge pile in the basket.

"Good." Melly heaved a sigh of relief. "I really don't think I'm much good at it."

Sophie bit her lip. Clarissa, she saw, was bent over her stitching. The last time Melly had "helped" with the mending, at least half the garments had had to be rewashed to removed the bloodstains. And if there was one task worse than darning, it was unpicking a tangled darn.

"Still, I don't suppose Mrs. Webb will have you darning in London. Oooh!" Melly hugged herself. "*How* I envy you, Clarissa! Just imagine being in the capital, surrounded by beaux and London swells—just like Mr. Lester."

Clarissa lifted her head, blue eyes alight. "Indeed, I really can't wait! It will be beyond anything great—to find oneself in such company, solicited by elegant gentlemen. I'm sure they'll eclipse the country gentlemen—well—" she shrugged "—how could they not? It will be *unutterably* thrilling."

The fervour behind the comment made Sophie glance up. Clarissa's eyes shone with innocent anticipation. Looking down at the tiny stitches she was inserting in a tear in one of Jeremy's cuffs, Sophie frowned. After a moment, she ventured, "You really should not judge all London gentlemen by Mr. Lester, Clarissa."

Unfortunately, her cousin mistook her meaning.

"But there *can't* be many more elegant, Sophie. Why, that coat he wore to the ball was top of the trees. And he did look so dashing this morning. And you have to admit he has a certain air." Clarissa paused for breath, then continued, "His bow is very graceful—have you noticed? It makes one wonder at the clumsiness of others. And his speech is very refined, is it not?"

"His voice, too," put in Melly. She shivered artistically. "So deep it reaches inside you and sort of rumbles there."

Sophie pricked her finger. Frowning, she put it in her mouth.

"And his waltzing must just be divine—so…so powerful, if you take my meaning." Clarissa frowned as she considered the point.

"We didn't hear much of his conversation, though," Melly cautioned.

Clarissa waved a dismissive hand. "Oh, that'll be elegant, too, I make no doubt. Why, Mr. Lester clearly moves in the best circles—good conversation would be essential. Don't you think so, Sophie?"

"Very likely." Sophie picked up her needle. "But you should remember that one often needs to be wary of gentlemen of manifold graces, like Mr. Lester."

But Clarissa, starry-eyed and rosy-cheeked, refused to accept the warning. "Oh, no," she said, shaking her head. "I'm sure you're wrong, Sophie. Why, with all his obvious experience, I'm sure one could trust Mr. Lester, or any gentleman like him. I'm sure they'd know just how things should be done."

Mentally Sophie goggled. She was quite sure Jack Lester, for one, would know just how "things" were done—but they certainly weren't the "things" Clarissa imagined. "Truly, Clarissa, trust me when I say that you would be very much safer with a gentleman *without* Mr. Lester's experience."

"Oh, come now, Sophie." Puzzled, Clarissa eyed her curiously. "Have you taken him in aversion? How could you? Why, you'll have to admit he's most terribly handsome."

When it became clear neither Clarissa nor Melly was going to be satisfied with anything short of an answer, Sophie sighed. "Very well. I'll concede he's handsome."

"And elegant?"

"And elegant. But—"

"And he's terribly…" Melly's imagination failed. "Graceful," she finally said.

Sophie frowned at them both. "And graceful. Yet—"

"And his conversation is elegant, too, is it not?"

Sophie tried a scowl. "Clarissa…"

"Is it not?" Clarissa was almost laughing, her natural exuberance bubbling through her recently acquired veneer of sophistication.

In spite of herself, Sophie could not restrain her smile. "Very well," she capitulated, holding up one hand. "I will admit that Mr. Lester is a paragon of manly graces. There— are you satisfied?"

"And you did enjoy your waltz with him, didn't you? Susan Elderbridge was in transports, and *she* had only a country dance."

Sophie didn't really want to remember that waltz, or any other of her interactions with Jack Lester. Unfortunately, the memories glowed bright in her mind, crystal clear, and refused to wane. As for his eyes, she had come to the conclusion that their image had, somehow, impinged on her brain, like sunspots. Whenever she closed her eyes, she could see them, that certain light which she trusted not at all in their deep blue depths.

She blinked and refocused on Clarissa's face, suffused with ingenuous curiosity. "Mr. Lester is very…skilled in such matters."

With that global statement, Sophie took up her needle, hoping her cousin would take the hint.

But Clarissa was not finished. Her arms sweeping wide to encompass all they had discussed, she concluded, her voice dramatic, her expression that of one convinced beyond doubt, "So we are agreed: Mr. Lester is a paragon, a maiden's dream. How then, Sophie can you not *yearn* to find happiness in his arms?"

"Well—his, or someone like him," Melly added, forever prosaic.

Sophie did not immediately raise her head. Her cousin's question was, indeed, very like the one she had been asking herself before Clarissa and Melly had entered. Was what she felt simply the inevitable response to such as Jack Lester? Or was it— Abruptly, she cut off the thought. "Indeed, Clarissa," she replied, shaking out Jeremy's shirt and folding it up, "Mr. Lester is the sort of gentleman of whom it's most unwise to have such thoughts."

"But why?"

Sophie looked up and saw genuine bewilderment in Clarissa's lovely face. She grimaced. "Because he's a rake."

There. It was said. Time and more that she brought these two down to earth.

Their reaction was immediate. Two pairs of eyes went round, two mouths dropped open.

Clarissa was the first to recover. "Really?" Her tone was one of scandalized discovery.

"No!" came from Melly. Then, "How can you tell?"

Clarissa's expression stated that was her question, too.

Sophie stifled her groan. How could she explain? A subtle something in his eyes? An undertone in his deep voice? Something in his suave manner? Then she recalled she had known instantly, in the moment she had seen him framed in Lady Asfordby's doorway. "His arrogant air. He carried himself as if the world were his oyster, the women in it his pearls."

His to enjoy at his whim. Sophie had surprised even herself with her words.

Both Clarissa and Melly fell silent. Then, frowning slightly, Clarissa glanced up. "I don't mean to doubt you, Sophie, but, you know, I don't think you can be right—at least, not in this instance."

Resigned to resistance, Sophie merely raised her brows.

Encouraged, Clarissa ventured, "If Mr. Lester *were* a rake, then surely Mama would not be encouraging him. And she is, you know. Why, she was perfectly thrilled to see him this morning—you know she was. And it was her suggestion he sit with us, beside you."

That, of course, had been the other niggling concern that had been inhabiting Sophie's mind. All Clarissa said was true; the only point Sophie was yet unsure of was what, exactly, her aunt was about. And that, as she well knew, could be just about anything. Given that Mr. Lester was a rake, one of the more dangerous of the species if her instincts were any guide, then Lucilla might just be grasping the opportunity to have her, Sophie, brush up on the social skills she would doubtless need once they were established in London. In the present circumstances, safe in the bosom of her family in their quiet country backwater, there was no real danger involved.

"Anyway," Clarissa said, drawing Sophie from her

thoughts, "what I said at first is still undeniably true. Experienced London gentlemen are *much* more interesting than country gentlemen."

Knowing there was one particular country gentleman Clarissa had in mind, Sophie felt compelled to point out, "But young country gentlemen do grow older, and gain experience in so doing. Even experienced gentlemen must once have been young."

The comment drew a spurt of laughter from Melly. "Can you imagine Mr. Marston young?"

Clarissa giggled. Sophie knew she should chide them but did not; she agreed far too well to make a rebuke sound sincere. As Clarissa and Melly fell to chattering, comparing various older men of their acquaintance and speculating on their younger incarnations, Sophie tried to visualize a younger Jack Lester. It was, she found, a very difficult task. She couldn't imagine his eyes without that certain gleam. With an inward snort, she banished such foolish thoughts and reached for the next garment to be mended.

Doubtless, Jack Lester had been born a rake.

CHAPTER THREE

FATE WAS DEFINITELY smiling upon him.

Tooling his curricle along the lane to the village, Jack squinted against the glare of the brittlely bright morning sunshine, his gaze locked on the group slowly making its way down the lane on the other side of the narrow valley, also bound for the village. A female figure in a familiar cherry-red pelisse was walking a horse of advanced years, hitched to the poles of a gig. A young girl skipped about, now beside the woman, now on the other side of the horse.

"Looks like a problem, Jigson." Jack threw the comment over his shoulder to his groom, perched on the box behind him.

"Aye," Jigson replied. "Likely a stone from the way he's favouring that hoof."

A tiny track joining the two main lanes across the narrow valley came into sight just ahead. Jack smiled and checked his team.

"Be we a-going that way, guv'nor? I thought we was for the village?"

"Where's your sense of chivalry, Jigson?" Jack grinned as he steered his highly strung pair onto the hedged track, then steadied them down a steep incline. "We can't leave a lady in distress."

Especially not *that* lady.

He should, of course, have left for London by now—or, at the very least, quit the scene. His experienced brother-in-law, for one, would certainly have recommended such a strategic retreat. "Women should never be crammed, any more than one's fences" had been a favourite saying of Jason's. He had, of course, been speaking of seduction, a fact that had given Jack pause. Given that he was, to all intents and purposes, wooing his golden head, he had elected to ignore the voice of experience, choosing instead to take heed of a new and unexpectedly strong inner prompting, which categorically stated that leaving the field free to Phillip Marston was not a good idea.

As he feathered his leader around a tight curve, Jack felt his expression harden.

According to Hodgeley, his head groom at the cottage, Marston was a gentleman farmer, a neighbour of the Webbs. He was commonly held to be a warm man, comfortably circumstanced. Village gossip also had it that he was on the lookout for a wife, and had cast his eye in Miss Winterton's direction.

Jack gritted his teeth. He took the tiny bridge at a smart clip, surprising a startled expletive from Jigson, but not so much as scratching the curricle's paintwork. Frowning, he shook aside the odd urge that had gripped him. For some reason, his mind seemed intent on creating monsters where doubtless none lurked. Fate wouldn't be so cruel as to parade his golden head before him, only to hand her to another. Besides, Jigson, who frequented the local tap, had heard no whispers of Mr. Marston heading south for the Season.

Deftly negotiating the tight turn into the lane, Jack relaxed. He came upon them around the next bend.

Sophie glanced up and beheld a team of matchless bays bearing down upon them. She grabbed Amy, then blinked as the team swung neatly aside, pulling up close by the ditch. Only then did she see the driver.

As he tossed the reins to his groom and swung down from the elegant equipage, she had ample time to admire the sleek lines of both carriage and horses. He strode across the narrow lane, his many-caped greatcoat flapping about the tops of his glossy Hessians, the cravat at his throat as neat and precise as if he were in Bond Street. His smile, unabashed, stated very clearly how pleased he was to see her. "Good day, Miss Winterton."

Stifling her response was impossible. Her lips curving warmly, Sophie countered, "Good morning, Mr. Lester. Dobbin has loosed a shoe."

He put a hand on the old horse's neck and, after casting an improbably apologetic glance her way, verified that fact. Releasing the horse's leg, he asked, "I can't remember—is the blacksmith in the village?"

"Yes, I was taking him there."

Jack nodded. "Jigson, walk Miss Winterton's horse to the

blacksmith's and have him fix this shoe immediately. You can return the gig to Webb Park and wait for me there."

Sophie blinked. "But I was on my way to see my mother's old nurse. She lives on the other side of the village. I visit her every Monday."

A flourishing bow was Jack's reply. "Consider me in the light of a coachman, Miss Winterton. And Miss Webb," he added, his gaze dropping to Amy, who was staring, open-mouthed, at his curricle.

"Oh, but we couldn't impose…." Sophie's protest died away as Jack lifted his head. The glance he slanted her brimmed with arrogant confidence.

Jack looked down at Amy. "What say you, Miss Webb? Would you like to complete your morning's excursion atop the latest from Long Acre?"

Amy drew in a deep breath. "*Oooh,* just wait till I tell Jeremy and George!" She looked up at Jack's face—a long way up from her diminutive height—and smiled brilliantly. She reached out and put her small hand in his. "My name is Amy, sir."

Jack's smile was equally brilliant. "Miss Amy." He swept her an elegant bow, and Amy's expression suggested he had made a friend for life. As he straightened, Jack shot Sophie a victorious grin.

She returned it with as much indignation as she could muster, which, unfortunately, was not much. The prospect of being driven in his curricle was infinitely more attractive than walking. And, after his conquest of Amy, nothing would suffice but that they should travel thus. The decision was taken out of her hands, though Sophie wasn't sure she approved.

His groom had already taken charge of old Dobbin. The man nodded respectfully. "I'll see the blacksmith takes good care of him, miss."

There was nothing to do but incline her head. "Thank you." Sophie turned and followed as Jack led Amy, skipping beside him, to the curricle. Abruptly, Sophie quickened her stride. "If you'll hand me up first, Mr. Lester, Amy can sit between us."

Jack turned, one brow slowly lifting. The quizzical laughter in his eyes brought a blush to Sophie's cheeks. "Indeed, Miss Winterton. A capital notion."

Relieved but determined not to show it, Sophie held out her hand. He looked at it. An instant later, she was lifted, as if she weighed no more than a feather, and deposited on the curricle's padded seat. Sophie sucked in a quick breath. He held her firmly, his fingers spread about her waist, long and strong. In the instant before his hands left her, his eyes locked with hers. Sophie gazed into the deep blue and trembled. Then blushed rosy red. She looked down, fussing with her skirts, shuffling along to make room for Amy.

He had taken up the reins and half turned the curricle before she recalled the purpose of her trip.

"The basket." Sophie looked back at the gig. "For Mildred. It's under the seat."

Jack smiled reassuringly. In a trice, Jigson had the basket out and transferred to the curricle's boot. "Now," Jack said, "whither away?"

Sophie bestowed a smile of thanks on Jigson. "The other side of the village and out along the road to Asfordby, a mile or so. Mildred lives very quietly; she's quite old."

Jack gave his horses the office. "Your mother's nurse, you said. Did your mother's family come from hereabouts?"

"No, from Sussex. Mildred came to Webb Park with Aunt Lucilla on her marriage. My aunt was the younger, so Mildred stayed with her."

Jack slanted a glance at the pure profile beside him— Amy's head was too low to interfere with his view. "Do you often do the duty visits for your aunt?"

Sophie considered the question. "I've often done so whenever I've stayed." She shrugged. "Aunt Lucilla is frequently very busy. She has twins younger than Amy— they're just six."

Jack grinned. "And quite a handful?"

"That," declared Sophie, "is a description insufficient to adequately convey the full glory of the twins."

Jack chuckled. "So you help out by taking on the role of the lady of the manor?"

"It's hardly an arduous task," Sophie disclaimed. "I've been doing much the same on my father's estate ever since my mother died."

"Ah, yes. I recall you mentioned helping your father."

Sophie threw him a quick frown. "That's not what I meant. Performing one's duty is hardly doing anything out of the ordinary." There had been something in his tone, a note of dismissal, which compelled her to explain. "I acted as his amanuensis in all matters concerning the estate and also for his studies. And, of course, since my mother's death, I've had charge of the house." It sounded like a catalogue of her talents, yet she couldn't help adding, "House parties, naturally, were impossible, but even living retired as we did, my father could not escape some degree of local entertaining. And the house, being so old and rambling, was a nightmare to run with the small staff we kept on." Sophie frowned at the memory.

Jack hid his keen interest behind an easy expression. "Who's running the house now?"

"It's closed up," Sophie informed him, her tone indicating her satisfaction. As the curricle rounded a corner, she swayed closer. "My father would have left it open—but for what? I finally managed to persuade him to leave just a caretaker and his agent and let the others go on leave. He may be away for years—who can tell?"

Jack slanted a curious glance at her. "If you'll forgive the impertinence, you don't seem overly troubled by the prospect."

Sophie grinned. "I'm not. Indeed, I'm truly glad Papa has gone back to his 'old bones.' He was so abjectly unhappy after my mother's death that I'd be a truly ungrateful wretch were I to begrudge him his only chance at contentment. I think his work carries him away from his memories, both physically and mentally." Her lips curved wryly; her gaze swung to meet Jack's. "Besides, even though I managed affairs for his own good, he could be a crusty old devil at times."

Jack's answering smile was broad. "I know exactly what you mean. My own father's in much the same case."

Sophie grasped the opportunity to turn the conversation from herself. "Are you his only son?"

"Oh, no." Jack turned his head to glance at her. "There are three of us." He was forced to look to his horses but continued, "I'm the eldest, then Harry. My sister, Lenore, came next; she's now married to Eversleigh. And the baby of the family is Gerald. Our mother died years ago but m'father's held on pretty well. Our Aunt Harriet used to watch over us, but Lenore did most of the work." He threw another glance at Sophie. "My sister is one of those women who shuns the bright lights of the *ton;* she was perfectly content to remain at home in Berkshire and keep the Hall going and the estates functioning. I'm ashamed to confess that, when she married two years ago, I was totally unprepared to take on the burden."

Noting the wry grimace that twisted his lips, Sophie ventured, "But you've managed, have you not?"

Jack's lips lifted. "I learn quickly." After a moment, he went on, his gaze still on the road, "Unfortunately, Aunt Harriet died last year. The estate I can manage—the house…that's something else altogether. Like your father's, it's a rambling old mansion—heaps of rooms, corridors everywhere."

To Jack's surprise, he heard a soft sigh.

"They're terribly inconvenient, but they *feel* like home, don't they?"

Jack turned his head to look at Sophie. "Exactly."

For a long moment, Sophie held his gaze, then, suddenly breathless, looked ahead. The first houses of the village appeared on their right. "The fork to the left just ahead leads to Asfordby."

Their passage through the small hamlet demanded Jack's full attention, his bays taking well-bred exception to the flock of geese flapping on the green, the alehouse's dray drawn up by the side of the road and the creak of the tavern's weatherbeaten sign.

By the time they were passing the last straggling cottages, Sophie had herself in hand. "Mildred's cottage is just beyond the next corner on the right."

Jack reined in the bays by the neat hedge, behind which a small garden lay slumbering in the sunshine. A gate gave on to a narrow path. He turned to smile ruefully at Sophie. "I'd come and lift you down, but these brutes are presently too nervy to be trusted on loose reins. Can you manage?"

Sophie favoured him with a superior look. "Of course." Gathering her skirts, she jumped down to the lane. Collecting her basket from the boot, she turned to Amy.

"I'll stay here with Mr. Lester," her cousin promptly said. "Old Mildred always wants to tidy my hair." Her face contorted in a dreadful grimace.

Sophie struggled to keep her lips straight. She glanced up at Jack, a questioning look in her eyes.

He answered with a smile. "I can manage, too."

"Very well. But don't be a nuisance," she said to Amy, then, unconsciously smoothed her curls, Sophie went to the gate.

The door opened hard on her knock; Mildred had obviously been waiting. The old dame peered at the curricle and all but dragged Sophie over the threshold. Mildred barely waited for Sophie to shut the door before embarking on a catechism. In the end, Sophie spent more time reassuring Mildred that Mr. Lester was perfectly trustworthy than in asking after Mildred herself, the actual purpose of her visit.

Finally taking her leave, Sophie reached the curricle to find Jack busy teaching Amy how to hold the reins. Depositing the empty basket in the boot, she climbed aboard.

Jack reached across Amy to help her up, then lifted a brow at her. "Webb Park?"

Sophie smiled and nodded. Amy relinquished the reins with sunny good humour, prattling on happily as the horses lengthened their stride.

About them, the March morning sang with the trills and warbles of blackbirds and thrush. The hedges had yet to unfurl their buds, but here and there bright flocks of daffodils nodded their golden heads, trumpeting in the spring.

"So tell me, Miss Winterton, what expectations have you of your stay in the capital?" Jack broke the companionable silence that had enveloped them once Amy had run her course. He flicked a quizzical glance at Sophie. "Is it to be dissipation until dawn, dancing until you drop, Covent Garden and the Opera, Drury Lane and the Haymarket, with Almack's every Wednesday night?"

Sophie laughed, and ducked the subtle query in his last words. "Indeed, sir. That and more."

"More?" Jack's brows rose. "Ah, then it'll be three balls every night, the Park and two teas every afternoon and more gossip than even Silence knows."

"You've forgotten the modistes."

"And the milliners. And we shouldn't forget the boot-makers, glovers and assorted emporia, the ribbon-makers and mantua-makers."

"Then there are the intellectual pursuits."

At that Jack turned to gaze at her, his expression one of stunned dismay. "Good heavens, Miss Winterton. You'll show us all up for the fribbles we are. No, no, my dear—*not* museums."

"Indeed," Sophie insisted, tossing her head, "I fully intend to view Lord Elgin's marbles."

"Oh, those. They don't count." When Sophie stared at him, Jack explained, "They're fashionable."

Sophie laughed again, a silvery sound. Jack smiled. He waited for a moment, then asked, "Will you be riding in the Park?"

"I should think nothing's more likely." Sophie glanced at him over Amy's head. "My cousins all rode before they could walk—literally. My uncle is a very keen horseman and I'm sure he'll be sending mounts down for us."

"So you won't be cutting a dash in a high-perch phaeton?"

"Alas," Sophie sighed. "Although I have always yearned to handle the ribbons, I've never had the opportunity to learn." Immediately, the curricle slowed. As it came to a halt, she turned to look at Jack.

His slow smile greeted her. "That sounded like a cry from the heart. Never let it be said that a Lester failed to respond to a damsel's plight."

Sophie blinked.

Jack's smile broadened. "I'll teach you."

"Here?"

"Now." He leaned across Amy. "Here, hold the reins like this."

Bemused, Sophie did as he said, taking the leather ribbons in her gloved fingers, looping them in accordance with his directions. It was a fiddle, with Amy between them.

"This will never work," Jack said, echoing Sophie's senti-ments. Leaving the reins in her hands, he sat back, his gaze considering. "Just hold them a moment. They won't bolt as long as they sense some weight on the reins." He swung down from the carriage as he spoke. "They're not particu-larly frisky now; they've been out for over an hour."

Sophie just hoped he knew what he was talking about. Her heart was in her mouth as the leader tossed his head.

Jack rounded the horses and came up beside her. "Shuffle up, Miss Amy, so I can give your cousin her first lesson."

Startled, Sophie glanced down at him. The leader imme-diately tugged on the loosened reins.

"Hoa, there."

One strong hand closed about her fingers, tightening the rein, steadying the restive horse.

Sophie knew she was blushing. With no alternative offering, she shuffled over, followed a delighted Amy across the seat, allowing her rakish mentor to sit beside her. Her first lesson—in what?

She risked a glance up from beneath her lashes; his eyes held a mocking gleam.

"Fie, Miss Winterton." His voice was low. One dark brow rose. "If I offered a guinea for your thoughts, would you take it?"

Sophie blushed even more. She abruptly transferred her gaze to the horses, thus missing Jack's smile.

"Now, the first thing to remember…"

To Sophie's surprise, despite the distraction of his nearness, she quickly mastered the reins, keeping the thoroughbreds well up to their bits. Even more amazingly, he kept strictly to his role of tutor; doubtless, she rationalized, he was sufficiently concerned over the welfare of his horses—and their sensitive mouths—to keep his mind on their safety. Whatever, her suspicions proved unfounded; caution evaporating, she quickly dropped her guard, absorbed in practising the skills he imparted.

Webb Park appeared far too soon.

Exhilarated, Sophie tooled the curricle up the drive, slowing to effect a sedate halt in the gravel forecourt. Her eyes were bright, her cheeks pink as she turned to her companion and, with real reluctance, handed back the reins.

"A most commendable first outing, my dear." Jack met her shy smile with a smile of his own, his eyes searching hers.

A groom came running to hold the horses. Recalled to his surroundings, Jack tied off the reins and leapt down.

Amy scrambled from her perch on the other side and went to natter to the groom.

Sophie slid to the side of the carriage. She made no demur when Jack reached for her and lifted her down. Her feet touched solid earth; she glanced up, and was overcome by flustered shyness. Sternly subduing the sensation, she accepted her empty basket and held out one gloved hand. "Thank you, Mr. Lester. You have indeed proved yourself a knight errant this day. Not only must I thank you for your timely rescue, but also for your excellent tuition."

Smiling down at her, Jack took her hand. "On the contrary, Miss Winterton, the gain was mine. I've rarely had the pleasure of an outing with a lady of such manifold talents."

Squelching the inner glow that rose in response to that compliment, Sophie shot him a sceptical glance. "Indeed, sir, I fear I'm no different from many another."

Jack's slow smile softened his features. "Now, there you are wrong, my dear." He trapped her gaze with his. "You are quite unique." Sophie's eyes widened; he felt her quiver.

Letting his lids veil his eyes, Jack lifted her hand, studying the slender palm, the long, slim fingers. Then his lids rose, his dark gaze again holding hers. Smoothly, he raised her hand and placed a kiss on her inner wrist, exposed above the edge of her glove. "You take the shine out of all the London belles, my dear."

Sophie's skin burned where his lips had touched. Her breathing suspended; light-headedness threatened. It took all the experience she possessed to summon an unaffected smile. "Why, thank you, sir. Will you come in and meet my aunt? I know she'll want to thank you for your help."

He accepted the dismissal without a blink, although the expression in his eyes was amused. "No, I thank you. I know your aunt will be busy; I will not press my presence on her at this time."

Holding hard to her composure, Sophie inclined her head. "Then I'll bid you a very good day, Mr. Lester."

He smiled then, his slow, teasing smile. "*Au revoir,* Miss Winterton."

Sophie turned and climbed the steps. On the threshold, she paused and looked back. He had climbed to the curricle's seat; as she watched, he flicked the reins. With a last wave, he was away, the carriage sweeping down the drive.

She watched until his dark head was no longer in sight. Then, lowering the hand she had automatically raised in farewell, Sophie frowned and turned indoors. She eventually located Amy in the kitchens, munching on a fresh-baked bun.

"Come, Amy. You should change."

Bustling the exuberant child, full of prattle, up the back stairs, Sophie was jolted from her thoughts by her cousin's bright voice, raised in innocent query.

"Is Mr. Lester courting you, Sophie?"

The breath caught in Sophie's throat. For an instant, she felt as if the world had lurched. She coughed. "Good heavens, Amy!" The dimness of the stairs hid her furious blush. "Of course not—he was just funning." She sought for more words—more convincing words—to deny the possibility; none were forthcoming. In desperation, she flapped her hands at Amy. "Come on now, up you go."

As she followed the little girl up the stairs, Sophie frowned. From the mouth of an innocent babe..?

CHAPTER FOUR

NOT CONTENT with her efforts thus far, Fate seemed intent on assisting him at every turn.

As he sat his black hunter in the shadows of a wind-break and watched the small cavalcade come thundering up Ashes' Hill, Jack couldn't keep the smile from his face.

Jigson, ever mindful of his place in the scheme of things, had been assiduous in his visits to the tap. Thus Jack had learned that the junior Webbs, accompanied by Miss Winterton and Miss Webb, were to be found on horseback most afternoons. Weather permitting, they would hack about the lanes and fields, but, according to one of the Webb grooms, the track over Ashes' Hill was currently their favoured route.

As he watched them canter up onto the green swath before him, Jack's smile broadened. His golden head was a delight in moss-green velvet, the long skirts of her habit brushing tan boots. On her guinea-gold curls perched a typically feminine contraption; he knew she'd call it a hat, but to his mind the wisp of fabric anchoring a pheasant's feather hardly qualified for the title. Turning, he lifted a brow at Percy mounted on a bay gelding beside him. "Shall we?"

Percy started; his abstracted gaze, very likely visualizing the rival merits of herringbone and country plaid, rapidly refocused. "What? Oh, yes. 'Bout time."

Jack smiled and led the way forward, out of the shadows of the firs.

Pulling up on the crest of the hill, then wheeling her horse to view her cousins, straggling up in her wake, Sophie did not immediately see him. Clarissa, who had reached the spot some moments ahead of her, had likewise turned to view the vista spread below them. Stone walls and still-dormant hedges divided the brown fields, their colour just tinged with the first hint of green. Jeremy and George, fourteen and twelve respectively, were but yards from the top; Amy, bouncing along on her placid cob, brought up the rear. The twins, yet to graduate from plodding ponies, were not included in these afternoon expeditions.

Reassured that all was well, Sophie relaxed her reins. Eyes bright, cheeks aglow, she drew in a deep breath, savouring the crisp freshness.

"Well met, Miss Winterton!"

The hail brought her head round; the deep voice sent the colour to her cheeks even before her eyes found him. He was mounted on a raking black hunter, sleek and powerful. As the animal walked towards her, neck proudly arched, black withers rippling, Sophie was struck by its harnessed power. Then her eyes lifted to its owner.

Broad shoulders encased in a hacking jacket of soft tweed, his powerful thighs, clad in buckskin breeches, effortlessly controlling the horse, he appeared the very epitome of a wealthy country gentleman. His face, features stamped with that coolly arrogant cast which identified his antecedents more definitively than his name. His eyes were very blue, dark, his gaze intent.

There was power there, too. As he brought his horse alongside hers, Sophie felt it reach for her.

"Good afternoon, Mr. Lester." She forced herself to extend a gloved hand, disconcerted by the warmth that caressed her cheeks and the breathlessness that had assailed her.

He took her hand and bowed over it, a difficult feat he performed with rare grace. His eyes quizzed her. "We saw you riding up and wondered if we might join you?"

"What a splendid idea!" From beside Sophie, Clarissa beamed ingenuously.

Feeling slightly helpless, Sophie could not resist the subtle laughter lurking in the blue eyes holding hers. Very much on her dignity, she retrieved her hand and indicated the track leading on over the hill. "If it pleases you, sir."

The smile she received in reply warmed her through and through.

Jack gestured to Percy, hanging back on his other side. "If you'll permit me to introduce Lord Percy Almsworthy?"

"Pleased to make your acquaintance, Miss Winterton."

Prepared to be wary, Sophie saw at a glance that Lord Percy was sprung from a mould quite different from his companion. Reassured, she smiled and held out a hand.

As he leant from the saddle to shake it, she thought she detected a look of keen appraisal in Lord Percy's mild gaze. "M'father's Carlisle," he said, giving her a peg on which to hang his hat.

Sophie dutifully introduced her cousins, in strict order of precedence. Jeremy and George barely waited for Amy's shy "Hello," before pouncing.

"What a bang-up set of blood and bones, sir!"

"Splendid hocks!"

"What stable does he hail from?"

"Is he a Thoroughbred?"

Jack laughed. "My brother bred him out of Jack Whistle."

"The winner of the Derby?" Jeremy's expression mirrored his awestruck tone.

Jack's eyes touched Sophie's. "The very same."

"Is your brother staying with you?" Gerald asked breathlessly.

Jack couldn't help his smile. "He was, but he's gone on to Belvoir."

"Oh." Both boys appeared crestfallen that they had missed the opportunity to badger a breeder who could turn out such a horse as the black.

"Never mind," Jack said. His eyes again met Sophie's. "I'll mention to him that you're interested in speaking with him, it's perfectly possible you may meet in him in Hyde Park."

"On Rotten Row?" George's eyes were round.

When Jack nodded, Jeremy put their seal of approval

firmly on the plan. He breathed out in a great sigh, his face alight. "Capital!"

Then, with the rapid change of direction that character-ised the young, Jeremy turned to George. "Race you to the oak." They were off on the words, thundering down the slope towards the distant tree.

As by unvoiced consent they set their horses ambling after the two boys, Sophie glanced up at Jack. "You'll have to excuse them—they're rather single-minded when it comes to horses."

Jack slanted her a smile. "Harry and I were the same."

Sophie let her glance slide away. She could hear Clarissa and Lord Percy conversing; they were only a step or so behind. It was true they had no real chaperon, yet she could not imagine there was any impropriety in the situation; the presence of the children lent a certain innocence to the gathering.

Jack had only just registered the absence of a groom. He suppressed an instinctive frown. "Tell me, Miss Winterton, do you commonly ride unescorted?"

Glancing up, Sophie caught the frown in his eyes. Her brows rose. "All my cousins are expert riders; there's little chance of calamity in a gentle ride about the lanes."

"The lanes?"

Sophie had the grace to blush. "You can hardly expect such high spirits—" she indicated Jeremy and George "—to be content with such mild entertainment." Somewhat defensively, she added, "Clarissa and I are experienced riders, and Amy's cob is so ancient it rarely gets above a canter."

That last was self-evident as Amy, not content with their ambling progress, was jigging along ahead of them as fast as the cob would go. Barely a canter, much to Amy's disgust.

"Besides, sir," Sophie added, slanting a glance up at him, "I cannot believe that you and your brother—Harry, was it not?—would have been content with the lanes."

To her surprise, Jack's lips firmed into a distinctly grim line. "Indeed, no, Miss Winterton. Which is why I feel peculiarly well-qualified to express an opinion on what disasters are possible—nay, probable—given two high-couraged youngsters on fine horses." He turned from his contemplation of the boys, now circling the oak ahead, to look down at her. "And," he added, "which is why I think you should most certainly have a groom with you."

A trifle nettled, Sophie reached down to pat the proud neck of her own mount, a raw-boned grey stallion. "You need have no fear of them getting away from me. Few horses can outrun the Sheik."

Her action drew Jack's gaze to her horse; until then, despite his frequent preoccupation with the species, he had not really noticed it. As his gaze took in the large head, the long legs and heavy shoulders and rump, he felt the hairs on his nape rise. Despite the fact he had heard the warning note in her voice, despite knowing she would not welcome his question, he cleared his throat and asked it. "Do you normally ride that beast, Miss Winterton?"

His curiously flat tone had Sophie glancing up, searching his face. "No," she admitted, after a moment's hesitation. "My uncle's stables are extensive. We all take turns helping to exercise the hunters."

Jack's jaw firmed. "And does your uncle know you're riding such a dangerous creature?"

Sophie stiffened. "Mr. Lester," she said, her accents precise, "I have grown up around horses—have been riding since my earliest days. I assure you I am perfectly capable of managing the Sheik, or any other of my uncle's horses."

"That horse is too strong for you." His brows lowered, Jack stated unequivocally, "You should not be riding such an animal."

In the sky above them, the larks swooped and carolled. Their horses, displaying a fine equine imperturbability, trotted on down the hill. Sophie, flags of colour in her cheeks, abruptly retrieved her dropped jaw. Wrenching her gaze from the deeply turbulent blue into which it had fallen, she looked ahead.

The froth of white lace covering her breast rose as she drew in a deep breath. "Mr. Lester," she began, her tone icy, her accents clipped, "I believe we would do well to leave this topic of conversation. I am perfectly capable of managing the Sheik. Now, if you don't mind, I think we should join my cousins."

Resisting the impulse to toss her head, she flicked her reins and the Sheik surged forward. She thought she heard an angry snort, then the black moved up beside her, long fluid strides eating up the turf. Irritation, consternation and something even more unnerving rasped her temper; Sophie kept her gaze fixed forward, ignoring the glowering presence beside her.

Through narrowed eyes, Jack viewed her chilly dignity with very real disapproval.

The two boys and Amy were waiting by the oak. Sophie drew rein and looked back. Clarissa and Lord Percy had followed them down. As his lordship drew up, she heard him remark, "The best bonnets are to be found at Drusilla's, in my opinion. Just off Bruton Street. All the crack at the moment." Her cousin and Lord Percy were clearly deep in fashion. His lordship appeared perfectly content; Clarissa was hanging on his every word. With a smothered snort, Sophie turned to her younger relatives.

"We'll walk along the hedge until we come to the ride. Then back beside the woods."

There was a definite edge to her tone. Jeremy, George and Amy cast her swift glances; without a word, they fell in behind her. Jack remained by her side; Sophie did not waste any effort in trying to dislodge him. Clarissa and Lord Percy brought up the rear, barely glancing up from their sartorial discussion.

Sophie slanted a wary and warning glance at Jack. He met it with a coolly inscrutable expression. With determined calm, Sophie lifted her chin and set off along the hedge.

The silence that engulfed them stretched ominously. She could feel the occasional touch of his glance; she knew there was a frown in his eyes. Sophie wondered why her throat felt so tight, why simply breathing seemed so difficult. Suppressing a grimace, she racked her brains for some suitably innocuous topic of conversation.

Behind her, George was idly threshing the hedge with his whip.

Later, Sophie learned that, entirely inadvertently, George had flushed a hare from the hedge. The animal darted out, straight under the Sheik's hooves.

The stallion reared, screaming.

Sophie fought for control. It was all she could do to keep her precarious seat.

Then the Sheik was off.

Like a steam engine, the huge stallion pounded down the line of the hedge. Sophie clung to his back. Mounted sidesaddle, she could not exert sufficient strength to rein in the panicked beast. The wind of their passing whistled in her ears and whipped her breath away. Desperate, she peered ahead through the wisps of hair flattened against her face, through the rough mane that whipped her cheeks. The hedge at the end of the field loomed ahead. Whispering a fervent prayer, Sophie dropped one rein and threw all her weight onto the other. Almost sobbing, she hauled back. The manoeuvre worked. The Sheik's head slewed, responding to the drag on the bit. But the stallion did not slow. Sophie felt herself tipping sideways. A scream stuck in her throat as she flung herself forward to cling once more to the Sheik's glossy neck. The ride they had been making for opened out before them; a single tug of the Sheik's powerful head pulled the rein from her grasp. Snorting, the stallion flew down the green turf.

Rattled, jolted, Sophie struggled to regain the reins. The ride eventually entered the woods, narrowing to a bridle track. She had to control the Sheik before that.

But the horse had the bit firmly between his teeth; even when she had the reins back in her hands, he refused to respond to her puny strength.

A flash of black to her left was her first intimation that help was at hand. Then Jack was beside her, the heavier black crowding the grey. He leaned across, one hand closing hard over her fingers as he added his weight to hers. Sophie felt him exert an increasing pressure, not jerking, as less experienced riders might. The Sheik felt the inexorable command.

Gradually, the grey slowed, finally stopping by the side of the ride.

Dragging in a ragged breath, Sophie sat up. Immediately the world tilted and spun. A ripe curse fell on her ears; it seemed to come from a long way away. Then strong hands fastened about her waist and weightlessness was added to the disconcerting sensations buffeting her.

Her feet touched firm earth. Shudder upon shudder racked her; she was trembling like a leaf.

The next instant she was enveloped in a warm embrace, locked against a hard frame. A large hand cradled her head, pressing her cheek against a firm male chest. The earthy scent of tweed and leather surrounded her, inexplicably comforting. With a gasp, stifled against his coat, Sophie clung to him, a solid anchor in her suddenly perilous world.

"*My God!* Are you all right?"

He sounded as shaken as she felt. Her throat was still closed; dumb, Sophie nodded. Dimly recalling the proprieties, she reluctantly drew away.

Hard fingers gripped her upper arms; abruptly Jack put her from him. Gasping, Sophie looked up, only to be subjected to a mercilous shake.

"*I thought you said you could handle that beast!*"

Numb, Sophie stared at him, at the fury that flamed in his eyes. A chill trickled through her veins, then spread; she felt the blood drain from her face. Cold blackness drew in; she blinked groggily.

Jack paled as she drooped in his hands. With a muttered curse, he gathered her to him.

Sophie didn't resist. Supporting her against him, Jack guided her to a fallen log. "Sit down!"

The harshness in his tone brought Sophie's head up. Simultaneously, her legs gave way and she complied with more haste than grace.

Jack stood over her, his face an icy mask. "You're white as a sheet. Put your head down."

Dizzy, disorientated, Sophie simply stared at him.

Jack cursed again.

The next thing Sophie knew her head was descending towards her knees, yielding to the insistent pressure of a large hand. He didn't let up until her forehead rested on her knees. As another wave of black nothingness swept over her, Sophie jettisoned any thought of resistance. She set her mind on breathing deeply, calming the turmoil inside. The world and her senses slowly returned to her. Only then did she become aware of the long fingers that had insinuated themselves beneath the collar of her habit and blouse, pushing aside her curls to gently caress her nape. Cool, firm, they traced sorcerous patterns on her sensitive skin. Faintness threatened again; his touch drew her back, anchoring her to reality, soothing her frayed nerves, promising security and safety.

They remained thus for what seemed like an age. Eventually, Sophie drew in a deep breath and sat up. The hand at her nape fell away. She glanced up through her lashes. His expression was closed, shuttered. Dragging in another breath, she gathered her skirts.

His hand appeared before her. After a moment's hesitation, she placed her hand in his and allowed him to assist her to her feet.

"I have to thank you, Mr. Lester, for your assistance." She managed the words creditably but could not look at him. Instead, eyes downcast, she fussed with her skirts, smoothing down the moss velvet.

"I would infinitely prefer, Miss Winterton, if, instead of your thanks, you would give me your promise not to ride that animal, or any like him, again."

The coolly arrogant tones left no doubt of the nature of that request. Slowly straightening, Sophie met his gaze. Inscrutable, distant, it told her little, as if he had brought a curtain down across his feelings, shutting her out. Lifting her head, she stated, "What befell, Mr. Lester, was purely an accident."

Jack bit back a caustic response. "The fact you were riding that horse, Miss Winterton, was no accident." His accents clipped, he viewed her through narrowed eyes. "He's too strong for you—and you knew it."

Sophie folded her lips, and gave him back stare for stare, her expression as remote as his.

Jack felt his temper slowly slip its leash. His expression hardened from mere flint to granite. "Before we leave here, Miss Winterton," he said, his voice low and commendably even, "I want your promise that you will not, in future, engage in such wanton recklessness." He saw her blink; he kept his gaze on hers. "Furthermore, I give you fair warning that should I ever find you on such a horse's back again, you have *my* promise you'll not sit a saddle for a sennight." He watched as her eyes widened, stunned disbelief in their depths. He raised one brow. "Is that perfectly clear, my dear?"

Sophie suppressed a shiver. Unable to hold his relentless gaze, her own dropped to his lips, compressed to a mere line in his ruggedly handsome face.

There was no more than a foot between them. Luckily, the shock of her recent terror was fading; Sophie felt her strength, her normal independence, returning, flooding back, stiffening her resolve. She raised her eyes once more to his. "You have no right to make such a demand of me, Mr. Lester—nor yet threaten me."

Her words were cool, her composure fragile but intact.

Gazing down at her, Jack made no answer, too engrossed in a ferocious inner struggle to subdue the tumultuous emotions raging through him. Every ounce of determination he possessed was required to keep his body still, his muscles locked against the impulse to sweep her into his arms, to demonstrate the validity of his claim on her.

Sophie sensed his turmoil. The odd flicker of the muscle along his jaw, his tightly clenched fists, the tension that gripped his whole frame bespoke her danger. The dark blue of his eyes had deepened, his gaze compelling, flames flickering elusively in the darkened depths. The hard line of his lips had not eased. His physical presence was overwhelming; even more than that, she sensed his strength, a tangible entity, emanating from his large, hard, masculine frame, an aura that reached out, surrounding her, threatening to engulf her, to trap her, to conquer her wilfulness and make her his.

"Sophie?" Clarissa's voice cut across her thoughts. "Sophie? Are you all right?"

A shiver slithered down Sophie's spine. She blinked and realized her heart was racing, her breasts rising and falling rapidly. For one last instant, she met that intense blue gaze. Then, with an effort, she looked away to where Clarissa, with the others in tow, was approaching. Struggling to reassemble her disordered wits, Sophie moved, walking the few feet to the side of her horse. "I'm all right. No harm done."

Jack moved with her, not touching her but ready to support her if needed. Sophie was aware of his protective presence. Recalling how much she owed him, for she was too honest not to acknowledge that it had, indeed, been a very near-run thing, she glanced up through her lashes.

Jack caught her gaze. "Are you able to ride home?"

Sophie nodded. His expression was hard, shuttered, concern the only emotion visible. She drew a shaky breath and raised her head. "I do thank you for your assistance, sir."

Her voice was low, soft, a quaver of awareness running beneath her words.

Jack acknowledged her thanks with a curt nod. Holding fast to the frayed reins of his control, he reached for her, lifting her effortlessly to the grey's back.

Unnerved by the streak of sensation that speared through her at his touch, Sophie made a production of arranging her skirts, using the time to draw every last shred of her experience about her.

As the party reformed, she was grateful to find Clarissa, openly concerned, between herself and Mr. Lester. Lord Percy, on her left, proved an unthreatening companion, chatting on a wide variety of subjects as they wended their way homeward through the golden afternoon.

No further words passed between herself and her rescuer, yet all the way back to the gates of Webb Park, Sophie was conscious of the touch of his brooding gaze.

ONCE SHE WAS SAFELY returned to the bosom of her family, circumstance conspired to afford Sophie no peace in which to ponder. As there were no guests that evening, dinner was served at the earlier hour of five o'clock, *en famille*. All the Webbs barring the twins sat down about the long table in the dining room.

Naturally, her aunt and uncle were immediately regaled with the details of her thrilling rescue. It was all Sophie could do to erase the embellishments with which the younger Webbs enthusiastically embroidered the tale. From their glowing faces and excited voices it was clear that Jack Lester, modern-day hero, could have no fault in their youthful eyes.

"Dear Sophie," Lucilla said, her customary calm intact. "You took no hurt of any kind, I hope?"

"None, aunt." Sophie laid down her soup-spoon. "It was an unfortunate accident but I was not in any way harmed."

"Thanks to Mr. Lester!" piped up Amy.

"You should have seen that black go, sir!" Jeremy addressed himself to his father. "A prime 'un—a real stayer."

"Indeed?' From the head of the table, Horatio Webb beamed his deceptively gentle smile upon them all. A shortish, distinctly rotund gentleman, with a face that somehow combined elements of both youth and wisdom, many, at first glance, relegated him to the rank of a genial country squire with few thoughts beyond his fields. Only those who looked closer, into his fine grey eyes, twinkling now as Sophie's delicately flushed cheeks assured him she had taken no hurt but was being made more than a little uncomfortable by the continuing fuss, saw a glimmer of the quick silver intelligence that lurked behind his outward appearance. The very intelligence that had made Horatio Webb a byword in certain rarefied financial circles and was, at some deeper level, part of the reason the beautiful and talented Lucilla Carstairs, capable of landing a dukedom with her smiles, had, instead, very happily married him. Peering at Jeremy over the top of his ever-present spectacles, Horatio replied, "I must say I would not mind getting a look at any horse that could run the Sheik down."

"Mr. Lester is staying in the neighbourhood, I believe," Clarissa volunteered.

Horatio nodded. "Rawling's Cottage, I expect." With bland calm, he picked up the carving implements and fell to carving the roast which had, that moment, been ceremonially placed before him.

To Sophie's relief, the healthy appetites of the younger Webbs thrust her adventure temporarily from their minds.

Dinner was followed by a noisy game of Speculation, after which, feeling positively exhausted, mentally and physically, Sophie took herself off to bed. She had expected to find time, in the quiet of her chamber, to review the afternoon's happenings—not the stirring events her cousins had described, but the far more unnerving moments she had spent alone with Jack Lester, a rescued damsel with her knight. Indeed, with her inner peace in disarray, she climbed the stairs determined to place the episode in proper perspective.

Instead, she fell deeply asleep, her dreams haunted by a pair of midnight-blue eyes.

THE FOLLOWING MORNING was filled to overflowing with the first of the tasks needed to be completed to allow them to remove to the capital at the end of the week as planned. Lucilla had the entire event organized, down to the last bottle of elderflower lotion needed to preserve their complexions against any breeze that might be encountered while being driven in gentlemen's curricles in the Park.

Excused from the first round of packing for a light luncheon, both Sophie and Clarissa were commanded to appear before the family's seamstress for a final fitting of the walking gowns, morning gowns, chemises and petticoats they had all agreed could be perfectly adequately supplied from home. The rest of their wardrobes, Lucilla had declared, must come from Bruton Street. As, after four years' absence from London, none of the gowns Sophie currently possessed could be considered presentable, she was as much in need of the modistes as Clarissa. Even Lucilla had murmured her intention of taking advantage of their time in the capital to refurbish her own extensive wardrobe.

It was midafternoon before Sophie was free. She had barely had time to wander down to the front hall before the younger Webbs found her. With the single-mindedness of the young, they claimed her for their accustomed ride. With an inward sigh, Sophie surveyed the bright faces upturned to hers, eyes glowing, eager to be off. "Very well," she said. "But I think we'll take a groom with us today. Jeremy, please tell John he's to accompany us. I'll get Clarissa and meet you at the stables."

To her relief, none of them commented on her departure from their established norm. Jeremy merely nodded, and all three departed with alacrity.

Glancing down at her morning gown, Sophie turned and started back up the stairs, refusing to dwell on what had prompted her caution, reflecting instead that, given that her aunt relied on her to ensure her cousins were exposed to no untoward occurrences, it was the least she should do.

When she appeared at the stables, Clarissa in tow, Old Arthur, the head groom, raised a questioning brow at her. Pulling on her gloves, Sophie nodded a greeting. "I'll take Amber out today. She hasn't had a run for some time, I believe."

Arthur blinked. Then, with a shrug which stated louder than words that it was not his place to question the vagaries of his betters, he went to fetch the mare. To Sophie's surprise, Clarissa, busy mounting her own high-bred chestnut, refrained from questioning her choice. Amber was as close to docile as any horse in the Webb stables. Taking her cue from her cousin, Sophie steadfastly ignored the niggling little voice which harped in her ear. Her choice of mount had nothing to do with Mr. Lester—and even less with that gentleman's too strongly stated opinions.

The tenor of his comments, both before and after dragging her from the Sheik's back, had stunned her. She had not before encountered such arrogantly high-handed behaviour, but she was quite certain what she thought of it. Yet her lingering reaction to the entire episode was equivocal, ambivalent, no help at all in restoring her equanimity.

Setting placid Amber to the task of catching up with the boys and Amy, already well ahead, Sophie frowned.

Until yesterday, she had been inclined to suspect Jack Lester of harbouring some romantic interest in her. Her conscience stirred, and Sophie blushed delicately. Irritated, she forced herself to face the truth: she had started to hope that he did. But his reactions yesterday afternoon had given her pause; whatever it was that had stared at her from the depths of his dark blue eyes—some deeply felt emotion that had disturbed his sophisticated veneer and wreaked havoc on her calm—it was not that gentle thing called love.

Sophie acknowledged the fact with a grimace as, with a wave and a whooping "halloo," Clarissa shot past. Twitching the reins, Sophie urged Amber into the rolling gait which, with her, passed for a gallop. Clarissa, meanwhile, drew steadily ahead.

Trapped in her thoughts, Sophie barely noticed. Love, as she understood it, was a gentle emotion, built on kindness, consideration and affection. Soft glances and sweet smiles was her vision of love, and all she had seen, between her uncle and aunt and her mother and father, had bolstered that image. Love was calm, serene, bringing a sense of peace in its wake.

What she had seen in Jack Lester's eyes had certainly not been peaceful.

As the moment lived again in her mind, Sophie shivered. What was it she had stirred in him? And how did he really view her?

HER FIRST QUESTION, had she but known it, was also exercising Jack's mind, and had been ever since he had returned from Webb Park the afternoon before. As soon as his uncharacteristically violent emotions had eased their grip on his sanity, he had been aghast. Where had such intense impulses sprung from?

Now, with the afternoon bright beyond the windows, he restlessly paced the parlour of Rawling's Cottage, inwardly still wrestling with the revelations of the previous day. He was deeply shocked, not least by the all but ungovernable strength of the emotion that had risen up when he had seen Sophie's slender figure, fragile against the grey's heaving back, disappear in the direction of the woods and possible death.

And he was shaken by what the rational part of his brain informed him such feelings foretold.

He had innocently supposed that courting the woman he had chosen as his wife would be a mild process in which his emotions remained firmly under his control while he endeavoured, through the skill of his address, to engage hers. A stranger, as he now realized, to love, he had imagined that, in the structured society to which they belonged, such matters would follow some neatly prescribed course, after which they could both relax, secure in the knowledge of each other's affections.

Obviously, he had misjudged the matter.

A vague memory that his brother-in-law had not surrendered to love without a fight glimmered at the back of his mind. Given Jason's undoubted conversion, and his equally undoubted acumen, Jack had always wondered what had made him hesitate—on the brink, as it were.

Now he knew.

Emotions such as he had felt yesterday were dangerous.

They boded fair to being strong enough to overset his reason and control his life.

Love, he was fast coming to understand, was a force to be reckoned with.

A knock on the front door interrupted his reverie. Glancing out of the window, he saw his undergroom leading a handsome bay around to the stables. The sight piqued Jack's interest.

A scrape on the parlour door heralded his housekeeper. "Mr. Horatio Webb to see you, sir."

Intrigued, Jack lifted a brow. "Thank you, Mrs. Mitchell. I'll receive him here."

A moment later, Horatio Webb was shown into the room. As his calm gaze swept the comfortable parlour, warm and inviting with its wealth of oak panelling and the numerous sporting prints gracing the walls, a smile of ineffable good humour creased Horatio's face. Rawling's Cottage was much as he remembered it—a sprawling conglomeration of buildings that, despite its name, constituted a good-sized hunting lodge with considerable stabling and more than enough accommodation for guests. Approaching his host, waiting by the fireplace, he was pleased to note that Jack Lester was much as he had imagined him to be.

"Mr. Webb?" Jack held out a hand as the older man drew near.

"Mr. Lester." Horatio took the proffered hand in a strong clasp. "I'm here, sir, to extend my thanks, and that of Mrs. Webb, for the sterling service you rendered in averting misadventure yesterday afternoon."

"It was nothing, I assure you, sir. I was there and merely did what any other gentleman, similarly circumstanced, would have done."

Horatio's eyes twinkled. "Oh, I make no doubt any other gentleman would have *tried,* Mr. Lester. But, as we both know, few would have succeeded."

Jack felt himself falling under the spell of the peculiarly engaging light in his visitor's eye. His lips twitched appreciatively. "A glass of Madeira, sir?" When Horatio inclined his head, Jack crossed to pour two glasses, then returned, handing one to his guest. "Phoenix is, perhaps, one of the few horses that could have caught your Sheik. I'm just dev'lish glad I was on him."

With a wave, he invited Sophie's uncle to a chair, waiting until the older man sat before taking a seat facing him.

With the contemplative air of a connoisseur, Horatio sipped the Madeira, savouring the fine wine. Then he brought his grey gaze to bear on Jack. "Seriously, Mr. Lester, I do, as you must understand, value your intervention of yesterday. If it weren't for the fact we'll be shortly removing to town, I'd insist you honour us for dinner one night." His words came easily, his eyes, calmly perceptive, never leaving Jack's face. "However, as such is the case, and we will depart on Friday, Mrs. Webb has charged me to convey to you her earnest entreaty that you'll call on us once we're established in Mount Street. Number eighteen. Naturally, I add my entreaty to hers. I take it you'll be removing to the capital shortly?"

Jack nodded, discarding the notion of urging Sophie's uncle to forbid her his more dangerous steeds. The shock she had so recently received should, with luck, suffice to keep her from the backs of murderous stallions, at least until the end of the week. "I intend quitting Melton any day, as it happens. However, as I must break my journey in Berkshire, I don't expect to reach the metropolis much in advance of your party."

Horatio nodded approvingly. "Please convey my greetings to your father. We were once, if not close friends, then certainly good acquaintances."

Jack's eyes widened. "You're *that* Webb!" Blinking, he hastily explained, "Forgive me—I hadn't realized. With so many Webbs in these parts, I wasn't sure which one had been my father's crony. I understand you and he shared many interests. He has told me of your devotion to the field."

"Ah, yes." Horatio smiled serenely. "My one vice, as it were. But I think you share it, too?"

Jack returned the smile. "I certainly enjoy the sport, but I feel my interest does not reach the obsessive heights of my father's."

"Naturally," Horatio acceded. "You younger men have other obsessions to compete with the Quorn, the Cottesmore and the Belvoir. But the Lester stud is still one of the best in the land, is it not?"

"Under my brother Harry's management," Jack replied. "Our kennels still produce some of the strongest runners, too."

While their conversation drifted into a discussion of the latest trends in breeding both hunters and hounds, Jack sized up Sophie's uncle. Horatio Webb, while younger than his own father, had been a long-time acquaintance of the Honorable Archibald Lester. More specifically, it had been he who had dropped that quiet word in his father's ear which had ultimately led to the resurrection of the family fortunes.

Taking advantage of a natural lull in the conversation, Jack said, "Incidentally, I must make you all our thanks for your timely advice in the matter of the Indies Corporation."

Horatio waved a dismissive hand. "Think nothing of it. What friends are for, after all." Before Jack could respond with a further expression of gratitude, Horatio murmured, "Besides, you've cleaned the slate. I assure you I would not have liked to have had to face my brother-in-law, eccentric though he is, with the news that his Sophie had broken her neck on one of my stallions. As far as I can see, the scales between the Webbs and the Lesters are entirely level."

Just for an instant, Jack glimpsed the reality behind Horatio Webb's mask. Understanding, then, that this visit had many purposes, perhaps even more than he had yet divined, Jack could do no more than graciously accept the older man's edict. "I'm pleased to have been able to be of service, sir."

Horatio smiled his deceptive smile and rose. "And now I must be off." He waited while Jack rang and gave orders for his horse to be brought round, then shook hands with his host. His eyes roving the room once more, he added, "It's nice to see this place kept up. It's been in your family for some time, has it not?"

Escorting Sophie's amazing uncle to the door, Jack nodded. "Five generations. All the Lester men have been bred to hunting."

"As it should be," Horatio said, and meant far more than the obvious. "Don't forget," he added, as he swung up to the back of his bay. "We'll look to see you in London."

Horatio nodded a last farewell and turned his horse's head for home. As he urged the bay to a canter, a subtle smile curved his lips. He was well pleased with what he had found at Rawling's Cottage. Aside from all else, the Lesters were obviously planning on remaining a part of the landscape, here as much as in Berkshire.

Lucilla would be pleased.

BY THE TIME she returned from their ride, Sophie had a headache. As she was not normally prey to even such minor ailments, she felt the constraint deeply. As she preceded Clarissa into the back parlour, she massaged her temples in an effort to ease the throbbing ache behind them.

It was, of course, all Jack Lester's fault. If she hadn't spent half her time worrying about how she would respond if he joined them, and the other half scanning the horizon for his broad-shouldered frame, metaphorically looking over her shoulder all the way, she would doubtless have taken her customary enjoyment in the ride. Instead, she felt dreadful.

Throwing her riding cap onto a chair, she sank gratefully into the overstuffed armchair in the shadows by the hearth.

"A pity Mr. Lester and Lord Percy didn't join us." Clarissa dropped onto the chaise, obviously ready to chat. "I was sure that, after yesterday, they would be waiting at Ashes' Hill."

"Perhaps they've already returned to London," Sophie suggested. "The ground's certainly soft enough to send the tail-chasers back to town."

"Tail-chasers" was the family term for those gentlemen whose only purpose in coming to Melton Mowbray was to chase a fox's tail. At the first sign of the thaw, such gentlemen invariably deserted the packs for the more refined ambience of the *ton*'s gaming rooms.

"Oh, but I don't think Mr. Lester and Lord Percy are tail-chasers, exactly. Not when they both ride such superb horses."

Sophie blinked and wondered if her headache was affecting her reason. "What have their horses to do with it?" she felt compelled to ask. "All tail-chasers, *ipso facto,* must have horses."

But Clarissa's mind was on quite a different track. "They're both terribly *elegant,* aren't they? Not just in the ballroom—well, everyone *tries* to be elegant there. But they both have that indefinable London polish, don't they?"

Sophie openly studied her cousin's lovely face. At the sight of the glowing expression inhabiting Clarissa's clear eyes, she stifled a groan. "Clarissa—please believe me—not all London gentlemen are like Lord Percy and Mr. Lester. Some of them are no better than…than any of the young gentlemen you've met at the local balls. And many are a great deal worse."

"Maybe so," Clarissa allowed. "But it's an indisputable fact that both Mr. Lester and Lord Percy put *all* the gentlemen hereabouts to shame."

Sophie closed her eyes and wished she could argue.

Clarissa rose, eyes shining, and twirled about the room. "Oh, Sophie! I'm so looking forward to being surrounded by all the swells—the dandies, the town beaux, even the fops. It will be so *thrilling* to be sought after by such gentlemen, to be twitted and teased—in a perfectly acceptable way, of course." Clarissa dipped and swirled closer. "And I know," she continued, lowering her voice, "that one is not supposed to say so, but I can't wait to at least try my hand at flirting, and I positively can't *wait* to be ogled."

As she squinted against the glare of the late afternoon

sun, her narrowed vision filled with Clarissa's svelte form, Sophie didn't think her cousin would have all that long to wait. She should, she supposed, make a push to bring Clarissa back to earth, and defend the local young gentlemen, Ned in particular. If she hadn't been feeling so ill, she would have. But with her head throbbing so, and her mind still tangled in her own confusion, she doubted she could find sufficient words to succeed.

"But what of you, Sophie?" Abruptly, Clarissa turned from rapt contemplation of her rosy future and plumped down on the chaise close by. "After his dramatically chivalrous rescue yesterday, aren't you just a *little* bit taken with Mr. Lester?"

Sophie let her lids fall; Clarissa, when she put her mind to it, could be quite as perspicacious as her mother. "Indeed," she forced herself to say. "Mr. Lester was everything that is gallant. However, that's hardly the only criterion I have for choosing a husband."

"So, what are your other criteria?"

Squinting through her lashes, Sophie studied Clarissa's grin. Her cousin, she reluctantly concluded, was unlikely to be diverted by any prevarication. "A liking for children," she stated. An obvious test; one, she suspected, Jack Lester would pass. He had handled Amy very well, and the boys, too. "And a sense of humour." He had that, too, reprehensible though it might sometimes be.

"And I would want a man who was steady and reliable, not given to fits of temper." Now *that* was a prerequisite her knight in shining armour might have trouble complying with. Rakes, she had always understood, were totally *un*reliable. Becoming absorbed with her catalogue, Sophie frowned. "Sufficiently handsome, although he needn't be an Adonis. Not mean or stingy. And he'd have to be able to waltz. There," she concluded, opening her eyes fully and fixing Clarissa with a mock glare. "Are you satisfied?"

Clarissa laughed and clapped her hands, making Sophie wince. "But that's famous! Mr. Lester might be just the man for you."

Abruptly, Sophie stood, disguising the sudden movement with a little laugh. "I pray you, Clarissa, don't let your imagination fly away with you. Mr. Lester's presence here—and our meetings—have been occasioned by nothing more than coincidence."

Clarissa looked slightly surprised by her vehemence but, to Sophie's intense relief, she forbore to argue. "I expect something must have detained them today." Clarissa's tone suggested she could see no other likelihood. As she fell to neatly folding the ribbons of her hat, she added, "I wonder when next we'll meet?"

As HE SAT DOWN to dinner that evening in the dining room of the cottage, Jack could have answered Clarissa's question without further thought. He was leaving Leicestershire on the morrow. Early.

He said as much to Percy, taking his seat on his right hand.

"What brought that on? Thought you were fixed here for another few weeks?"

"So did I," Jack returned. "But something's come up." Before Percy could ask what, he added, "And the weather's turned, so I think I'll do better to look in at Lester Hall before hying up to town."

"There is that," Percy agreed knowledgeably. "Ground's softening up. Not many good runs left in the season."

Jack nodded, unexpectedly grateful for the thaw. As he rode very heavy, the going for his mounts would become noticeably harder in the coming weeks.

"Think I'll take a look in on the old man," Percy mused, his expression distant. "Gets a bit obstreperous if we forget him. I'll go and do my filial duty, then meet you in town."

Jack nodded again, his mind busy with his plans. There was no need to hurry up to town. The Webbs would not be receiving for at least another week.

His decision to quit the field in Leicestershire was prompted by a firm conviction that such a scene as had occurred when he'd hauled Sophie from her stallion's back could not be repeated. However, thanks to the incident, he was now on good terms with the Webbs and had been all but commanded to call, once in town. Assuming Mrs. Webb approved, there would, he felt sure, be no impediment placed in his path should he desire to further his interest with Sophie in the usual way.

It was his first, albeit small, advance.

However, given his turbulent and presently unpredictable

reactions, it seemed the course of wisdom to suspend all further activity until his golden head was safe in the bosom of the *ton*. His home ground, as it were.

The strictures of Society reached a pinnacle of stringency in London—the strict mores and unwavering practices would undoubtedly prove sufficiently rigid to ensure his wooing followed acceptable paths.

So, for her sake, and, he reluctantly admitted, his own, he had determined to forgo the sight of Sophie's fair face until she appeared in London.

It would be safer for everyone that way.

CHAPTER FIVE

CLIMBING THE STAIRS of Entwhistle House, Sophie looked about her, at the silks and satins, the jewels and curls, and knew she was back in the *ton*. About her, the refined accents and dramatic tones of the elite of society, engaged in their favourite pastime, drowned out the plaintive strains of a violin, struggling through from the ballroom ahead. Immediately in front of her, Lucilla, clad in an exquisite gown of deep blue silk overlaid with figured lace, forged steadily onward, stopping only to exchange greetings with the acquaintances, both close and distant, who constantly hailed her.

Close beside Sophie, Clarissa frankly stared. "Isn't it *wonderful?*" she breathed. "So many beautiful gowns. And the men look just as I imagined—precise to a pin. Some are very handsome, are they not?"

As she whispered the words, Clarissa caught the eye of an elegant buck, who, noticing her wide-eyed stare, ogled her shamelessly. Clarissa blushed and retreated behind her fan.

Following her gaze, Sophie caught the gentleman's eye, and raised a coolly superior brow. The man smiled and bowed slightly, then turned back to his companions. Sophie slipped an arm through Clarissa's. "Indeed, and you look very handsome, too, so you must expect to be ogled, you know. The best way to deal with such attentions is to ignore them."

"Is it?" Clarissa sent a cautious glance back at the gentleman, now fully engaged with his friends. Relieved, she relaxed and looked down at her gown, a delicate affair in palest aquamarine muslin, a demure trim of white lace about the neckline and tiny puffed sleeves. "I must admit, I did wonder at Madame Jorge's choice, but it really does suit me, doesn't it?"

"As that gentleman has just confirmed," Sophie replied. "I told you you should never argue with Madam Jorge. Aside from anything else, it's wasted breath."

Clarissa giggled. "I never imagined she would be like that."

Looking ahead, Sophie smiled. They had quit Leicestershire on Friday, spending two nights on the road in a stately progress that had delivered them up in Mount Street on Sunday afternoon. The rest of that day had gone in the predictable chaos of unpacking and installing the family in their home for the Season. Lucilla had shooed them all off to bed early, warning both Sophie and Clarissa, "We'll be out first thing, off to Madame Jorge. I refuse to permit either of you to step into a *ton* ballroom unsuitably gowned. We shall have to hope Jorge can come to our aid, for we're promised to Lady Entwhistle tomorrow night if you recall."

And so, that morning, immediately after breakfast at the unheard-of hour of ten, they had arrived before the small door on Bruton Street that gave on to Madame Jorge's salon.

"I only hope she can help us at such short notice," Lucilla had said as she led the way up the stairs.

Her aunt needn't have worried; Madame Jorge had fallen on her neck with unfeigned delight.

Madame Jorge was the modiste who for years had been her mother's and aunt's favourite; her own wardrobe for her ill-fated first Season had come from Madame Jorge's salon. But Madame Jorge was definitely not what one expected of a modiste who made for a very select clientele amongst the *ton*.

For a start, she was huge, a massive bosom balanced by immense hip and brawny arms. But her small hands and thick, short fingers were remarkably nimble. She had almost no neck that one could see; her neat grey hair was perennially coiled in a tight bun upon her round head. Small blue eyes twinkled in a rosy-cheeked face. Only the shrewd gaze and the determined set of Madame Jorge's mouth gave her away.

"And Miss Sophie, too!" she had exclaimed, once she had finished greeting Lucilla. "*Ma pauvre* little one, how good it is to see you again."

Jorge had hugged her to her massive bosom, neatly covered in black bombazine, and then held her at arm's length, the better to survey her. "But, yes! This is wonderful—*wunderbar*!" Jorge had never settled entirely into any one language. She was a polyglot and spoke at least three, often all at once. She took a step back, eyes narrowing, then whipped the tape measure which always hung about her neck into her hands. "For you, my *liebschen,* we will have to retake the measurements." Jorge's eyes had gleamed. "You will turn the gentlemen on their heads, no?"

She had murmured that she hoped not, but was not sure Jorge heard. The modiste had spied Clarissa, hanging back, a little overwhelmed. Her cousin had promptly been even more overwhelmed by Jorge's bear-like embrace.

"Oh—the *petit chou!* You are your mother's daughter, but yes! Very young—but the bloom is worth something, *hein?*"

Utterly bewildered, Clarissa had glanced at her mother. Lucilla had taken Jorge in hand, rapidly explaining their requirements and the need for haste.

Jorge had understood immediately. "*Quelle horreur!* To go to the ball without a gown—it is not to be thought of! No, no, somehow we will contrive."

Contrive she certainly had.

Glancing down at her own silk skirts, in a delicate pale-green hue that was the perfect foil for her colouring, making the blue of her eyes more intense and setting off the true gold of her curls, Sophie felt more than content. The long lines of the skirts, falling from the high waist beneath an unusual square-cut neckline, displayed her slender figure to perfection. Jorge, as always, had come to the rescue; she was a wizard and had waved her magic wand. Their new ball gowns had been delivered at six that evening, the first of their day gowns would be on the doorstep by nine the next morn.

"Sophie! Look!"

Following Clarissa's gaze, Sophie beheld another young

girl, weighed down by a gown in frothy pink muslin, a heavy flounce about the neckline repeated twice about the hem making her appear wider than she was tall. The gown was precisely what Clarissa had gone to Madame Jorge's salon determined to have for her first ball.

"Oh, dear." Clarissa viewed the apparition with empathetic dismay. "Would I have looked like that?"

"Very likely," Sophie replied. "Which all goes to show that one should never, ever, argue with Madam Jorge."

Clarissa nodded, carefully averting her gaze from the unfortunate young lady to study, somewhat nervously, the crowd still separating them from their hostess. "I'd never imagined to see so many elegant people in one place at one time."

Sophie felt her lips twitch. "I hesitate to mention it, but this is only a small gathering by *ton* standards, and an informal one at that. There could only be a hundred or so present."

The look Clarissa sent her did not exactly glow with anticipation. They had gained the top of the stairs and were now slowly shuffling across the upper foyer. Then the curtain of bodies before them parted and they found themselves facing Lady Entwhistle.

"Lucilla dear, so glad you could come." Her ladyship and Lucilla touched scented cheeks. Casting a knowledgeable eye over Lucilla's gown, Lady Entwhistle raised a brow. "Dashed if you aren't capable of giving these young misses a run for their money."

Lucilla's eyes flew wide. "*Run*, Mary? Gracious heavens,

my dear—*so* enervating!" With a smile that was almost mischievous, Lucilla passed on to greet the young gentleman next in line—Lord Entwhistle's cousin's boy, Mr. Millthorpe—leaving both Sophie and Clarissa to make their curtsies to her ladyship.

Rising, Sophie once more found herself subjected to her ladyship's lorgnette. As before, no item of her appearance escaped Lady Entwhistle's scrutiny, from the green ribbon in her curls to her beaded satin dancing slippers.

"Hmm, yes," Lady Entwhistle mused, her expression brightening. "*Excellent,* my dear. No doubt but that you'll have a truly *wonderful* Season this time."

Her ladyship's tone left little doubt as to what, in her mind, constituted a "wonderful" Season. Having known what to expect from her mother's old friends, Sophie smiled serenely. Together with Clarissa, she moved on to Mr. Millthorpe.

A young gentleman of neat and pleasant aspect, Mr. Millthorpe was clearly overawed at finding himself thus thrust upon the notice of the *ton.* He replied to Sophie's calm greeting with a nervously mumbled word; she saw him fight to keep his hand from tugging his cravat. Then he turned to Clarissa, who was close on her heels. Mr. Millthorpe's colour promptly fled, then returned in full measure.

"Indeed," he said, his bow rendered awkward by his determination to keep Clarissa's face in view. "I'm very glad to meet you Miss…Miss…." Mr. Millthorpe's eyes glazed.

"Miss Webb!" Triumph glowed in his smile. "I hope you won't mind…that is, that you might have a few minutes to spare later, Miss Webb. Once I get free of this." His expression earnest, he gestured ingenuously at his aunt.

A little taken aback, Clarissa sent him a shy smile.

That was more than enough encouragement for Mr. Millthorpe. He beamed, then was somewhat peremptorily recalled to his duties.

Bemused, Clarissa joined Sophie where she waited at the top of the shallow flight of steps leading down into the ballroom.

Poised above the room, Sophie resisted the impulse to send a questing glance out over the sea of heads. Looking down, she raised her skirts and commenced the descent in her aunt's wake. Beside her, Clarissa was tensing with excitement, her eyes, bright and wide, drinking in every sight. The sensation of tightness about her own lungs informed Sophie that she, too, was not immune to expectation. The realization brought a slight frown to her eyes.

The odds were that Mr. Lester would not be present. Even if he was, there was no reason to imagine he would seek her out.

With an inward snort, Sophie banished the thought. Jack Lester was a rake. And rakes did not dance attendance on young ladies—not, that is, without reason. She, however, was in town to look for a husband, the perfect husband for her. She should devote her thoughts to that goal, and forget all about engaging rakes with dark blue eyes and unnerving tempers.

Determination glimmered in her eyes as she lifted her head—only to have her gaze fall headlong into one of midnight blue.

Sophie's heart lurched; an odd tremor shook her. He filled her vision, her senses, tall and strong, supremely elegant in black coat and pantaloons, his dark locks in fashionable disarray, the white of his cravat a stark bed on which a large sapphire lay, winking wickedly.

Jack watched as, her surprise at seeing him plainly writ in her large eyes, Sophie halted on the second-last stair, her lips parting slightly, the gentle swell of her breasts, exposed by her gown, rising on a sharp intake of breath.

His eyes on hers, he slowly raised a brow. "Good evening, Miss Winterton."

Sophie's heart stuttered back to life. Large, dark and handsome, he bowed gracefully, his gaze quizzing her as he straightened. Giving her wits a mental shake, she descended the last step, dipping a curtsy, then extending her hand. "Good evening, Mr. Lester. I had not expected to see you here, sir."

His brow lifted again; to her relief, he made no direct reply. "Might I request the pleasure of a waltz, my dear? The third, if you have it to spare."

She had not even had time to look at her dance card. Shooting him a cool glance, Sophie opened it, then, meeting his eyes briefly, she lifted the tiny pencil and marked his name in the appropriate spot.

The answer to the question in her mind came with his

smooth, "And, perhaps, if you're not already bespoken, I might escort you to supper at the conclusion of the dance?"

Blinking, Sophie found she had unthinkingly surrendered her hand to his. Her gaze flew to his as he drew her gently to his side. Her heart leapt to her throat and started beating erratically there. "That will be most pleasant, Mr. Lester," she murmured, looking away.

"It will, you know."

His tone was gently teasing, on more levels than one. Elevating her chin, Sophie drew her composure more firmly about her. Ahead of them, her aunt was strolling through the crowd, Clarissa by her side.

To Sophie's surprise, having escorted her as far as the chaise where her aunt finally deigned to rest, Mr. Lester exchanged a few pleasantries with Lucilla, then, with an elegant bow, excused himself, leaving her to weather a spate of introductions as a small host of gentlemen gravitated to her side.

Despite the nature of Lady Entwhistle's little ball, despite the fact that the *ton* was only just beginning to desert its winter playgrounds to return to the capital, there were sufficient eligible bachelors present to fill her card long before the first dance began.

Clarissa, by her side, proved a potent attraction for the younger gentlemen. She was soon casting anxious glances at Sophie.

Keeping her voice firm and clear, Sophie calmly apologized to Mr. Harcourt. "Indeed, sir, I'm most sorry to disappoint you but I fear my card is full."

Minutes later, she heard Clarissa copy her words, prettily turning Lord Swindon away.

As her equilibrium, momentarily undermined, returned, Sophie became conscious of a niggling disquiet, a sense that something was not entirely right. Only when, for the third time, she found her gaze scanning the room, searching automatically, did she realize just what it was she felt.

Feeling very like muttering a curse, she instead pinned a bright smile on her lips and, with renewed determination, gave her attention to her court. "Will your sister be coming up to London, Lord Argyle? I should be delighted to meet her again."

She was here to find a husband, not to fall victim to a rake's blue eyes.

By dint of sheer determination, Jack managed to keep himself occupied until the country dance preceding the supper waltz was in progress. He was, he kept reminding himself, far too experienced to cram his leaders. Instead, he had forced himself to circulate, artfully sidestepping subtle invitations to lead other young ladies onto the floor. Now, as the last strains of the music died, he threaded his way through the crowd to come up by Sophie's side. Fate was smiling on him again; she had just finished thanking her partner, Lord Enderby.

"Miss Winterton." With a slight bow, Jack reached for Sophie's hand. "Evening, Enderby." A nod was enough to distract her recent partner.

"Eh?" Squinting slightly, Lord Enderby switched his

near-sighted stare from Sophie to Jack. "Oh, it's you, Lester. Surprised to see *you* here. Thought you'd be at Newmarket."

Jack smiled—into Sophie's eyes. "I discovered that, this Season, there was to be an unlooked-for distraction in London."

"Really?" Lord Enderby's eyes were too weak to appreciate the action taking place before them. "What's that?"

Feeling the warmth rise to her cheeks, Sophie held her breath, her gaze daring her next partner to say anything untoward.

Jack's gaze grew more intent. "Far be it from me to reveal any secrets," he said. "You'll learn the truth soon enough." His gaze remained on Sophie's face. "But I'm come to steal Miss Winterton from you, Enderby. My dance is next, I believe, my dear?" With a calmly proprietorial air, Jack tucked Sophie's hand into the crook of his elbow and, with the barest of nods for Lord Enderby, now thoroughly bemused, turned her down the room.

Sophie blinked and grabbed her wandering wits. "I believe you're right, Mr. Lester. But shouldn't we return to my aunt?"

"Why?"

She glanced up to find an improbably mild expression inhabiting her companion's patrician features as, undeterred by her remonstrance, he led her further and further from her aunt. "Because it's expected," she replied.

He smiled then, a slow, devilish smile, and looked down, meeting her gaze. "You're not a deb, my dear." His voice had deepened; she felt as well as heard it. Then his intent look softened and he looked ahead. "And, despite the throng, the room is not so crowded your aunt cannot keep you in view, if she's so inclined."

That, Sophie realized as she calmed her leaping heart, was true. A quick glance over her shoulder revealed Lucilla, with Clarissa beside her, almost at the other end of the room. There were many bodies between, but the crowd was not so thick it blocked them off.

"I don't intend to kidnap you, you know."

The soft statement pulled her gaze back to his face.

Jack smiled and tried his best to make the gesture reassuring. "I merely thought you might like to see who else is here tonight."

Her "Oh," was there in her eyes. Then, with a last, still-suspicious glance, she gave up her resistance, her hand settling on his arm.

He did as he had indicated, embarking on a gentle perambulation of the room. "Lady Entwhistle's lucky to see so many here so early in the Season. Lord Abercrombie," Jack indicated that well-known huntsman. "Have you met him before?" Sophie nodded. "He, for one, rarely leaves Northamptonshire until late April. The thaw must be extensive to have driven him south this early."

Sophie had, indeed, been surprised to find so many of the *ton*'s more mature yet eligible bachelors present. "I hadn't realized that the weather was to blame."

Again, she was aware of his gaze. "For some," he said,

his voice low. Sternly quelling a shiver, Sophie pretended to look about.

"So, how do you find Society after four years away? Does it still hold some allure?"

Sophie glanced up at the question; a cynical ripple in his smooth tones gave her pause. "Allure?" she repeated, putting her head on one side. "I do not know that that is the right term, Mr. Lester." She frowned slightly. "There's glamour, perhaps." With one hand, she gestured about them. "But any with eyes must see it is transitory, an illusion with no real substance." They strolled on and Sophie smiled wryly. "I have long thought the Season society's stage, where we all come together to impress each other with our standing before summer draws us back to our true professions, to the management of our estates."

His gaze on her face, Jack inclined his head, his expression enigmatic. "You are wise beyond your years, my dear."

Sophie met his gaze; she arched a sceptical brow. "And you, sir?" She let her gaze slide away. Greatly daring, she continued, "I find it hard to believe that your view of the Season agrees with mine. I have always been told that gentlemen such as yourself pursue certain interests for which the Season is indispensible."

Jack's lips twitched. "Indeed, my dear." He let a moment stretch in silence before adding, "You should not, however, imagine that such interests are behind my presence here in town this early in the year."

Resisting the urge to look up at him, Sophie kept her gaze

on those surrounding them. "Indeed?" she replied coolly. "Then it was boredom that fetched you south?"

Jack glanced down at her. "No, Miss Winterton. It was not boredom."

"Not boredom?" Determination not to allow him to triumph, Sophie swung about and, disregarding the crazed beating of her heart and the constriction which restricted her breathing, met his blue gaze. "Indeed, sir?"

He merely raised an arrogant brow at her, his expression unreadable.

She met his gaze coolly, then allowed hers to fall, boldly taking in his large, immaculately clad frame. The sapphire glinted in the white folds of his cravat; he wore no fobs or other ornament, nothing to detract from the image created by lean and powerful muscles. "Ah," she declared, resisting the urge to clear her throat. Settling her hand once more on his sleeve, she fell in by his side. "I see it now. Confess, sir, that it is the prospect of your mounts having to wade through the mire that has driven you, in despair I make no doubt, from Leicestershire."

Jack laughed. "Wrong again, Miss Winterton."

"Then I greatly fear it is the lure of the gaming rooms that has brought you to town, Mr. Lester."

"There's a lure involved, I admit, but it's not one of green baize."

"What, then?" Sophie demanded, pausing to look up at him.

Jack's gaze rose to touch her curls, then lowered to her

eyes, softly blue. His lips lifted in a slow smile. "The lure is one of gold, my dear."

Sophie blinked and frowned slightly. "You've come seeking your fortune?"

Jack's gaze, darkly blue, became more intent. "Not my fortune, Miss Winterton." He paused, his smile fading as he looked into her eyes. "My future."

Her gaze trapped in his, Sophie could have sworn the polished parquetry on which she stood quivered beneath her feet. She was dimly aware they had halted; the crowd about them had faded, their chattering no longer reaching her. Her heart was in her throat, blocking her breath; it had to be that that was making her so lightheaded.

The midnight blue gaze did not waver; Sophie searched his eyes, but could find no hint, in them or his expression, to discount the wild possibility that had leapt into her mind.

Then he smiled, his mouth, his expression, softening, as she had seen it do before.

"I believe that's our waltz starting, Miss Winterton." Jack paused, then, his eyes still on hers, his voice darkly deep, he asked, "Will you partner me, my dear?"

Sophie quelled a shiver. She was not a green girl; she was twenty-two, experienced and assured. Ignoring her thudding heart, ignoring the subtle undertones in his voice, she drew dignity about her and, calmly inclining her head, put her hand in his.

His fingers closed strongly over hers; in that instant, Sophie was not at all sure just what question she had answered. Yet she followed his lead, allowing him to seep her into his arms. With a single deft turn, he merged them with the circling throng; they were just one couple among the many on the floor.

Time and again, Sophie told herself that was so, that there was nothing special in this waltz, nothing special between them. One part of her mind formed the words; the rest wasn't listening, too absorbed in silent communion with a pair of dark blue eyes.

She only knew the dance was over when they stopped. They had spoken not a word throughout; yet, it seemed, things had been said, clearly enough for them both. She could barely breathe.

Jack's expression was serious yet gentle as he drew her hand once more through his arm. "It's time for supper, my dear."

His eyes were softly smiling. Sophie basked in their glow. Shy yet elated, off balance yet strangely assured, she returned the smile. "Indeed, sir. I rely on you to guide me."

His lips lifted lightly. "You may always do so, my dear."

He found a table for two in the supper room and secured a supply of delicate sandwiches and two glasses of champagne. Then he settled back to recount the most interesting of the past year's *on-dits,* after which they fell to hypothesizing on the likely stance of the various protagonists at the commencement of this Season.

Despite her blithe spirits, Sophie was grateful for the distraction. She felt as if she was teetering on some invisible brink; she was not at all sure it was wise to take the next step. So she laughed and chatted, ignoring the sudden moments when breathlessness attacked, when their gazes met and held for an instant too long.

Her elation persisted, that curious uplifting of her spirits, as if her heart had broken free of the earth and was now lighter than air. The sensation lingered, even when Jack, very dutifully, escorted her back to Lucilla's side.

With what was, she felt, commendable composure, Sophie held out her hand. "I thank you for a most enjoyable interlude, sir." Her voice, lowered, was oddly soft and husky.

A small knot of gentlemen hovered uncertainly, awaiting her return.

Jack eyed them, less than pleased but too wise to show it. Instead, he took Sophie's hand and bowed elegantly. Straightening, for the last time that evening he allowed his gaze to meet hers. "Until next we meet, Miss Winterton."

His eyes said it would be soon.

To SOPHIE'S CONSTERNATION, he called the next morning. Summoned to join her aunt in the drawing-room, she entered to find him, garbed most correctly for a morning about town in blue Bath superfine and ivory inexpressibles, rising from a chair to greet her, a faint, challenging lift to his dark brows.

"Good morning, Miss Winterton."

Determined to hold her own, Sophie bludgeoned her wits

into order and plastered a calm, unflustered expression over her surprise. "Good day, Mr. Lester."

His smile warmed her before he released her hand to greet Clarissa, who had entered in her wake.

Aware that her aunt's deceptively mild gaze was fixed firmly upon her, Sophie crossed to the chaise, cloaking her distraction with a nonchalant air. As she settled her skirts, she noted that susceptibility to Mr. Lester's charms appeared strangely restricted. Despite her inexperience, Clarissa showed no sensitivity, greeting their unexpected caller with unaffected delight. Released, her cousin came to sit beside her.

Jack resumed his seat, elegantly disposing his long limbs in a fashionably fragile white-and-gilt chair. He had already excused his presence by turning Lucilla's edict to call on them to good account. "As I was saying, Mrs. Webb, it is, indeed, pleasant to find oneself with time to spare before the Season gets fully under way."

"Quite," Lucilla returned, her pale gaze open and innocent. In a morning gown of wine-red cambric, she sat enthroned in an armchair close by the hearth. "However, I must confess it took the small taste of the *ton* that we enjoyed last night to refresh my memories. I had quite forgotten how extremely fatiguing it can be."

From behind his urbane facade, Jack watched her carefully. "Indeed." He gently inclined his head. "Coming direct from the country, the *ton*'s ballrooms can, I imagine, take on the aspect of an ordeal."

"A very stuffy ordeal," Lucilla agreed. Turning to the chaise, she asked, "Did you not find it so, my dears?"

Clarissa smiled brightly and opened her mouth to deny any adverse opinion of the previous evening's entertainment.

Smoothly, Sophie cut in, "Indeed, yes. It may not have been a crush, yet the crowd was not inconsiderable. Towards the end, I found the atmosphere positively thick."

It was simply not done to admit to unfettered delight, nor to dismiss a kindly hostess's entertainments as uncrowded.

Jack kept his smile restrained. "Just so. I had, in fact, wondered, Miss Winterton, if you would like to blow away any lingering aftertaste of the crowd by taking a turn in the Park? I have my curricle with me."

"What a splendid idea." Lucilla concurred, turning, wide-eyed, to Sophie.

But Sophie was looking at Jack.

As she watched, he inclined his head. "If you would care for it, Miss Winterton?"

Slowly, Sophie drew in a breath. And nodded. "I…" Abruptly, she looked down, to where her hands were clasped in the lap of her morning gown, a concoction of lilac mull-muslin. "I should change my gown."

"I'm sure Mr. Lester will excuse you, my dear."

With a nod to her aunt, Sophie withdrew, then beat a hasty retreat to her chamber. There, summoning a maid, she threw open the doors of her wardrobe and drew forth the carriage dress Jorge had sent round that morning. A golden umber, the heavy material was shot with green, so that, as she moved, it appeared to bronze, then dull. Standing before her cheval-glass, Sophie held the gown to her, noting again how its colour heightened the gold in her hair and emphasized the creaminess of her complexion. She grinned delightedly. Hugging the dress close, she whirled, waltzing a few steps, letting her heart hold sway for just a moment.

Then she caught sight of the maid staring at her from the doorway. Abruptly, Sophie steadied. "Ah, there you are, Ellen. Come along." She waved the young girl forward. "I need to change."

Downstairs in the drawing-room, Jack made idle conversation, something he could do with less than half his brain. Then, unexpectedly, Lucilla blandly declared, "I hope you'll excuse Clarissa, Mr. Lester. We're yet very busy settling in." To Clarissa, she said, "Do look in on the twins for me, my love. You know I never feel comfortable unless I know what they're about."

Clarissa smiled in sunny agreement. She rose and bobbed a curtsy to Jack, then departed, leaving him wondering about the twins.

"They're six," Lucilla calmly stated. "A dreadfully *imaginative* age."

Jack blinked, then decided to return to safer topics. "Allow me to congratulate you on your daughter, Mrs. Webb. I've rarely seen such beauty in conjunction with such a sweet disposition. I prophesy she'll be an instant success."

Lucilla glowed with maternal satisfaction. "Indeed, it

seems likely. Fortunately for myself and Mr. Webb, and I dare say Clarissa, too, her Season is intended purely to—" Lucilla gestured airily "—broaden her horizons. Her future is already all but settled. A young gentleman from Leicestershire—one of our neighbours—Ned Ascombe."

"Indeed?" Jack politely raised his brows.

"Oh, yes," his redoubtable hostess continued in a comfortably confiding vein. "But both my husband and I are firmly of the opinion that it does no good for a young girl to make her choice before…surveying the field, as it were." With every appearance of ingenuousness, Lucilla explained, "The chosen suitor may be the same as before she looked but she, certainly, will feel much more assured that her choice is the right one if she's given the opportunity to convince herself it is so." Lucilla's pale eyes swung to Jack's face. "That's why we're so keen to give Clarissa a full Season—so that she'll know her own mind."

Jack met her level gaze. "And your niece?"

Lucilla frowned delicately but approval glimmered in her eyes. "Indeed. Sophie's first Season was cut so very short it hardly signified. She was presented, and had her come-out and even braved the trial of Almack's, but it was barely three weeks in all before my sister succumbed to a chill. So very tragic."

Her sigh was sorrowful; Jack inclined his head and waited.

"So, you see, Mr. Lester," Lucilla continued, raising her head to look him in the eye. "Both Mr. Webb and I hope very much that any gentleman who truly appreciates dear Sophie will allow her to have her Season this time."

Jack held her coolly challenging gaze for what seemed like an age. Then, reluctantly, he inclined his head. "Indeed, ma'am," he replied, his tone even. "Your arguments are hard to deny." When it became clear his hostess was waiting for more, he added, his expression impassive, "Any gentleman who valued your niece would, I feel sure, abide by such wisdom."

Gracious as ever, Lucilla smiled her approbation, then turned as the latch lifted. "Ah, there you are, Sophie."

Smoothly, Jack rose and went forward, his eyes feasting on the vision hovering on the threshold. She had donned a forest green half-cape over her carriage dress, which was of a strange bronzy-gold shade with piping of the same dark green at collar and cuffs. Green gloves and green half-boots completed her outfit. Jack felt his lips soften in a smile; his Sophie was fashionable elegance incarnate.

Reassured by his smile, and the appreciative light in his eyes, Sophie smiled back and gave him her hand. Together, they turned to Lucilla.

"I will engage to take all care of your niece, Mrs. Webb." Jack sent an arrogantly questioning glance across the room.

Lucilla studied the picture they made, and smiled. "I trust you will, Mr. Lester. But do not be too long; Lady Cowper is to call this afternoon, and we must later attend Lady Allingcott's at-home." With a graciously benevolent nod, she dismissed them.

It was not until they reached the Park and Jack let his horses stretch their legs that Sophie allowed herself to believe it was real. That she was, in truth, bowling along the well-tended carriageway with Jack Lester beside her. The brisk breeze, cool and playful, twined in her curls and tugged little wisps free to wreath about her ears. Above and about them, arched branches were swelling in bud; the sky, a clear, crisp blue, formed a backdrop for their nakedness. Slanting a glance at her companion, she wondered, not for the first time, just what he intended.

He had, most correctly, escorted her down the steps of her aunt's house, then blotted his copybook by ignoring her hand and lifting her instead to his curricle's seat. On taking his own seat beside her and being assured she was comfortable, he had smiled, a slow, proudly satisfied smile, and clicked the reins. The bustle in the streets had made conversation unwise; she had held her peace while they travelled the short distance to the gates of the Park.

Now, with the first fashionable carriages looming ahead, she said, her tone merely matter-of-fact, "I had not looked to see you so soon, sir."

Jack glanced down at her. "I couldn't keep away." It was, he somewhat ruefully reflected, the literal truth. He had fully intended to allow the Webbs reasonable time to settle in the capital; instead, he had not been able to resist the compulsion to take Sophie for a drive, to show her the *ton,* and display her to them, safely anchored by his side. Staking his claim—and in such uncharacteristically blunt fashion that Sophie's aunt had seen fit to metaphorically wag her finger at him. Even the weather was conspiring to make him rush on with his wooing, the bright sunshine more redolent of April and May than chilly March.

He had expected some confusion in response to his forthright answer. Instead, to his delight, Sophie raised her chin and calmly stated, "In that case, you may make yourself useful and tell me who all these people are. My aunt has had little time to fill me in, and there are many I don't recognize."

Jack grinned. It was close on noon, a most fashionable time to be seen driving in the Park. "The Misses Berry you must recall," he said as they swept down on an ancient landau drawn up by the verge. "They're always to be found at precisely that spot, morning and afternoon throughout the Season."

"Of course I remember them." With a gay smile, Sophie nodded to the two old dames, bundled up in scarves and shawls on the seat of the landau. They nodded back. As the curricle swept past, Sophie saw the gleam in their bright eyes.

"Next we have Lady Staunton and her daughters. You don't need to know them, although doubtless your cousin will make the younger girls' acquaintance."

Sophie bestowed a distant smile on the bevy of girlish faces turned to stare in open envy as she went by. Despite Jorge's undoubted expertise, she doubted it was her new carriage dress that had excited their interest.

As she looked ahead once more, she saw a tall woman, modishly gowned in bright cherry-red, strolling the lawns just ahead. Her hand rested on the arm of a rakishly handsome buck. Both looked up as the carriage neared.

The woman's face lit up; she raised her hand in what appeared, to Sophie, a distinctly imperious summons.

The reaction on her right was immediate; Jack stiffened. As it became clear the carriage was not about to stop, nor even slow, Sophie glanced up. Chilly reserve had laid hold of Jack's features; as Sophie watched, he inclined his head in the most remote of greetings.

The carriage swept on, leaving the couple behind. Relaxing against the padded seat, Sophie forced her lips to behave. "And that was?" she prompted.

The glance she received was dark with warning. She met it with a lifted brow—and waited.

"Harriette Wilson," came the answer. "Someone you definitely do *not* need to know."

His repressive tone evoked a gurgle of laughter; Sophie swallowed it and airly looked around. Lady Cowper's barouche was drawn up in a curve of the carriageway; Sophie waved as they passed, pleased to note her ladyship's answering smile. Lady Cowper was yet another old friend of her late mama's.

They passed many others; Jack knew them all. His running commentary kept Sophie amused and distracted. She was content to enjoy his company and his apparent liking for hers; she would dwell on what it might mean later. So she smiled and laughed up at him, basking in the glow of his very blue eyes.

"Jack!"

The hail jolted them from their absorption.

It emanated from a young, dark-haired gentleman, clearly of the first stare, who, together with his similarly well-turned-out companion, was perched on the driving seat of a swan-necked phaeton, approaching at a clipping pace. Jack reined his horses to the side of the track; the elegant equipage executed a neat turn and came to a swooping stop beside them.

"Been searching for you forever," the young gentleman declared, his eyes, also deeply blue, passing from Jack to Sophie. He smiled with cheery good-humour. "Dashed if I'd thought to find you here!"

Glancing up at her escort's face, Sophie saw a whimsical smile soften his hard features.

"Gerald." Jack nodded to his brother, his knowledgeable gaze roving over the finer points of the pair of high-bred horses harnessed between the long shafts of the phaeton, itself spanking new if its gleaming paintwork was to be believed. "Where'd you get this rig?"

"The phaeton's fresh out of old Smithers's workshop. The nags are Hardcastle's. He'll let me have them for a tithe their true value—five hundred the pair. The phaeton'll be full price, though, and you know what Smithers is like."

Brows lifting, Jack nodded. With a deft twirl of his wrist, he looped his reins and offered them to Sophie. "Will you do me the honour, my dear?"

Scrambling to hide her surprise, greatly pleased for she well knew that few gentlemen would entrust their horses to a mere female, Sophie graciously nodded and took the reins.

With a reassuring smile, Jack climbed down. The horses shifted slightly; determined to keep them in line, Sophie kept her eyes firmly on them, her brow furrowing in concentration.

Hiding his grin, Jack paced slowly around Gerald's carriage and horses, his blue eyes shrewdly assessing. Gerald and his friend watched with bated breath, their eagerness barely suppressed. Then, rejoining Sophie and retaking possession of the reins with a warm smile, Jack nodded at his brother. "Not a bad set-up."

Gerald grinned delightedly.

"But allow me to make you known to Miss Winterton." Jack paused to allow Gerald to bow, lithely graceful. "My youngest brother, Gerald Lester."

Having had time to note the similarity between Jack and the youthful gentleman, also dark-haired, blue-eyed and broad-shouldered, but without the heavy musculature that characterized her escort's more mature frame, Sophie showed no surprise.

While his brother introduced Lord Somerby, his companion, Jack cast a last glance over the phaeton and pair. His lips quirked. Turning to Gerald, he smoothly said, "And now you'll have to excuse us. I'm overdue to return Miss Winterton to her home."

"Jack!" Gerald's pained exclamation was heartfelt. "Dash it all—don't tease. May I have them or not?"

Jack chuckled. "You may. But make sure you get an account from Smithers. Drop by this evening and I'll give you a draft." Although it was his own money Gerald would be spending, as his trustee until his twenty-fifth birthday, Jack had to approve all his youngest brother's transactions.

Gerald's smile was ecstatic. "I'll be around at seven." With an insouciant wave of his whip, he touched his horses' ears. As the phaeton disappeared along the avenue, his gay carolling rolled back to them.

Smiling at Jack's exuberance, a sort of boundless *joie de vivre,* Sophie glanced up at her companion.

As if sensing her regard, Jack's smile, distant as he contemplated his brother's delight, refocused on her face. "And now, I fear, I really should return you to Mount Street, my dear."

So saying, he whipped up his horses; they took the turn into the main avenue in style. As they bowled along, a stylish matron chatting idly with an acquaintance in her carriage, glanced up, then waved them down. Jack politely drew in beside the lady's barouche.

"Sophia, my dear!" Lady Osbaldestone beamed at her. "I take it your aunt has finally arrived in town?"

"Indeed, ma'am." Sophie leant from the curricle to shake her ladyship's hand. "We'll be here for the Season."

"And a good thing, too! It's entirely more than time you were amongst us again." Her ladyship's eyes gleamed with a fervour to which Sophie was innured.

Jack was not so fortunate. He exchanged nods with Lady Osbaldestone, wryly resigned to being ignored for at least the next ten minutes. Lady Osbaldestone's lack of concern in finding a young lady with whom she clearly claimed more than a passing acquaintance alone in his presence registered—and made his inner smile even more wry. There had been a time, not so very far distant, when she would not have been so sanguine. However, over the past year, his acknowledged search for a wife had gained him, if not immunity from all suspicion, then at least a certain acceptance amongst the *grandes dames*. He suspected they viewed him as a leopard who, at least temporarily, had changed his spots.

That much, he was willing to concede, might be true. Nevertheless, the underlying temperament remained.

As he heard her ladyship's plans for Sophie's future unfurl, his instincts rose to shake his complacency.

He waited until they had, at last, parted from his ladyship and were once more rolling towards the gates before saying, "Lady Osbaldestone seems quite determined to see you well wed."

Totally unconcerned by her ladyship's grand schemes, which had even stretched as far as the Duke of Huntington, Sophie smiled gaily. "Indeed. They are all of them busy hatching schemes."

"All of them?"

There was something in his flat tones that made her glance up but her companion's expression was inscrutable. Light-hearted still, even light-headed, the aftermath, no doubt, of an uninterrupted hour of his company, Sophie grinned. "All of my mother's old friends," she explained. "They all look upon me as a motherless chick—one and all, they're determined to see me 'properly established'." She uttered the last words in a passable imitation of Lady Osbaldestone's haughty accents.

She glanced up, expecting to see him smiling, laughing with her at the prospect of so many matrons busily scheming on her behalf. Instead, his face remained stony, devoid of expression. Jack felt her glance. His emotions straining at the leash, he looked down.

Sophie met his dark gaze, and felt a vice slowly close about her heart. Avid, eager to find the reason, for that and the force that held them in a curious hiatus, out of time, she searched his face and his deeply glowing eyes. Jack watched as her smile slowly faded, to be replaced with puzzlement—and a clear query.

"Sophie—" He drew in a deep breath and glanced ahead, just in time to avoid colliding with a natty trilby, swung through the gates far too fast.

Jack swore. In the ensuing chaos as he calmed his own horses, then received the shrill and abject apologies of the trilby's owner, a young sprig barely old enough to shave and, in Jack's pithily offered opinion, of insufficient experience to be entrusted with the reins, the purport of Lucilla's words returned to him.

As the trilby crept away, Jack turned to Sophie, his expression carefully blank. "Are you all right?"

"Yes." Sophie smiled brightly up at him, while inwardly she wondered if that was strictly true. The instant before the trilby's advent had left her nerves stretched and quivering.

Jack forced his lips into an easy smile. "I'd better get you back to Mount Street forthwith, or your aunt will doubtless forbid me your company. It's well past our allotted hour."

Sophie kept her own smile light. "My aunt is very understanding."

That, Jack thought, as he eased into the traffic, was undoubtedly the greatest understatement he had ever heard. He made no effort to break the silence until they reached Mount Street. Even then, relinquishing the reins to Jigson, whom he had left awaiting his return, he eschewed comment, reaching up to lift Sophie down to the pavement in what was rapidly becoming a charged silence.

As he expected, she showed no signs of fluster. Instead, she stood before him, her face turned up to his, her query contained in the gentle lift of her delicate brows.

Despite himself, Jack smiled—his slow, sensuous smile, the one he was usually careful to hide from well-bred young ladies.

Sophie didn't disappoint him; she studied his face, openly gauging his smile, then, lifting her eyes to his, merely raised her brows higher.

Jack laughed softly but shook his head. "The time is not yet," was all he dared say. Holding her eyes with his, he raised her gloved hand and, most reprehensibly, placed a kiss on her bare wrist. Then, placing her hand on his sleeve, he covered it with his and strolled with her up the steps. As the door opened to admit her, he bowed. "Once again, my dear—until next we meet."

CHAPTER SIX

FOR SOPHIE, the rest of Tuesday and all of Wednesday passed in a rosy-hued blur. As expected, Lady Cowper called, promising vouchers for Almack's and her most earnest endeavours. Lucilla and her ladyship spent a full hour with their heads close together; Sophie stared absent-mindedly at the window, her expression distant. Recalled to the present when her ladyship rose, she flashed a bright smile and bade Lady Cowper farewell. The smile lingered, muted but nevertheless present, long after her ladyship's carriage rattled away down the street.

"Well then, my dears." Lucilla swept back into the drawing-room. Clarissa followed with Sophie trailing in the rear. "In the light of Lady Cowper's remarks, we had best reconsider our strategy."

Closing the door, Sophie made for the chaise, a slight blush tinting her cheeks. "How so, aunt?" She could not, in truth, recall all that much of Lady Cowper's conversation.

With a long-suffering air, Lucilla raised her brows. "Because, my dear, if the *ton* is already in town then there's no reason not to steal a march on those who have planned their entertainments to coincide with the usual start of festivities and already sent out their invitations." Reclaiming her seat, she gestured to the pile of white cards upon the mantelshelf. "The list grows every day. I have it in mind to make our mark with a tactical manoeuvre, if I have the phrase correctly."

Sophie tried to concentrate on her aunt's meaning. Yet at every pause, her mind slid sideways, to ponder the subtleties in a certain deep voice, and the light that had glowed in his eyes. Frowning, she struggled to banish her distracting fascination. "So you mean to bring Clarissa's come-out forward?"

Deep in thought, Lucilla nodded. "It seems strategically imperative—if she's not out, she cannot be present at the rush of balls and parties which, as dear Emily pointed out, are this year going to precede the usual commencement." Lucilla pulled a face. "Yet it's not the sort of decision one takes lightly." She pondered a moment, one elegant fingernail tapping on the chair arm. Then she straightened. "We have Lady Allingcott's at-home this afternoon and Lady Chessington's little party tonight, then Almack's tomorrow—even they have started early this year. I pray you both to keep your ears open. Depending on what we all hear, I think we might start with an impromptu party, just for the younger folk, next week. And plan Clarissa's ball for the week after that. My ideas are already well advanced; it will simply be a matter of bringing them forward a trifle." Nodding to herself, Lucilla turned to Clarissa. "What say you to that, my dear?"

"It sounds *wonderful!*" Clarissa's eyes radiated excited relief. "Indeed, I wasn't looking forward to missing the balls in the next weeks."

"And why should you?" Lucilla spread her hands wide. "This is your Season, my love; you're here to enjoy it." She smiled her subtlest smile. "As Madame Jorge said; we will contrive."

Sophie had nothing to say against her aunt's plans. Mr. Lester, of course, would not be present at the small, informal parties and dances held by the families with young girls making their come-out, to help the young ladies gain their social feet. Until Clarissa was officially out, the Webb ladies would be restricted to such tame affairs, which were all very well if there was nothing else on offer. But this year, this Season, was going to be different—and it wasn't only the weather that would make it so for her.

They attended Lady Allingcott's and Lady Chessington's entertainments, and on Wednesday called on Lady Hartford and the Misses Smythe, then danced at Almack's, all the while listening to what their peers had to say of projected entertainments.

Over breakfast the next morning, Lucilla called a council of war. "Now pay attention, Sophie."

Thus adjured, Sophie blinked. And endeavored to obey the injunction.

"I've consulted with your father, Clarissa, and he's in full agreement. We will hold your come-out ball at the end of the week after next."

Clarissa crowed. Her younger brothers pulled faces and taunted.

"In the meantime, however," Lucilla raised her voice only slightly; as her eagle eye swept the table the din subsided. "We'll hold a dance at the end of next week—on Friday. An informal affair—but we need not restrict the guest list solely to those making their come-out. I see no reason not to invite some of those amongst the *ton* with whom you are already acquainted."

Sophie knew her smile was almost as bright as Clarissa's. Her aunt's gaze, pausing meaningfully on her, sent her heart soaring. Ridiculous—but there was no other word for it— the exhilarating excitement that gripped her at the mere thought of seeing him again. She lived for the moment but, given he had not appeared at Almack's—faint hope though that had been—it had seemed likely they would not meet again until Clarissa was out and they could move freely in society's mainstream.

Unless, of course, he called to take her driving again.

She spent all morning with one ear tuned to the knocker. When the time for luncheon arrived and he had not called, she put her disappointment aside and, her smile still bright, descended to the dining-room. She was determined none of her cousins would guess her true state. As for her aunt, she had directed one or two pointed glances at her niece and once, she had surprised a look of soft satisfaction upon Lucilla's face. That, of course, was inevitable.

It was at Mrs. Morgan-Stanley's at-home later that day that her bubble of happiness was punctured.

On entering the Morgan-Stanleys' large drawing-room, Lucilla immediately joined the circle of fashionable matrons gathered about the fireplace. Clarissa drifted across to the windows, to where the youngest of those present had shyly retreated to trade dreams. With a confident smile, Sophie joined a small group of young ladies for whom this was not their first Season. She was taking tea with them in their corner when, in the midst of a discussion on the many notables already sighted in town, Miss Billingham, a thin young lady with severe, pinched features, cast her an arch glance.

"Indeed! Miss Winterton, I fancy, can testify to the fact. Why, we saw you in the Park just the other morning, my dear, driving with Mr. Lester."

"Mr. Lester?" Miss Chessington, a bright, cheerful soul, short, good-natured and of an indefatigably sunny temperament, blinked in amazement. "But I thought he *never* drove mere females."

"Not previously," Miss Billingham conceded with the air of one who had made a thorough study of the matter and was unshakeably certain of her facts. "But it's clear he has, at last, realized he must change his ways. My mama commented on the point, even last Season." When the others, Sophie included, looked their question, Miss Billingham consented to explain. "Well, it's common knowledge that he must marry well. More than well—real money—for there are his brothers, too, and everyone knows the Lesters have barely a penny to bless themselves with. Good breeding, good estates—it's the blunt that's wanting."

Sophie was not the only one who blinked at the crude term and the hard gleam in Miss Billingham's eyes but, in her case, the action was purely reflex. Her mind was reeling; a horrible sinking feeling had taken up residence in the pit of her stomach. Her features froze in a polite mask, and a sudden chill swept through her.

"My mama has long maintained," Miss Billingham declaimed, "that he'd have to come about. Too high in the instep by half, he spent all last Season searching for some goddess. Likely he's come to the understanding that he cannot look so high."

Miss Billingham looked at Sophie. The others, following her lead, did the same. Caught on a welling tide of despair, Sophie did not notice.

"I suppose, it being so early in the Season, he thought to amuse himself—get his hand in at the practice in safety, so to speak—by squiring you about, Miss Winterton."

It was the rustling of skirts as the others drew back, distancing themselves from the snide remark, that shook Sophie from her trance. As Miss Billingham's words registered, she felt herself pale. A cattish gleam of satisfaction flared in Miss Billingham's eyes. Pride came to Sophie's rescue, stiffening her spine. She drew in a steadying breath, then lifted her chin, looking down at Miss Billingham with chilly hauteur. "I dare say, Miss Billingham." Her tone repressively cool, Sophie continued, "I can only assume that

Mr. Lester could find no other to suit his purpose, for, as you say, I hardly qualify as a rich prize."

At first, Miss Billingham missed the allusion; the poorly suppressed grins of the other young ladies finally brought Sophie's words home. Slowly, Miss Billingham's sallow complexion turned beet-red, an unhappy sight. She opened her mouth, casting a glance around for support. As she found none, her colour deepened. With a few muted words, she excused herself to return to the safer precincts close by her mother, a woman of battleship proportions.

"Don't pay any attention to her," Miss Chessington advised as their little circle closed comfortably about Sophie. "She's just furious Jack Lester paid her no heed whatever last year. Set her cap at him, and fell flat on her face."

Valiantly, Sophie struggled to return Miss Chessington's bright smile. "Indeed. But what of your hopes? Do you have anyone in your sights?"

Belle Chessington grinned hugely. "Heavens, no! I'm determined to enjoy myself. All that bother about a husband can come later."

Reflecting that, a few months ago, she, too, would have been as carefree, Sophie dragged her thoughts away from what had focused her mind on marriage. She clung to Miss Chessington's buoyant spirits until it was time to depart.

Once enveloped in the quiet of her aunt's carriage, cool reason returned to hold back the misery that threatened to engulf her. Sophie closed her eyes and laid her head back on the squabs.

"Aren't you feeling quite the thing, my dear?"

Lucilla's calm voice interrupted Sophie's thoughts. Sophie tried to smile, but the result was more like a grimace. "Just a slight headache. I found Mrs. Morgan-Stanley's drawing-room a trifle close." It was the best she could do. To her relief, her aunt seemed to accept the weak excuse.

Lucilla reached over and patted her hand. "Well, do take care. I hope you'll both remember that one never appears to advantage while a martyr to ill health." After a moment, Lucilla mused, "I don't think our schedule is overly full, but if you do feel the need, you must both promise me you'll rest."

Together with Clarissa, Sophie murmured her reassurances.

As the carriage rolled steadily onward, she kept her eyes closed, hiding her frown. Despite her often outrageous machinations, Lucilla was ever supportive, always protective. If Jack Lester was, indeed, totally ineligible as a suitor for her hand—or, more specifically, if, as a mere lady of expectations, *she* was ineligible to be his bride, then Lucilla would not have allowed him to draw so close. Her aunt was as clever as she could hold together. Surely she could trust in Lucilla's perspicacity?

Perhaps Miss Billingham had it wrong?

That possibility allowed Sophie to meet the rest of her day with equanimity, if not outright enthusiasm. Until the evening, when Lady Orville's little musical gathering brought an end to all hope.

It was, most incongruously, old Lady Matcham who squashed the bubble of her happiness flat. A tiny little woman, white-haired and silver-eyed with age, her ladyship was a kindly soul who would never, Sophie knew, intentionally cause anyone harm.

"I know you won't mind me mentioning this, Sophia, my dear. You know how very close I was to your mother—well, she was almost a daughter to me, you know. So sad, her going." The old eyes filled with tears. Lady Matcham dabbed them away with a lace-edged handkerchief. "Silly of me, of course." She smiled with determined brightness up at Sophie, sitting beside her on a chaise along the back wall of the music room.

Before them, the very select few whom Lady Orville had invited to air their musical abilities along with her two daughters were entertaining the gathering, seated in rows of little chairs before the pianoforte. Now, to the sound of polite applause, Miss Chessington took her seat at the instrument and laid her hands upon the keys.

Expecting a comment on the colour of her ribbons, or something in similar vein, Sophie smiled reassuringly at Lady Matcham, returning the squeeze of one birdlike claw.

"But that's why I feel I have to say something, Sophia," Lady Matcham continued. "For I would not rest easy thinking you had got hurt when I could have prevented it."

An icy hand closed about Sophie's heart, all expression leached from her face. Numb, paralyzed, she gazed blankly at Lady Matcham.

"I must say," her ladyship went on, her washed-out eyes widening. "I had thought Lucilla would have warned you but, no doubt, having only just returned to the capital, she's not yet up with the latest."

The chill creeping through Sophie had reached her mind; she couldn't think how to interrupt. She didn't want to hear any more, but her ladyship pressed on, her soft, gentle, undeniably earnest tones a death-knell to all hope.

"It's about Mr. Lester, my dear. Such a handsome man—quite the gentleman and so very well-connected. But he needs a rich wife. A very rich wife. I know, for I am acquainted with his aunt, dear soul—she's passed on now. But it was always understood the Lester boys would have to marry money, as the saying goes." Lady Matcham's sweet face grimaced with distaste. "Such a disheartening thought."

Sophie could only agree. Her heart was a painful lump in her breast; her features felt frozen. She couldn't speak; she could only gaze blankly as Lady Matcham lifted her wise old eyes to her face.

Lady Matcham patted her hand. "I saw you in the Park, in his curricle. And I just had to say something, my dear, for it really won't do. I dare say he's everything a gal like you might wish for. But indeed, Sophia dear, he's not for you."

Sophie blinked rapidly and sucked in a quick breath. Her heart was aching; all of her hurt. But she could not give way to her pain in the middle of Miss Chessington's sonata. Sophie swallowed; with an effort, she summoned a weak smile. "Thank you for the warning, ma'am." She couldn't trust herself to say more.

Her ladyship patted her hand, blinking herself. "There, there. It's not the end of the world, although I know it may feel that way. Such unfortunate happenings are best nipped in the bud—before any lasting damage can be done. I know you're too wise, my dear, not to know that—and to know how to go on. Why, you've all the Season before you. Plenty of opportunity to find a gentleman who suits you."

Sophie would have given the earth to deny it, all of it, but nothing could gainsay the sincerity in Lady Matcham's old eyes. With a wavering smile, Sophie gave the old lady a brief hug, then, with a mute nod, rose. Dragging in a steadying breath, she drifted to a corner of the room.

By dint of sheer will-power, she did not allow herself to dwell on Lady Matcham's revelations until, together with her aunt and Clarissa, she was enclosed in the protective shadows of the carriage and bound for home.

Then misery engulfed her, tinged with black despair.

As they alighted in Mount Street, the light from a street flare fell full on her face. Lucilla glanced around; her eyes narrowed. "Sophie, you will lie in tomorrow. I will not have you coming down with any ailment at this time of year."

Fleetingly, Sophie met her aunt's gaze, sharp and concerned. "Yes, Aunt," she acquiesced, meekly looking down. Ignoring Clarissa's concerned and questioning glance, Sophie followed her aunt up the steps.

THE NEXT DAY dawned but brought with it no relief. From behind the lace curtain at her bedchamber window, Sophie watched as Jack Lester descended the steps to the street. He climbed up into his waiting curricle and, as his groom scrambled up behind, deftly flicked his whip and drove away. Sophie watched until he disappeared around the corner, then, heaving a heavy sigh, turned back into the room.

He had called to take her for a drive, only to be met with the news of her indisposition.

Sophie sniffed. Aimless, she drifted across the room towards her bed, her sodden handkerchief wadded in her fist. As she passed her dressing-table, she caught a glimpse of her face in the mirror. Dark shadows circled her eyes; her cheeks were wan, her lips dry. Her head felt woosy and throbbed uncomfortably; her limbs seemed heavy, listless.

Lady Matcham's warning had come too late. In the dark hours of the night, she had faced the dismal fact: the delicate bud rooted in her heart, influenced by the weather and the warmth of his smile, had already flowered. Now it lay crushed, slain by the weight of circumstance. Soon, she supposed, it would wither.

She was not a wealthy catch, a bride who would bring as her dower the ready cash necessary to rescue a gentleman's estates. Nothing could change that cold, hard fact. She was her father's heiress, a lady of expectations, possessed of no more than moderate fortune, and even that was prospective, not immediately accessible as capital.

Sophie sniffed again, then determinedly blew her nose. She had spent too much of the night weeping, not an occupation she had had much experience of, not since her mother's death. Now, she felt emptied, desolate, as she had then. But she knew she would recover. She would allow herself one day in which to mope, and by tonight, she would be back on her feet, her smile bright. As the Season unfolded, she would devote herself to her search for a husband with all due diligence. And forget about a handsome rake with dark blue eyes.

That was the way things were in her world; she knew it well enough. And after all Lucilla's and Clarissa's kindnesses, she would not allow her unhappiness to cloud Clarissa's Season. She would do her best to ensure it did not sink her own, either.

Feeling oddly better to have such clear goals before her, Sophie perched on the end of her bed. Her fingers pulled at her wrinkled handkerchief; her gaze grew abstracted. There was one point she had yet to consider: how best to deal with him when they met, as, inevitably, they would.

After deep and lengthy cogitation, she had absolved him of all blame. She could not believe he had sought to cause her pain. She it was who had misread his purpose; she was, in reality, no more experienced in such matters than Clarissa. It was, very likely, as Miss Billingham had said—to him, she was a safe and agreeable companion, one with whom to pass the time until the Season was fully under way and he could set about choosing his bride. Indeed, Lady Matcham's observations left little room for any other interpretation.

There were, admittedly, his curious words when he had last left her. *The time is not yet.* She had thought he had meant…. Abruptly, Sophie cut off the thought, setting her teeth against the pain. What he *had* probably meant was to propose some outing, some excursion which their present early stage of friendship would not stretch to encompass. She had read more—much more—into his innocent words than he could ever have intended.

Which meant that, given his innocence, she would have to treat him as if nothing was wrong. Pride dictated she do so. Any awkwardness she felt must be suppressed, hidden, for she couldn't bear him to know what she had thought—hoped.

Somehow, she would cope. Like Madame Jorge, like Lucilla, she could contrive.

With a sigh, Sophie climbed onto her bed and tugged the covers over her. She snuggled down, settling her head on the pillows; calmly determined, she closed her eyes. She forced herself to relax, to allow the furrows in her forehead to ease away. If she was going to contrive, she would need some sleep.

The days ahead would not be easy.

CHAPTER SEVEN

EVEN PICCADILLY WAS CROWDED. Jack frowned as, leaving the shady avenues of the Park behind him, he was forced to rein in his horses by the press of traffic, vehicular and pedestrian, that thronged the wide street. Manoeuvring his curricle into the flow, he sat back, resigned to the crawling pace. To his right, Green Park luxuriated in the unseasonable heat, green buds unfurling as the fashionable strolled its gentle paths. Its calm beckoned, but Jack ignored it. The clamour of the traffic more suited his mood.

Grimacing at his inching progress, he kept his hands firm on his horses' reins. Just as he did on his own. He supposed his wooing of Sophie Winterton was progressing satisfactorily, yet this snail's pace was hardly what he had had in mind when he had exchanged the informality of the country for the *ton*'s structured delights. Lady Entwhistle's small ball had raised his hopes; at its conclusion he had felt decidedly smug. Thus, he felt sure, should a lady be wooed.

That success had been followed by his admittedly precipitous invitation to go driving, prompted by the unexpectedly tempestuous feelings which lay beneath his reasoned logic. He could justify to his own and anyone else's satisfaction just why Sophie Winterton would make him an excellent wife but, underneath it all, that peculiarly strong emotion which he hesitated to name simply insisted she was his.

Which was all very well, but Sophie's aunt, while not disputing his claim, had made it clear she would not assist him in sweeping Sophie off her feet.

Which, given his present state, was a serious set-back.

His horses tossed their heads impatiently, tugging at the reins. Reining them in, Jack snorted, very much in sympathy.

That drive in the Park, that gentle hour of Sophie's company, had very nearly tripped him up. If he was to obey her aunt's clear injunction and allow her to enjoy her Season unencumbered by a possessive fiancé—he had few illusions about that—then he would have to keep a firmer grip on himself. And on his wayward impulses.

Not that that was presently proving a problem; he had not set eyes on Sophie since that morning nearly a week ago. After her aunt's warning, he had held off as long as he could—until Friday, when he had called only to learn she was ill. That had shaken him; for an instant, he had wondered if her indisposition was real or just one of those tricks ladies sometimes played, then had dismissed the thought as unworthy—of Sophie and himself. He knew she liked him; it was there in her eyes, a warm, slightly wary but nonetheless welcoming glow that lit up her face whenever they met. Chiding himself for his ridiculous sensitivity, he had dispatched his man, Pinkerton, to scour the town for yellow roses. As always, Pinkerton, despite his perennial gloom, had triumphed. Three massive sprays of yellow blooms had duly been delivered in Mount Street with a card, unsigned, wishing Miss Winterton a speedy recovery.

He had looked for her in the Park, morning and afternoon, on both Saturday and Sunday but had failed to come up with the Webb carriage.

So, feeling distinctly edgy, all but champing on his metaphorical bit, he had called in Mount Street this morning—only to be informed that Miss Winterton had gone walking with her cousins.

Fate, it seemed, had deserted him. Despite the bright sunshine, his view of the Season was growing gloomier by the minute.

Lord Hardcastle, driving his greys, hailed him; they spent a few minutes exchanging opinions on the unusual press of traffic before said traffic condescended to amble onward, parting them. An organ-grinder, complete with monkey, was playing to an attentive crowd, blocking the pavement, much to the disgust of merchants and those less inclined to dally. Jack smiled and returned his attention to his horses. As he did so, a flash of gold caught his eye.

Turning, he searched the throng bustling along the pavement—and saw Sophie with Clarissa beside her, the two boys and Amy reluctantly following, casting longing glances back at the organ-grinder. As he watched, the little cavalcade halted before a shop door, then, leaving the maid and groom who had brought up the rear outside, Sophie led the way in.

Jack glanced up and read the sign above the shop, and smiled. He pulled his curricle over to the kerb. "Here—Jigson! Take charge of 'em. Wait here." Tossing the reins in Jigson's general direction, Jack leapt down and, threading his way through the traffic, entered the door through which Sophie had passed.

The door shut behind him, abruptly cutting off the noisy bustle outside. Calm and well-ordered, the refined ambience of Hatchard's Book Shop and Circulating Library enfolded him. No raised voices here. A severely garbed man behind a desk close to the door eyed him, disapproval withheld but imminent. Jack smiled easily and walked past. Despite its relative peace, the shop was quite crowded. He scanned the heads but could not find the one he sought. An eddy disturbed the calm; Jack spotted Jeremy, George and Amy huddling in a nook by the window, noses pressed to the pane, gazes locked on the entertainment on the pavement opposite.

Glancing around, Jack discovered that the disapproving man had been joined by an equally severely garbed woman. They were now both regarding him askance. With another urbane smile, he moved into the first aisle and pretended to scan the spines until he was out of their sight.

At the end of the third aisle, Sophie frowned up at the novel she most expressly wished to borrow. It was wedged tightly between two others on the topmost shelf, barely within reach. She thought of summoning the clerk to retrieve it for her, and grimaced; he was, she had discovered, quite cloyingly admiring. Sophie smothered a snort. She would make one last effort to prise the book loose before she surrendered to the attentions of the clerk.

Sucking in a breath, she stretched high, her fingers grappling to find purchase above the leather-covered tome.

"Allow me, my dear."

Sophie jumped. Snatching back her hand, she whirled, her colour draining then returning with a rush. "Oh! Ah…" her eyes widened as they met his. Abruptly, she dropped her gaze and stepped back, determinedly shackling her wayward wits. "Why thank you, Mr. Lester." With all the calm she could command, Sophie raised her head. "This is quite the last place I had thought to meet you, sir."

Tugging the book free of its fellows, Jack presented it to her with a bow. "Indeed. Not even *I* would have thought to find me here. But I saw you enter and was filled with an unquenchable desire—" Jack trapped her gaze, a rakish smile dawning "—to view such apparently attractive premises. Strange, was it not?"

"Indeed." Sophie sent him a cool glance. "Most strange." She accepted the volume, reminding herself of her sensible conclusion, and her determination to view him as he viewed her: as a friendly acquaintance. "I do, most sincerely, thank you for your assistance, sir. But I must not keep you from your business."

"Rest assured you are not doing so, my dear." As he fell in beside her, Jack slanted her a glance. "I have what I came in to find."

The tenor of his deep voice tightened the vice about Sophie's heart. She glanced up, meeting his blue gaze, and abruptly realized that her vision of a "proper distance" might differ considerably from his. A sudden revelation of what that might mean—the effect his warm regard and teasing ways would inevitably have on her—set her chin rising. With commendable hauteur, she bestowed a repressively chilly glance on him. "Indeed? I take it you are not particularly fond of reading?"

Jack grinned. "I confess, my dear, that I'm a man of action rather than introspection. A man of the sword rather than the word."

Sophie ignored his subtle tone. "Perhaps that's just as well," she opined. "Given you have large estates to manage."

"Very likely," Jack conceded, his lips twitching.

"There you are, Sophie. Oh, hello, Mr. Lester." Clarissa appeared around the corner of the aisle. She smiled blithely up at Jack and dropped a slight curtsy.

Jack shook her hand. "Have you found sufficient novels to keep you entertained, Miss Webb?" He eyed the pile of books Clarissa carried in her arms.

"Oh, yes," Clarissa replied ingenuously. "Are you ready, Sophie?"

Sophie considered replying in the negative, but was convinced that, rather than leave, Jack Lester would insist on strolling with her up and down the aisles, distracting her from making any sensible selection. She glanced about; her gaze fell on her younger cousins, glued to the prospect outside. "I suspect we *had* better leave before Jeremy falls through the window."

While Sophie and Clarissa went through the process of borrowing their chosen novels, Jack smiled smugly at the disapproving assistant.

To her relief, Sophie found the assistant disinclined to conversation, a fact for which she gave mute thanks. Clarissa summoned her brothers and sister and they all started for the door. As she stepped over the threshold and paused to get her bearings, Sophie felt her packaged novel lifted from her hands.

"Allow me, my dear." Jack smiled as Sophie glanced up, consternation in her wide, slightly startled gaze. Puzzled, Jack inwardly frowned. "If you have no objection, I'll escort you to Mount Street."

Sophie hesitated, then, her lids veiling her gaze, inclined her head. "Thank you. That would be most kind." With a determinedly light air, she surrendered her hand into his warm clasp and allowed him to settle it on his sleeve. While she waited beside him as he dismissed his groom and, with a simple admonition, succeeded in convincing Jeremy, George and Amy to leave the crowd about the organ-grinder, Sophie prayed that her momentary dismay had not shown; she did not wish to hurt him any more than she wished him to guess how much her heart had been bruised. As their little party got under way, she flashed Jack a bright smile. "Did you see Lady Hemminghurst's new carriage?"

To her relief, his rakish smile appeared. "And those nags she insists are high-steppers?"

With Clarissa beside them, they chatted easily, more easily than she had hoped, all the way back to Mount Street. Indeed, the steps leading up to her uncle's door appeared before them far sooner than she had expected. Jeremy and George bounded up the steps to ring the bell, Amy close behind. With a cheery smile, Clarissa bade their escort farewell and followed her siblings as they tumbled through the door.

Acutely conscious of the gentleman before her, of Ellen and the groom, still standing decorously a few steps behind, and of Minton, the butler, holding open the door, Sophie held firm to her composure and, receiving her book, presented with a flourish, calmly said, "Thank you for your escort, Mr. Lester. No doubt we'll run into each other at the balls once they start."

Jack's slow smile twisted his lips. "I fear, my dear, that I'm not endowed with as much patience as you credit me." He hesitated, his eyes narrowing as he searched her face. "Would you be agreeable if I called to take you driving again?"

Sophie held her breath and wished she could lie. When one dark brow rose, a gentle prompt, his gaze steady on hers, she heard herself say, "That would be most pleasant, sir." His smile was triumphant. *"But,"* she hurried on. "My time is not always my own. My aunt has decided to start entertaining and I must assist her if required."

Jack's smile did not fade. "Indeed, my dear. But I'm sure she'll not wish you to hide yourself away." With smooth authority, he captured her hand. His eyes met hers; he raised her fingers, then turned them.

"No!" As surprised as he by her breathless denial, Sophie stared up at him, her heart thudding wildly. Abruptly, she dropped her gaze, quite unable to meet the startled question in his. Head bowed, she withdrew her hand from his and dropped a slight curtsy. "Good day, Mr. Lester."

The words were barely audible.

Jack felt as if he'd taken a blow to the head. He forced himself to execute a neat bow. Sophie turned and quickly climbed the steps, disappearing inside without a backward glance.

Finding himself standing stock-still, alone in the middle of the pavement, Jack drew in a ragged breath. Then, his expression stony, he turned and strode briskly away.

WHAT IN THE NAME of all creation had gone wrong?

The question haunted Jack through the next three days and was still revolving incessantly in his brain as, the evening chill about him, he climbed the steps to knock on the Webbs' oak-panelled door. Despite his initial intentions, it was the first time he had called in Mount Street since his unexpected expedition to Hatchard's. He had returned home in a most peculiar mood, a mood that had been only slightly alleviated by the white and gold invitation he had discovered awaiting him.

"Mrs. Horatio Webb takes great pleasure in inviting Mr. Jack Lester to an impromptu dance to be held on Thursday evening."

The words had not dissipated the cloud that had settled over him, but had, at least, given him pause. Thus, he had not pressed the, albeit minor, intimacy of a drive on Sophie but had waited instead to come up with her in her aunt's ballroom, where, surely, she would feel more confident, less likely to take fright at his advances.

Quite clearly he had been too precipitate. He had put a foot wrong somewhere, although he wasn't entirely sure where.

From now on, he would woo her according to the book, without any subtle deviations. He would simply have to conceal his feelings; he would not risk panicking her by heeding them.

Admitted by the butler, who recognized him well enough to greet him by name, Jack climbed the stairs, slightly mollified by the man's cheery demeanour. Not what one was accustomed to in a butler but probably inevitable, given the junior Webbs. They would undoubtedly give any overly stuffed shirt short shrift.

Entering the salon on the first floor, Jack paused on the threshold and glanced around. A warm, welcoming atmosphere blanketed the room; it was not overly crowded, leaving adequate space for dancing, yet his hostess was clearly not going to be disappointed by the response to her summons. He discovered Sophie immediately, talking with some others. To his eyes, there was none to match her, her slim form sheathed in silk the colour of warm honey. With an effort, he forced his gaze to travel on, searching out his hostess. As he sighted her, Lucilla excused herself from a small knot of guests. She glided forward to greet him, regally gowned in satin and lace.

"Good evening, Mr. Lester." Lucilla smiled benevolently. She watched approvingly as he bowed over her hand.

"Mrs. Webb." Jack straightened. "May I say how honoured I was to receive your invitation?"

Lucilla airily waved her fan. "Not at all, Mr. Lester. It is I who am very glad to see you. I've been a trifle concerned that dear Sophie might be finding our present round of engagements somewhat stale. Dare I hope you might feel inclined to relieve her boredom?"

Jack forced his lips to behave. "Indeed, ma'am, I would be happy to do whatever I may in that endeavour."

Lucilla smiled. "I knew I could rely on you, Mr. Lester." With an imperious gesture, she claimed his arm. "Now you must come and speak with Mr. Webb."

As she led him into the crowd, Jack suppressed the thought that he had been conscripted.

On the other side of the room, Sophie chatted with a small group of not-so-young ladies. Some, like Miss Chessington, her aunt had invited specifically to keep her company, while others, like Miss Billingham, had younger sisters making their come-out this year. Gradually, they had attracted a smattering of the gentlemen present. Most of these were either carefully vetted Webb connections or unexceptionable young men who were the sons of Lucilla's closest cronies. There was no danger lurking among them.

Stifling an inward sigh, Sophie applied herself to keeping the conversation rolling; not a difficult task, supported as she was by the ebullient Miss Chessington.

"I had heard," that ever-bright damsel declared, "that there's to be a duel fought on Paddington Green, between Lord Malmsey and Viscount Holthorpe!"

"Over what?" Miss Billingham asked, her long nose quivering.

Belle Chessington looked round at the gentlemen who had joined them. "Well, sirs? Can no one clear up this little mystery?"

"Dare say it's the usual thing." Mr. Allingcott waved a dismissive hand, his expression supercilious. "Not the sort of thing you ladies want to hear about."

"If *that's* what you think," Miss Allingcott informed her elder brother, "then you know *nothing* about ladies, Harold. The reason for a duel is positively *thrilling* information."

Discomfited, Mr. Allingcott frowned.

"Has anyone heard any further details of the balloon ascension from Green Park?" Sophie asked. In less than a minute, her companions were well launched, effectively diverted. Satisfied, Sophie glanced up—and wished she could tie a bell about Jack Lester's neck. A bell, a rattle, anything that would give her warning so that her heart would not lurch and turn over as it did every time her gaze fell into his.

He smiled, and for an instant she forgot where she was,

that there were others standing only feet away, listening and observing intently. An odd ripple shook her, stemming from where his fingers had closed over hers. She must, she realized, have surrendered her hand, for now he was bowing over it, making every other gentleman look awkward.

"Good evening, Mr. Lester," she heard herself say, as if from a distance. She sincerely hoped her smile was not as revealing as her thoughts.

"Miss Winterton."

His smile and gentle nod warmed her—and made her suspect she had been far too transparent. Taking herself firmly in hand, Sophie turned and surprised an avid gleam in Miss Billingham's eyes. "Have you made the acquaintance of Miss Billingham, sir?"

"Oh, yes!" Augusta Billingham gushed. "Indeed," she said, her expression turning coy. "Mr. Lester and I are *old* acquaintances." She held out her hand, her smile sickly sweet, her eyes half-veiled.

Jack hesitated, then took the proffered hand and curtly bowed over it. "Miss Billingham."

"And Miss Chessington."

Belle's bright smile had nothing in common with Augusta Billingham's. "Sir," she acknowledged, bobbing a curtsy.

Jack smiled more naturally and allowed Sophie to introduce him to the rest of the company. By the time she had finished, he was feeling a trifle conspicuous. Nevertheless, he stuck it out, loath to leave Sophie's side.

When the musicians struck up, he bent to whisper, "I do hope, Miss Winterton, that you'll return. I would be quite overcome—utterly at a loss in such company as this—if it weren't for the reassurance of your presence."

Sophie lifted her head and looked him in the eye. "Gammon," she whispered back. But her lips quirked upward; Jack let her go with a smile.

While she danced the cotillion and then a country reel, he endeavoured to chat to some of the younger gentlemen. They were slightly overawed. His reputation as a devotee of Jackson's and one of Manton's star pupils, let alone his memberships in the Four-in-Hand and Jockey Clubs were well-known; their conversation was consequently stilted. It made Jack feel every one of his thirty-six years—and made him even more determined to bring his dazzling career as a bachelor of the *ton* to a close as soon as might be.

The prospect was still too far distant for his liking. A quadrille had followed hard on the heels of the reel; Sophie had been claimed for it before she had left the floor. With a brief word, Jack excused himself and wandered over to the musicians. The violinist was the leader; a few quick words were all that was needed, and a guinea sealed their bargain.

When the music stopped, Jack was passing the point where Sophie came to rest. She turned towards the end of the room, where her small group was once again gathering, her youthful partner at her side; she was laughing, her expression open and carefree. Her eyes met his—and a subtle change came over her.

Sophie forced a laugh to her lips, denying the sudden tightening about her lungs, the sudden constriction in her throat. She shot Jack a quizzical glance. "Have you survived thus far, sir?"

With a single, fractionally raised brow, Jack dispensed with her companion. Flustered, the young man bowed and murmured something before taking himself off.

Turning from thanking him, Sophie frowned a warning at her nemesis. "That was most unfair, taking advantage of your seniority."

Jack hid a wince. "I fear, my dear, that my…ah, experience marks me irrevocably." Making a mental note to be more careful in future, he took her hand and settled it in the crook of his elbow. "I feel very much like the proverbial wolf amongst the sheep."

His glance left Sophie breathless. Coolly, she raised a brow at him, then fixed her gaze on her friends. He led her in their direction but made no haste. Nor did he make any attempt at conversation, which left her free, not to regain her composure, as she had hoped, but, instead, to acknowledge the truth of his observation.

He did stand out from the crowd. Not only because of his manner, so coolly arrogant and commanding, but by virtue of his appearance—he was precise as always in a dark blue coat over black pantaloons, with a crisp white cravat tied in an intricate knot the envy of the younger men—his undeniable elegance and his expertise. No one, seeing him, could doubt he was other than he was: a fully fledged and potentially dangerous rake.

Sophie frowned, wondering why her senses refused to register what was surely a reasonable fear.

"Why the frown?"

Sophie looked up to find Jack regarding her thoughtfully.

"Would you rather I left you to your younger friends?"

There was just enough hesitation behind the last words to make Sophie's heart contract. "No," she assured him, and knew it was the truth.

A flame flared in his eyes, so deeply blue.

Shaken, Sophie drew her eyes from the warmth and looked ahead to where her friends waited. In her eyes, the younger gentlemen were no more than weak cyphers, cast into deep shade by his far more forceful presence.

After a moment, Jack bent his head to murmur, "I understand there's a waltz coming up. Will you do me the honour of waltzing with me, my dear?"

Sophie fleetingly met his gaze, then inclined her head. Together, they rejoined her little circle, Jack withdrawing slightly to stand by her side, a little behind. He hoped, thus, to feature less in the conversation himself, commendably doing his best not to intimidate the younger sparks who, he kept telling himself, were no real threat to him.

Twenty minutes of self-denial later, he heard the musicians again put bow to string. Sophie, who knew very well that he had not moved from his position behind her, turned to him, shyly offering her hand.

With a smile of relief and anticipation both, Jack bowed and led her to the floor.

His relief was short-lived. A single turn about the small floor was enough to tell him something was seriously amiss. True, there was a smile on his partner's face; now and again, as they turned, she allowed her gaze to touch his. But she remained stiff in his arms, not softly supple, relaxed, as previously. She was tense, and her smile was strangely brittle.

His concern grew with every step. Even the cool glance her aunt directed at him as they glided gracefully past, held no power to distract him.

Eventually, he said, his voice gentle, "I had forgot to ask, Miss Winterton—I sincerely hope you've fully recovered from your indisposition?"

Momentarily distracted from the fight to guard her senses against his nearness, Sophie blinked, then blushed. Guilt washed through her; his tone, his expression, were touchingly sincere. "Indeed," she hastened to reassure him. "I..." She searched for words which were not an outright lie. "It was nothing serious, just a slight headache." She found it hard to meet his eyes.

Jack frowned, then banished the notion that once more popped into his brain. Of course she had been truly ill; his Sophie was not a schemer.

"And indeed, sir, I fear I've been remiss in not thanking you before this for your kind gift." Sophie's words died as she stared up at his face, strangely impassive. "You did send them, did you not? The yellow roses?"

To her relief, he nodded, his smile real but somehow distant. "I only hope they lightened your day." His gaze focused on her face. "As you do mine."

His last words were whispered, yet they clanged like bells in Sophie's head. She suddenly felt absolutely dreadful. How could she go on pretending like this, trying to hide her heart? It would never work. She was not strong enough; she would trip and he would find out…

Her distress showed very clearly in her eyes. Jack caught his breath. He frowned. "Sophie?"

The music came to an end. He released her only to trap her hand firmly on his sleeve. "Come. We'll stroll a little."

Sophie's eyes flared wide. "Oh, no, really. I'd better get back."

"Your friends will survive without you for a few minutes." Jack's accents were clipped, commanding. "There's a window open at the end of the room. I think you could do with some air."

Sophie knew fresh air would help, yet the fact that he was sensitive enough to suggest it didn't help at all. She murmured her acquiescence, not that he had waited for it, and told herself she should be grateful. Yet being so close to him, and cut off from ready distraction, her senses were being slowly rasped raw. His effect on them, on her, seemed to get worse with every meeting.

"Here. Sit down." Jack guided her to a chair set back by

the wall, not far from where a set of fine draperies billowed gently in the breeze.

Sophie sank onto the upholstered seat, feeling the cool wood of the chair back against her shoulders. The sensation helped her think. "Perhaps, Mr. Lester, if I could impose on you to get me a drink."

"Of course," Jack said. He turned and snapped his fingers at a waiter. With a few terse words, he dispatched the man in search of a glass of water. Sophie hid her dismay.

"And now, Sophie," Jack said, turning to look down at her. "You're going to tell me what's wrong."

It was a command, no less. Sophie dragged in a deep breath and forced herself to meet his gaze calmly. "Wrong?" She opened her eyes wide. "Why, Mr. Lester, nothing's wrong." She spread her hands in a gesture of bewilderment. "I'm merely feeling a trifle…warm." That, she suddenly realized, was the literal truth. He stood over her, his dark brows drawn down, and she was violently reminded of their interlude in the glade in Leicestershire. That same something she had glimpsed then, behind the intense blue of his eyes, was there again tonight. A prowling, powerful, predatory something. She blinked and realized she was breathing rapidly. She saw his lips compress.

"Sophie…"

His eyes locked with hers; he started to lean closer.

"Your glass of water, miss."

Sophie wrenched her gaze away and turned to the waiter. She dragged in a quick breath. "Thank you, John." She took the glass from the man's salver and dismissed him with a weak smile.

It took considerable concentration to keep the glass steady. With her gaze fixed, unfocused, on the couples now dancing a boulanger, Sophie carefully sipped the cool water. An awful silence enfolded them.

After a few minutes, Sophie felt strong enough to glance up. He was watching her, his expression utterly impassive; he no longer seemed so threatening. She inclined her head. "Thank you, sir. I feel much better now."

Jack nodded. Before he could find words for any of his questions, his attention was diverted by a group of younger folk who descended amid gusts of laughter to cluster not ten paces away.

Sophie looked, too, and saw her cousin surrounded by a group of young gentlemen, each vying for Clarissa's attention. Noting the frenetic brittleness that had infused Clarissa's otherwise bright expression, Sophie frowned. She looked up, and met an arrogantly raised brow.

She hesitated, then leaned closer to say, "She doesn't really like having a fuss and flap made over her."

Jack looked again at the fair young beauty. His lips twisted wryly as he watched her youthful swains all but cutting each other dead in an effort to gain her favour. "If that's the case," he murmured, "I fear she'll have to leave town." He turned back to Sophie. "She's going to be a hit, you know."

Sophie sighed. "I know." She continued to watch Clarissa, then frowned as a particularly petulant expression settled firmly over her cousin's features. "What…?" Sophie followed Clarissa's gaze. "Oh, dear."

Following Sophie's gaze, Jack beheld a well-set-up young man, unquestionably recently up from the country if his coat was any guide, bearing determinedly down on the group about Sophie's cousin. The young man ignored the attendant swains as if they didn't exist, an action that won Jack's instant respect. Directly and without preamble, the youngster addressed Clarissa; to Jack's disappointment, they were too far away to hear his words. Unfortunately, the young man's grand entrance found no favour in Clarissa's eyes. As Jack watched, Clarissa tossed her silvery curls, an indignant flush replacing the sparkle of moments before.

"Oh, dear. I do hope he didn't call her 'Clary' again."

Jack glanced down. Sophie was watching the unfolding drama, small white teeth absent-mindedly chewing her lower lip. "Whatever," he said. "It appears that his embassy has failed."

Sophie sent him a worried frown. "They've known each other since childhood."

"Ah." Jack glanced back at the tableau being enacted but yards away. A wisp of remembered conversation floated through his mind. "Is that young sprig by any chance Ned Ascombe?"

"Why, yes." Sophie stared up at him. "The son of one of my uncle's neighbours in Leicestershire."

Jack answered the question in her eyes. "Your aunt mentioned him." Glancing again at the young couple, Jack felt an empathetic twinge for the earnest but callow youth who was, quite obviously, under the impression he held pride of place in the beautiful Clarissa Webb's heart. As he watched, Ned gave up what was undeniably a losing fight and, with a galled but defiant expression, retired from the lists. Looking down at Sophie, Jack asked, "I take it he was not expected in London?"

Sophie considered, then said, "Clarissa didn't expect him."

Jack's brows lifted cynically. "Your aunt gave me to understand that their future was all but settled."

Sophie sighed. "It probably is. Clarissa does not really care for racketing about and she has never been one to enjoy being the centre of attention for very long. My aunt and uncle believe that, by the end of the Season, she'll be only too happy to return to Leicestershire."

"And Ned Ascombe?"

"And Ned," Sophie confirmed.

Considering the colour that still rode Clarissa Webb's cheeks, Jack allowed one brow to rise.

Sophie finished the last of her water. It was time and more to return to the safety of her circle. "If you'll excuse me, Mr. Lester, I should return to my friends."

Jack could have wished it otherwise but he was, once more, under control. Without a blink, he nodded, removing the glass from her fingers and placing it on a nearby table. Then he held out a hand.

Steeling herself against the contact, Sophie put her hand in his. He drew her to her feet, then tucked her hand into his elbow, covering her fingers with his. Hers trembled; with an effort, she stilled them. She glanced up and saw him frown.

Jack studied her face, still pale. "Sophie, my dear—please believe I would never knowingly do anything to cause you pain."

Sophie's heart turned over. Tears pricked, but she would not let them show. She tried to speak, but her throat had seized up. With a smile she knew went awry, she inclined her head and looked away.

He escorted her to her friends, then, very correctly, took his leave of her.

Jack did not immediately quit the house. Something was wrong, and Sophie wouldn't confide in him. The unpalatable fact ate at him, gnawing at his pride, preying on his protective nature, prompting all manner of acts he was far too experienced to countenance. His restless prowling, disguised beneath an air of fashionable boredom, took him by the alcove where Ned Ascombe stood, keeping a glowering watch over his prospective bride.

His gaze on the dancers, Jack propped one broad shoulder against the other side of the alcove. "It won't work, you know."

The laconic comment succeeded in diverting Ned's attention. He turned his head, his scowl still in evidence, then abruptly straightened, his face leaching of expression. "Oh, excuse me, sir."

Jack sent the youngster a reassuring grin. "Boot's on the other foot. It was I who interrupted you." Briefly scanning

Ned's face, Jack held out his hand. "Jack Lester. An acquaintance of the Webbs. I believe I saw you at Lady Asfordby's, as well."

As he had expected, the mention of two well-known and well-respected Leicestershire names was enough to ease Ned's reticence.

Ned grasped his hand firmly, then blushed. "I suppose you saw…" He abruptly shut his mouth and gestured vaguely, his gaze once more on the dancers. "You were with Sophie."

Jack smiled, more to himself than Ned. "As you say, I saw. And I can tell you without fear of contradiction that your present strategy is doomed to failure." He felt rather than saw Ned's curious glance. Straightening, Jack extricated a notecase from an inner pocket and withdrew a card. This he presented to Ned. "If you want to learn how to pull the thing off, how to win the blond head you've set your eye on, then drop by tomorrow. About eleven." Very used to younger brothers, Jack ensured his worldly expression contained not the slightest hint of patronage.

Taking the card, Ned read the inscription, then raised puzzled eyes to Jack's face. "But why? You've never even met me before."

Jack's smile turned wry. "Put it down to fellow-feeling. Believe me, you're not the only one who's feeling rejected tonight."

With a nod, very man-to-man, Jack passed on.

Left by the alcove, Ned stared after him, his gaze abstracted, Jack's card held tight in his fingers.

"WELL, M'DEAR? Did Jack Lester disappoint you?" Propped against the pillows in the bed he most unfashionably shared with his wife, Horatio Webb slanted a questioning glance at his helpmate, sitting sipping her morning cocoa beside him.

A slight frown descended upon Lucilla's fair brow. "I don't expect to be disappointed in Mr. Lester, dear. I really should have organized that waltz myself. However, matters do seem to be progressing along their customary course." She considered, then banished her frown to cast a smiling glance at her spouse. "I dare say I've just forgotten how agonizingly painful it is to watch these things unfold."

Lowering the business papers he had been perusing, Horatio peered at her over the top of his gold-rimmed spectacles. "You haven't been meddling, have you?"

The slightest suspicion of a blush tinged Lucilla's cheeks. "Not to say *meddling*." She dismissed the notion with an airy wave. "But I really couldn't allow Mr. Lester to sweep Sophie into matrimony before the child had even had a taste of success. Not after her last Season was so tragically curtailed."

"Humph!" Horatio shuffled his papers. "You know how I feel about tampering with other people's lives, dear. Even with the *best* of intentions. Who knows? Sophie might actually *prefer* to have her Season curtailed—if it were Jack Lester doing the curtailing."

Head on one side, Lucilla considered the idea, then

grimaced. After a moment, she sighed. "Perhaps you're right. When did you say the horses will be here?"

"They're here now. Arrived yesterday." Horatio had gone back to his papers. "I'll take the troops to view them this morning if you like."

Lucilla brightened. "Yes, that *would* be a good idea. But we'll have to give some consideration to escorts." She touched her spouse's hand. "Leave that to me. I'm sure I can find someone suitable."

Horatio grunted. "Wonder if Lester brought that hunter of his up to town?"

Lucilla grinned but said nothing. Finishing her cocoa, she laid her cup and saucer on the bedside table and snuggled down beneath the covers. Smiling, she reached out to pat her husband's hand. "I'm really quite in awe of your far-sightedness, dear. So clever of you to help the Lesters to their fortune. Now there's no impediment at all to concern you, and you may give Jack Lester your blessing with a clear conscience." An expression of catlike satisfaction on her face, Lucilla settled to doze.

Horatio stared down at her, a faintly astonished expression on his face. He opened his mouth, then abruptly shut it. After a long moment of staring at his wife's exquisite features, Horatio calmly picked up his papers and, settling his spectacles firmly on the bridge of his nose, left his wife to her dreams.

CHAPTER EIGHT

AT PRECISELY ELEVEN the next morning, the doorbell of Jack's townhouse in Upper Brook Street jangled a summons. Jack looked up, his brows lifting. "I believe that will be a Mr. Ascombe, Pinkerton. I'll see him here."

Here was the parlour; Jack sat at the head of the table, Pinkerton, his gentleman's gentleman, had just finished clearing the remains of Jack's breakfast and was lovingly glossing the mahogany surface.

"Very good, sir," Pinkerton returned in his usual sepulchral tones.

Jack nodded and returned to his perusal of the latest edition of the *Racing Chronicle.* "Oh—and bring a fresh pot of coffee, will you?"

"Yes, sir." A sober individual who considered it a point of professional etiquette to carry out his duties as inconspicuously as possible, Pinkerton slipped noiselessly from the room. As the sounds of voices penetrated the oak door, Jack folded the *Chronicle* and laid it aside. Easing his chair back from the table, he stretched, trying to relieve the tension that seemed to have sunk into his bones.

The door latch lifted; Pinkerton ushered Ned Ascombe in, then departed in search of more coffee.

"Good morning, sir." Feeling decidedly awkward, not at all sure why he had come, Ned surveyed his host. Jack Lester was clearly not one of those town beaux who considered any time before noon as dawn. He was dressed in a blue coat which made Ned's own loosely-fitting garment look countrified in the extreme.

Jack rose lazily and extended a hand. "Glad to see you, Ascombe—or may I call you Ned?"

Grasping the proffered hand, Ned blinked. "If you wish." Then, realizing that sounded rather less than gracious, he forced a smile. "Most people call me Ned."

Jack returned the smile easily and waved Ned to a chair.

Dragging his eyes from contemplation of his host's superbly fitting buckskin breeches and highly polished Hessians, Ned took the opportunity to hide his corduroy breeches and serviceable boots under the table. What had Clary called him? Provincial? His self-confidence, already shaky, took another lurch downwards.

Jack caught the flicker of defeat in Ned's honest brown eyes. He waited until Pinkerton, who had silently reappeared, set out a second mug and the coffee-pot, then, like a spectre, vanished, before saying, "I understand from Miss Winterton that you would wish Miss Webb to look upon you with, shall we say, a greater degree of appreciation?"

Ned's fingers tightened about the handle of his mug. He

blushed but manfully met Jack's gaze. "Sophie's always been a good friend, sir."

"Quite," Jack allowed. "But if I'm to call you Ned, I suspect you had better call me Jack, as, although I'm certainly much your senior, I would not wish to be thought old enough to be your father."

Ned's smile was a little more relaxed. "Jack, then."

"Good. With such formalities out of the way, I'll admit I couldn't help but notice your contretemps with Miss Webb last night."

Ned's face darkened. "Well, you saw how it was," he growled. "She was encouraging an entire company of flatterers and inconsequential rattles."

There was a pause, then Jack asked, "I do hope you didn't tell her so?"

Ned fortified himself with a long sip of coffee and nodded darkly. "Not in those precise words, of course."

"Thank heaven for small mercies." Jack fixed his guest with a severe glance. "It seems to me, my lad, that you're in desperate need of guidance in the matter of how to conduct a campaign in the *ton*."

"A campaign?"

"The sort of campaign one wages to win a lady's heart."

Ned glowered. "Clarissa's heart has always been mine."

"I dare say," Jack replied. "The trick is to get her to recognize that fact. From what I saw last night, if you continue as you are, you're liable to go backwards rather than forwards."

Ned frowned at his mug, then glanced up at Jack. "I'm

not really cut out to shine in town. I don't know how to do the pretty by the ladies; I'm more at home in the saddle than in a ballroom."

"Aren't we all?" At Ned's questioning look, Jack elaborated. "The vast majority of gentlemen you'll see at any evening's entertainments would rather be somewhere else."

"But why attend if they don't wish to?"

"Why were you at Mrs. Webb's little affair?"

"Because I wanted to see Clarissa."

"Precisely. The only inducement capable of getting most of us across the threshold of a ballroom is the lure of the ladies. Where else do we get a chance to converse, to establish any connection? If you do not meet a lady first at a ball, it's dashed difficult to approach her anywhere else, at least in town. So," Jack concluded, "if you're set on winning Clarissa Webb, you'll have to accept the fact that you'll be gracing the *ton*'s ballrooms for the Season."

Ned wrinkled his nose. "My father was against my coming up to town—he thought I should just wait for Clarissa to come back. Mr. and Mrs. Webb are very sure she'll not appreciate the racketing about and will want to return to the country."

"I have inestimable faith in the senior Webb's perspicacity. However, don't you think you're extrapolating just a little too far? Taking Clarissa just a little too much for granted?"

Ned flushed again. "That's what worried me. It's why I came to town."

"And your instincts were right." Jack eyed him straitly. "From what little I've seen, I would predict that, whatever her inclinations, Clarissa Webb is sure to be one of the hits of the Season. That means she'll have all the puppies fawning at her feet, eager to paint unlikely pictures of a glowing future should she bestow her hand on them. And, despite the fact she may remain at heart a country miss, one should not lose sight of the fact that there's no shortage of gentlemen who are also inclined to the country. Such men would not baulk at taking a wife who dislikes town life. Most, in fact, would consider her a find."

Ned's brow furrowed. After a moment's cogitation, he looked Jack in the eye. "Are you telling me Clarissa will be sought after by other gentlemen who would wish to retire to the country?"

Jack nodded decisively.

"And if I don't make a…a push to fix her interest, she may accept one of them?"

Again came a definite nod.

Ned looked slightly shaken. After a long silence in which he studied the coffee at the bottom of his mug, and during which Jack sat back, at ease, and waited patiently, Ned raised his head, his jaw set, and regarded Jack with determined honesty. "I thank you for your warning, Jack. You've given me a great deal to think about." Despite his efforts, Ned's features contorted in a grimace which he immediately hid behind his mug. "Dashed if I know what I'm to do about it, though," he mumbled from behind the mug.

"No need to panic." Jack waved a languid hand. "I've loads of experience I'm perfectly willing to place at your disposal. I dare say once you learn the ropes, you'll find the whole business a challenge."

Surprised, Ned looked up from his mug. "Do you mean…" he began, then took the bull by the horns. "Are you suggesting you'd be willing to help me?"

"Not suggesting. I'm *telling* you I'm prepared to stand your mentor in this."

Ned's open face clouded. "But…why?" He flushed vividly. "I mean…"

Jack laughed. "No, no. A perfectly understandable question." He viewed his guest with a quietly assessing eye. Then he smiled. "Let's just say that I can't bear to see one so young so tangled in the briars. And, of course, I, too, have an interest in the Webb household." He made the admission with easy assurance and was rewarded by Ned's instant comprehension.

"Sophie?" His eyes growing round, his gaze openly speculative. Ned considered Jack—and his revelation.

Jack inclined his head.

"Oh."

As Jack had hoped, Ned seemed to accept that his interest in Sophie was sufficient excuse for his interest in him. While he was certainly drawn to Ned's open earnestness, it was Sophie's transparent concern for her cousin that had prompted him to take Ned under his wing. It formed no part of his own campaign to have Sophie in a constant fidget over her cousin, always keeping one eye on the younger girl. It was natural enough that she do so; to one who was himself imbued with a strong sense of sibling responsibility, Sophie's concern for Clarissa demonstrated a highly laudable devotion. Nevertheless, Sophie's cousinly concern could rapidly become a distraction.

And Jack was quite certain he did not wish to share Sophie's attention—not With Clarissa, nor anyone else.

Ned was frowning, clearly still uncertain.

"Consider my offer in the light of one doing his damned-est to ensure his lady is not distracted by unnecessary ructions amongst her family," Jack suggested somewhat drily.

Ned glanced up, struggling to hide a grin. "I suppose that's true enough. Sophie's always been like an elder sister to Clarissa."

Jack inclined his head. "I'm so glad you see my point."

Ned nodded. "If that's the way it is, I have to admit it wouldn't sit well to walk away from a fight. But I do feel totally at sea." He grinned at Jack. "Do you think you can turn me into a dandy?"

Jack grinned back. "Not a chance. What I'm sure we *can* do is to turn you out as a gentleman of the *ton*." Sobering, he fixed Ned with a meaningful glance. "You should never forget, nor attempt to hide, your origins. There is, if you'll only stop to consider, no taint attached to being a husbander of acres. Most of the highest in the *ton* are also the largest landholders in England and I can assure you they're not the least apologetic for the fact. Many spend considerable amounts of time managing their estates. Drawing one's fortune directly from the land is nothing to be ashamed of."

Ned coloured slightly. "Thank you. I don't know how you knew but that's exactly what I felt."

"I know because I've been there before you. I, too, have an estate to manage. That, however, has never stopped me from feeling at home in London."

"Oh." The revelation that Jack, too, had firm links with the country eased Ned's mind of its last doubt. "So, what do I do first?"

"A tailor," Jack declared. "Then a barber. You can't do anything until you look the part. And then we'll see about introducing you to some of the necessary establishments a gentleman of the *ton* must needs frequent—like Manton's and Jackson's Boxing Saloon. After that, we shall plan your campaign in more detail." Jack smiled. "You're going to have to learn that finessing the feminine mind takes the wiles of a fox and the devotion of a hound."

"I'll do whatever I need to," Ned averred. "Just as long as I can make Clarissa stop looking at those trumped-up popinjays as she was last night."

Jack laughed and rose. "Onward, then. No time like the present to make a start."

WHILE NED WAS sipping coffee in Upper Brook Street, Horatio Webb was busy introducing his children and his niece to the mounts he had had brought down from the country.

"These should be just the ticket for jaunts in the Park," he said as he ushered his charges into the stables. "Quite the thing, I hear, to be seen riding in the morning."

"Golly, yes!" returned Jeremy, eyes aglow. "All the crack."

Horatio's eyes twinkled. "Now these two, you two should recognize."

"By Jupiter! They're the ones you bought from Lord Cranbourne, aren't they, sir?" George, together with Jeremy, stared round-eyed at the two glossy-coated chestnut geldings their father had indicated.

Horatio beamed. "I thought they needed a little exercise. Think you can handle them?"

A garbled rush of words assured him that they could.

"We'll cut a dash on these," Jeremy declared.

With both boys absorbed, Horatio smiled down at Amy, clutching his hand. "Now for you, my miss, I've brought down Pebbles. Old Maude wouldn't have appreciated the traffic, you know."

Struck dumb at the thought of advancing beyond Old Maude's plodding gait, Amy stared at the placid grey mare who ambled up to look over the stall door. "Look!" she piped, as the mare reached down to nudge hopefully at her pockets. "She knows me!"

That, of course, took care of Amy. Leaving her to get properly acquainted with the mare, Horatio smiled at his two remaining charges. "Now, my dear," he said, beckoning Clarissa forward. "I fear I couldn't improve on Jenna, so I brought her down for you. I do hope you're not disappointed."

Clarissa smiled delightedly as she reached up to stroke the velvety nose of her beautiful chestnut mare. "How could I possibly be disappointed with you, my pet," she crooned softly as the mare nudged her cheek. "I was afraid you would want to spell her for a bit," she told her father. "I rode her all winter."

"Old Arthur seemed to think she was moping, missing all her rides. You know how soft-hearted he is." Horatio patted Jenna's nose, then turned to Sophie.

"And now for you, my dearest Sophie." Taking her arm, he led her to the next stall, where an elegant roan mare was bobbing her head curiously. "I hope Dulcima here suits you. Not as powerful as the Sheik, of course, but rather more suited to the confines of the Park."

Sophie was staring at the beautiful horse. "But…she's new, isn't she?"

Horatio waved dismissively. "Found her at Tattersall's. She's well broken and used to being ridden in town. Quite a find."

"Well, yes. But I would have been quite happy with one of your other horses, uncle. I do hope you didn't buy her just for me?"

"No, no. Nonsense—of course not." Under Sophie's disbelieving gaze, Horatio looked down and tugged at his waistcoat. "Besides," he said, looking up, a sudden impish twinkle in his eye. "Dare say Mr. Lester will be riding in the Park on the odd occasion. Never do for him to think I don't take all care of you, m'dear."

The comment cut off Sophie's protests. Taken aback, she frowned, opened her mouth, then closed it again.

"Leave you to get acquainted." With a farewell pat for the mare, Horatio strode back to see how his sons were faring.

Sophie looked after him, her eyes narrowing. Then she snorted disgustedly and turned back to the mare. As if in argument, the mare shook her head, then snorted once, ears pricking forward. Sophie grinned. "Aren't you a clever creature?" she crooned.

The mare nodded vigorously.

When, at length, they were ready to leave their equine partners, they strolled together back along the mews and around to the house, Horatio with them.

In reply to Jeremy and George's eager question, Horatio replied, "You should give them a day or two to get over their journey, and for those not used to the noise to become more accustomed, before you take them out."

The boys whooped. "Monday, then!"

"However," Horatio smoothly continued, cutting across their transports. "You cannot, I'm afraid, simply take off with a groom here in town." He glanced first at Sophie, then at Clarissa, walking on either side of him. "Neither your aunt nor I would be happy with that."

"But Toby will be here soon, will he not?" Clarissa ventured.

Horatio nodded. His eldest son, presently at Oxford, was expected to join the family any day. "True. But even so, you must remember that Toby is barely twenty. It would hardly be fair to foist the responsibility for all of you onto his shoulders. Indeed, although your mother and I have no doubt of his willingness to act as your escort, he is not yet experienced enough to adequately guard against the dangers which might face you here in the capital. This is not Leicestershire, as you know."

"What, then?" Sophie asked, knowing he was right. "Where will we find a suitable escort?"

Horatio smiled his most inscrutable smile. "Your aunt has promised to see to it."

TUESDAY AFTERNOON saw the Webb ladies taking the air in the Park. The weather continued unseasonably mild; everyone was out to take advantage. Bright walking gowns splashed colour across the lawns. One or two ladies had even felt the need for parasols.

From her perch in the barouche beside her aunt, with Clarissa gaily smiling from the opposite seat, Sophie nodded and waved greetings, determined thus to keep her mind on noting any newcomers, rather than allowing her gaze to wander farther afield, searching for one she would do well to forget.

After completing a leisurely circuit, her aunt directed her coachman to pull up alongside Lady Abercrombie's carriage.

Her ladyship, as sociable as her husband was not, was all smiles. "Lucilla, dear! How positively delightful! Do you intend to remain all Season?"

While Lucilla exchanged gossip with her ladyship, both

Sophie and Clarissa did what young ladies were supposed to do on such occasions: they responded to any query directed their way but otherwise allowed their gaze to idly roam the passing scenery, which was to say, the passing crowd.

Engaged in this necessary occupation, Sophie greeted any acquaintances who passed, exchanging commonplaces all but automatically, while her wandering gaze became gradually more intent. When it finally occurred to her what she was doing, she frowned and shook herself.

With a determined air, she looked about for distraction. And discovered Mr. Marston, waiting, sober and serious as a judge, to greet her.

"Oh, good day, sir." Annoyed at her awkwardness—she was surely more experienced than this!—Sophie summoned a smile. "I did not know you had intended to come to London."

Phillip Marston took her hand and bowed. He shook hands with both Clarissa and Lucilla, who, on hearing his voice, had turned, brows flying upward. After exchanging a few words, Lucilla turned back to Lady Abercrombie, leaving Mr. Marston to gravely tell Sophie, "Indeed, Miss Winterton, it was not my intention to join the frivolity." A disdainful glance at two young gentlemen who came up to speak to Clarissa declared his opinion very clearly. "Nevertheless, I felt that, in this case, my presence was necessary."

Sophie was mystified. "Indeed, sir?"

"I flatter myself that I am fully cognizant of the inherent

sensibility of your mind, Miss Winterton. I greatly fear that you will find little to entertain a lady of your refined nature here in the capital." Phillip Marston cast a glance at Lucilla, once more deeply engrossed with Lady Abercrombie, and lowered his voice. "As your aunt was determined to bring you to town, I felt that the least I could do, as I assured my dear mama, was to journey here to do what I may to support you through this time."

Utterly dumbfounded, Sophie silently searched for the prescribed reply to that revelation, and discovered that there wasn't one. In fact, as the full implication of Mr. Marston's declaration impinged on her mind, she decided she did not approve—of him or it. Drawing herself up, she fixed him with a distinctly frosty gaze. "I must inform you, sir, that I find the entertainments to which my aunt escorts me quite fascinating."

A condescending smile lifted Mr. Marston's thin lips. "Your loyalty to your aunt does you credit, my dear, but I feel I must point out that the Season has not yet begun. The entertainments thus far are doubtless mild enough. You will understand my concern once the more…rackety gentlemen are included. Then, I venture to say, you will be only too glad of my escort."

Sophie struggled for words. She dragged in a deep breath, glanced up—and felt a surge of inexpressible relief. Her heart leapt. She promptly tried to dampen her reaction, only to see the corners of Jack Lester's lips lift.

With determined calm, Sophie coolly extended one hand. "Good afternoon, Mr. Lester."

"Miss Winterton." With suave grace, Jack bowed. "I had hoped to discover you here." He ignored Mr. Marston beside him.

Mr. Marston, Sophie noticed, was not ignoring him. He drew himself up, his nostrils pinched as if Mr. Lester's appearance was offensive. Just what he could find amiss with that supremely elegant figure Sophie was at a loss to guess. "Ah…I believe you have met Mr. Marston before, Mr. Lester? He's down from Leicestershire. I was just commenting on what a surprise it was to see him here." Sophie watched as the two men exchanged glances, Marston visibly bristling.

"Marston." With a brief nod, Jack dismissed the fellow from his thoughts and turned to Clarissa as her two admirers withdrew. "Miss Webb." Jack shook her hand, then indicated the figure beside him. "I believe Mr. Ascombe is known to you both?"

Sophie blinked, then smiled delightedly. From the corner of her eye, she saw Clarissa's jaw drop. Ned had been to a tailor—a good one. His coat of Bath superfine now hugged his shoulders, doing far more justice to his lean frame than his previous suiting ever had. And he had had a haircut—his crisp brown locks were now in fashionable disarray. His breeches, his boots—all were new and all contributed to a remarkable transmogrification. Taking it all in with one comprehensive glance, Sophie retained sufficient wit to respond to the subtle prompt in Jack's steady blue gaze. She held out her hand and smiled warmly. "Indeed, yes. It's good to see you, Ned."

Some of Ned's stiffness faded. He slanted Sophie a grin. "You look ravishing, Sophie. Determined to cut a swath through the *ton?*"

Sophie was impressed by the clear confidence in Ned's tone. A quick glance to her right showed that she wasn't alone. Clarissa was staring at Ned, confusion clearly writ in her large blue eyes. "I'm certainly determined to enjoy myself this Season," Sophie responded. "Will you be in town for the duration?"

"I expect so," Ned replied, his gaze fixed on Sophie. "I hadn't realized before just how many distractions there were to be found in the capital."

"Hello, Ned."

At Clarissa's somewhat tentative greeting, Ned turned to her with an easy but in no way especial smile. "Good afternoon, Miss Webb. You're looking quite splendid. Have you been enjoying your stay thus far?"

Sophie bit her lip. The quick glance she sent Jack was a mistake. The devilish light in his blue eyes very nearly overset her control.

Clarissa, clearly bemused by the change in her childhood companion, mumbled a disjointed response, lost as Mr. Marston cut in.

"Afternoon, Ascombe." Phillip Marston eyed Ned's new finery with a critical eye. "Your father, I suspect, would be quite surprised to see you thus decked out."

Used to Phillip Marston's sober declarations, Ned merely grinned and shook his hand.

Sophie smothered a giggle. Jack caught her eye; she looked away, her jaws aching.

Then Lucilla joined the fray. She greeted Jack as an old acquaintance, complimented Ned on his good sense, and, under cover of a rapid-fire monologue on the varied entertainments to be found in the capital, managed to divulge that her charges would dearly like to ride in the Park in the mornings but lacked suitable escorts. "For even when Toby arrives," she declared, "I would not be happy to allow a group of such innocents to brave the Park without someone more experienced to handle the reins, as it were."

Stunned, Sophie directed a look of pointed reproof at her aunt. Lucilla pretended not to notice. Predictably, a deep voice answered.

"Mr. Ascombe and I would be only too happy to be of assistance, Mrs. Webb. Would you be content to release your charges to our care?"

Impotent, Sophie watched as Lucilla bent a look of shining approval on Jack. "Indeed, Mr. Lester. I cannot think of anyone I'd trust more."

Jack very nearly winced but inclined his head in acceptance of her commission. In this instance, her stipulation that he was being entrusted with her charges and therefore, as a gentleman, expected to respect her confidence, was no handicap.

And there was hay yet to be made from the situation. "Perhaps Miss Winterton and Miss Webb would care to stroll the lawns while we discuss the most appropriate time to meet?"

Lucilla's eyes widened slightly.

Sophie was not at all certain of the wisdom of strolling beside Jack Lester, even in the middle of the Park. Maintaining an appropriate distance was imperative; closing the physical distance between them was unlikely to help her cause.

"What a perfectly splendid idea!" Clarissa turned to Lucilla, her eyes bright and eager.

With a sigh and a lifted brow, Lucilla relaxed against the squabs. "By all means—but only for fifteen minutes. I'll await you here."

To Sophie's immense relief, Phillip Marston said nothing, merely frowning into the distance in an abstracted fashion. Then, rather abruptly, he bowed and took his leave of them.

Jack barely noticed. He handed Sophie down from the carriage, his satisfaction implicit in his smile. She was a picture in muslin the colour of old gold, a fairy princess with a touch of rose in her cheeks.

With her hand snugly tucked in his arm, they strolled across the broad expanse of clipped grass. Beside them, Clarissa, on Ned's arm, kept shooting shy glances up at him. Very correctly, the party remained together, clearly within sight of Lucilla in the barouche.

Aware, again, as she paced beside him of that strength that seemed an integral part of Jack Lester, impinging on her senses as if she had no defence, Sophie struggled to remain calmly aloof. Just friends—only friends. To her surprise, her companion proved to have a ready line of patter to meet even this occasion, one she doubted he had had much previous experience of.

"The *ton* seems uncommonly eager to commence this Season." Jack commented, idly scanning the host dotting the lawns. "I don't think I've seen such a turnout this early for years."

"My aunt was commenting on that fact," Sophie returned, keeping her gaze firmly on their surroundings. "I believe that a number of ladies are considering holding coming-out balls next week."

"My own ball will be held on Friday," Clarissa volunteered, suppressed excitement quivering in her tone. "Mama says there's no reason not to get into the swing of things."

"Your mother is indeed very wise, Miss Webb." Jack smiled down at Clarissa's delicately flushed face. A few days of Ned's company had more than sufficed to bolster his instinctive liking into solid support. He was quite determined that, come the end of the Season, Ned would retire from the lists with Clarissa's favour firmly in his possession. "I suspect there are few subjects on which you would not be wise to heed your mother's advice."

"Have you been on an excursion to the Royal Exchange, Miss Webb? I'm told the wild beasts are a fearsome spectacle." Ned's tone was commendably even, devoid of overeagerness.

Hearing Clarissa, still warily suspicious but too unsure of this new Ned to risk any airs, answer with unaffected openess, Sophie was hard put to hide her grin.

Seeing her lips quirk, and deciding he had done enough today in furthering Ned's enterprise, Jack slowed his pace.

Sophie noticed. Her head came up. Looking her escort firmly in the eye, she raised a brow at him. When he merely smiled back, maddeningly, she surrendered to temptation. "Am I right, sir, in supposing you are helping Ned to adjust to town life?"

Jack smiled and leaned closer, lowering his voice. "Ned's a likeable chap. But having come up fresh from the country, he was facing opposition of unfair proportions. I thought it only fair to even the odds a little."

Sophie felt her lips soften. "Indeed?" she replied, her eyes on his. "So your actions are prompted by nothing more than a passing interest in righting an inequity?"

"I'm very keen on righting inequities," Jack informed her, his brows rising arrogantly. Then, abandoning his haughty attitude, he added, his tone deepening, "Not that I don't have reasons of my own to wish Clarissa settled."

"Oh?" Sophie held his gaze, warmly blue. Caution went winging. "And what might those be, sir?"

"Jack." Glancing ahead, Jack asked, "Do you think I'm succeeding?"

Although his glance had taken in Clarissa and Ned immediately ahead of them, his gaze had swung back to her on his question. Sophie, her heart increasing its tempo, was not sure how to reply. With a determined effort, she switched her gaze forward to where Clarissa was still viewing Ned curiously, like some specimen she did not yet understand. "My cousin certainly seems enthralled by Ned in his new guise."

A heartfelt sigh came from beside her. "Perhaps I should take a leaf out of his book? Mayhap Percy could give me some hints."

At his defeated tone, Sophie swung about, her eyes automatically travelling the length of his elegantly accoutred frame before, realizing she had fallen into his trap, her gaze snapped up to meet his. Warm amusement, and a clear invitation to play this game—with him—glowed in the deep blue. Abruptly, Sophie dropped her gaze and murmured, "Time is flying; we should return to my aunt, sir."

A gentle, somewhat wry smile softened Jack's lips. "I dare say you're right, Miss Winterton." So saying, he drew her hand once more through his arm. A few quick strides brought them up with the younger couple.

Ned turned, a glimmer of relief showing briefly in his eyes. But before they could retrace their steps to the barouche, they were hailed from the nearby carriageway.

"Jack!"

They all turned. Sophie recognized Gerald Lester—and his new phaeton. Ned had noticed the phaeton, too—and Gerald had noticed Clarissa. Naturally, they had to pause while introductions were performed and accolades on the phaeton and pair duly exchanged.

"No doubt but that I'll see you at one of the balls," Gerald said, impartially addressing them all. Then he flicked his whip and waved. "Tally-ho!"

"Puppy!" Jack snorted, but he was grinning.

Sophie watched the expensive carriage roll away, then turned towards the barouche.

One more reason why Jack Lester would have to marry well.

She risked a glance up at him; he was scanning the couples between them and the barouche. With Ned and Clarissa in tow, he steered her clear of any interference, making directly for the carriage where Lucilla sat awaiting them. Sophie bit her lip and looked down.

Gerald Lester was clearly a young gentleman unaccustomed to habits of economy. Jack's elegance declared that he, too, was not one to count the cost in presenting himself to the *ton*. The Lesters, at least those she had thus far encountered, knew their place, knew to a nicety how to behave within the circles into which their birth and estates elevated them. Equally obviously, they thought nothing of financing their expensive style of life on tick.

Well, she amended moodily, perhaps not on tick—but there was little doubt that Jack needed a rich wife.

It was not, Sophie reflected dourly, an uncommon occurrence in the *ton*—families innured to living well beyond their means. She could only curse the fate that had made the Lesters one of them.

Then the barouche was before them and it was all she could do to behave normally, agreeing to ride the next morning in the Park, then acknowledging the farewells, smiling as he bowed over her hand, as if there were no black cloud lowering on her horizon, about to deprive her of the warmth of his gaze.

CHAPTER NINE

RESIGNED TO THE INEVITABLE, Sophie was the first of the
Webb contingent to appear in the hall the next morning. As
she came down the stairs, buttoning her gloves, a wary
smile twisted her lips. She should have expected Lucilla to
seize the opportunity to throw Ned and Clarissa together,
especially now that Ned had captured Clarissa's attention
in what was, for her cousin, a wholly novel way. And Jack
Lester, of course, was an undeniably capable escort. The
children, for some mystical reason, had accorded him
favoured status; he had only to speak and they tumbled to
obey. Sophie grimaced. Descending the last flight, she tried
to ease the knot of nervous tension that was tightening
within her. The situation, she told herself, could have been
worse. Mr. Marston might have spoken first.

Busy with her thoughts, her gaze abstracted, she did not
see the young gentleman who emerged from the library.

"Sophie! Just the person! How are you?"

Before she could answer, Sophie was engulfed in a hug
which owed more to enthusiasm than art. "Toby!" she gasped,
recognizing her assailant. "Watch my hat, you clunch!"

"That wispy thing ain't a *hat,* Sophie." Toby flicked her

riding hat, composed of a pheasant's feather and a scrap of velvet, with one finger. "Wouldn't keep the rain off you for a moment."

"As I should hope you are by now aware, Tobias Webb, having attained the years of wisdom, the importance of a modish hat lies not in its ability to protect one from the elements." Sophie's severity was belied by the affectionate twinkle in her eyes. "How was the trip down?"

"Enjoyable enough." Toby assumed a nonchalant air. "Peters and Carmody and I all came down together."

"I see." Sophie hid her smile. "Have you seen your father and mother yet?"

Toby nodded. "Papa told me you were planning to ride this morning with Ned Ascombe and a Mr. Lester. Thought I might join you."

"By all means," Sophie replied, only too glad of another distraction to counteract Jack Lester. "But they should be here with the horses any moment."

"I've already sent around to the stables for mine, so I shouldn't keep you. I'll just change my coat."

As Sophie stood in the hall watching Toby briskly climb the stairs, pausing at the top to greet Clarissa, about to descend, the clop and clash of many hooves on the cobbles beyond the massive oak door heralded the arrival not only of their mounts, but also of Jeremy, Gerald and Amy, who had been keeping watch from a window upstairs.

After whooping in greeting about their eldest brother, who admonished them with mock severity, the tribe descended to whirl about Sophie, eager to be off on this, their first excursion in the Park.

Thus it was that, admitted by a benignly beaming Minton, Jack, with Ned behind, came upon his golden head knee-deep in commotion. However, the expression of resigned calm on Sophie's face assured him she was not about to succumb to the vapours, despite the din.

"Quiet, you vexatious imps!" His firm greeting immediately transformed said imps into angels.

Sophie struggled to keep her lips straight. Jack's eyes lifted to meet hers and she lost the battle, her lips curving in a generous smile. "Good morning, sir. You see us almost ready."

"Almost?" Taking her hand, Jack lifted an eyebrow, then turned to nod to Clarissa.

"My eldest cousin, Toby, has rejoined the family. He's just gone to change." Nodding to Ned, Sophie wondered if it would be possible to tug her fingers free of the warm clasp which held them trapped. Despite her firm intention to remain aloof, her heart, unreliable organ that it was whenever he was near, was accelerating. "Toby's a keen rider and would not wish to miss our outing."

"Naturally not," Jack agreed, his gaze touching the children's eager faces. "Not when we've such an august and intrepid company as shall make all the *ton* stare."

He smiled as he made the statement, which was greeted with hoots from the younger Webbs. Sophie, however, was suddenly visited by a vision of how their cavalcade would appear to others in the Park. With a sudden sinking feeling, she realized that Lucilla, in her usual cryptic manner, had made no mention of the children.

As the children fell to fitting on their hats and gloves and swishing their skirts, Sophie lowered her voice to say, "Indeed, Mr. Lester, I would understand if you feel my aunt was not sufficiently open with you—she did not mention the children, and I dare say you will not care to be seen with such an entourage in the Park."

Jack turned to regard her in genuine surprise. Then he smiled. "If I were a Tulip of the *ton,* I might be concerned. However, such as I am, I feel sure my standing is sufficient to weather being seen with the Webbs, *en famille.* Besides which, my dear, I like your cousins."

Gazing up into his face, and seeing the gentle amusement therein, Sophie could not doubt his sincerity. It eased her mind and brought a calm smile back to her lips.

Which, to Jack's mind, was a perfectly satisfactory recompense for the trouble he could see looming before him.

Then Toby came bounding down the stairs, his enthusiasm only slightly less than that of his younger siblings. Introduced to Jack, he wrung his hand good-naturedly, nodded to Ned with easy familiarity and suggested they be off.

By Jack's side, Sophie was the last to quit the house. Standing at the top of the steps, she beheld a scene of veritable pandemonium. Luckily, her uncle's grooms had come to hold the horses; used to their master's children, the grooms did not blink as the youngsters rowdily mounted.

As Jack drew her protectively closer, Sophie quieted her misgivings with the reflection that, once on horseback, she would not have to deal with her apparently inevitable reactions to his nearness. Riding, when all was said and done, should be safe enough.

It was not until they paused beside Dulcima that Sophie realized that there were hurdles, even when riding in London. Hurdles such as gaining her saddle atop the tall mare.

Jack, of course, saw no obstacle before him. He placed his hands about Sophie's slim waist and easily lifted her up.

Gently deposited in her saddle, Sophie tried to hide her blush, vowing to make a special effort, as of today, to stop reacting that way to his touch. Her heart was thudding madly; the tension within her had twisted tight. She felt the warmth of Jack's blue gaze upon her face but refused to meet it. By the time she had settled her skirts, he had swung up to the saddle of his black and the party was ready to depart.

Determined to appear unaffected by his proximity, she forced herself to look up and smile. She watched as Jack brought his sleek black alongside her mare; with the others ranged neatly before them, they brought up the rear of the procession as it clattered, eager but restrained, down Mount Street, towards the leafy precincts of the Park.

Grateful to feel her cheeks cool once more, Sophie kept her gaze fixed ahead. Jack's black swung his head towards Dulcima's, then snorted and shook his mane, setting his harness jingling. Dulcima calmly trotted on. The black repeated the manoeuvre, this time nudging Dulcima's shoulder. Sophie frowned. Four paces on, as the black turned to her mare again, Dulcima whinnied and tossed her head.

"Mr. Lester." Sophie felt compelled to support her mare's protest. She turned to Jack, gesturing to the black. "Your horse, sir."

Jack's expression turned rueful. He obligingly tightened his reins, leaning forward to pat the black's glossy neck. "Never mind, old boy. Delicately reared ladies are always the hardest to win over. Pretend they don't even see one. I know just how you feel."

For an instant, Sophie's mind went quite blank. Finding her gaze locked with Jack's, she glared at him. Then, with a toss of her head that came perilously close to mimicking her mare, she looked straight ahead, thereby proving Jack's point.

To her immense relief, the gates of the Park appeared ahead. They entered and proceeded down a ride at a leisurely pace, glorying in the sunshine that continued to defy all predictions. About them, the rich smell of warming earth spiced the air, while birds trilled in the branches arching high overhead.

Glancing at Sophie, Jack inwardly smiled. Prey to an unnerving uncertainty, he had not again called to take her driving. But their stroll in the Park had reassured him, even though she had pulled back the instant he had drawn closer. Feminine nerves—that was the problem. He would just have to bide his time, and give her time to grow accustomed to his interest, to become more at ease with him.

So, holding his restless black to a sedate walk, he ambled beside her, his thoughts filled not with the joys of burgeoning spring, but with resigned acceptance of the tales that would no doubt be told in his clubs that night. He consoled himself with the reflection that, as his pursuit of Sophie would keep him in the ballrooms for most of the Season, he would not be spending much time at his clubs.

And if his pursuit of his bride did not keep him sufficiently busy, there was always his self-imposed task of keeping Ned Ascombe from doing himself an injury.

"I dare say the preparations for your coming-out ball must be exercising your imagination, Miss Webb." Jack cut across Ned to put a stop to what, to his experienced eyes, had been all too much like backsliding.

Caught out, reminded of the role he had been instructed it was in his best interests to play, Ned looked guilty.

"Yes, indeed," Clarissa readily replied. "But Mama had taken care of all the details. The theme is to be classical, although personally I would rather have had the Rites of Spring. But Mama held that that has been quite done to death these last years."

Clarissa glanced at Ned.

"I'm sure Mrs. Webb knows what's best" was his verdict.

Sophie bit her lip.

After a moment's blank astonishment, Clarissa stiffened slightly. When no expression of empathetic understanding joined Ned's bare statement, she pointedly looked ahead.

Jack grinned and drew back, sure Ned would not again lapse into his habitually easy relationship with Clarissa. At least, not today.

"Are we allowed to gallop in the Park sir?" Toby brought his bay hunter up alongside Jack's black.

At twenty, brown-haired and blue-eyed with the same innate elegance that characterized Lucilla, Toby struck Jack as the sort to be up to all the usual larks, yet wise enough to avoid the grief that often overtook his peers. There was a glimmer of wisdom already detectable in his blue-grey eyes. No doubt, Jack mused, he had inherited his parents' brains. "You and your younger brothers and sister could conceivably do so. However, neither Miss Webb nor Miss Winterton would be wise to attempt the feat."

Toby wrinkled his nose. "The usual stuffy notions?"

Jack nodded. "As you say."

Lifting a brow at Sophie, and seeing her smile, Toby grinned ruefully. "Sorry, Sophie." Then, turning to his younger siblings, he waved his quirt and challenged, "Last to the oak at the other end of the turf gets to tell Mama what happened today!"

His three juniors responded immediately. All four thundered off.

Exchanging an indulgent smile, Jack and Sophie set their horses into a mild canter in their wake. Ned and Clarissa fell in behind. As they broke from the cover of the long ride and slowed, Sophie noticed their presence was attracting considerable interest. She did her best to appear unaware, until she realized that surprise was the predominant emotion on the faces of the gentlemen they passed.

Turning, she lifted a brow at her companion.

Jack smiled. "I fear I'm not noted for escorting boisterous families on jaunts through the Park."

"Oh." Uncertain, Sophie blinked up at him.

"I don't regret it in the least," Jack supplied, his smile somewhat wry. "But, tell me, my dear Miss Winterton, if you had to make the choice, would it be town or country for you?"

"Country," Sophie immediately replied. "Town is pleasant enough, but only…" she paused, putting her head on one side, "as a short period of contrast." After a moment, she shook herself free of her thoughts and urged Dulcima into a trot. "But what of you, sir? Do you spend much time in the country?"

"*Most* of my time." Jack grinned. "And, although you might not credit it, quite willingly. The estates, of course, need constant attention. When my sister left, she bequeathed me a list as long as my arm of all the improvements required." His brow darkening as a subject that, now, was very close to his heart claimed him, Jack continued, "I'm afraid, before Lenore left, I had not paid as much attention as I should have. She kept us together financially, which was no small feat. Consequently, my brothers and I left the decisions on what projects the family could afford to undertake to her. Although she was not to blame in any way, I should have realized that she did not have an extensive grasp of the estate as a whole, but was entirely familiar with all matters pertaining to the Hall itself. Hence, our ancestral home is in very good repair, but, for my money, I would have given some, at least, of the improvements necessary on the estate a higher priority."

Glancing down at Sophie's face, Jack added, "I fully intend to resuscitate the estate. I know what's needed; now it's simply a matter of getting things done."

A steel vice closed about Sophie's heart. She let her lids veil her eyes. Her features frozen in an expression of rapt attention, she inclined her head.

Encouraged, Jack briefly described those improvements he felt most urgent. "I think it has something to do with being the one to inherit the land," he concluded. "I feel an attachment—a responsibility—now that it's virtually mine. I know Harry feels the same about the stud farm, which will one day be his."

Woodenly Sophie nodded, clutching her reins tightly. From her experience of her father's estates, she knew the cost of Jack's dreams. His words settled, a leaden weight about her heart.

Distraction arrived in a most unexpected form. A brusque hail had them drawing rein; turning, they beheld Mr. Marston astride a showy dun trotting quickly towards them. As he approached, Sophie inwardly admitted that Phillip Marston looked his best on horseback; his best, however, had never been sufficient to raise her pulse. Now, with her expectations conditioned by the likes of Jack Lester, she knew it never would.

"Good day, Mr. Marston." Her expression calmly regal, Sophie held out one hand, refusing to embellish the brief greeting with any hypocritical phrases.

"My very dear Miss Winterton." Phillip Marston attempted the difficult feat of bowing over her hand, but was forced to release it quickly as his horse jibbed. Frowning, he restrained the restive animal and, with obvious reluctance, nodded at Jack. "Lester."

Jack returned the nod with a perfectly genuine smile. "Marston."

The dun continued to jib and prance.

Phillip Marston did his best to ignore it—and the fact the dun was no match on any level with the even-tempered black Jack Lester rode. He nodded gravely to Ned and Clarissa, then fixed his pale gaze on Sophie. "I thought I'd take the trouble to find a mount and join you, my dear. I have not, as you know, previously had much experience of town, but I felt sure you would feel more easy in the company of one with whom you share a common background."

Inwardly bridling, Sophie refrained from glancing heavenwards and searched for some acceptable response. She was delivered from her unenviable predicament by the arrival of her younger cousins, whooping gleefully, their faces alight with exuberant joy.

Phillip Marston frowned bleakly. "Really, you young barbarians! Is this the way you behave when out from under your parents' eye?"

Their transports abruptly cut short, their joy fading,

Jeremy, George and Amy instinctively looked not to Sophie, but to Jack.

He reassured them with a smile. "Nonsense, Marston," he said, his tone equable but distant. "The Park at this hour is a perfectly acceptable venue for the young to let off steam. Later, perhaps, such behaviour would be frowned upon, but now, with mainly young people and families about, there's nothing the least untoward in such high spirits."

The crestfallen trio were miraculously revived. They shot Jack a grateful glance and fell in beside him, as far as they could get from Mr. Marston. For a moment, Sophie allowed herself to envy them, before regretfully banishing the thought.

Phillip Marston received Jack's wisdom with a stiff little bow. His pinched lips and the slant of his brows left little doubt of his feelings. A charged moment passed in which Sophie bludgeoned her brains for some safe topic—not an easy task with Mr. Marston on one side and Jack Lester on the other—before Marston's particular devil prompted him to say: "I dare say, Lester, not being a *family* man, you don't realize the importance of discipline in handling the young."

Jack controlled his countenance admirably, bending a look of blandly polite enquiry on Marston. As Jack had hoped, Phillip Marston continued, airily declaiming, apparently unaware of Sophie's stunned silence.

"Natural enough, of course. After all, discipline's hardly your style, is it? I mean to say," he hurried on, "that doubtless, having little need for such in your own life, it's hard for you to understand that others live by a different code."

"Indeed?" Jack lifted a brow, his expression remote and slightly bored. "I hadn't, I confess, thought my life so very different from that of the rest of my class."

Phillip Marston laughed condescendingly. "Oh, but it is." He waved airily. "Why, I dare say you'd be stunned to know that some of us spend months on our estates, grappling with such matters as tenants and bailiffs and crop rotation." Oblivious to the flags flying in Sophie's cheeks, Marston continued, "Not all of us can spend our lives in London, frittering away our money at the tables, sipping, unrestrained, from the bowl of life's pleasures."

That was far too much for Sophie. *"Mr. Marston!"* She regarded him with icy indignation. "I'm surprised, sir, that you even know of such things as life's pleasures." The words—so uncharacteristically sniping—shocked her, but she had no intention of recalling them. However, it immediately became clear Mr. Marston stood in no danger of being crushed.

He inclined his head, smiling unctuously. "Quite so, my dear. Such pastimes hold no allure for me. However, I am aware that others find them much more to their taste." He lifted his pale gaze to Jack's face. "No doubt, Lester, you find this squiring of innocents not at all to your liking. Playing nursemaid to a pack of brats is hardly your style, after all." Marston leant forward and spoke across Sophie. "I heard Mrs. Webb trap you into this little jaunt. Dare say you'd rather be anywhere but here. However, as I've nothing better to do with my time, I'll be only too happy to take the responsibility off your hands."

Ned and Clarissa had drawn closer; along with Toby, who had silently rejoined the company, they held their breath and looked, slightly stunned, at Jack. Indeed, every eye in the party was fixed upon him.

They all saw his slow smile.

"On the contrary, Marston," Jack drawled. "I believe you're labouring under a misapprehension. Believe me, there's nothing I would rather be doing than squiring this particular party of innocents. In fact," he went on, his expression growing pensive, "I believe if you consider the matter more closely, you'll see that one such as I, to whom the…ah, pleasures of life are well known, is precisely the most suitable escort."

The relief that swept the party, all except Marston, was palpable.

Jack's smile broadened as he met the other man's gaze. "Indeed, Marston, I wouldn't have missed this morning's jaunt for the world."

Confounded, Phillip Marston glanced at Sophie. Her glacial expression awoke the first inklings of understanding in his brain. His hand tightened on his reins.

The dun, having behaved reasonably for all of ten minutes, reacted predictably, jibbing, then twisting, prancing sideways. Marston struggled to subdue the animal, muttering perfectly audible curses beneath his breath.

Sternly quelling her laughter, Sophie grasped the opportunity. "Mr. Marston, I believe you would be wise to return that horse to the stables forthwith. I confess its antics are making me quite nervous." She managed to imbue her tones with perfectly specious feminine fear.

Which left Phillip Marston with little choice. His expression grim, he nodded curtly. He left, heading straight for the gate.

"Phew!" Toby came up beside Sophie, a grin lighting his face. "I wouldn't want to be the stableman when he returns that horse."

The comment drew laughter all round, banishing any lingering restraint. Restored to their usual high spirits, the youngsters were soon off again. By mutual consent, the party ambled slowly in Mr. Marston's wake.

Summoning the children, coercing them into an orderly retreat, then supervising them through the traffic kept Sophie fully occupied. But when they turned the corner into Mount Street and the youngsters drew ahead, she glanced up at her companion. His features were relaxed; he looked every bit as content as he had claimed. "I feel I must apologize for Mr. Marston's behaviour, sir."

Jack looked down at her. "Nonsense, my dear. It was hardly something you could control. Besides," he continued, his blue gaze holding hers, "I have yet to see you encouraging him."

"Heaven forbid!" Sophie shuddered, then, seeing the calm satisfaction that infused Jack's expression, wished she'd been rather more circumspect. It was, after all, no business of Jack Lester's whom she encouraged. Taking refuge in the banal, she said, "So the balls are starting at last."

With a slow smile, Jack inclined his head. "Indeed. And your cousin's come-out will be one of the first. Your aunt seems set to steal a march on her peers."

Thinking of Lucilla and her careful scheming, Sophie smiled. "As you say. She's quite determined to make the most of this Season."

Clarissa nudged her horse up beside Jack's. "Indeed," she declared, unusually pert. "Mama is quite set on my come-out being an *unenviable crush*."

Sophie exchanged a wry smile with Jack.

Turning to Clarissa, Jack raised a laconic brow. Obviously, Ned had been faithfully adhering to instructions. "Is that so?" Jack asked. "And what do you know of crushes, Miss Webb?"

Clarissa coloured, then waved a dismissive hand. "Sophie told me all about them."

"Ah." Lips quirking, Jack turned back to Sophie as they halted their mounts before the Webbs' steps.

The junior Webbs had already gone in, leaving the grooms with their hands full. Sophie steeled herself and managed to survive the ordeal of being lifted down to the pavement by Jack Lester with commendable composure.

She looked up—and beheld his slow smile.

"Well, my dear?" Jack lifted a brow. "Was it bearable, riding with me?"

Sophie blushed rosily but was determined to give no ground. Lifting her chin, she looked him in the eye. "Indeed, sir. It was most enjoyable."

Jack chuckled. "Good. Because from what I understand, your cousins wish it to be a frequent event."

With an inclination of her head, Sophie indicated her acquiescence.

Her hand in his, Jack looked down at her, his smile a trifle crooked. "Until your aunt's crush, then, Miss Winterton. Rest assured that, despite the sea of humanity that will no doubt be thrown up between us, I will endeavour to win through to your side." With a rakish grin, he bowed over her hand.

And let her go.

With a very correct nod, Sophie escaped up the steps, refusing to give in to her heart and look back.

At the corner of the street, two horsemen sat their mounts, apparently discussing the weather. In actuality, their interest was a great deal more focused.

"Well, that's a relief! It's the older one Lester's got his eye on—fancy that." Hubert, Lord Maltravers, blinked blearily up at his companion. "A hard night followed by an ungodly early start may have taken its toll on my wits," his lordship mused. "But stap me if I can see why."

Captain Terrence Gurnard's lips lifted in a sneer. "Tarnished his image, that's why. The Webbs are a deal too downy to let their chick fly too close to his snare. But obviously the cousin has enough of the ready to satisfy Lester."

"Odd." His lordship frowned. "Thought she had nothing

more than the usual. You know what I mean—expectations but no more. Would've thought Lester needed rather more than that."

"Obviously not. The point, thank Heaven, doesn't concern me. As long as he's *not* got his eye on that juicy little plum, he can have the rest of London for all I care. Come, let's get moving. We've seen all we need."

Side by side, they steered their mounts through the streets in the direction of Hubert's lodgings, the slightly rumpled figure of Lord Maltravers slumped in his saddle, the handsome, broad-shouldered guardsman towering over him.

"Y'know, Gurnard, I've been thinking."

"I thought you didn't do that until after noon."

Hubert snorted. "No. I'm serious. This start of yours—sure there isn't a better way? I mean, you could always try the cent per cents—doesn't hurt to ask."

"In this case, I fear it could hurt." Gurnard winced. "A very great deal."

Realization was slow but it eventually broke on Hubert. "Oh," he said. "You're already on their books?"

"Let's just say that one or two moneylenders could scrape an acquaintance."

"Hmm." Hubert grimaced. "That does rather cut down on your options." As they turned into Piccadilly, he ventured, "No chance this last opponent of yours would consider holding your vowels for latter payment?"

Slowly, Terrence Gurnard turned his head and looked his friend in the eye. "My last opponent was Melcham."

Hubert blanched. "Oh," he said. Then, "Ah." Switching his gaze to the traffic, he nodded. "In that case, I quite see your point. Well, then—when's the wedding?"

CHAPTER TEN

HER AUNT, SOPHIE MUSED, was not to be trusted. At least, not when it came to Jack Lester. Although she had expected to see Mr. Lester at her cousin's come-out ball, Sophie had had no inkling that he would feature among the favoured few who had been invited to dine before the event. Not until he walked into the drawing-room, throwing all the other gentlemen into immediate shade.

From her position by the fireplace, a little removed from her aunt, Sophie watched as Jack bowed over Lucilla's hand. His coat was of midnight blue, the same shade as his eyes at night. His smallclothes were ivory, his cravat a minor work of art. His large sapphire glowed amid the folds, fracturing the light. Beyond the heavy gold signet that adorned his right hand, he wore no other ornament, nothing to distract her senses from the strength of his large frame. After exchanging a few words, Lucilla sent him her way.

Stilling an inner quiver, Sophie greeted him with a calm smile. "Good evening, Mr. Lester."

Jack's answering smile lit his eyes. "Miss Winterton." He bowed gracefully over her hand, then, straightening, looked down at her. "Sophie."

Sophie's serene expression did not waver as she drew her gaze from his; she had had practice enough in the past few days in keeping her emotions in check. Seeing Ned, who had followed his mentor into the room, turn from Lucilla to make his way to Clarissa's side, Sophie glanced up at her companion. "Ned has told me how much you have done for him, even to the extent of putting him up. It's really very kind of you."

Having drunk his fill of Sophie's elegance, Jack reluctantly looked out over the room. Tonight, his golden head appeared warm yet remote, priestess-like in a classically styled ivory sheath, draped from one shoulder to fall in long lines to the floor. Forcing himself to focus on his protégé, Jack shrugged. "It's no great thing. The house is more than large enough, and the proximity increases the time we have to…polish his address."

Sophie arched a sceptical brow. "Is that what you term it?"

Jack smiled. "Polish is all Ned needs."

Sophie slanted him a glance. "And that's the secret of gentlemanly success—polish?"

Jack looked down at her. "Oh no, my dear." His gaze grew more intent. "Such as I, with more sophisticated game in sight, often need recourse to…weapons of a different calibre."

Sophie tilted her chin. "Indeed, sir? But I was thanking you for helping Ned—and must also convey all our thanks for your assistance this morn. How we would have coped had you not removed Jeremy, George and Amy from the house, I simply do not know."

Meeting his eyes, Sophie smiled serenely.

Jack smiled back. "As I've told you before, your cousins are the most engaging urchins; playing nursemaid, as Marston had it, is no great undertaking. I trust all came right in the end?"

With Ned in tow, Jack had arrived on the Webbs' doorstep that morning, as he had for the past two, to find the house in the grip of the usual mayhem coincident with a major ball. Knowing neither Sophie nor Clarissa would be free, he and Ned had nevertheless offered to take the youngsters to the Park—a boon to all as, with the house full of caterers, florists and the like, and the servants rushed off their feet, the youthful trio had been proving a severe trial. They had already caused havoc by pulling the bows on the sheaves of flowers the florists had prepared all undone, then been threatened with incarceration when they had discovered the pleasures of skidding across the newly polished ballroom floor.

"Yes, thank Heaven," Sophie replied, watching further arrivals greet her aunt. "I don't know how Aunt Lucilla manages to keep it all straight in her head. But the storm and tempest did eventually abate, leaving order where before there was none."

Jack's grin was wry. "I'm sure your aunt's order is formidable."

Sophie smiled. "I rather suspect the ball tonight ranks as one of her more spectacular undertakings."

"With both your cousin and yourself to launch, it's hardly surprising that she's pulled out all stops."

Sophie blinked, her smile fading slightly. Then, with determined brightness, she inclined her head. "Indeed. And both Clarissa and I are determined she will not be disappointed."

A subtle reminder that she, too, was expected to find a husband. Just as he would have to find a wife. Sophie was all too well aware that, through shared moments, shared laughter and some indefinable attraction, she and Jack Lester had drawn far closer than was common between gentlemen and ladies who remained merely friends. Nevertheless, that was all they could be, and the time was fast approaching when their disparate destinies would prevail. She was steeling herself to face the prospect.

"Sophia, my dear!" Lady Entwhistle bustled up, her silk skirts shushing. "You look positively radiant, my dear—doesn't she, Henry?"

"Set to take the shine out of the younger misses, what?" Lord Entwhistle winked at Sophie, then shook her hand.

"And Mr. Lester, too—how fortunate." Her ladyship presented her hand and looked on with approval as Jack bowed over it. "A pleasure to see you again, sir. I hear Lady Asfordby's in town; have you run into her yet?"

Jack's eyes briefly touched Sophie's. "I have not yet had that pleasure, ma'am."

"A deuced shame about the hunting, what?" Lord Entwhistle turned to Jack. "Not that you younger men care—just change venues, far as I can see." His lordship cast a genial eye over the room.

"As you say, sir," Jack replied. "I fear there are few foxes to be found in London, so naturally we're forced to shift our sights."

"What's that? Forced? *Hah!*" His lordship was in fine fettle. "Why, I've always heard the tastiest game's to be found in the capital."

Sophie struggled to keep her lips straight.

"Really, Henry!" Her ladyship unfurled her fan with an audible click.

"But it's true," protested Lord Entwhistle, not one whit abashed. "Just ask Lester here. Few would know better than he. What say you, m'boy? Don't the streets of London offer richer rewards than the fields of Leicestershire?"

"Actually," Jack replied, his gaze returning to Sophie, "I'm not sure I would agree with you, sir. I must confess I've recently discovered unexpected treasure in Leicestershire, after a year in the *ton*'s ballrooms had yielded nothing but dross."

For an instant, Sophie could have sworn the world had stopped turning; for a moment, she basked in the glow that lit Jack Lester's eyes. Then reality returned, and with it awareness—of the conjecture in Lord Entwhistle's eyes, the startled look on her ladyship's face, and the role she herself had to play. Smoothly, she turned to Lady Entwhistle. "I do hope Mr. Millthorpe has found his feet in London. Will he be here tonight?"

The surprise faded from her ladyship's eyes. "Yes, indeed. Lucilla was kind enough to invite him for the ball.

I'm sure he'll attend. He was very much taken with Clarissa, you know." She glanced across the room to where Clarissa was surrounded by a small coterie of young gentlemen. "Mind you, I expect he'll be in good company. As I told your aunt, fully half the young men in town will be prostrating themselves at Clarissa's feet."

Sophie laughed and steered the conversation towards the social events thus far revealed on the *ton*'s horizon. She was somewhat relieved when Jack chipped in with the news of the balloon ascension planned for May, thus distracting Lord Entwhistle, who declaimed at length on the folly of the idea.

His lordship was still declaiming when Minton entered, transcending the impression conveyed by his severe grab to announce in jovially benevolent vein that dinner was served.

Lord and Lady Entwhistle went together to join the exodus. Jack turned to Sophie. "I believe, dear Sophie, that the pleasure of escorting you in falls…to me."

Sophie smiled up at him and calmly surrendered her hand. "That will be most pleasant, sir."

With her hand on his arm, Jack steered her into the shuffling queue.

Laughing chatter greeted them as they strolled into the dining-room. The surface of the table, polished to a mellow glow, reflected light fractured by crystal and deflected by silver. A subtle excitement filled the air; this was, after all, the first of the large gatherings, and those present were the chosen few who would start the ball of the Season rolling. Horatio, genially rotund, took his place at the table's head;

Lucilla graced the opposite end, while Clarissa, sparkling in a gown of fairy-like silvered rose silk, sat in the middle on one side. Ned beside her. Jack led Sophie to her place opposite Clarissa, then took the seat on her right.

As she glanced about, taking note of her neighbours, Sophie took comfort from Jack's presence beside her. Despite his apparently ingrained habits, he always drew back whenever she baulked—smoothly, suavely, ineffably rakish, yet a gentleman to his very bones. She now felt confident in his company, convinced he would never press her unduly nor step over that invisible line.

There was, indeed, a certain excitement to be found in his games, and a certain balm in the warmth of his deep blue gaze.

The toast to Clarissa was duly drunk; her cousin blushed prettily while Ned looked on, a slightly stunned expression on his face.

As she resumed her seat, Sophie glanced at Jack. He was watching her; he raised his glass and quietly said, "To your Season, dear Sophie. And to where it will lead."

Inwardly Sophie shivered, but she smiled and inclined her head graciously.

On her left was Mr. Somercote, a distant Webb cousin, a gentleman of independent means whom her uncle had introduced as hailing from Northamptonshire. While obviously at home in the *ton,* Mr. Somercote was reserved almost to the point of rudeness. Sophie applied herself but could tease no more than the barest commonplaces from him.

The lady on Jack's right was a Mrs. Wolthambrook, an

elderly widow, another Webb connection. Sophie wondered at the wisdom of her aunt's placement, but by the end of the first course, her confidence in Lucilla had been restored. The old lady had a wry sense of humour which Jack, in typical vein, recognized and played to. Sophie found herself drawn into a lively discussion, Mrs. Wolthambrook, Jack and herself forming a nexus of conversation which served to disguise the shortcomings of others in the vicinity.

It was almost a surprise to find the dessert course over. With a rustle of silk skirts, Lucilla rose and issued a charming directive sending them all to the ballroom.

While ascending the stairs on Jack's arm, Sophie noticed the glimmer of a frown in Lady Entwhistle's sharp eyes. It was, Sophie decided, hardly to be wondered at: installing Jack Lester as her partner at dinner had clearly declared her aunt's hand. Lucilla was playing Cupid. It was inconceivable that, after nearly three weeks in the capital, her aunt was not *au fait* concerning Jack Lester's state. But Lucilla was not one to follow the conventions in matters of the heart; she had married Horatio Webb when he was far less well-to-do than at present, apparently without a qualm. Sophie's own mother, too, had married for love. It was, in fact, something of a family trait.

Unfortunately, Sophie thought, casting a fleeting glance at Jack's darkly handsome profile, it was not one she was destined to follow. Hiding her bruised heart behind a serene smile, she crossed the threshold of the ballroom.

Under the soft flare of candlelight cast by three huge

chandeliers, the efforts of the florists and decorators looked even better than by day. The tops of the smooth columns supporting the delicately domed ceiling had been garnished with sprays of white and yellow roses, long golden ribbons swirling down around the columns. The minstrels' gallery above the end of the room was similarly festooned with white, yellow and green, trimmed with gold. Tall iron pedestals supporting ironwork cones overflowing with the same flowers filled the corners of the room and stood spaced every few yards along the long mirrored wall, with chaises and chairs set between. The opposite wall contained long windows giving onto the terrace; some were ajar, letting in the evening breeze.

The guests dutifully oohed and aahed, many ladies taking special note of the unusual use of ironwork.

Jack's blue eyes glinted down at her. "As I said, my dear, your aunt's efforts are indeed formidable."

Sophie smiled, but her heart was not in it; it felt as if her evening was ending when, with a graceful bow, Jack surrendered her to her duty on the receiving line.

He had bespoken a waltz, she reminded herself, giving her emotions a mental shake. Conjuring up a bright smile, she dutifully greeted the arrivals, taking due note of those her aunt introduced with a certain subtle emphasis. Lucilla might be encouraging Jack Lester, but it was clear she was equally intent on giving Sophie a range of suitable gentlemen from which to make her choice.

Which was just as well, Sophie decided. Tonight was the

start of her Season proper; she should make a real start on her hunt for a husband. There was no sense in putting off the inevitable. And it would no doubt be wise to make it abundantly plain that she was not infected with Lucilla's ideals. She could not marry Jack Lester, for he needed more money than she would bring. Embarking on her search for a husband would clarify their relationship, making it plain to such avid watchers as Lady Entwhistle and Lady Matcham that there was nothing to fear in her friendship with Jack.

Stifling a sigh, Sophie pinned on a smile as her aunt turned to greet the latest in the long line of guests.

"Ah, Mr. Marston," Lucilla purred. "I'm so glad you could come."

Sophie swallowed a most unladylike curse. She waited, trapped in line, as Mr. Marston greeted Clarissa with chilly civility, his glance austerely dismissing the enchanting picture her cousin made.

Then his gaze reached her—and Sophie privately resolved to send a special thank-you to Madame Jorge. Mr. Marston's distant civility turned to frigid disapproval as he took in her bare shoulders and the expanse of ivory skin exposed by the low, slanting neckline of her gown.

Sophie smiled sunnily. "Good evening, sir. I trust you are well."

Mr. Marston bowed. "I…" He drew himself up, his lips pinched. "I will look to have a few words with you later, Miss Winterton."

Sophie tried her best to look delighted at the prospect.

"Lady Colethorpe—my niece, Sophia Winterton."

With a certain relief, Sophie turned to her aunt's next guest and put Mr. Marston very firmly from her mind.

Down in the ballroom, Jack wended his way through the throng, stopping here and there to chat with old acquaintances, constantly hailed as the *ton,* one and all, found their way to the Webbs' ball. Percy, of course, was there. He greeted Jack with something akin to relief.

"Held up with m'father," Percy explained. "He was having one of his turns—convinced he was going to die. All rubbish, of course. Sound as a horse." Smoothing down his new violet silk waistcoat, Percy cast a knowledgeable eye over Jack's elegance, innate, as he well knew—and sighed. "But what's been going on here, then?" he asked, raising his quizzing glass to look about him. "Seems as if every squire and his dog have already come to town."

"That's about the sum of it," Jack confirmed. "I just met Carmody and Harrison. The whole boiling's in residence already, and raring to get started. I suspect that's what's behind the eagerness tonight. Lucilla Webb's gauged it to a nicety."

"Hmm. Mentioned the Webbs to m'father. Very knowing, he is. He had a word for Mrs. Webb."

"Oh?" Jack looked his question.

"Dangerous," Percy offered.

Jack's lips twitched. "That much, I know. To my cost, what's more. Nevertheless, unless I'm greatly mistaken, the lady approves of yours truly. And, dangerous or not, I fear I'm committed to further acquaintance."

Percy blinked owlishly. "So you're serious, then?"

"Having found my golden head, I'm not about to let her go."

"Ah, well." Percy shrugged. "Leave you to it, then. Where'd you say Harrison was?"

After sending Percy on his way, Jack looked over the heads, curled and pomaded, and discovered that Sophie and her family had quit the doorway to mingle with their guests. He located Sophie on the other side of the room, surrounded by a small group of gentlemen. Eminently eligible gentlemen, he realized, as he mentally named each one. Jack felt his possessive instincts stir. Immediately, he clamped a lid on them. He had already claimed a waltz and the right to take Sophie to supper; Lucilla would frown on any attempt to claim more.

With an effort, Jack forced himself to relax his clenched jaw. To ease the strain on his temper, he shifted his gaze to Clarissa, a little way along the wall. Sophie's cousin was glowing, radiating happiness. As well she might, Jack thought, as he viewed her not inconsiderable court. Puppies all, but Clarissa was only seventeen. She was unquestionably beautiful and, to her and her mother's credit, blissfully free of the silly affectations that often marred others of her calibre. Whether she was as talented as her mother, Jack had no notion—he had seen no evidence of it yet.

Seeing Ned holding fast to his place by Clarissa's side despite all attempts to dislodge him, Jack grinned. As long as

Ned circulated when the dancing began, there was no harm in his present occupation. His protégé was maintaining a coolly distant expression, which had made Clarissa glance up at him, slightly puzzled, more than once. Ned was learning fast, and putting his new-found knowledge to good use.

Making a mental note to drop a word of warning in Ned's ear, to the effect that any female descended from Lucilla Webb should be treated with due caution, Jack allowed his mind to return to its preoccupation.

Was Sophie like her aunt, capable of manipulation on a grand scale? Jack shook aside the silly notion. His Sophie was no schemer—he would stake his life on that. To him, she was open, straightforward, all but transparent. As he watched her smile brightly up at the Marquess of Huntly, Jack's satisfied expression faded. Abruptly executing a neat about-face, he strolled deeper into the crowd.

The first waltz was duly announced, and Clarissa, blushing delicately, went down the floor with her father, a surprisingly graceful dancer. At the conclusion of the measure, Horatio beamed down at her. "Well, my dear. You're officially out now. Are you pleased?"

Clarissa smiled brilliantly. "Indeed, yes, Papa," she said, and meant it.

The crowd parted and she looked ahead. To see Ned leading another young lady from the floor. Clarissa's smile faded.

Horatio noticed. "I had better return you to your court, my dear." Blandly, he added, "But do spare a thought for your old father. Don't line up too many suitors for your hand."

Apparently unaware of Clarissa's startled glance, Horatio guided her back to her circle, then, with a blithely paternal pat on her hand, left her to them.

"I say, Miss Webb." Lord Swindon was greatly smitten. "You waltz divinely. You must have been practising incessantly up in Leicestershire."

"May I get you a glass of lemonade, Miss Webb? Thirsty work, dancing." This from Lord Thurstow, a genial red-haired gentleman whose girth explained his conjecture.

But the most frightening comment came from Mr. Marley, a young sprig who considered himself a budding poet. "An ode…I feel an ode burgeoning in my brain. To your incomparable grace, and the effect it has on your poor followers who have to watch you take the floor in another's arms. *Argh!*"

Clarissa eyed the flushed young man in alarm. Gracious, were they all so unutterably silly?

As the evening wore on, she decided that they were. This was not what she had come to London to find. Being mooned over by gentlemen she classed as barely older than Jeremy and George was hardly the stuff of her dreams. Stuck with her court, surrounded on all sides, Clarissa met their sallies with guileless smiles, while inwardly she considered her options.

When Ned reappeared and rescued her, leading her into the set forming for a country dance, the truth dawned.

Smiling up at him, Clarissa shyly said, "It's such a relief to dance with someone I know."

Mindful of his instructions, Ned merely raised a brow. "Is it?" Then he smiled, a touch of condescension in his manner. "Don't worry, you'll soon get used to all the attention."

Stunned, Clarissa stared at him.

"Not a bad ball, this," Ned cheerily remarked. "Your mother must be pleased at the turnout. Don't think I've seen so many young ladies all at once before."

It was, perhaps, as well for Ned that the dance separated them at that point. When they came together again, Clarissa, her nose in the air, treated him to a frosty glance. "As you say," she said, "I'm sure I'll learn how to respond suitably to all the compliments the gentlemen seem so intent on pressing on me. I must ask Mama how best to encourage them."

Again the dance averted catastrophe. By the time the music finally died, Ned, chilly and remote, led Clarissa, equally distant and frigid, back to her circle. After perfunctorily bowing over her hand, Ned quit the vicinity, leaving Clarissa to deal with her importunate followers, her cheeks flushed, a dangerous glint in her large eyes.

A little distance away, Sophie had started to compile a list of potential suitors. The task was not difficult, for they promptly presented themselves before her, all but declaring their interest. The basis for their attraction had her mystified until Lord Annerby confessed, "The young misses are not really my style." When the movements of the quadrille brought them together again, he admitted, "Been hoping a lady like you would hove on my horizon. Not just in the common way, and not likely to giggle in a man's ear, if you take my meaning."

After that, Sophie paid a little more attention to her would-be swains, and discovered that many were, indeed, like his lordship: gentlemen who had been waiting for a lady such as she, not in the first flush of youth but yet young, presentable and altogether acceptable, to appear and walk up the aisle with them. With their reasons explained, she turned her attention to their attributes.

"I understand your estates are in Northamptonshire, Mr. Somercote. I hail from that county myself."

"Do you?" As they glided through the steps of the cotillion, Mr. Somercote made a visible effort to produce his next statement. "Somercote Hall lies just beyond the village of Somercote in the northwesternmost corner of the county."

Sophie nodded and smiled encouragingly, but apparently that was the full extent of Mr. Somercot's loquacity. As they returned through the crowd to where her admirers were waiting, she mentally crossed his name off her list.

The Marquess of Huntly was her next partner. "Tell me, Miss Winterton, do you enjoy the amenities of London?"

"I do indeed, my lord," Sophie replied. The marquess was Lord Percy's elder brother and, despite his bluff appearance and a tendency to stoutness, was unquestionably eligible.

"I've heard that you ride in the Park. Mayhap we'll meet one fine morning."

"Perhaps," Sophie returned, her smile noncommittal.

As they left the floor, Sophie decided the marquess could remain on her list for the present. Perhaps a meeting in the Park, with her younger cousins in tow, would be useful? She was pondering the point when a deep voice cut across her thoughts.

"I believe our waltz is next, Miss Winterton." Jack nodded to the marquess. "Huntly."

"Lester." The marquess returned his nod. "Seen Percy about?"

"He was chatting with Harrison earlier in the evening."

"Suppose I should go and have a word with him. M'brother, you know," the marquess confided to Sophie. "M'father's been at death's door—should see how he is. If you'll excuse me, m'dear?"

Even as she stared at Lord Huntly's retreating back, Sophie's mental pencil was scrubbing out his name. Such callousness was appalling.

Seeing her shocked expression, Jack abruptly shut his lips on the explanation he had been about to make. He did not consider Huntly a rival—but why make a whip for his own back? Appropriating Sophie's hand, he laid it on his sleeve. "Perhaps we could stroll about the room until the waltz commences?"

Sophie blinked, then frowned. "I really should return to my aunt."

His own frown hidden behind an urbane smile, Jack inclined his head and dutifully led her to where her court was waiting.

An unwise move. He was not impressed by the small crowd of eligibles who apparently could find nothing better to do at the first major ball of the Season than congregate about his Sophie. His temper was not improved by having to listen to them vie to heap accolades upon their compliments. For their part, they ignored him, secure in the knowledge that Sophie's expectations were insufficient to permit him to woo her. The thought made Jack smile inwardly. The smile turned to a suppressed growl when he heard Sophie say, "I do indeed enjoy the opera, Lord Annerby."

She then smiled serenely at his lordship.

"I'll be sure to let you know when the season begins, my dear Miss Winterton." Lord Annerby all but gloated.

Jack gritted his teeth. He had avoided the opera for years— a fact that owed nothing to the performances but rather more to those performing. To his immense relief, the strains of the waltz heralded his salvation. "Miss Winterton?"

Surprised, Sophie blinked up at him even as she put her hand in his. His fingers closed tightly about hers. His words had sounded like a command. An inkling of a difficulty she had not previously considered awoke in Sophie's brain.

Without further speech, Jack led Sophie to the door, drawing her into his arms with an arrogance that bespoke his mind far too well. He knew it, but did not care. The relief as she settled into his arms was balm to his lacerated feelings.

As they joined the swirling crowd on the floor, Jack considered closing his eyes. He would wager he could waltz round any ballroom blindfolded, so accustomed was he to the exercise. And with his eyes closed, his senses would be free to concentrate solely on Sophie—on the soft warmth of her, on how well she fitted in his arms, on the subtle caress of her silk-encased thighs against his.

Stifling a sigh, he kept his eyes open.

"Are you enjoying the ball, Mr. Lester?"

Sophie's calm and rather distant comment drew Jack's eyes from contemplation of her curls. He considered her question, simultaneously considering her invitingly full lips. "I'm enjoying this waltz," he replied.

Raising his eyes to hers, Jack watched a frown form in the sky-blue orbs. Puzzled, he continued, "But when are you going to call me Jack? I've been calling you Sophie for weeks."

He had never before seen a lady blush and frown simultaneously.

"I know," Sophie admitted, forcing herself to throw him a disapproving glance. "And you know you should not. It's not at all acceptable."

Jack simply smiled.

Sophie shot him an exasperated glance, then transferred her gaze to the safe space above his shoulder. As always, being in his arms had a distinctly unnerving affect on her. A fluttery, shivery awareness had her in its grip; breathless excitement threatened her wits. His strength reached out and enfolded her, seductively beckoning, enticing her mind to dwell on prospects she could not even dream of without blushing.

She blushed now, and was thankful to hear the closing bars of the waltz.

Jack saw her blush but was far too wise to comment. Instead, he smoothly escorted her into supper, adroitly snaffling a plate of delicacies and managing to install plate, glasses of champagne and Sophie at a small table tucked away near the conservatory.

He had reckoned without her court. They came swarming about, sipping champagne and, to Jack's mind, making thorough nuisances of themselves. He bore it stoically, repeatedly reminding himself that Lucilla would not consider the first major ball of the Season a suitable venue for him to declare his intentions. When the light meal was over, he insisted on escorting Sophie all the way back to her aunt's side.

The look he bent on Lucilla made her hide a grin.

With Sophie and Clarissa both claimed for the next dance, Lucilla turned her large eyes on Jack. "I must say, Mr. Lester, that you're doing a very good job on Ned."

Somewhat stiffly, Jack inclined his head. "I'm glad the transformation meets with your approval, ma'am."

"Indeed. I'm most grateful. *Immensely* grateful."

Seeing Lady Entwhistle fast approaching, clearly intent on having a word in Lucilla's ear, Jack bowed briefly and drifted into the crowd. As he passed the dancers, he heard a silvery laugh. Glancing up, he saw Sophie, smiling brightly up at Lord Ainsley, a handsome and very rich peer.

Muting his growl, Jack swung into an alcove. What numbskull had invented the practice of wooing? Lucilla's comment, which he felt confident in interpreting as open encouragement, was welcome enough. However, the last thing his passions needed right now was further encouragement, particularly when the object of said passions was behaving in a manner designed to enflame them.

Suppressing his curses, he set himself to endure. He could have left, but the night was yet young. Besides, he was not sufficiently sure of Ned to leave his protégé unsupported. At the thought, Jack drew his gaze from Sophie's bright curls and scanned the dancers for Clarissa.

Predictably, Sophie's cousin was smiling up at an elegant youth as she went down the floor in the dance. Jack silently harrumphed, then switched his gaze back to Sophie. Clarissa was clearly absorbed with her partner.

In so thinking, Jack erred.

Although Clarissa smiled and nodded at Mr. Pommeroy's stilted conversation, her attention was far removed from that blameless young gentleman. From the corner of her eye, she could see Ned dancing with Miss Ellis in the next set. The sight filled Clarissa with a sort of quiet fury she had never before experienced. Regardless of its import, it was quite clearly time to refocus Ned's attention on that which had brought him to town.

Her eyes narrowing, Clarissa herself refocused—on Mr. Pommeroy. She grimaced. Startled, Mr. Pommeroy stumbled and almost fell. Guiltily, for she had not meant to grimace openly, Clarissa applied herself to soothing her partner's ruffled feathers while looking about her for inspiration.

Her court, unfortunately, had little to offer. They were so young; not even in her wildest dreams could she cast them in the role she was rapidly becoming convinced she needed filled. Back amongst them, responding to their quips with but half her mind, Clarissa grimly watched as Ned joined the crowd about two sisters also making their come-out this year. Inwardly sniffing, Clarissa shifted her gaze—and saw Toby coming towards her, a positive Adonis in tow.

"Ah, Clarissa?" Toby came to an uncertain halt before his sister. "Might I make known to you Captain Gurnard? He's with the Guards." Toby was unsure how his sister would react, but the captain had been keen to gain a personal introduction, something Toby could see no harm in.

Clarissa's wide eyes took in every detail of the tall, broad-shouldered figure bowing before her. The captain was clad in scarlet regimentals; his tightly curled hair gleamed like fool's gold in the candlelight. As he straightened, Clarissa caught the hard gleam in his eyes and the cynical tilt of his mouth before unctuous gratification overlaid them.

Clarissa smiled brilliantly and held out her hand. "How do you do, Captain? Have you been with the Guards long?"

Blinking, Toby inwardly shrugged and took himself off.

Dazzled, Captain Gurnard saw nothing beyond Clarissa's guileless china-blue eyes and her delicately curved lips. He could only conclude that Fate had taken pity on him. With a consciously charming smile, he reluctantly released

Clarissa's hand. "I've been with my regiment for some years, my dear."

"Some years?" Clarissa's expression was all innocent bewilderment. "But—" She broke off and shyly put one hand to her lips. "Indeed," she whispered, half-confidingly. "I had not thought you so old as all that, Captain."

Gurnard laughed easily. "Indeed, Miss Webb. I greatly fear I must admit to being quite in my dotage compared with such a sweet child as yourself." His expression sobered. "In truth," he added, his voice low, "I fear I cannot compete with these young pups that surround you. The blithe and easy words of youth have long ago left me."

Ignoring the rising hackles of said pups, Clarissa smiled sweetly and leaned towards the captain to say, "Indeed, sir, I find a little of such blithe and easy words is more than a surfeit. Honest words are always more acceptable to the hearer."

The smile on Captain Gurnard's face grew. "Perhaps, my dear, in order to hear such honest words, you would consent to stroll the room with me? Just until the next dance begins?"

Plastering a suitably ingenuous smile on her lips, Clarissa nodded with apparent delight. Rising, she placed her fingertips on the captain's scarlet sleeve.

As he led her into the crowd, Captain Gurnard could not restrain the smugness of his smile. He would have been supremely disconcerted had he known that Clarissa's inner smile outdid his.

Sophie, meanwhile, had run into a problem, an obstacle

to her endeavours. Large, lean and somehow oddly menacing, Jack had left his retreat, where he had been propping up the wall, to gravitate to her side, a hungry predator lured, she suspected, by the smiles she bestowed on the gentlemen about her.

Under her subtle encouragement, her potential suitors preened.

Jack looked supremely bored. Having by dint of superior experience won through to her side, he towered over her, his expression rigidly controlled, his eyes a chilly blue.

Sophie felt distinctly irate. He was intimidating her suitors. She did not *like* her current course, but it was the only one open to her, a fact she felt Jack should acknowledge, rather than get on his high ropes because… Well, the only conclusion she *could* reach was that he was jealous of the attention she was paying the other men.

But it was from among *them* she would have to chose a husband, and she felt increasingly annoyed when Jack continued to make her task more difficult. When Sir Stuart Mablethorpe, a distinguished scholar, met Jack's gaze and promptly forgot whatever lengthy peroration he had been about to utter, Sophie shot her nemesis a frosty glance.

Jack met it with bland imperturbability.

Thoroughly incensed, Sophie was only too ready to smile at Lord Ruthven, a gentleman she suspected had much in common with Jack Lester, in all respects bar one. Lord Ruthven did not need a wealthy bride.

One of Lord Ruthven's dark brows rose fractionally.

"Perhaps, Miss Winterton," he said as he straightened from his bow, "you might care to stroll the room?" His gaze flicked to Jack, then returned to Sophie's face.

Ignoring the glint in Ruthven's eyes, Sophie replied, "Indeed, sir. I'm becoming quite fatigued standing here."

Ruthven's lips twitched. "No doubt. Permit me to offer you an escape, my dear." Thus saying, he offered her his arm.

With determined serenity, Sophie placed her hand on his lordship's sleeve, refusing to acknowledge the charged silence beside her. She was too wise to even glance at Jack as, with Ruthven, she left his side.

Which was just as well. Only when he was sure his emotions were once more under control did Jack allow so much as a muscle to move. And by then, Sophie and Ruthven were halfway down the room. His expression stony, Jack considered the possibilities; only the glint in his eyes betrayed his mood. Then, with his usual languid air, he strolled into the crowd, his course set for a collision with his golden head.

By the time she reached the end of the room, Sophie had realized that Ruthven's green eyes saw rather more than most. All the way down the room, he had subtly twitted her on her keeper. She suspected, however, that his lordship's indolent interest was more excited by the prospect of tweaking Jack's nose than by her own inherent attractions. Which was both comforting and a trifle worrying.

Together, she and Lord Ruthven paused beneath the minstrels' gallery and turned to survey the room.

"Ah, there you are, Ruthven." Jack materialized out of the crowd. He smiled easily at his lordship. "I just saw Lady Orkney by the stairs. She was asking after you."

Sophie glanced round in time to see an expression compounded of chagrin and suspicion flit across his lordship's handsome face. "Indeed?" One brow elevated, Ruthven regarded Jack sceptically.

Jack's smile grew. "Just so. Quite insistent on speaking with you. You know how she is."

Lord Ruthven grimaced. "As you say." Turning to Sophie, Ruthven said, "I fear I must ask you to excuse me, Miss Winterton. My aunt can become quite hysterical if denied." Again one of his lordship's brows rose, this time in resignation. "I dare say Lester will be only too happy to escort you about." With a wry smile, he bowed gracefully over her hand and departed.

Sophie eyed his retreating back through narrowed eyes. She had not seriously considered Ruthven as a suitor but she would certainly not consider a man who aggravated a lady's position, then deserted her, leaving her to face the consequences alone.

As Jack's fingers closed about her hand, she glanced up at his face. His impassive expression didn't fool her for a moment. Then he looked down at her, his eyes hard and very blue.

"Come with me, Miss Winterton." Her hand trapped on his sleeve, Jack headed towards the windows leading onto the terrace.

Sophie dug in her heels. "I have no intention of going anywhere private with you, Mr. Lester."

"Jack." The single syllable left Sophie in no doubt of his mood. "And if you would rather air our differences in public…" he shrugged. "…who am I to deny a lady?"

Looking up into his eyes, and seeing, as she had twice before, the dark brooding presence that lurked behind them, Sophie felt her throat constrict. But her own temper was not far behind his—he was behaving like a dog in a manger. "Very well, *Mr. Lester,*" she replied, holding his gaze. "But not on the terrace." From the corner of her eye, Sophie could see the rippling curtains that sealed off the music room, built out at the end of the ballroom under the minstrels' gallery. Half-concealed as it was by the gallery above and a row of ironwork urns, it was doubtful anyone else had thought to use the room. They could be private there while still remaining in the ballroom. Her lips firming, Sophie nodded to the curtain. "This way."

Jack followed her into the shadows beneath the gallery, then held back the curtain as she slipped through. He followed her. The heavy curtain fell to, deadening the noise from the ballroom. Candelabra shed ample light about the room, casting a mellow glow on the polished surfaces of the pianoforte and harpsichord. It was a comfortable little nook furnished with well-stuffed chaises and two armchairs. Sophie ignored its amenities and strode to the middle of the Aubusson rug in the centre of the floor.

Chin high, she swung to face Jack. "Now, Mr. Lester. Perhaps we may speak plainly."

"Precisely my thinking," Jack replied, strolling forward until he stood directly before her, no more than a foot away.

Mentally cursing, Sophie had to lift her head higher to meet his eyes.

"Perhaps," Jack suggested, "we could start with what, precisely, you think to achieve with all the gentlemen you've been so busily collecting?"

"A most pertinent point," Sophie agreed. She took a moment to marshall her thoughts, then began, her tone calm and quietly determined. "As I believe I told you, my first Season, four years ago, was cut very short."

Jack nodded curtly.

"As you also know, not only my aunt, but all my mother's friends are very keen…" Sophie paused, then amended, "Positively *determined* that I should wed. Indeed—" she met Jack's gaze challengingly "—I can see no other alternative."

A muscle shifted in Jack's jaw. "Quite."

"Thus," Sophie continued, "I must set about…er, gathering suitable suitors." She frowned slightly. Put like that, it sounded decidedly cold.

Jack frowned too. "Why?"

Sophie blinked. "I beg your pardon?"

Jack gritted his teeth and hung onto his temper. "Why do you need a whole *pack* of eligibles? Won't one do?"

Sophie frowned again, but this time at him. "Of course not," she answered, irritated by what could only be deliberate obtuseness. She drew herself up, her own eyes glittering. "I refuse to marry a man who does not have at least *some* of the attributes I consider appropriate."

Jack's frown intensified. "What attributes?"

"Attributes such as having estates in the country and a willingness to spend most of the year there. And being fond of children." Sophie blushed and hurried on, "And who can…can…well, who likes riding and…"

"Who can waltz you off your feet?" Jack's expression relaxed.

Sophie shot him a wary glance and saw the taunting gleam in his eye. She put up her chin. "There is a whole *host* of attributes I consider necessary in the gentleman I would wish to marry."

Jack nodded. "Nevertheless, coming to appreciate the attributes of the gentleman you're going to marry does not, for my money, necessitate gathering a small crowd with which to compare him."

"But *of course* it does!" Sophie glared. "How *do* you imagine I'm going to know that the one I accept is the right one if I do not—" she gestured with one hand "—look over the field?" Her tone was decidedly belligerent.

Jack frowned, recalling Lucilla's words. Did Sophie really need to compare him with others to be sure?

"And how," Sophie demanded, "am I supposed to do *that,* other than by talking and dancing with them?"

Jack's lips compressed into a thin line.

Sophie nodded. "Precisely. And I have to say," she continued, her nose in the air, "that I consider it most unfair of you to get in my way."

A moment's silence followed.

"Sophie," Jack growled, his voice very low, his eyes fixed on Sophie's face. "Believe me when I say that I have no intention *whatever* of letting you loose amongst the *ton*'s bachelors."

Sophie very nearly stamped her foot. Dragging in a portentous breath, she fixed him with a steely glare. "You are behaving *outrageously!* You do understand that I must marry, do you not?"

"Yes. But—"

"And that I must therefore choose between whatever suitors I may have?"

Jack's expression darkened. "Yes. But—"

"Well, then—with all your remarkable experience, perhaps you'd like to tell me *how* I'm to learn enough about each of them to discover which one will make the best husband?"

Jack's eyes narrowed. "It's very easy."

"Indeed?" Sophie's brows flew. "How?"

Jack focused on her lips, lushly full and all but pouting. "You should marry the man who loves you the most."

"I see," Sophie said, her temper still in alt. "And *how,* pray tell, am I supposed to identify him?" Her tone stated very clearly that she expected no sensible answer.

Very slowly, Jack's lips curved. His eyes lifted to Sophie's. "Like this," he said. Bending his head, he touched his lips to hers.

Sophie shivered, then went quite still. Her lids lowered, then shut as a wave of sweet longing swept through her. His lips were warm, smooth and firm against the softness of hers. His fingers found hers and laced through them; her fingers curled about his, clinging as if to a lifeline. She knew she should draw back, but made no move to do so, held, trapped, not by his desire, but her own. The realization made her tremble; his hands left hers to gently frame her face, holding her still as his lips teased and taunted, soothed and sipped.

Another wave of longing swept through her, keener, sweeter, more urgent. Sophie felt her senses start to slide into some blissful vale; she raised her hands and gripped his lapels as she leant into the kiss, offering her lips, seeking his.

Jack shuddered as his passions surged. Ruthlessly he quelled them, refusing to rupture the magic of the moment by allowing them free rein. Sophie's lips were warm and inviting, as sweet as nectar, just as he had imagined they would be. She drew nearer, her breasts brushing his chest. Her lips softened under his, she shivered delicately—and he knew he had been right from the start. She was his.

He felt his passions swell, possessively triumphant; he stood firm against their prompting, even though his arms ached to hold her. Unable to completely resist the beguiling temptation of her lips, he allowed the kiss to deepen by imperceptible degrees, until he had to struggle to shackle the need to taste her passionate sweetness.

Reluctantly he drew back, bringing the kiss to an end, his breathing sounding harsh in his ears. He forced his hands from her face, willing them to his sides.

Slowly Sophie's eyes opened. Her wise, starry gaze searched his face.

Bemused, bewildered, Sophie eased her grip on his lapels and lowered her hands. But she did not step back. She stared up at him and struggled to understand. She was teetering on the brink of some abyss; her senses pushed her on, urging her into his arms. Dimly she wondered what magic it was that could so overset her reason.

She wanted him to kiss her again. She needed to feel his arms close about her—even though she knew it would only further complicate an already difficult situation.

Jack read her desire in her eyes, in the parting of her full lips. He tensed against his instincts, against the building urge to sweep her into his arms.

Sophie saw the dark prowling beast that raged, caged, behind his eyes. And suddenly she understood. She caught her breath, fighting the excitement the welled within her, an unknown, never-before-experienced longing to meet his passion with her own. To fling herself into the dark depths of his gaze.

Jack saw the spark that lit her eyes, the glow that softened her face. The sight shredded his will. His control wavered.

The curtain cutting off the ballroom lifted and the noise of the ball rushed in.

As one, Sophie and Jack turned to see Phillip Marston holding the curtain back. His expression could only be described as severely disapproving.

"There you are, Miss Winterton. Permit me to escort you back to your aunt."

Sophie did not move. She drew in a breath, then slanted a glance at Jack. He met it, his expression arrogantly distant. Sophie held her breath; she thought she saw one brow lift slightly. Then, to her relief, he offered her his arm.

"You're mistaken, Marston; Miss Winterton needs no other escort than mine."

A delicious little thrill coursed down Sophie's spine; sternly, she suppressed the sensation and placed her hand on Jack's sleeve.

"Miss Winterton was overcome by the heat in the ballroom," Jack glibly explained. "We retired here to allow her to recover." He glanced down at Sophie's slightly flushed cheeks. "If you're feeling up to it, my dear, I'll take you back to your circle."

But not willingly, said his eyes. Sophie ignored the message and graciously inclined her head. "Thank you, sir." At least he wasn't abandoning her to Mr. Marston.

Jack allowed Marston to hold back the curtain as they emerged into the cacophony of the ball, now in full swing.

Sophie held her head high as they slowly wended their way through the crowd. Phillip Marston kept close by her other side.

Jack bided his time until Sophie's little group of would-be suitors, vaguely at a loss having misplaced their focus, loomed large before them. Then he adroitly lifted Sophie's hand from his sleeve and, stepping behind her, interposed himself between her and Phillip Marston. "We have not yet finished our discussion, Sophie."

His words were muted as he raised her hand.

Sophie, her expression once more calm and remote, lifted her chin. "Indeed, sir, I urge you to believe that we have had all the discussion we are ever likely to have on that particular topic."

Jack's expression remained impassive but his eyes held hers. Very deliberately, he lifted her hand and, turning it, pressed a brief kiss to her palm. "I'll speak with you later."

Sophie snatched her hand back, grateful that his bulk shielded them from almost everyone. She opened her mouth to protest—only to find him bowing gracefully. The next thing she knew, she was surrounded on all sides by gentlemen trying to claim her attention. By the time she had smoothed over her absence, Jack had disappeared.

But he hadn't left.

From an alcove by the steps, shielded by a potted palm, Jack kept a brooding watch over his golden head until the last note had sounded and the last of her would-be suitors had been dismissed.

CHAPTER ELEVEN

WITHIN TWENTY-FOUR HOURS, Jack had come to the conclusion that Fate had decided to live up to her reputation. He had fully intended to pursue his discussion with Sophie, rudely interrupted by Phillip Marston, the very next morning. Fickle Fate gave him no chance.

True, they went riding as usual, a mere ball being insufficient to dampen the Webbs' equestrian spirits. The children, however, prompted, Jack had no doubt, by Sophie, hung about him, bombarding him with questions about the projected balloon ascension. When Percy hove in sight, Jack ruthlessly fobbed the children off on his friend, who, by pure chance, was an amateur enthusiast. But by that time, the gentlemen who had discovered Sophie and Clarissa the night before had caught up with them.

Jack spent the rest of the ride po-faced by Sophie's side.

And there was worse to come.

As Jack had predicted, Clarissa Webb's come-out ball became the de facto beginning of the Season. It had been voted an horrendous crush by all; every hostess with any claim to fame rushed to lay her own entertainments before the *ton*. The days and evenings became an orgy of Venetian breakfasts, alfresco luncheons, afternoon teas and formal dinners, all crowned by a succession of balls, routs, drums and soirées. And beneath the frenzy ran the underlying aim of fostering suitable alliances—an aim with which Jack was, for the first time in his career, deeply involved.

Indeed, as he leaned against the wall in an alcove in Lady Marchmain's ballroom, his gaze, as always, on Sophie, presently gliding through a cotillion, the only thing on Jack's mind was a suitable alliance. He had come to town to use the Season as a backdrop for his wooing of Sophie. By his reckoning, the Season was now more than a week old. Then how much longer did he have to hold off and watch her smile at other men?

"I wonder…need I ask which one she is? Or should I make an educated guess?"

At the drawled words, Jack shifted his gaze to frown at Harry. Observing his brother's interrogative expression, Jack snorted and returned to his occupation. "Second set from the door. In amber silk. Blond."

"Naturally." Harry located Sophie by the simple expedient of following Jack's gaze. His brows slowly rose. "Not bad at all," he mused. "Have I complimented you recently on your taste?"

"Not so I've noticed."

"Ah, well." Harry slanted Jack a rakish smile. "Perhaps I'd better converse with this paragon before I pass judgement."

"If you can shake the dogs that yap at her heels."

Harry shook his head languidly. "Oh, I think I'll manage. What's her name?"

"Sophie Winterton."

With a smile which Jack alone could view with equanimity, Harry sauntered into the crowd. His lips twisting wryly, Jack settled to watch how his brother performed a feat he himself was finding increasingly difficult.

"Thank you, Mr. Somercote. An excellent measure." Sophie smiled and gave Mr. Somercote her hand, hoping he would accept his dismissal. He was, unfortunately, becoming a trifle pointed in his interest.

Mr. Somercote gazed earnestly into her face, retaining her hand in a heated clasp. He drew a portentous breath. "My dear Miss Winterton…"

"It is Miss Winterton, is it not?"

With abject relief, Sophie turned to the owner of the clipped, somewhat hard tones, beneath which a certain languidness rippled, and beheld a strikingly handsome man, bowing even more elegantly than Jack Lester.

This last was instantly explained.

"Harry Lester, Miss Winterton," the apparition offered, along with a rakish grin. "Jack's brother."

"How do you do, Mr. Lester?" As she calmly gave him her hand, Sophie reflected that in any contest of handsomeness, it would be exceedingly difficult to decide between Jack and Harry Lester, not least because they were so unalike.

The gentleman currently shaking her hand, then appropriating it in a manner she recognized all too well, was fair where Jack was dark, with green eyes where Jack's were blue. He was as tall as Jack, but leaner, and there hung about him an aura of dangerous elegance that was distinctly more sharp-edged than Jack's easy assurance. This Lester possessed an elegance that was almost extreme, an aesthetic's adherence to Brummel's dictates, combined with a well-nigh lethal grace.

Harry's glance flicked to Mr. Somercote, then returned to Sophie's face. "Perhaps you would care for a stroll about the rooms, Miss Winterton?"

The arrogant smile that curved his fatally attractive lips assured Sophie that, despite their physical dissimilarity, the Lesters were certainly brothers beneath the skin. "Indeed, sir. That would be most pleasant." He had already settled her hand on his sleeve. With a gentle nod for the deflated Mr. Somercote, Sophie allowed Harry to lead her along the floor.

"You've come to town with your aunt and cousins, have you not?"

Sophie glanced up to find a pair of green eyes lazily regarding her. "Yes, that's right. The Webbs."

"I'm afraid I've not had the pleasure of making their acquaintance. Perhaps you could introduce me if we meet?"

Sophie quickly discovered that Harry, like his brother, had a ready facility for filling in time in a most agreeable, and surprisingly unexceptionable, manner. As they chatted, threading their way through the crowd, she found herself relaxing, then laughing at a tale of a most hilarious excursion in the Park when he and Jack had first come to town. It was only the arrival of her next partner, Mr. Chartwell, that put an end to their amble.

Jack's brother yielded her up with a flourish and a wicked smile.

Smiling herself as she watched him disappear into the crowd, Sophie wondered at the steely danger so apparent in him. It contrasted oddly with Jack's strength. Not that she had felt the least threatened by Harry Lester—quite the opposite. But she did not think she would like to lose her heart to him.

Her mind had little respite from thoughts of Lesters; Jack claimed her immediately the dance with Mr. Chartwell concluded, barely giving that gentleman time to take his leave. However, having detected an expression of chagrin in Mr. Chartwell's mild grey eyes, Sophie was too grateful for her rescue to remonstrate.

Her gratefulness diminished markedly when it became apparent that Jack's difficulties in accepting their fate had not yet been resolved.

"Sophie, I want to talk to you. Privately." Jack had given up trying to manoeuvre such an interlude subtly. Sophie had proved the most amazingly stubborn female he had ever encountered.

Sophie lifted her chin. "You know that would be most unwise, let alone inappropriate."

Jack swallowed a curse. "Sophie, I swear…" The music for the waltz started up; Jack shackled his temper long enough to sweep Sophie into his arms. Once they were whirling slowly down the room, hemmed in on all sides, he continued, "If I have to put up with much more of this, I'll—"

"You'll do nothing that would force me to cut the connection, I hope?" Sophie kept her eyes wide and her expression serene; they might have been discussing the weather for all anyone could see. But her chest felt tight and her heart had sunk. She held Jack's gaze and prayed he'd draw back.

A savage light lit his eyes. Then, with a muttered curse, he looked away. But the tightening of his arm about her told Sophie the argument was far from over. He was holding her far too tight. Sophie made no demur. She had long ago given up hypocritically protesting his transgressions—such as his insistence of using her first name.

She felt a quiver run through her, felt her body respond to his nearness. That, she supposed, was inevitable. He wanted her—as she wanted him. But it wasn't to be; their world did not operate that way. They would both marry others, and Jack had to accept the fact gracefully. If he did, then perhaps they could remain friends. It was all she could hope for, and she was selfish enough to cling to his friendship. He shared so many of her interests, much more so than any of the gentlemen vying for her hand. Indeed, she was loweringly aware that not one of them measured up to Jack Lester and that whenever they gave signs of wanting to fix their interest, she felt an immediate aversion for their company. Her heart, no longer hers, was proving very difficult to reconquer.

Sensing an easing in the tension surrounding her, Sophie slanted a glance at Jack's face.

He was watching her, waiting. "Sophie…I'll accept that you need time to look about you. But I'm not an inherently patient man." The muscle along his jaw twitched; he stilled it, his eyes never leaving hers. "If you could find some way to hurry up this phase, I'd be eternally grateful."

Sophie blinked, her eyes widening. "I…I'll try."

"Do," Jack replied. "But just remember, Sophie—you're mine. *Nothing,* no amount of pretty phrases, will *ever* change that."

The possessiveness in his expression, intransigent, unwavering, stunned Sophie even more than the essence of his arrogant demand. A slow shudder shook her. "Please, Jack…" She looked away, her whisper dying between them.

Jack shackled the urge to haul her into his arms, to put an end to this wooing here and now. Instead, as the music ceased, he drew her hand through his arm. "Come. I'll escort you back to your aunt."

At least she had called him Jack.

"SOMETHING'S WRONG."

It was two nights after Lady Marchmain's ball. Horatio, already propped amid the pillows, turned to study his wife as she sat at her dressing-table, brushing out her mane of silver-blond hair. "What makes you say that?" he asked, unperturbed by her intense expression.

Lucilla frowned. "Sophie isn't happy."

"Isn't she?" Horatio blinked behind his glasses. "Why not? I would have thought, with a horde of would-be suitors, Jack Lester to the fore, she'd be as happy as a young lady could be."

"Well, she's not—and I think it has something to do with Jack Lester, although I cannot, for the life of me, imagine what it could be. Why, the man's positively eaten by jealousy every time she so much as smiles at another. Anyone with eyes can see it. I really don't know what more Sophie wants. Jack Lester will be the catch of the Season."

"Hmm." Horatio frowned. "You're quite sure it's Jack Lester she wants?"

Lucilla snorted. "Believe me, my dear, there's no man Sophie wants even a tenth as much. Indeed, if I was intent on doing my job by the book, I should have warned her long ago not to be so blatant in her preference."

"Ah, well." Horatio shuffled his ever-present documents and laid them aside as Lucilla stood and came towards the bed. "I dare say it'll work itself out. These things generally do."

Lucilla slipped beneath the covers and snuggled down. She waited until Horatio had blown out the candle before saying, "You don't think I should…well, find out what the problem is?"

"You mean *meddle?*" Horatio's tone made his opinion quite clear even before he said, "No. Let the young make their own mistakes, m'dear. How else do you expect them to learn?"

Lucilla grimaced in the dark. "Doubtless you're right, dear." She reached under the covers and patted Horatio's hand. She waited all of a minute before saying, "Actually,

I was thinking of organizing a short respite from town. The circus of the Season can become a mite tedious without a break. And I wouldn't want Sophie or Clarissa to become jaded just yet. What say you to a little house party at Aunt Evangeline's?"

Protected by the dark, Horatio slowly smiled. "Whatever you think best, m'dear."

It wouldn't hurt for the young people to have a little time together—time enough to correct their mistakes.

BUT FATE HAD NOT yet consented to smile again on Jack. And as for Sophie, she was finding it hard to smile at all.

The thought that Jack wanted her to marry as soon as possible was depressing enough. The idea of what he imagined would happen after was even more so. Her dreams were in tatters; Sophie found it increasingly hard to support her serene façade. She had made a habit of joining circles with Belle Chessington, relying on her friend's unquenchably cheery constitution to conceal her flagging spirits. But her glow was entirely superficial. Inside was all deepening gloom.

She had just returned to her circle on the arm of Mr. Chartwell, who was becoming more assiduous with every passing day, when a deep voice set her heart thumping.

"I do hope, Miss Winterton, that you've saved me a dance." Jack smiled into Sophie's eyes as he took her hand and drew her away from her court. "I've been teaching Ned how to tie his cravat, and it took rather longer than either of us expected."

Sophie felt her nerves knot and pull tight. Was this, she wondered, as they strolled down the room, how it was going to be later? Would he simply arrive and appropriate her at will? Tensing, she lifted her chin. "I'm afraid my card is full, Mr. Lester."

Jack frowned slightly. "I had rather supposed it would be. But you have kept a dance for me, haven't you?"

They both nodded to Miss Berry, ensconced on a chaise, then continued onward in silence. Sophie struggled to find words for her purpose.

Somewhat abruptly, their progress halted and her escort drew her to face him.

"Sophie?" Jack's frown was gathering force.

Sophie's eyes met his, cloudy, turbulent, intensely blue. Her heart thudding uncomfortably in her throat, she slid her gaze from his. "As it happens, I have not yet accepted anyone for the second waltz."

"You have now." Smothering the dark, almost violent passion that had threatened to erupt, Jack trapped her hand on his sleeve and continued their stroll.

He pointedly returned Sophie to her aunt, some little way from her cloying court. Surrendering her up for their delectation was presently beyond him. His expression somewhat grim, he bowed over Sophie's hand. "Until the second waltz, Miss Winterton."

With that, he left her, his mood even more savage than when he had arrived.

For Sophie, the second waltz arrived far too soon. She

had not yet regained her composure, seriously strained by the events of the past weeks and now close to breaking. Jack's arm about her whirled her effortlessly down the floor; Sophie held herself stiffly, battling the impulse to surrender to his strength.

So absorbed was she with her struggle that the first she knew of their departure from the ballroom was the cool touch of the night air on her face.

"Where…?" Distracted, Sophie glanced about and discovered they were on a terrace. But that, apparently, was not their destination, for Jack, his arm still hard about her waist, urged her on. "Jack!" Sophie tried to dig in her heels.

Jack stopped and looked down at her. "You were obviously finding the waltz a trial. I thought you might need some air."

Sophie relaxed slightly, and found she was moving again. "Where are we going?"

The answer was a garden room, built onto the house beyond the end of the terrace. Walls of windows let the moonlight pour in, silvering everything in sight. A few padded cane chairs and two little tables were scattered about the small room, which was, Sophie realized as she heard the door click behind them, mercifully empty.

Which was just as well, for Jack demanded without preamble, "How much longer, Sophie?"

Sophie swung about and found him advancing on her.

"How much longer are you going to make me suffer?"

Her hand rose as if to ward him off; it came to rest on his

chest as he halted directly before her. Feeling the warmth of his body through his coat, Sophie shivered. She looked up into his shadowed face, the planes hard and unyielding, and a small spurt of temper flared inside. How did he think *she* felt, having to give up the man she loved—and having that man urge her to do it? Her chin lifted. "I'm afraid the decision is not that simple. In fact, I find the attentions of my present admirers not at all to my taste."

That admission went a long way towards easing the tension that held Jack in its grip. He could feel it flowing from him, the muscles of his shoulders and back relaxing.

Still considering her suitors, Sophie frowned. "I'm afraid I would not be happy accepting any of my present suitors."

An icy chill stole over Jack's heart. It beat three times before he asked, "None?"

Sophie shook her head. "I don't know what to do. I must accept *someone* by the end of the Season."

The chill was slowly spreading through Jack's veins. He touched his tongue to his lips, then asked, "Why not me?"

Startled, Sophie glanced up at him. "But..." She frowned. "I can't marry you—you know I can't." She could see very little of his expression through the shadows veiling his face. And nothing at all of his eyes.

"Why not?" Sight wouldn't have helped her; Jack's expression was hard, impassive, all emotion suppressed. "We both know I've all the attributes you seek in a husband: a country estate, a wish to reside in the country, a desire for children, to have a family about me. That's what you want, isn't it?"

Sophie stared up at him.

"And, of course," Jack continued, his lips twisting in an uncertain smile, "we have something else between us." Raising a hand, he delicately drew the tip of one finger from the point of Sophie's shoulder, exposed by her wide neckline, across to the base of her throat, then down to where the deep cleft between her breasts was visible above her gown. Sophie shivered and caught her breath.

"A...compatibility," Jack said, "that makes all the rest fade into insignificance." His eyes rose to trap Sophie's stunned gaze. "Isn't it so, Sophie?"

Sophie swallowed. "But I have no fortune. Nothing but expectations."

"That doesn't matter." Jack's gaze sharpened. He drew a deep breath. "Sophie—"

In a sudden breathless rush, Sophie put her fingers over his lips. "No!" she squeaked, and cursed her quavering voice. At last she understood—and knew what she must do. Drawing in a determined breath, consciously steeling herself, she drew back, forcing herself to hold his gaze. "I'm afraid you don't understand, Jack. I've never been wealthy in my life—I came to London determined to marry well." The lie came out so easily. Her eyes falling from his, Sophie searched for more words to shore it up. "I know I didn't say so, but I thought you understood. Nothing..." She paused to make sure her voice would not waver. "Nothing I've seen in London has changed my mind; I require that my preferred suitor has considerable wealth."

The words came out more than creditably. Sophie heard them; her heart thudded painfully in her breast but she held herself erect, head high. Far better he think her lost to all sensibility than that he offer to marry her, mortgaging his future, turning his back on those responsibilities that were so very important to him. He was just like Lucilla—ready to sacrifice all for love. She wouldn't allow it.

"But…" Jack couldn't have felt more stunned had she slapped him. His brain reeled, grappling with the fact that Sophie did not know of his true circumstances. He had assumed Horatio would tell Lucilla, who in turn would have told Sophie. Obviously not. The facts were on his lips. Chill reason froze them there.

He looked down at Sophie's face, calm and serene in the moonlight, the face of the woman he had thought he understood. But she was intent on marrying for money—so intent she would happily put aside what was between them, turn away from his love, and hers, in exchange for cold hard cash. Fate was playing games with him; his golden head had gold on her mind. Did he really want to win her by revealing his disgusting wealth? How would he feel when she smiled and came to his arms, knowing that it had taken money to get her there?

There was a bitter taste in his mouth. Jack drew a sharp breath and looked up, over Sophie's head. He felt cold. A steel fist had closed about his heart, squeezing unmercifully.

He took a jerky step back. "I regret, Miss Winterton, if my…attentions have been unwelcome. I will not trouble you more. I realize my actions must have complicated your search for…a suitable suitor. You have my apologies." With a curt bow, Jack turned to leave. And hesitated.

His face in profile, Sophie saw his lips twist in the travesty of a smile. Then he turned his head to look down at her. "I can only hope, my dear, that when you find your pot of gold at the end of the rainbow you're not disappointed." With a curt nod, he strode away, opening and shutting the door carefully.

Leaving Sophie in the centre of the empty room.

For a long moment, she remained as she was, proudly erect, then her shoulders slumped. Sophie bowed her head, drawing in an aching breath, squeezing her eyes tight against the pain that blossomed inside.

Ten minutes later, she returned to the ballroom, no trace of misery on her face. Coolly composed, she joined her little circle, brightly responding to Belle Chessington's quips. A quick glance about revealed the fact that Jack's dark head was nowhere to be seen. Sophie crumpled inside. She had done the right thing. She must remember that.

If this was what it took to ensure he prospered and lived the life he should live, so be it.

From an alcove by the card room, almost at the other end of the floor, Jack brooded on Sophie's ready smiles. If he had needed any further proof of the superficiality of her feelings for him, he had just received it. Raising his glass, he downed a mouthful of the golden liquor it contained.

"There you are. Been looking all over." Ned ducked

round the palm that blocked the opening of the alcove. His eyes fell on Jack's glass. "What's that?"

"Brandy," Jack growled and took another long sip.

Ned raised his brows. "Didn't see any of that in the refreshment room."

"No." Jack smiled, somewhat grimly, across the room and said no more. Ned didn't need to drink himself into a stupor.

"I danced the last cotillion with Clarissa," Ned said. "Her blasted card was virtually full and that bounder Gurnard's taking her in to supper. Should I hang around here or can we leave?"

His gaze on Sophie, Jack considered the point. "I don't advise leaving until after supper, or it'll be said you only came to dance with Clarissa."

"I *did* only come to dance with Clarissa," Ned groaned. "Can we just cut and run?"

Very slowly, Jack shook his head, his attention still fixed across the room. "I told you, this game's not for the faint-hearted." For a long moment, he said no more; Ned waited patiently.

Abruptly, Jack shook himself and straightened from the wall. He looked at Ned, his usual arrogant expression in place. "Go and join some other young lady's circle. But whatever you do, don't be anywhere near Clarissa at suppertime." At Ned's disgusted look, Jack relented. "If you survive that far, I don't suppose it would hurt to talk to her afterwards—but no more than fifteen minutes."

"Wooing a young lady in the *ton* is the very devil," Ned declared. "Where do all these rules come from?" With a disgusted shake of his head, he took himself off.

With his protégé under control, Jack leaned back into the shadows of the alcove, and kept watch on the woman who, regardless of all else, was still his.

FOUR DAYS LATER, Sophie sat in the carriage and stared gloomily at the dull prospect beyond the window. Lucilla's little excursion, announced this morning, had taken the household by surprise. In retrospect, she should have suspected her aunt was planning something; there had been moments recently when Lucilla had been peculiarly abstracted. This three-day sojourn at Little Bickmanstead, the old manor belonging to Lucilla's ancient Aunt Evangeline, was the result.

Despondent, Sophie sighed softly, her gaze taking in the leaden skies. In perfect accord with her mood, the unseasonably fine spell had come to an abrupt end on the night she had refused to let Jack offer for her. A rainstorm had swept the capital. Ever since, the clouds had threatened, low and menacing, moving Lucilla to veto their rides.

Glumly, Sophie wondered if Jack understood—or if he thought she was avoiding him. The miserable truth was, she did not think she could cope with any meeting just now. Perhaps Fate had sent the rain to her aid?

Certainly Jack himself seemed in no hurry to speak with her again. Perhaps he never would. He had been present at the balls they had attended over the past three nights. She had seen him in the distance, but he had not approached her. Indeed, once, when they had passed close while she had been strolling the floor on one of her would-be suitors' arms, and their gazes had met, he had merely inclined his head in a distant fashion. She had replied in kind, but inside the ache had intensified.

Sophie closed her eyes and searched for peace in the repetitive rocking of the coach. She had done the right thing—she kept telling herself so. Her tears, perforce, had been shed discreetly, far from Lucilla's sharp eyes. She had stifled her grief, refusing to dwell on it; suppressed, it had swelled until it pervaded her, beating leaden in her veins, a cold misery enshrouding her soul. A misery she was determined none would ever see.

Which meant she had to face the possibility that Jack might take up the invitation Lucilla had extended to join them at Little Bickmanstead. The guest list numbered some twenty-seven souls, invited to enjoy a few days of rural peace in the rambling old house close by Epping Forest. But Jack wouldn't come, not now. Sophie sighed, feeling not relief, but an inexpressible sadness at the thought.

The well-sprung travelling carriage rolled over a rut, throwing Clarissa against her shoulder. They disentangled themselves and sat up, both checking on Lucilla, seated opposite, her dresser, Mimms, by her side. Her aunt, Sophie noted, was looking distinctly seedy. A light flush tinted Lucilla's alabaster cheeks and her eyes were overbright.

Touching a lace-edged handkerchief to her nose, Lucilla sniffed delicately. "Incidentally, Clarissa, I had meant to mention it before now—but you really don't want to encourage that guardsman, Captain Gurnard." Lucilla wrinkled her nose. "I'm not at all sure he's quite the thing, despite all appearances to the contrary."

"Fear not, Mama." Clarissa smiled gaily. "I've no intention of succumbing to the captain's wiles. Indeed, I agree with you, there's definitely something 'not quite' about him."

Lucilla shot her daughter a narrow-eyed glance, then, apparently reassured, she blew her nose and settled back against the cushions.

Clarissa continued to smile sunnily. Her plans were proceeding, albeit not as swiftly as she would have liked. Ned was proving remarkably resistant to the idea of imitating her other swains; he showed no signs of wanting to prostrate himself at her feet. However, as she found such behaviour a mite inconvenient, Clarissa was perfectly ready to settle for a declaration of undying love and future happiness. Her current problem lay in how to obtain it.

Hopefully, a few days in quieter, more familiar surroundings, even without the helpful presence of the captain to spur Ned on, would advance her cause.

The carriage checked and turned. Sophie looked out and saw two imposing gateposts just ahead. Then the scrunch of gravel announced they had entered the drive. The house lay ahead, screened by ancient beeches. When they emerged in the forecourt, Sophie saw a long, two-storey building in a hotchpotch of styles sprawling before them. One thing was instantly apparent: housing a party of forty would not stretch the accommodations of Little Bickmanstead. Indeed, losing a party of forty in the rambling old mansion looked a very likely possibility.

Drops of rain began spotting the grey stone slabs of the porch as they hurried inside. A fleeting glance over her shoulder revealed a bank of black clouds racing in from the east. The other members of the family had elected to ride from town, Horatio keeping a watchful eye on his brood. Minton and the other higher servants had followed close behind, the luggage with them. The forecourt became a scene of frenzied activity as they all hurried to dismount and stable the horses and unpack the baggage before the storm hit.

The family gathered in the hall, looking about with interest. The rectangular hall was dark, wood panelling and old tapestries combining to bolster the gloom. An ancient butler had admitted them; an even more ancient house-keeper came forward, a lamp in her hand.

As the woman bobbed a curtsy before her, Lucilla put out a hand to the table in the centre of the room. "Oh, dear."

One glance at her deathly pale face was enough to send them all into a panic.

"My dear?" Horatio hurried to her side.

"Mama?" came from a number of throats.

"Mummy, you look sick," came from Hermione, gazing upwards as she held her mother's hand.

Lucilla closed her eyes. "I'm dreadfully afraid," she began, her words very faint.

"Don't say anything," Horatio advised. "Here, lean on me—we'll have you to bed in a trice."

The old housekeeper, eyes wide, beckoned them up the stairs. "I've readied all the rooms as instructed."

Minton was already sorting through the bags. Sending Clarissa ahead with Mimms and the housekeeper, Sophie came to her aunt's other side. Together, she and Horatio supported a rapidly wilting Lucilla up the stairs and along a dim and drafty corridor to a large chamber. Mimms was in charge there; the bed was turned down, the housekeeper dispatched for a warming pan. A fire was cracking into life in the grate.

They quickly helped Lucilla to bed, laying her back on the soft pillows and tucking the covers about her. Once installed, she regained a little colour. She opened her eyes and regarded them ruefully. And sniffed. "This is terrible. I've organized it all—there are twenty-seven people on their way here. They'll all arrive before dinner. And if the rain persists, they'll need to be entertained for the next two days."

"Don't worry about anything," Horatio said, patting her hand. But even he was frowning as the ordeal before them became clear.

"But you haven't a hostess." Lucilla put her handkerchief to her nose, cutting off what sounded like a tearful wail. She blinked rapidly.

Sophie straightened her shoulders. "I'm sure I can manage, with Uncle Horatio and Great Aunt Evangeline behind me. It's not as if you were not in the house—I can check any details with you. And it's not as if there were no chaperons. You told me yourself you've invited a number of matrons."

Lucilla's woeful expression lightened. Her frown turned pensive. "I suppose…" For a moment, all was silent. Then, "Yes," she finally announced, and nodded. "It just might work. But," she said, raising rueful eyes to Sophie's face, "I'm awfully afraid, my dear, that it will be no simple matter."

Relieved to have averted immediate catastrophe, for if Lucilla broke down, that would certainly follow, Sophie smiled with totally false confidence. "You'll see, we'll contrive."

Those words seemed to have become a catchphrase of her Season, Sophie mused as, an hour later, she sat in the front parlour, off the entrance hall, the guest list in her hand.

After assuring themselves that Lucilla was settled and resigned to her bed, she and Clarissa and Horatio had gone to pay their respects to Aunt Evangeline. It had been years since Sophie had met her ageing relative; the years had not been kind to Aunt Evangeline. She was still ambulatory, but her wits were slowly deserting her. Still, she recognized Horatio, even though she was apparently ineradicably convinced that Clarissa was Lucilla and Sophie her dead mother, Maria. They had given up trying to correct the misapprehension, concentrating instead on explaining their current predicament. Whether or not they had succeeded was moot, but at least Aunt Evangeline had given them a free hand to order things as they wished.

Nevertheless, the prospect of having to keep a weather eye out for an old dear who, so the housekeeper had gently informed them, was full of curiosity and prone to wandering the corridors at all hours draped in shawls that dragged their fringes on the floor, was hardly comforting.

A sound came from outside. Sophie lifted her head, listening intently. The wind was rising, whistling about the eaves. Rain fell steadily, driving in gusts against the windows, masking other sounds. Then came the unmistakable jingle of harness. Sophie rose. The first of her aunt's guests had arrived. Girding her loins, she tugged the bell-pull and went out into the hall.

From the very first, it was bedlam. The Billinghams—Mrs. Billingham and both of her daughters—were the first to arrive. By the time they had descended from their carriage and negotiated the steps, their carriage dresses were soaked to the knees.

"Oh, how dreadful! Mama, I'm *dripping!*" The younger Miss Billingham looked positively shocked.

Mrs. Billingham, if anything even damper than her daughters, was not disposed to give comfort. "Indeed, Lucy, I don't know what you're complaining about. We're all wet—and now here's a to-do with Mrs. Webb ill. I'm not at all sure we shouldn't turn round and return to town."

"Oh no, Mama—you couldn't be so cruel!" The plaintive wail emanated from the elder Miss Billingham.

"Indeed, Mrs. Billingham, there's really no need." Smoothly, Sophie cut in, clinging to her usual calm. "Everything's organized and I'm sure my aunt would not wish you to withdraw purely on account of her indisposition."

Mrs. Billingham humphed. "Well, I suppose with your uncle present and myself and the other ladies, there's really no impropriety."

"I seriously doubt my aunt would ever countenance any," Sophie replied, her smile a trifle strained.

"We'll stay at least until the morning." Mrs. Billingham cast a darkling glance out of the open door. "Perhaps by then the weather will have eased. I'll make a decision then."

With that declaration, Mrs. Billingham allowed herself to be shown to her chamber.

Hard on the Billinghams' heels came Lord Ainsley. His lordship had unwisely driven out in his curricle, and he was soaked to the skin. He tried hard to smile, but his chattering teeth made it difficult.

Sophie was horrified, visions of guests catching their deaths whirling through her mind. Issuing orders left and right—for hot baths and mustard to ward off chills, for the staff to make sure all the fires were blazing—she turned from the sight of Lord Ainsley's back disappearing up the stairs to behold a bedraggled Lord Annerby on the doorstep.

And so it went, on through the afternoon, while outside a preternatural darkness descended.

Belle Chessington and her equally cheery mother were amongst the last to arrive.

"What a perfectly appalling afternoon," Mrs. Chessington remarked as she came forward with a smile, hand outstretched.

Sophie heaved an inward sigh of relief. The Marquess of Huntly, another who had unwisely opted to drive himself, was dripping all over the hall flags. Her little speech now well rehearsed, Sophie quickly made Lucilla's indisposition known, then smoothed away their exclamations with assurances of their welcome. Horatio had retreated to the main parlour to play host to those gentlemen who had already descended, looking for something to warm themselves while they waited for the dinner gong.

The Chessingtons and the marquess took the news in their stride. They were about to head upstairs when a tremendous sneeze had them all turning to the door.

Mr. Somercote stood on the threshold, a pitiful sight with water running in great rivers from his coattails.

"My dear sir!" Belle Chessington swept back along the hall to drag the poor gentleman in.

His place in the doorway was immediately filled by Miss Ellis and her mother, closely followed by Mr. Marston, Lord Swindon and Lord Thurstow. Of them all, only Mr. Marston, clad in a heavy, old-fashioned travelling cloak, was less than drenched. Sophie left the marquess; she tugged the bell-pull twice, vigorously, then hurried forward to help the others out of their soaked coats.

Mentally reviewing the guest list, she thought most had now arrived.

Mr. Marston moved to intercept her, unwrapping his

cloak as he came. He was frowning. "What's this, Miss Winterton? Where is your aunt?"

His question, uttered in a stern and reproving tone, silenced all other conversation. The latest arrivals glanced about, noting Lucilla's absence. Suppressing a curse, Sophie launched into her explanation. Mr. Marston did not, however, allow her to get to her reassurances. He cut across her smooth delivery to announce, "A sad mischance indeed. Well—there's nothing for it—we'll all have to return to town. Can't possibly impose on the family with your aunt so gravely ill. And, of course, there are the proprieties to consider."

For an instant, silence held sway. The others all looked to Sophie.

With an effort, Sophie kept her smile in place. "I assure you, Mr. Marston, that my aunt has nothing more than a cold. She would be most unhappy if such a trifling indisposition were to cause the cancellation of this party. And with my great-aunt, my uncle and Mrs. Chessington and the other matrons all present, I really don't think the proprieties are in any danger of being breached. Now," she went on, smiling around at the others, "if you would like to retire to your chambers and get dry—"

"You'll pardon me, Miss Winterton, but I must insist that you fetch your uncle. I cannot be easy in my mind over this most peculiar suggestion that the party proceed as planned." Supercilious as ever, Phillip Marston drew himself up. "I really must insist that Mr. Webb be consulted at once. It is hardly a minor matter."

An utterly stunned silence ensued.

It was broken by a stupendous thunderclap—then the night outside lit up. The blaze in the forecourt threw the shadow of a man deep into the hall.

As the brilliance beyond the door died, Sophie, along with everyone else, blinked at the newcomer.

"As usual, Marston, you're mistaken," Jack drawled as he strolled forward. "Mrs. Webb's indisposition undoubtedly is, as Miss Winterton has assured us, entirely minor. Our kind hostess will hardly thank you for making an issue of it."

A most peculiar *frisson* frizzled its way along Sophie's nerves. She could not drag her gaze from the tall figure advancing across the floor towards her. The long folds of his many-caped greatcoat were damp, but it was clear he, alone amongst the gentlemen invited, had been wise enough to come in a closed carriage. Beneath the greatcoat, his dark coat and breeches were dry and, as usual, immaculate.

With his usual grace, he bowed over her hand. "Good evening, Miss Winterton. I trust I see you well?"

Sophie's mind froze. She had convinced herself he wouldn't come, that she would never see him again. Instead, here he was, arriving like some god from the darkness outside, sweeping difficulties like Mr. Marston aside. But his expression was impassive; his eyes, as they touched her face, held no particular warmth. Sophie's heart contracted painfully.

Glancing about, Jack bestowed a charming smile on the other, much damper, guests. "But pray don't let me detain you from giving succour to these poor unfortunates." His smile robbed the term of any offence.

Gently, he squeezed Sophie's hand.

Sophie dragged in a sharp breath. She retrieved her hand and pinned a regal smile to her lips. "If you and Mr. Marston don't mind, I shall see these others to their rooms."

Still smiling, Jack politely inclined his head; Phillip Marston hesitated, frowning, then nodded curtly.

Determinedly calm, Sophie moved forward to deal with the last of her aunt's guests. As she did so, Ned slipped in through the door. He grinned at her. "Shall I shut it? Jack was sure we'd be last."

Sophie smiled and nodded. "Please." As she helped Minton ease Lord Thurstow from his sodden coat, she wondered whether Jack Lester had purposely arrived last for greatest effect—or whether his lateness was a reflection of reluctance.

The heavy door clanged shut on the wild night; to Sophie, it's resounding thud sounded like the knell of an inescapable doom.

CHAPTER TWELVE

SHE BARELY HAD TIME to scramble into an evening gown and brush out her curls before the dinner gong sounded, echoing hollowly through the long corridors. The meal had already been put back twice to accommodate the travellers and their recuperation.

With a last distracted glance at her mirror, Sophie hurried out. The corridor was dark and gloomy, the ubiquitous wood panelling deepening the shadows cast by the candles in the wall sconces. Feet flying over the worn carpet, Sophie turned a corner only to find a cordon, formed by two determined figures, across her path.

Jeremy frowned, threatening sulky. "We can come down to dinner, can't we, Sophie?"

Sophie blinked.

"It's not as if we'd cause any ruckus," George assured her.

"It's *boring* here, Sophie. Having dinner with Amy and the twins—well, it's just not fair." Jeremy's jaw jutted pugnaciously.

"It's not as if we're children." George fixed his blue eyes on her face and dared her to contradict him.

Sophie swallowed a groan. With all the trials of the afternoon, and those yet to come, she had precious little patience left to deal with the boys' prickly pride. But she loved them too well to fob them off. Draping an arm about each, she gave them a quick hug. "Yes, I know, loves—but, you see, we're a bit rushed this evening, and although the party's informal, I don't really think it's quite the same as when we're at Webb Park."

They both turned accusing eyes on her. "I don't see why not," Jeremy stated.

"Ah—but if you don't get an early night, you won't be up in time to go shooting tomorrow."

Sophie jumped. The deep, drawling voice brought goosebumps to her skin. But both boys turned eagerly as Jack strolled out from the shadows.

"Shooting?"

"You mean you'll take us?"

Jack raised a brow. "I don't see why not. I was discussing the outing with your father earlier. If the rain eases, we should have tolerable sport." Jack's blue gaze flicked to Sophie, then returned to the boys' glowing faces. "But you'd have to get an early night—and that, I fear, means dining in the nursery. Of course, if that's beneath you..."

"Oh, no," Jeremy assured him. "Not if we're to go shooting tomorrow."

George tugged his brother's sleeve. "Come on. We'd better let Jack and Sophie get to dinner and go find ours before the twins scoff all the buns."

Restored to good humour, the boys hurried off.

Sophie breathed a sigh of relief, then glanced up at Jack. "Thank you, Mr. Lester."

For a moment, Jack's gaze rested on her face, his expression impassive. Then he inclined his head. "Think nothing of it, my dear. Shall we?"

He gestured towards the stairs. With a nod, Sophie started forward. As they strolled the short distance in silence, she was excruciatingly aware of him, large and strong beside her, her skirts occasionally brushing his boots. He made no move to offer her his arm.

They descended the stairs and turned towards the drawing-room. Minton was hovering in the hall. "Could I have a word with you, miss?"

Sophie's heart sank. "Yes, of course." With a half smile for Jack, she glided across the tiles. "What is it?"

"It's the footmen, miss. That's to say—there aren't any." Looking supremely apologetic, Minton continued, "The old lady apparently didn't see the need and Mrs. Webb didn't imagine we'd need more. Even with old Smithers— that's the old lady's butler—there'll only be two of us and that'll make service very slow. Naughton—Mr. Webb's man—said as he'd help, but still…"

Minton didn't need to spell it out; Sophie wondered what next the evening had in store. Where on earth could she find footmen to wait at table at a minute's notice "I don't suppose the coachman…"

Minton looked his answer. "I'd rather have the maids. But you know how it'll look, miss, having women wait at table."

She did indeed. Sophie's shoulders slumped.

"If I could make a suggestion?"

Sophie turned as Jack strolled forward. He glanced at her, his expression merely polite. "I couldn't help overhearing. I suggest," he said, addressing Minton. "That you ask my man, Pinkerton, to assist. Huntly's man, too, will be well-trained, and Ainsley's and Annerby's. The rest I can't vouch for, but Pinkerton will know."

Minton's worried expression cleared. "Just the ticket, sir. I'll do that." He bobbed to Sophie. "All under control, miss, never fear." And with that, Minton hurried off.

Sophie knew a moment of blessed relief, superceded by the knowledge that more hurdles doubtless awaited her. She glanced up at Jack. "I have to thank you again, Mr. Lester. I would never have thought of such a solution; I only hope it serves." The last was uttered softly, a slight frown playing about her brows.

Not a glimmer of expression showed on Jack's face as, looking down, he studied hers. "Don't worry. Such arrangements are not uncommon—no one will remark on it."

From beneath her lashes, Sophie glanced up. "Thank you," she murmured, a tentative smile touching her lips.

Jack's hand closed about the knob of the drawing-room door. "After you, Miss Winterton."

Sophie entered to find most of the company already assembled. She moved among the guests, seeing that all had everything they needed. Most had recovered from their soaking and regained their spirits. Only Mrs. Billingham and Mrs. Ellis, a delicate lady, had elected to take trays in their rooms. Clarissa was surrounded by her usual little band, Ned included. Her cousin had drawn the other younger ladies into the charmed circle; the sound of shy laughter now ran as a counterpoint to more sober conversations. Her uncle, together with the more mature gentlemen, was deep in discussion of the sport to be found in the vicinity.

Great-Aunt Evangeline provided an unexpected distraction. She had come down to examine the guests who had invaded her home. Blithely calling Sophie "Maria" and Clarissa "Lucilla," she happily chatted with the ladies, her remarkable shawls threatening to trip her at every step.

When Minton announced dinner, the old lady squeezed Sophie's arm. "I'll take mine in my room, dear. Now remember, Maria—you're in charge. Keep an eye on Lucilla, won't you?" With a motherly pat, Great-Aunt Evangeline retired.

Dinner, as it transpired, posed no further problems. As one course was smoothly followed by the next, Sophie gradually relaxed. She had led the way into the dining-room on the Marquess of Huntly's arm. He was now seated on her right with Lord Ainsley on her left. A hum of good-natured conversation hovered over the table; everyone was reasonably well acquainted and, so it seemed, determined to enjoy themselves. Further down the board, Belle Chessington had taken on the challenge posed by Mr. Somercote; she was bending his ear unmercifully. Sophie smiled and let her gaze travel on, to where Clarissa and Ned, together with Lord Swindon and Mr. Marley, were deep in discussion of some passingly serious subject. Beyond them, Jack Lester was devoting himself primarily to Mrs. Chessington. Sophie had seen him offer that lady his arm in the drawing-room even as she herself had placed her hand on the Marquess's sleeve.

Rousing herself from her thoughts, Sophie conjured a smile and beamed at the marquess. "Do you intend to make one of the shooting party tomorrow, my lord?"

Once the covers were removed, Sophie led the ladies back to the drawing-room. The gentlemen were disposed to linger over their port, yet there was still an hour before the tea trolley was due when they strolled back into the room.

As ladies and gentlemen merged, then fractured into the inevitable smaller groups, Sophie wondered how to keep them amused. She hadn't had time to organize any of the fashionable little games that were so much a part of country-house parties. She was cudgelling her brains for inspiration when Ned stopped by her chair.

"We thought we might try charades, Sophie. Jack mentioned it was all the thing for the younger crowd."

Relieved, Sophie smiled. "By all means; that's an excellent idea."

She watched as Ned and Clarissa rounded up the younger members of the party and cleared an area of the large room. Many of the matrons seemed disposed to look on indulgently. Rising, Sophie glanced about—and found her uncle approaching.

Horatio beamed and took her hand. "You're doing magnificently, my dear." He squeezed her fingers, then released them. "Lester's taken Huntly, Ainsley and Annerby off to try their luck at billiards. I'll just go and have a word with Marston." Horatio glanced about the drawing-room. "The rest I fear I'll have to leave to you—but I'm sure you can manage."

With Mr. Marston off her hands, Sophie was sure of it, too. Belle Chessington seemed reluctant to let Mr. Somercote escape, which left only Mr. Chartwell, Miss Billingham and a few relaxed matrons for her to take under her wing. Sophie smiled. "Indeed, Uncle, it seems we've contrived amazingly well."

"Indeed." Horatio grinned. "Your aunt will be delighted."

To Sophie's relief, the rain cleared overnight. The morning was damp and dismal, but sufficiently clement to allow the shooting party to proceed. By the time the ladies descended to the breakfast parlour, the gentlemen had taken themselves off. Even Mr. Marston had seized the opportunity to stretch his legs.

The ladies were content to stroll the gardens. Sophie went up to check on the twins and Amy. She eventually ran them to earth in the attics; their nurse, who had been with the Webbs for many years, had had the bright idea of turning them loose in such relatively safe surrounds. The trio were engaged in constructing a castle, later to be stormed. Great-Aunt Evangeline was with them. Sophie left them to it and went to look in on her aunt. She found Lucilla sleeping, which of itself spoke volumes. Mimms confirmed that her aunt's indisposition had eased, but she was still very weak.

The gentlemen returned in time for luncheon, an informal meal at which their prowess with their guns was discussed and admired, the ladies smiling good-naturedly at claims of prizes flushed from coverts or taken on the wing.

Listening to the genial chatter, Sophie spared a thought for Lucilla's expertise. Her aunt had selected her guests with a knowing hand; they had melded into a comfortable party despite the presence of such difficult elements as Mr. Marston and Mr. Somercote.

But by the end of the meal, the rain had returned, gusting in from the east in leaden sheets. By unvoiced consensus, the gentlemen retired to the library or billiard room, while the ladies took possession of the morning-room and parlour, to chat in little groups ensconced in the comfortable armchairs or wander in the adjoining conservatory.

With everyone settled, Sophie went to the kitchens to confer with Cook. Belowstairs, she stumbled on an army, the depleted ranks of Aunt Evangeline's aged servitors swelled beyond imagining by the maids, coachmen and valets of the guests, as well as the doyens of the Webb household. But all seemed to be cheery, the bulk of the men gathered about the huge fire in the kitchen. Minton, beaming, assured her all was well.

Climbing back up the stairs, her chores completed, Sophie decided she could justifiably seize a moment for herself. The conservatory had proved a most amazing discovery; it was huge and packed with ferns and flowering creepers, many of kinds Sophie had not before seen. She had had time for no more than a glimpse; now, she pushed open the glass door and slipped into the first avenue, half an hour of peace before her.

As the greenery surrounded her, Sophie closed her eyes and breathed deeply. The humid scent of rich earth and green leaves, of growing things, tinged with the faint perfume of exotic flowers, filled her senses. A smile hovered on her lips.

"There you are, Miss Winterton."

Sophie's eyes flew open; her smile vanished. Swallowing a most unladylike curse, she swung round to see Mr. Marston advancing purposefully upon her. As usual, he was frowning.

"Really, Miss Winterton, I cannot tell you how very displeased I am to find you here."

Sophie blinked; one of her brows rose haughtily. "Indeed, sir?"

"As you should *know,* Miss Winterton." Mr. Marston came to a halt before her, giving Sophie an excellent view of his grim expression. "I do not see how your uncle can reconcile this with his conscience. I knew from the first that continuing with this affair was unwise in the extreme. Unconscionable folly."

Sophie straightened her shoulders and looked him in the eye. "I fear, sir, that I cannot allow you to malign my uncle, who, as everyone knows, takes exceptional care of me. In truth, I cannot follow your reasoning at all."

Mr. Marston appeared to have difficulty restraining himself. "What I mean, Miss Winterton," he finally replied, his tones glacially condemnatory, "is that I am *shocked* to find you—a young lady whom I consider of sound and elevated mind and a naturally genteel manner—here." He paused to gesture about them. "Quite alone, unattended, where any gentleman might come upon you."

Sophie hung onto her patience. "Mr. Marston, may I point out that I am in my great-aunt's house, within easy call not only of servants but many others whom I consider friends? Is it not all the same thing as if I had chosen to walk the pavements of Covent Garden unattended?"

Mr. Marston's grey eyes narrowed; his lips were set in a thin line. "You are mistaken, Miss Winterton. No lady can afford to play fast and loose with her reputation by courting—"

"Really, Marston. No need to bore Miss Winterton to tears by reciting the Young Ladies' Catechism. They all have to learn it by heart before being admitted to Almack's, you know." Jack strolled forward, green leaves brushing his shoulders. His expression was easy and open, but Sophie saw a glint of something harder in his eyes.

The sudden rush of mixed emotions—relief, nervousness and anticipation among them—on top of her rising temper, left her momentarily giddy. But she turned back to Mr. Marston, lifting her chin challengingly. "Mr. Lester is correct, sir. I assure you I need no lectures on such topics."

She made the comment in an even voice, giving Mr. Marston the opportunity to retreat gracefully. He, however, seemed more intent on glowering at Jack, a futile gesture for, as she shifted her gaze to her rescuer's face, Sophie found he was watching her.

She would have given a great deal, just then, for one of his smiles. Instead, he simply bowed, urbanely elegant, and offered her his arm. "I came to collect you, my dear. The tea trolley has just been brought in."

Sophie tried a small smile of her own and placed her fingers on his sleeve.

Phillip Marston snorted. "Ridiculous! Taking lessons in comportment from a—" He broke off as he met Jack's gaze.

One of Jack's brows slowly rose. "You were saying, Marston?"

The quiet question made Phillip Marston glower even more. "Nothing, nothing. If you'll excuse me, Miss Winterton, I find I am not in the mood for tea." With a curt bow, he turned on his heel and disappeared into the greenery.

Sophie didn't bother to stifle her sigh. "Thank you again, Mr. Lester. I must apologize for Mr. Marston. I fear he's labouring under a misapprehension."

As they strolled towards the parlour, Sophie glanced up at her knight-errant. He was looking down at her, his expression enigmatic.

"No need for apologies, my dear. Indeed, I bear Marston no ill-will. Strange to say, I know just how he feels."

Sophie frowned, but she got no chance to pursue his meaning; the tea trolley and the bulk of her aunt's guests were waiting.

WHEN SOPHIE AWOKE the next morning, and tentatively peeked out from under the covers, she was met by weak sunshine and a pale, blue-washed sky. She relaxed back against her pillows, feeling decidedly more confident than she had the morning before.

The previous evening had passed off smoothly, much in the manner of the first. The only exceptions had been the behaviour of her suitors, who, one and all, had recovered from the dampening effects of their arrival and were once more attempting to pay court to her. That and the behaviour of the elder Miss Billingham, who had all but thrown herself at Jack Lester.

Sophie grimaced, her eyes narrowing. After a moment, she shook herself. And rose to meet the day.

She looked in on Lucilla on her way downstairs. Her aunt was sitting up in bed sipping her morning cocoa. "Indeed, I would love to see how things are progressing, but I still feel quite weak." Lucilla pulled a face. "Maybe this evening?"

"You will remain abed until you are well," declared Horatio, coming through the door with a laden tray.

Leaving her aunt to her husband's fond care, Sophie descended to the breakfast parlour. There, her suitors lay in waiting.

"This kedgeree is quite remarkable, m'dear," offered the marquess. "Quite remarkable."

"Perhaps you would care for some bacon and an egg or two, Miss Winterton?" Mr. Chartwell lifted the lid of a silver platter and glanced at her enquiringly.

Sophie smiled on them all, and managed to install herself between Mr. Somercote, engaged in silent communication with Belle Chessington, who was chattering enough for them both, and Mrs. Chessington, who smiled understandingly.

Further down the board, Jack was apparently absorbed with Mrs. Ellis and her daughter. Beside him, Ned was chatting to Clarissa, Lord Swindon and Mr. Marley openly eavesdropping. Sophie hid a smile at her cousin's rapt expression.

She escaped the breakfast parlour unencumbered, using the pretext of having to check on her younger cousins. Jeremy and Gerald had been tired out by a day in woods and fields; they had happily eaten with Amy and the twins the night before. When she reached the nursery she was greeted by an unnatural silence, which was explained by Nurse when she hunted that worthy down. The children had been taken on a long ride by the grooms; peace, therefore, was very likely assured. Smiling with both relief and satisfaction, Sophie descended—into the arms of her suitors.

The marquess took the lead. "My dear Miss Winterton, may I interest you in a stroll about the gardens? I believe there are some early blooms in the rose garden."

"Or perhaps you would rather stroll about the lake?" Mr. Chartwell directed a quelling look at the marquess.

"There's a very pretty folly just the other side of the birch grove," offered Lord Ainsley. "Nice prospect and all that."

Mr. Marston merely frowned.

Sophie resisted the urge to close her eyes and invoke the gods. Instead, she favoured them all with a calm smile. "Indeed, but why don't we all go together? The gardens, after all, are not that large; doubtless we can see the rose garden, the lake and the folly before lunch."

They mumbled and shot frowning glances at each other but, of course, they had to agree. Satisfied she had done what she could to improve the situation, Sophie resigned herself to an hour or two's insipid conversation. At least she would get some fresh air.

As they wandered the lawns and vistas, they came upon little groups of their companions likewise employed. They nodded and smiled, calling out information on the various sights to be found, then continued with their ambles. In the distance, Sophie saw the unmistakable figure of Jack Lester, escorting Mrs. Ellis and Mrs. Doyle. Neither lady had her daughter with her, but Miss Billingham the elder had attached herself to the group. Viewing the gown of quite hideous puce stripes that that young lady had donned, along with a chip bonnet from under which she cast sly glances up at Jack Lester, Sophie gritted her teeth and looked elsewhere. To her mind, her own walking gown of pale green was far superior to Miss Billingham's attire, and she would never cast sheep's eyes at any man—particularly not Jack Lester.

Swallowing a humph, Sophie airily remarked, "The light is quite hazy, is it not?"

Her court immediately agreed, and spent the next five minutes telling her so.

Nevertheless, the brightness seemed to have gone out of her day. Not even the spectacle of her suitors vying for the right to hand her up the steps could resuscitate her earlier mood. She forced herself to smile and trade quips throughout luncheon but, as soon as the meal was over and it became clear that the guests were quite content, she escaped.

Donning a light cloak, she gathered her embroidery into a small basket and slipped out of the morning-room windows.

IN THE SMALL summer-house at the very end of the birch grove, hidden from the house by the shrubbery, Jack paced back and forth, his expression decidedly grim. He wasn't all that sure what he was doing at Little Bickmanstead. He had taken refuge in the summer-house—refuge from Miss Billingham, who seemed convinced he was just waiting to make her an offer.

Not a likely prospect this side of hell freezing over—but she did not seem capable of assimilating that fact.

It was another woman who haunted him, leaving him with a decision to make. A pressing decision. Sophie's suitors were becoming daily more determined. While it was clear she harboured no real interest in them, she had declared her requirement for funds and they each had plenty to offer. It could only be a matter of time before she accepted one of them.

With a frustrated sigh, Jack halted before one of the open arches of the summer-house and gripped the low sill; unseeing, he gazed out over the wilderness. He still wanted Sophie—regardless.

A movement caught his eye. As he watched, Sophie came into view, picking her way along the meandering path that led to the summer-house.

Slowly, Jack smiled; it seemed for the first time in days, Fate had finally remembered him, and his golden head.

Then he saw the figure moving determinedly in Sophie's wake. Jack cursed. His gaze shifted to the left, to the other path out, but the thought of leaving Sophie to deal with Marston alone occurred, only to be dismissed. Besides, Horatio had had to leave for Southampton on business immediately after lunch; it was, Jack decided, undoubtedly his duty to keep watch over his host's niece.

Glancing about, he noticed a small door in the back wall of the summer-house. Opened, it revealed a small room, dark and dim, in which were stored croquet mallets, balls and hoops. Shifting these aside, Jack found he could stand in the deep shadow thrown by the door and keep the interior of the summer-house in view. Propping one shoulder against a shelf, he settled into the dimness.

On reaching the summer-house, Sophie climbed the stairs, listlessness dogging her steps. With a soft sigh, she placed her basket on the small table in the centre of the floor. She was turning to view the scene from the arch when footsteps clattered up the steps behind her.

"Miss Winterton."

In the instant before she turned to face Phillip Marston, Sophie permitted herself an expressive grimace. Irritation of no mean order, frustration and pure chagrin all had a place in it. Then she swung about, chilly reserve in her glance. "Mr. Marston."

"I must protest, Miss Winterton. I really cannot condone your habit of slipping away unattended."

"I wasn't aware I was a sheep, nor yet a babe, sir."

Phillip Marston frowned harder. "Of course not. But you're a lady of some attraction and you would do well to bear that in mind. Particularly with the likes of Mr. Lester about."

Her accents frigid, Sophie stated, "We will, if you please, leave my aunt's other guests out of this discussion, sir."

With his usual superior expression, Mr. Marston inclined his head. "Indeed, I'm fully in agreement with you there, my dear. In fact, it was precisely the idea of leaving your aunt's other guests entirely that has prompted me to seek you out."

Sophie felt her spirits, already tending to the dismal, slump even further. She searched for some soothing comment.

Mr. Marston fell to pacing, his hands clasped behind him, his frowning gaze fixed on the floor. "As you know, I have not been at all easy in my mind over this little party. Indeed, I did not approve of your aunt's desire to bring you to town. It was quite unnecessary. You did not need to come to London to contract a suitable alliance."

Sophie cast a pleading glance heavenward. Her mind had seized up; no witty comment occurred to her.

"But I will say no more on what I fear I must term your aunt's lack of wisdom." Phillip Marston pursed his lips. "Instead, I have resolved to ask you to leave your aunt and uncle's protection and return to Leicestershire with me. We can be married there. I believe I know you too well to think you will want a large wedding. Such silly fripperies might be well enough for the *ton* but they are neither here nor there. My mother, of course, fully approves—"

"Mr. Marston!" Sophie had heard quite enough. "Sir, I do not know when I have given you cause to believe I would welcome an offer from you, but if I have, I most sincerely apologize."

Phillip Marston blinked. It took him a moment to work through Sophie's words. Then he frowned and looked more severe than ever.

"A-hem!"

Startled, both Sophie and Marston turned as first the marquess and then Mr. Chartwell climbed the steps to the summer-house. Sophie stared. Then, resisting the urge to shake her head, she drifted to the table, leaving her three most eager suitors ranged on the other side.

"Er, we were just strolling past. Couldn't help overhearing, m'dear," Huntly explained, looking most apologetic. "But felt I had to tell you—no need to marry Marston here. Only too happy to marry you myself."

"Actually," cut in Mr. Chartwell, fixing the marquess

with a stern eye. "I was hoping to have a word with you later, Miss Winterton. In private. However, such as it is, I pray you'll consider my suit, too."

Sophie thought she heard a smothered snort, but before she could decide who was responsible, Mr. Marston had claimed the floor.

"Miss Winterton, you will be much happier close to your family in Leicestershire."

"Nonsense!" Huntly exclaimed, turning to confront his rival. "No difficulty in travelling these days. Besides, why should Miss Winterton make do with some small farmhouse when she could preside over a mansion, heh?"

"Chartwell Hall is very large, Miss Winterton. Fifty main rooms. And of course I would have no qualms in giving you a free hand redecorating—there and at my London residence." Mr. Chartwell's attitude was one of ineffable superiority.

"Marston Manor," Phillip Marston declaimed, glaring at Huntly and Chartwell, "is, as Miss Winterton knows, a sizeable establishment. She shall want for nothing. My resources are considerable and my estates stretch for miles, bordering those of her uncle."

"Really?" returned the marquess. "It might interest you to know, sir, that my estates are themselves considerable, and I make bold to suggest that in light of my patrimony, Miss Winterton would do very much better to marry me. Besides, there's the title to consider. Still worth something, what?"

"Very little if rumour is to be believed," Mr. Chartwell cut in. "Indeed, I fear that if we are to settle this on the basis of monetary worth, then my own claims outshine you both."

"Is that so?" the marquess enquired, his attitude verging on the belligerent.

"Indeed." Mr. Chartwell held his ground against the combined glare of his rivals.

"Enough!" Sophie's declaration drew all three to face her. Rigid with barely suppressed fury, she raked them with a glinting, narrow-eyed gaze. "I am *disgusted* with all of you! How *dare* you presume to know my thoughts—my feelings—my requirements—and to comment on them in such a way?"

The question was unanswerable; all three men shuffled uncomfortably. Incensed, Sophie paced slowly before them, her glittering gaze holding them silent. "I have never in my life been so insulted. Do you actually believe I would marry a man who thought *I* was the sort of woman who married for *money?"* With an angry swirl, Sophie swung about, her skirts hissing. "For wealth and establishments?" The scorn in her voice lashed at them. "I would draw your attention to my aunt, who married for love—and found happiness and success. My mother, too, married purely for love. My cousin Clarissa will unquestionably marry for love. *All* the women in my family marry for love—and I am no different!"

Sophie blinked back the tears that suddenly threatened. She was not done with her suitors yet. "I will be perfectly frank with you gentlemen, as you have been so frank with me. I do not love any of you, and I will certainly not marry any of you. There is no earthly use persisting in your pursuit of me, for I will not change my mind. I trust I make myself plain?"

She delivered her last question with a passable imitation of Lucilla at her most haughty. Head high, Sophie looked down her nose and dared them to deny her.

Typically, Phillip Marston made the attempt. As startled as the others, he nevertheless made an effort to draw his habitual superiority about him. "You are naturally over-wrought, my dear. It was unforgivable of us to subject you to such a discussion."

"Unforgivable, ungentlemanly and totally unacceptable." Sophie wasn't about to quibble. Mr. Chartwell and the marquess shuffled their feet and darted careful, placating glances at her.

Heartened, Mr. Marston grew more confident. "Be that as it may, I strongly advise you to withdraw your hasty words. You cannot have considered. It is not for such as us to marry for love; that, I believe is more rightly the province of the *hoi polloi.* I cannot think—"

"*Mr.* Marston." Sophie threw an exasperated glance at the heavens. "You have not been listening, sir. I care not what anyone thinks of my predilection for love. It may not be conventional, but it is, I should point out, most fashionable these days. And I find I am greatly addicted to fashion. You may think it unacceptable, but there it is. Now," she contin-ued, determined to give them no further chance to remonstrate, "I fear I have had quite enough of your company for one afternoon, gentlemen. If you wish to convince me that you are, in fact, the gentlemen I have always believed you, you will withdraw and allow me some peace."

"Yes, of course, my dear."

"Pray accept our apologies, Miss Winterton."

Both the marquess and Mr. Chartwell were more than prepared to retreat. Phillip Marston was harder to rout.

"Miss Winterton," he said, his usual frown gathering, "I cannot reconcile it with my conscience to leave you thus unguarded."

"Unguarded?" Sophie barely restrained her temper. "Sir, you are suffering from delusions. There is no danger to me here, in my great-aunt's summer house." Sophie glanced briefly at Mr. Chartwell and the marquess, then returned her gaze, grimly determined, to her most unwanted suitor. "Furthermore, sir, having expressed a desire for your absence, I will feel perfectly justified in requesting these gentlemen to protect me—from you."

One glance was enough to show Phillip Marston that Mr. Chartwell and the marquess would be only too pleased to take out their frustrations on him. With a glance which showed how deeply against the grain retreat went with him, he bowed curtly. "As you wish, Miss Winterton. But I will speak with you later."

Only the fact that he was leaving allowed Sophie to suppress her scream. She was furious—with all of them. Head high, she stood by the table and watched as they clattered down the steps. They paused, exchanging potent looks of dislike, then separated, each heading towards the house by a different route.

With a satisfied humph, Sophie watched them disappear. Slowly, her uplifting fury drained. The tense muscles in her shoulders relaxed. She drew in a soft breath.

It tangled in her throat as she heard a deep voice say from directly behind her,

"You're wrong, you know."

With a strangled shriek, Sophie whirled round. One hand at her throat, she groped with the other for the table behind her. Eyes wide, she stared up at Jack's face. "Wh—what do you mean, wrong?" It was an effort to calm her thudding heart enough to get out the words.

"I mean," Jack replied, prowling about the table to cut off her retreat, "that you overlooked one particular danger in assuring Marston of your safety." He met Sophie's stare and smiled. "Me."

Sophie took one long look into his glittering eyes and instinctively moved to keep the table between them. As the truth dawned, she lifted her chin. "How *dare* you eavesdrop on my conversations!"

Jack's predatory smile didn't waver. "As always, your conversation was most instructive, my dear. It did, however, leave me with one burning question."

Sophie eyed him warily. "What?"

"Just what game are you playing, my dear?"

The sudden flare in his eyes startled Sophie anew. "Ah—

you're a gentleman, Mr. Lester." It seemed the time to remind him.

"Gentleman *rake*," Jack replied. "There's a difference."

Sophie was suddenly very sure there was. Eyes wider than ever, she took a step back, then smothered a yelp as, with one hand and a single shove, Jack sent the table shooting over the floor.

Sophie's gaze followed it, until it came to a quivering halt by the wall, her basket still balanced upon it. Then she looked round—and jumped back a step when she found Jack directly in front of her. He advanced; she retreated another step. Two more steps and Sophie found the wall of the summer-house at her back. Jack's arms, palms flat against the wall, one on either side, imprisoned her. She eyed first one arm, then the other. Then, very cautiously, she looked up into his face.

His expression was intent. "Now, Sophie—"

"Ah—Jack." Any discussion was potentially dangerous; she needed time to consider just what he had heard, and what he might now think. Sophie fixed her gaze on his cravat, directly before her face. "I'm really quite overset." That was the literal truth. "I—I'm rather overwrought. As you heard, I just turned away three suitors. Three offers. Not a small thing, after all. I fear my nerves are a trifle strained by the experience."

Jack shifted, leaning closer, raising one hand to catch Sophie's chin. He tipped her face up until her wise gaze met his. "I suggest you steel yourself then, my dear. For you're about to receive a fourth."

Sophie's lips parted on a protest; it remained unuttered. Jack's lips closed over hers, sealing them, teasing the soft contours, then ruthlessly claiming them. Head whirling, Sophie clutched at his lapels. She felt him hesitate, then his head slanted over hers. Sophie shuddered as he boldly claimed her warmth, tasting her, teasing her senses with calculated expertise. Her fingers left his lapels to steal upwards, to clutch at his shoulders. He released her chin; he shifted, straightening, pulling her against him, one large hand gripping her waist. The kiss deepened again; her senses whirling, Sophie wondered how much deeper it could go. Then his hand swept slowly upward to firm about her breast, gently caressing even as he demanded her surrender.

Sophie tried to stiffen, to pull away, to refuse as she knew she should. Instead, she felt herself sink deeper into his arms, deeper into his kiss. Her breast swelled to his touch, her body ached for more.

Jack drew her hard against him, then lifted his head to breathe against her lips, "Will you marry me, Sophie?"

Sophie's heart screamed an assent but she held the words back, hanging on to her wits by her fingernails. Slowly, she opened her eyes, blinking up into the warm blue of his. She licked her lips, then blushed as his gaze followed the action. She tried to speak, but couldn't find her voice. Instead, she shook her head.

Jack's blue eyes narrowed. "No? Why not?" He gave her no chance to answer but kissed her again, just as deeply, just as imperiously.

"You said you would only marry for love," he reminded her when he again consented to lift his head. His eyes rose to hers. satisfaction flaring at her dazed expression. "You're in love with me, Sophie. And I'm in love with you. We both know it."

His head lowered again; Sophie realized she was in desperate straits. Faced with another of his kisses, and their increasingly debilitating effect on her wits, she seized the first word that crossed her mind. "Money," she gasped.

Jack stopped, his lips a mere inch from hers. Slowly, he drew back, enough to look into her eyes. He studied them for a long moment, then slowly shook his head. "Not good enough this time, Sophie. You told them—your three importunate suitors—that you would never marry for money. You said it very plainly. They had money, but not your love. I've got your love—why do I need money?"

His gaze did not leave hers. Sophie could barely think. Again, she shook her head. "I can't marry you, Jack."

"Why not?"

Sophie eyed him warily. "You wouldn't understand if I explained."

"Try me."

Pressing her lips together, Sophie just shook her head. She knew she was right; she also knew he wouldn't agree.

To her dismay, a slow, thoroughly rakish smile lit Jack's face. He sighed. "You'll tell me eventually, Sophie."

His tone was light, quite unconcerned. Sophie blinked and saw him look down. She followed his gaze—and gasped.

"*Jack!* What on earth are you doing?" Sophie batted in-effectually at his hands, busy with the buttons of her gown. Jack laughed and drew her closer, so that she couldn't reach his nimble fingers. Then the gown was open and his long fingers slipped inside. They closed about her breast; Sophie's knees shook.

"Sophie—" For an instant, Jack closed his eyes, his hand firming about her soft flesh. Then he bent his head and caught her lips with his.

For a giddy moment, a tide of delight caught Sophie up and whirled her about. Then Jack drew his lips from hers and the sensation receded, leaving a warm glow in its wake. Desperate, Sophie clung to reality. "What are you doing?" she muttered, her voice barely a whisper.

"Seducing you," came the uncompromising reply.

Sophie's eyes flew open. She felt Jack's lips on her throat, trailing fire over her suddenly heated skin. She shuddered, then glanced wildly about the room—what she could see of it beyond his shoulders. "Here?" Her mind refused to accept the notion. The room was bare of all furniture, no chaise or day-bed, not even an armchair. He had to be teasing.

She felt rather than heard Jack's chuckle. "The table."

The *table?* Sophie's shocked gaze swung to the innocent wooden table, now standing by the wall. Then she looked back at Jack, into his heated gaze. "No," she said, then blushed furiously at the question in her tone.

Jack's gaze grew warmer. "It's easy," he murmured,

bending his head to drop wicked little kisses behind her ear. "I'll show you."

"No." This time, Sophie got the intonation right. But her eyes closed and her fingers sank into Jack's shoulders as he continued to caress her.

"But yes, sweet Sophie," Jack whispered in her ear. "Unless you can give me a good reason why not."

Sophie knew there had to be hundreds of reasons—but she could think of only one. The one he wanted to hear. She opened her eyes and found his face. She tried to glare. His fingers shifted beneath her bodice; Sophie sucked in a breath. She didn't have the courage to call his bluff. He probably wasn't bluffing. "All right," she said and felt his fingers still. She leaned against him, seeking his strength as she sought for her words. "I told you I'm a lady of expectations, nothing more," she began.

"And I've told you that doesn't matter."

"But it does." Sophie glanced up, into the warm blue eyes so close to hers. She put all the pleading sincerity she could into her eyes, her voice. "Your dreams are mine: a home, a family, estates to look after. But they'll remain nothing but *dreams* if you don't marry well. You know that."

She saw his face still, his expression sober. Sophie clung to him and willed him to understand.

Her heart was in her eyes, there for Jack to see. He drank in the sight, then closed his eyes against the pain behind. He dropped his forehead to hers and groaned. "Sophie, you have my heartfelt apologies."

Sophie felt like sagging—with relief or was it defeat?

"I should have told you long ago." Jack pressed a soft kiss against her temple, hugging her to him.

Sophie frowned and pushed back to look up at him. "Told me what?"

Jack smiled crookedly. "That I'm horrendously wealthy—disgustingly rich."

Sophie's face crumpled; her eyes filled with tears. "Oh, Jack," she finally got out around the constriction in her throat. "Don't." Abruptly, she buried her face in his shoulder.

It was Jack's turn to frown and try to hold her away. "Don't what?"

"Don't lie," Sophie mumbled against his coat.

Jack stiffened. Thunderstruck, he stared down at the woman in his arms. "Sophie, I'm not lying."

She looked up, her eyes swimming, softly blue, her lips lifting in a heart-rending smile. She raised a hand to his face. "It's no use, Jack. We both know the truth."

"No, we do not." Jack withdrew his hand from her breast and caught her hand, holding it tightly. "Sophie, I swear I'm rich." When she simply smiled, mistily disbelieving, he swore. "Very well. We'll go and ask your aunt."

The look Sophie sent him made Jack grimace. "All right, not Lucilla. Horatio, then. I assume you'll accept your uncle's word on my finances?"

Surprised, Sophie frowned. Horatio, she well knew, was a man of his word. Not even for love would he so much as bend the truth. And Jack was suggesting Horatio would bear out his claims. "But my uncle's just left. We don't know when he'll return."

Jack swore some more, distinctly colourfully. He considered his options, but the only others who knew of his recent windfall were relatives, friends or employees, none of whom Sophie would believe. "Very well." Grimly, he surveyed Sophie's doubting expression. "We'll wait until he returns."

Her mind reeling, Sophie nodded, struggling to see her way forward. She glanced down, and blushed rosily. Tugging her fingers from Jack's clasp, she drew back enough to do up the buttons of her gown. Whatever the truth, she would have to keep Jack at arm's length until Horatio returned—or it wouldn't matter what her uncle said.

"Sophie?" Jack sensed her withdrawal. He had half a mind to draw her back to him, back into his arms where she belonged.

From under her lashes, Sophie glanced up at him almost guiltily. "Ah, yes." She tried to step back but Jack's arm was firm about her waist. "Now, Jack," she protested, as she felt his arm tighten. She braced her hands against his chest. "We've agreed, have we not?" The light in his eyes left her breathless. "We'll wait until my uncle returns."

Jack's blue eyes narrowed. "Sophie…" His gaze met hers, full of breathless anticipation, yet, for all that, quite determined. Jack heaved a disgusted sigh. "Very well," he bit out. "But *only* until your uncle returns—agreed?"

Sophie hesitated, then nodded.

"And you'll marry me three weeks after that."

It was not a question; Sophie only just stopped her nod.

"And furthermore," Jack continued, his blue gaze holding hers, "if I'm to toe the line until your uncle gets back, then so shall you."

"Me?"

"No more flirting with your suitors—other than me."

"I do not flirt." With an offended air, Sophie drew back.

"And no more waltzing with anyone but me."

"That's outrageous!" Sophie disengaged from Jack's arms. "You don't know what you're asking."

"I know only too well," Jack growled, letting her go. "Fair's fair, Sophie. No more going to supper with any gentleman but me—and certainly no driving or going apart with anyone else."

Smoothing down her skirts, Sophie humphed.

Jack caught her chin on his hand and tipped her head up until her eyes met his. "Are we agreed, Sophie?"

Sophie could feel her pulse racing. Her eyes met his, intensely blue, and she felt like she was drowning. His face, all hard angles and planes, was very near, his lips, hard and finely chiselled, but inches away. "Yes," she whispered and breathed again when he released her.

With his customary grace, Jack offered her his arm.

Drawing her dignity about her, Sophie picked up her basket and placed her hand on his sleeve. She allowed him to lead her down the steps and back towards the house, all the way struggling to cope with the sensation of being balanced on a knife-edge. Determined to give the reprobate by her side no inkling of her difficulty, she kept her gaze on the scenery and her head very high.

Jack viewed the sight through narrowed eyes. Then he smiled, slowly, and started to plan.

CHAPTER THIRTEEN

THE PARTY broke up the next morning. By then, everyone was aware that something had changed, that Jack stood, in some unspecified way, as Sophie's protector. Despite her disapproval of his tactics, Sophie could not help feeling grateful, especially when he helped shoulder the responsibility for their return to the capital. Even with Lucilla all but fully recovered, with her uncle absent, she had not been looking forward to travelling with all her cousins, Toby the only adult male in sight.

But by mid-morning, when she emerged from the door of her great-aunt's home, all was under control. Her younger cousins were to ride as before, much to their delight. With Jack, Toby and Ned to keep them in line, Sophie had no residual qualms. The carriage stood waiting, Clarissa already aboard. Her arms full of rugs and cushions, Sophie glanced back.

Lucilla came slowly through the hall, leaning heavily on Jack's arm. Although still wan, her aunt showed no signs of faintness. Sophie turned and hurried down the steps to prepare Lucilla's seat in the carriage.

At the top of the steps, Lucilla paused to breathe in the

crisp morning air. Blue skies had returned; fluffy white clouds held no lingering menace. With a small, highly satisfied smile, she glanced at Jack beside her. "I'm very glad you did not disappoint me, Mr. Lester."

Recalled from his study of Sophie's curvaceous rear, neatly outlined as she stood on the carriage step and leaned in, Jack looked down at Lucilla, one brow slowly rising. "That was never my intention, ma'am."

Lucilla's smile broadened. "I'm so glad," she said, patting his arm. "Now, if you'll give me your arm…?"

Jack got his revenge by lifting her easily and carrying her down the steps. As he settled her amid Sophie's cushions and rugs, Lucilla favoured him with a dignified glare. Then her lips twitched and she lay back on the seat, waving him away.

His own lips curving, Jack handed Sophie up, resisting the temptation to bestow a fond pat on her retreating anatomy. And then they were away.

FIVE NIGHTS LATER, under the glare of the chandeliers in the Duchess of Richmond's ballroom, Sophie dimly wondered why she had imagined awaiting her uncle's return in the bosom of the *ton* would be safer than at Little Bickmanstead. Mere hours had sufficed for Jack to make it patently clear that he had meant every word he had uttered in Great-Aunt Evangeline's summer-house. Twenty-four hours had been enough for her to realize that, that being so, the possibility of ever denying him receded even further with every successive day.

Casting a glance up at him as he stood, planted immovably by her side, starkly handsome in severe black and white, Sophie stifled a sudden tremor.

Jack caught her glance. He bent his head to hers. "There's another waltz coming up."

Sophie shot him a warning glance. "I've already danced one waltz with you."

His rakish grin surfaced. "You're allowed two dances with any gentleman."

"But not two waltzes, if I'm wise."

"Don't be wise, my Sophie." His eyes gently teased. "Come dance with me. I promise you no one will remark unduly."

Resistance, of course, was useless. Sophie allowed him to lead her to the floor, knowing any show of reluctance would be pure hypocrisy. She loved being held in his arms; at the moment, waltzing was the only safe way to indulge her senses.

As they circled the floor, she noted the looks of resignation many of her mother's old friends turned upon them. In contrast, Lady Drummond-Burrell, that most haughty of Almack's patronesses, smiled with chilly approval.

"Amazing," Jack said, indicating her ladyship with an inclination of his head. "Nothing pleases them more than the sight of a fallen rake."

Sophie tried to frown but failed. "Nonsense," she said.

"No, it's not. They'll all approve once the news gets out."

Sophie did frown then. Jack had told her how the change

in his fortune had come about. "Why hasn't it got out by now? Presuming it's real, of course."

The arm about her tightened, squeezing in warning. "It's real," Jack replied. "But I confess I purposely neglected to mention it to anyone."

"Why?"

"You've met the elder Miss Billingham; just imagine her sort, multiplied by at least a hundred, all with yours truly in their sights."

Sophie giggled. "Surely you weren't afraid?"

"Afraid?" Jack raised an arrogant brow. "Naturally not. I merely have an innate dislike of tripping over debs at every turn."

Sophie laughed, the delicious sound teasing Jack's senses, tightening the tension inside him until it was well-nigh unbearable. He metaphorically gritted his teeth. The wait, he promised himself, would be worth it.

At the end of the dance, he escorted Sophie back to her aunt and took up his position—by her side.

Sophie knew better than to argue. Lord Ruthven stopped by, then Lord Selbourne joined them. With practised ease, Sophie laughed and chatted. While there were many gentlemen who still sought her company, her suitors, not only the three she had already dismissed but all the others who had viewed her with matrimony in mind, rarely hove in sight. Jack's presence, large and dark by her shoulder, was more than enough to make them think twice. Their rides in the Park every morning continued, but with Jack by her side, she found herself blissfully free of encumbrances. It was impossible to misinterpret his interest; as he was so tall, whenever he spoke with her, he bent his head to hers, and she, motivated by her instincts, naturally turned into his strength, reinforcing the image that they were one, wanting only the official announcement. Horatio's absence explained their present hiatus; none doubted the announcement would eventually come, as her mother's old friends' attitudes clearly showed.

She was his, and every passing day made her more aware of that truth. And that much more nervous of her uncle's return. She still doubted Jack's story; she had seen the passion in him and knew his love to be strong enough to motivate the most enormous lie. Regardless of what he said, it was possible. Only Horatio could lay her doubts to rest—and none knew when he would return.

With an inward sigh, Sophie mentally girded her loins. She glanced across at Clarissa, holding court on the other side of her aunt's chaise. Her cousin looked radiant, charming her many youthful swains yet, as Sophie had noticed, careful to give none any particular encouragement. Beside her, Ned occupied a position that had much in common with Jack's. Sophie's lips twitched; she returned her gaze to Lord Selbourne. There was a light in Ned's eyes that she did not think Clarissa had yet noticed.

Ned, in fact, was almost as impatient as Jack. But both his and Clarissa's parents had agreed that no formal offer should be considered until after Clarissa's Season. Which meant he had a far longer wait ahead of him; and, to his mind, far less assurance of gaining the prize at the end.

Which left him feeling distinctly uneasy. His silver princess still smiled on her court; he had even heard her laugh with that bounder Gurnard.

"This wooing business seems to drag on forever," he later grumbled to Jack as they both kept watch over their ladies, presently gracing the floor in other men's arms.

Jack shot him a sympathetic glance. "As you say." After a moment, he continued, "Has Clarissa let slip any information as to when they might retire to Leicestershire?"

"No," Ned replied. He cast a puzzled glance at Jack. "But I thought they were staying until the end of the Season. That's more than a month away, isn't it?"

Jack nodded. "Just a thought." As Sophie whirled past in Ruthven's arms, Jack's easy expression hardened. "As you say, this business of wooing is an ordeal to be endured."

While Jack, Ned and the ladies of his family were thus engaged, Toby had embarked on amusement of a different kind. At that moment, he was strolling along the pavement of Pall Mall, along the stretch which housed the most notorious gaming hells in town, in company with Captain Terrence Gurnard.

The captain stopped outside a plain brown door. "This is the place. A snug little hell—very exclusive."

Toby smiled amiably and waited while the captain knocked. After a low-voiced conversation with the guardian of the portal, conducted through a grille in the door, they were admitted and shown into a sizeable room, dimly lit except for the shaded lamps which shed their glow onto the tables. There were perhaps twenty gentlemen present; few raised their heads as Toby followed Gurnard across the room.

With his usual air of interested enquiry, Toby glanced about him, taking in the expressions of grim determination with which many of the gentlemen applied themselves to their cards and dice. There was a large table devoted to Hazard, another to Faro. Smaller tables attested to the hell's reputation for variety; there were even two older gentlemen engaged in a hand of Piquet.

This was the third night Toby had spent with Gurnard, and the third hell they had visited. He was, as usual, following one of his father's maxims, that which declared that experience was the best teacher. After tonight, Toby felt, he would have learned all he needed of gaming hells. His real interest tonight lay in the play. Gurnard had allowed him to win for the past two nights; Toby had begun to suspect the captain's motives.

Initially, Gurnard had brushed against him with apparently no particular intent; they had subsequently struck up an acquaintance. It was after their sojourn at Little Bickmanstead that the captain had sought him out and, being apparently at a loose end, had offered to show him the sights. Toby had accepted the offer readily; he had not previously spent much time in the capital.

Now, however, he wondered whether the captain had taken him for a flat.

By the end of the evening, which Toby promptly declared once his losses had, almost mysteriously, overtaken his current allowance, he was quite sure the captain had done just that. Comforting himself with the reflection that, as his father was wont to say, there was no harm in making mistakes just as long as one didn't make the same mistake twice, he frowned slightly as he looked across at Gurnard. "I'm afraid I won't be able to meet that last vowel until the pater returns to town—but he should be back any day."

He hadn't expected to outrun his ready funds. However, as his father had settled a considerable sum on him two years before, and managed it for him under his direction the better to teach him the ways of finance, Toby had no real qualms about asking Horatio for an advance. "I'll speak to him as soon as he returns."

Gurnard sat back, his face flushed with success and the wine he had steadily consumed. "Oh, you don't want to do that." He held up his hand in a fencer's gesture. "Never let it be said that I caused father and son to fall out over the simple matter of a few crowns."

Toby could have set him straight—he fully expected his father to have a good laugh over his adventure—but some sixth sense made him hold back. "Oh?" he said guilelessly. There were rather more than "a few crowns" involved.

Gurnard frowned, his face a mask of concentration. "Perhaps there's some way you can repay the debt without having to apply to your pater?"

"Such as?" Toby asked, a chill stealing down his back.

Gurnard looked ingenuous. He frowned into space. Then his face cleared. "Well, I know I'd count it a blessing to have a few minutes alone with your sister."

He leant across the table and, with just the slightest hesitation, conspiratorially lowered his voice. "Your sister mentioned that your party are planning to attend the gala at Vauxhall. Perhaps, in repayment of your debt, you could arrange for me to meet with her in the Temple of Diana—just while the fireworks are on. I'll return her to you when the show's over, and no one will be any the wiser."

Not only a flat—a foolish flat. Toby hid his reaction behind a vacant expression. The poor light concealed the steely glint in his eyes. "But how will I get Clarissa to agree?"

"Just tell her you're taking her to meet her most ardent admirer. Don't tell her my name—I want to surprise her. Women like the romantic touch." Gurnard smiled and waved a languid hand. "Dare say you haven't noticed, but your sister and I are deeply in love. You needn't fear I'll take advantage. But with all the attention that's focused on her we've found it hard to find the time to talk, to get to know each other as we'd like."

Concluding that the captain was the sort of gentleman he should hand over to higher authorities, Toby slowly nodded. "All right," he agreed, his tone bland. He shrugged. "If you'll be happy with that instead of the money…?"

"Definitely," Gurnard replied, his eyes suddenly gleaming. "Ten minutes alone with your sister will be ample recompense."

"TOBY, is anything wrong?"

Bringing up the rear as his exuberant siblings tumbled back into the house after their morning ride, Toby jumped and cast a startled glance at Sophie. Seeing the conjecture in her cousin's open face, she nodded.

"I thought so." With a glance at the horde disappearing up the stairs, Clarissa trailing absent-mindedly behind, she linked her arm with Toby's. "Come into your father's study and tell me all."

"It's nothing really dreadful," Toby hurried to assure her as they crossed the threshold of his father's sanctum.

"Then there's probably no reason for you to be so worried about it," Sophie returned. Sinking into one of the armchairs by the hearth, she fixed Toby with a commanding if affectionate eye. "Open your budget, my dear, for I really can't let this go on. Doubtless I'm imagining all sorts of unlikely horrors; I'm sure you can set my mind at rest."

Toby grimaced at her, too used to Lucilla to take offence. He fell to pacing before the hearth, his hands clasped behind his back. "It's that bounder Gurnard."

"Bounder?" Sophie looked her surprise. "I know Ned's been calling him that for ages, but I thought that was just Ned."

"So did I—but now I know better. Dashed if Ned wasn't right."

Sophie looked pensive, then cast a glance up at Toby.

"I've just remembered. Your mother said she didn't trust the man, and Clarissa agreed."

"Did she?" Toby brightened. "Well, that makes it easier, then."

"Makes what easier?" Sophie stared at Toby, consternation in her eyes. "Tobias Webb, just what is going on?"

"No need to get into a flap. At least, not yet."

When Toby said no more but continued to pace the hearthrug, Sophie straightened her shoulders. "Toby, if you don't tell me what this is all about immediately, I'll feel honour bound to speak to your mother."

Toby halted, his expression horrified. "Saints preserve us all," he said. And proceeded to tell Sophie the story.

"That's *iniquitous!*" Sophie was incensed. "The man's worse than a mere bounder."

"Undoubtedly. He's a dangerous bounder. That's why I want to wait until Papa gets back to lay this before him. I think it would be best for all concerned if Gurnard is stopped once and for all."

"Unquestionably," Sophie agreed. After a moment, she added, "I don't think it would serve any purpose to tell Clarissa. She doesn't like the man as it is; I can't see her doing anything rash."

Toby nodded.

"And I really don't think telling your mama would be a good idea."

"Definitely not." Toby shuddered at the thought.

"I suppose," Sophie suggested. "We could seek professional assistance."

"The Runners? And risk a brouhaha like they made over Lady Ashbourne's emeralds?" Toby shook his head. "That's not a decision I'd like to make."

"Quite," Sophie agreed. "Still, at least we know Gurnard's unlikely to make a move before the gala."

"Precisely." Toby's blue gaze rested consideringly on Sophie. "All we really need do is hold the fort until then."

AN HOUR LATER, Jack sat in his chair in his parlour in Upper Brook Street, the table before him spread for an early luncheon, and attacked the slices of sirloin on his plate with an air of disgruntled gloom. "Permit me to warn you, brother mine, that this wooing business is definitely plaguesome."

Harry, who had looked in on his way down to the country, raised an amused brow. "You've only just discovered that?"

"I cannot recall having wooed a lady—nor any other kind of female—before." Jack scowled at a dish of roast potatoes, then viciously skewered one.

"I take it all is not proceeding smoothly?"

For a full minute, Jack wrestled with a conscience that decreed that all matters between a lady and a gentleman were sacrosant, then yielded to temptation. "The damned woman's being noble," he growled. "She's convinced herself that I really need to marry an heiress and is determined not to ruin my life by allowing me to marry her."

Harry choked on his ale. Jack rose to come around the

table and thump his back but Harry waved him away. "Well," he said, still breathless, "that was the impression you wanted to give, remember."

"That was then, this is now," Jack answered with unshakeable logic. "Besides, I don't care what the *ton* thinks. My only concern is what goes on in one particular golden head."

"So tell her."

"I've already told her I'm as rich as Croesus, but the witless woman doesn't believe me."

"Doesn't believe you?" Harry stated. "But why would you lie about something like that?"

Jack's expression was disgusted. "Well might you ask. As far as I can make out, she thinks I'm the sort of romantic who would marry a 'lady of expectations'—her words—and then valiantly conceal the fact we were living on tick."

Harry grinned. He reached for the ale jug. "And if things had been different? If we hadn't been favoured by fortune and you'd met her—what then? Would you have politely nodded and moved on, looking for an heiress, or would you do as she suspects and conceal the reckoning?"

Jack shot him a malevolent glance. "The subject doesn't arise, thank God."

When Harry's grin broadened into a smile, Jack scowled. "Instead of considering hypothetical situations, why don't you turn that fertile brain of yours to some purpose and think of a way to convince her of our wealth?"

"Try a little harder," Harry offered. "Be your persuasive best."

Jack grimaced. "Can't be done that way; believe me, I've tried." He had, too—twice. But each time he resurrected the subject, Sophie turned huge eyes full of silent reproach upon him. Combined with a brittlely fragile air, such defences were more than enough to defeat him.

"I need someone to vouch for me, someone she'll believe. Which means I have to wait until her uncle returns to town. He's off looking over the Indies Corporation's next venture at Southampton. The damnable situation is that no one has any idea of when he'll be back."

Viewing his brother's exasperated expression, evoked, so it seemed, by the prospect of having to wait a few days to make a certain lady his, Harry raised a laconic brow. Everything he had heard thus far suggested that Jack was poised to take the final momentous step into parson's mousetrap and, amazing though it seemed, he would have a smile on his face when he did so. Love, as Harry well knew, was a force powerful enough to twist men's minds in the most unexpected ways. He just hoped it wasn't contagious.

The sound of the knocker on the door being plied with determined force disrupted their peace.

Jack looked up.

Voices sounded in the hall, then the door opened and Toby entered. He glanced at Jack, then, noticing Harry, nodded politely. As the door shut behind him, Toby turned to Jack. "I apologize for the intrusion, but something's come up and I'd like your opinion on the matter. But if you're busy I can come back later."

"No matter." Harry made to rise. "I can leave if you'd rather speak privately."

Jack raised a brow at Toby. "Can you speak before Harry?"

Toby hesitated for only an instant. Jack had spent all the Season at Sophie's feet, concentrating on nothing beyond Sophie and her court. Harry Lester, on the other hand, was by reputation as much of a hellion as Jack had been and had not shared his brother's affliction. Toby's gaze swung to Harry. "The matter concerns a Captain Gurnard."

Harry's eyes narrowed. "Captain Terrence Gurnard?" The words sounded peculiarly flat and distinctly lethal. When Toby nodded, Harry settled back into his seat. "What, exactly, is that bounder up to?"

Jack waved Toby to a seat. "Have you eaten?" When Toby shook his head, his eyes going to the half-filled platters still on the table, Jack rang for Pinkerton. "You can eat while you fill us in. I take it the problem's not urgent?"

"Not that urgent, no."

While he fortified himself, Toby recounted his outings with Gurnard and the ultimate offer to discount his losses against an arranged clandestine meeting with Clarissa.

"So you won for the first two nights but lost heavily on the third?"

Toby nodded at Harry. "He was setting me up, wasn't he?"

"It certainly sounds like it."

Jack glanced at his brother. "I've not heard much of Gurnard—what's the story?"

"That, I suspect, is a matter that's exercising the minds of quite a few of the man's creditors." Harry took a long sip of his ale. "There are disquieting rumours doing the rounds about the dear captain. Word has it he's virtually rolled up. Fell in with Duggan and crew. A bad lot," Harry added in an aside to Toby. "But the last I heard, he'd been unwise enough to sit down with Melcham."

"Melcham?" Jack tapped a fingernail against his ale mug. "So Gurnard's very likely up to his eyebrows in debt."

Harry nodded. "Very possibly over his head. And if Melcham holds his vowels, as seems very likely, his future doesn't look promising."

"Who's Melcham?" Toby asked.

"Melcham," Jack said, "is quite a character. His father was a gamester—ran through the family fortune, quite a considerable one as it happened, then died, leaving his son nothing but debts. The present earl, however, is cut from a different cloth than that used to fashion his sire. He set out to regain his fortune by winning it back from those who had won it from his father. Them and their kind, which is to say the sharps who prey on the susceptible. And he wins. Virtually always."

"The sharps can't resist the challenge," Harry added. "They line up to be fleeced, knowing Melcham's now worth a not-so-small fortune. The catch is that he's also won a lot of powerful friends—and paying one's debts is mandatory."

"In other words," Jack summed up, straightening in his chair, "Gurnard is in a lot of trouble. And once the news gets out, he'll no longer be the sort of escort wise mamas view with equanimity."

"But not yet," Harry said. "The news hasn't hit the clubs. That was privileged information, courtesy of some friends in the Guards."

Jack nodded. "All right. So Gurnard has decided that the most sensible way to get himself out of the hole he has nearly buried himself in is to marry an heiress—a very wealthy heiress."

"Clarissa?" asked Toby.

"So it appears." Jack's expression was as grim as Harry's. "And time is not on his side. He'll have to secure his heiress before his pressing concerns become public knowledge." Jack turned to Toby. "Exactly how did he want this meeting arranged?"

Toby had started to repeat the directions Gurnard had been at pains to impress upon him when the door opened and Ned walked in. Toby broke off in midsentence. Ned's amiable smile faded as he took in Toby's expression and Harry's grim face. He looked at Jack.

Jack smiled, a predatory glint in his eye. "What did Jackson say today?"

Drawing a chair up to the table, Ned dropped into it. "I have to work on my right hook. The left jab's coming along well enough." Ever since Jack had introduced him to Gentleman Jackson's Boxing Saloon, Ned had been taking lessons, having uncovered a real aptitude for the sport. His eyes slid around the table once more.

"Excellent." Jack's gaze was distant, as if viewing some invisible vista. Then he abruptly refocused on Ned. "Strangely, I believe we may have found a use for your newly discovered talents."

"Oh?" Jack's smile was making Ned uneasy.

The smile grew broader. "You want to consolidate your position in Clarissa's affections, don't you?"

"Yes," Ned admitted, somewhat cautiously.

"Well, I'm pleased to announce that a situation has arisen which calls for a knight-errant to rescue a fair damsel from the unwanted attentions of a dastardly knave. And as the fair damsel is Clarissa, I suspect you had better polish up your armour."

"What!"

It took another ten minutes to explain all to Ned's satisfaction and by then Jack had been sidetracked. "You told all this to Sophie?" he asked, fixing Toby with a disbelieving stare.

Toby looked guilty. "I couldn't avoid it—she threatened to speak to Mama."

Jack looked disgusted. "Meddlesome female," he growled, and he didn't mean Lucilla.

"I pointed out that we needn't worry until the gala. If Papa returns before that, there'll be no reason for Sophie to worry at all."

Jack nodded. "Well, don't tell her anything more. We can take care of it—and the fewer complications the better."

Toby nodded, entirely in agreement.

"But how, exactly, are we to take care of it?" Ned's expression was grimly determined.

Succinctly, assisted by helpful suggestions from his inventive brother, Jack laid their campaign before them.

By the time he'd finished, even Ned was smiling.

"Argh!" Jack stretched his arms above his head, then relaxed into his chair. "At last I think I see the light."

Harry grinned. "Think Ned can pull it off?"

The brothers were once more alone, Ned and Toby having taken themselves off with some vague intention of keeping a watchful eye on Clarissa during her afternoon's promenade in the Park.

"Think?" Jack replied. "I know it! This performance should land Clarissa firmly in his arms, relieving Sophie of further anxiety on the point and myself of the charge of overseeing that youthful romance once and for all."

"Has it been such a burden?" Harry drained his tankard.

"Not a burden, precisely. But it hurts to watch one of us succumb so young."

Harry chuckled. "Well, at least neither of us fell young, and I don't think you need worry about Gerald."

"Thank God. At least I have the excuse of being the head of the family—it's expected, after all."

"Rationalize it any way you want, brother mine; I know the truth."

Jack's blue eyes met Harry's green ones across the width

of the table. Their gazes locked, then Jack sighed. "Well, at least with Ned safely settled, I'll be able to give my full attention to a certain golden head. And with Horatio Webb's help, I'll conquer her stubbornness."

"Let me be the first to wish you happy."

Jack glanced at Harry and realized his brother was serious. He smiled. "Why thank you, brother mine."

"And I'll give you a warning, too."

"Oh?"

"The news is out."

Jack grimaced. "Are you sure?"

"Put it this way." Harry set his tankard down. "I was at Lady Bromford's affair last night, and lo and behold, Lady Argyle made a play for me. Not a blush in sight, what's more. She had her daughter in tow, a chit just out of the schoolroom." Harry wrinkled his nose. "Her ladyship was as clinging as Medusa. Totally unaccountable, *unless* she'd heard rather more than a whisper of our affairs."

"And if she's heard, others will, too." Jack grimaced even more.

"Which means it won't be long before we're the toast of the tea parties. If I were you, I'd secure your golden head with all speed. An announcement in the *Gazette* should just be enough to buy your escape. As for myself, I've decided to run for cover."

Jack grinned. "I did wonder over your sudden penchant for the lush green fields."

"In the circumstances, Newmarket looks considerably

safer than London." Harry's grin was crooked as he rose. "Given the danger, I feel confident I'll find enough in the country to keep me amused for the rest of the Season."

Jack shook his head. "You won't be able to run forever, you know."

Harry raised an arrogant brow. "Love," he declared, "is not about to catch me." With a last, long look, he turned to the door. His hand on the knob, he paused to look back, his grin distinctly wry. "Good luck. Just don't get so distracted by the excitement at the gala that you forget to keep your back covered. Until your golden head says yes, you're no safer than I."

Jack had raised his hand in farewell; now he groaned. "God help me! Just when I thought I was home and hosed."

HARRY'S DIRE PREDICTION was confirmed that evening at Lady Summerville's ball. Jack bowed gracefully over her ladyship's hand, disturbingly aware of the relish in her gimlet gaze. Luckily her duties prohibited her from pursuing him immediately, but her promise to look him up later left little doubt that his news was out. Fully alert, Jack artfully avoided two ostriched-plumed matrons, as imposing as battleships, waiting to ambush him just yards from the ballroom steps. He was congratulating himself on his escape when he walked straight into Lady Middleton's clutches.

"My dear Mr. Lester! I declare, Middleton and I have not seen much of you this year."

Biting back the retort that, if he had had his eyes about him, her ladyship would have seen even less of him, Jack bowed resignedly. On straightening, he was subjected to the scrutiny of her ladyship's protuberant eyes, grotesquely magnified by lorgnettes deployed like gunsights. "Indeed, ma'am, I fear I have been greatly occupied thus far this Season."

"Well! I hope you're not going to be too *occupied* to attend my niece's coming-out ball. She's a sweet thing and will make some gentleman an unexceptionable wife. Your Aunt Harriet was particularly fond of her, y'know." This last was accompanied by a pointed glance. Jack looked politely impressed. Her ladyship nodded, apparently satisfied. "Middleton and I will expect you."

With a snap, she shut her lorgnettes and used them to tap him on the sleeve.

Choosing to interpret this as a dismissal, Jack bowed and slid into the crowd. It was, indeed, as Harry had foreseen; despite his efforts to make his intentions crystal clear, he was not yet safe. Doubtless, nothing less than the announcement of his betrothal would convince the matchmaking mamas that he had passed beyond their reach. Yet another good reason to add to the increasingly impressive tally indicating that the speedy curtailment of Miss Sophia Winterton's Season was a highly desirable goal.

Looking about him, he spotted his quarry, elegant as ever in a gown of pale green figured silk, her curls glowing warmly in the candlelight. His height was both advantage and disadvantage, allowing him to scan the crowds but making him far too conspicuous a target. By dint of some rapid tacking by way of evasive action, he gained Sophie's side without further difficulty.

As always, his appearance coincided with a thinning of the ranks about her. Sophie no longer noticed. She gave him her hand and a warmly welcoming smile. "Good evening, Mr. Lester."

"Actually," Jack said, straightening and scanning their surroundings. "It probably isn't."

"I beg your pardon?" Sophie stared at him.

"As an evening, I've probably faced better," Jack replied, tucking her hand into his arm. "Ruthven, Hollingsworth— I'm sure you'll excuse us." With a nod for those two gentlemen, Jack led Sophie into the crowd.

Hearing Lord Ruthven chuckle, Sophie glanced back to see his lordship explaining something to a puzzled Mr. Hollingsworth. "What is it?" she asked, looking up at Jack.

"I've been pegged up for target practice."

"Whatever do you…" Sophie's words trailed away as she noticed the simpering glances thrown Jack's way—mostly by debutantes who, two days ago, would certainly not have dared. She shot a suspicious glance at Jack. "You've put the story of your fortune about?"

Under his breath, Jack growled. "No, Sophie. I have not *put* the news about. It *got* out—doubtless from the other investors involved in the Indies Corporation." He cast an exasperated glance down at her. His temper was not improved by the wary frown he saw in her eyes. "Devil take it, woman!" he growled. "No rake in his right mind, having declared his intention to wed, would then call the dragons down on his head by *inventing* a fortune."

Sophie swallowed her giggle. "I hadn't thought of it in quite that way."

"Well, do," Jack advised. "It's the truth—and you're not going to escape it. And speaking of escape, I do hope you realize that, until your uncle returns and our betrothal can be announced, I expect you to assist my cause."

"In what way?" Sophie asked.

"By lending me your protection."

Sophie laughed, but the smile was soon wiped from her face. A succession of cloying encounters set her teeth on edge; some of the warm hints directed at Jack left her positively nauseous. Somehow, he managed to keep a polite expression on his face and, by dint of his quick wits and ever-ready tongue, extricated himself from the ladies' clutches. She admired his address, and was more than ready to acquiesce to his unvoiced plea. She remained fixed by his side, anchored by his hand on his sleeve, and defied all attempts to remove her. That she managed to do so while restraining her comments to the realms of the acceptable was, she felt, no reflection on the provocation provided. Indeed, on more than one occasion she found herself blushing for her sex. Miss Billingham proved the last straw.

"My mama was quite bowled over to hear of your windfall, sir," she declared, batting her sparse lashes and simpering. "In light of our time spent together at Mrs. Webb's house party, she has charged me to ask you to call. Indeed," she went on, dropping her coy smile long enough to shoot a venomous glance at Sophie, "Mama is very keen to speak to you immediately." Greatly daring, Miss Billingham placed her hands about Jack's arm and smiled acidly at Sophie. "If you'll excuse us, Miss Winterton?"

Sophie stiffened, then smiled sweetly back. "I greatly fear, Miss Billingham," she said, before Jack would speak, "that I cannot release Mr. Lester. There's a waltz starting up." With calculated charm, Sophie smiled dazzlingly up at Jack. "Our waltz, I believe, Jack."

Jack's slow smile was triumphant. "Our waltz, dear Sophie."

They left Miss Billingham, open-mouthed, staring after them.

Sophie was seething as they took to the floor. "How *dare* she? How can they? They're all quite shameless. I thought it was only rakes who were so."

Jack chuckled and drew her closer. "Hush, my sweet Sophie." When she glared in reply, her full breasts swelling with indignation, he brushed a most reprehensible kiss across her curls. "It doesn't matter. You're mine—and I'm yours. When your uncle returns, we can tell the world."

Sophie took comfort in the warmth of his gaze, and in the delight she saw behind it. Did he really find it so surprising that she would fly to his aid?

Whatever the case, she thought, as she felt the waltz, and

him, weave their accustomed magic, Horatio had better return soon. In such difficult circumstances, there was no telling what scandalous declaration she might feel obliged to make.

CHAPTER FOURTEEN

GALA NIGHT AT VAUXHALL was a treat few among the *ton* cared to miss. With their party, swollen by the presence of Jeremy and Gerald, who had been included by special dispensation, Sophie strolled beside Jack down the Grand Walk. She saw many familiar faces, all bright with expectation of the night's revelries. None were as bright as hers.

She glanced up at Jack and smiled, feeling her brittle tension tighten. Horatio was due back tonight; her uncle had sent word that despite the business that had delayed him, he would return this evening to join them at the Gardens. Jack smiled back, his hand warm over hers where it rested on his sleeve. He said nothing, but the expression in his eyes left her in no doubt of his thoughts.

Determined at least to appear calm, Sophie gave her attention to their surroundings, duly exclaiming at the brightly lit colonnade, which had been added since her last visit. Jeremy and George, and, to a lesser extent, Toby, Ned and Clarissa, looked about with avid interest, speculating on the age of the elms lining the gravelled promenade and eyeing the dense shrubbery separating the walks.

"I think the booth your uncle has rented is this way."

Jack steered her to the right of the section of promenade known as the Grove. Toby followed with Lucilla on his arm, Ned and Clarissa behind with the two boys bringing up the rear. In the centre of the Grove, a small orchestra was setting up. Arranged about the perimeter were a large number of wooden booths, many already filled with patrons come to enjoy the night's entertainments.

Their booth proved to have an excellent view of the orchestra.

"Ah, yes." Lucilla settled herself on a chair by the wide front window. "A most satisfactory location. From here, one can see almost everything."

Sophie noticed her aunt's gaze was not on the musicians. Indeed, it seemed as if all of fashionable London were a part of the passing scene. Gentlemen and ladies of all degrees strolled upon the paths; many stopped to exchange pleasantries with her aunt before moving on. Then there were the bucks and their ladybirds, the bright lights of the *demi-monde*. Sophie found herself fascinated by one particular redhead—or rather her gown, a wispy concoction of silk and feathers that barely concealed her charms. Until she noticed the interest the lady evinced in return, and realized it was not for her. A frown threatening, Sophie glanced at her companion—the focus of the red-head's attention—only to find he was watching her. A slow smile lifted his lips; one dark brow rose.

Sophie blushed vividly, and pointedly transferred her gaze to the orchestra. As if sensing her need, they promptly laid bow to string, filling the night with their magic. Soon, a bevy of couples was whirling in the light of the Chinese lanterns, suspended high overhead.

Jack rose. "Come," he said, holding out his hand, a smile and an invitation in his eyes. "No one counts the dances at Vauxhall."

For an instant, Sophie met his gaze. Then, with a calm decisiveness that surprised even her, she lifted her chin and put her hand in his. "How accommodating."

Her uncle had better arrive soon; she couldn't bear to wait much longer.

Luckily, Jack proved most efficient at distracting her, until her mind was filled with nothing beyond thoughts of him, of his teasing smile and the beckoning warmth behind his blue eyes. He danced with her twice, then relinquished her to Ned, who in turn passed her to Toby before Jack once more drew her into his arms.

Sophie laughed. "I find myself quite breathless, sir."

Jack smiled down at her, a slow crooked smile. "Jack," he said.

Sophie looked into his eyes; her breath vanished altogether. "Jack," she whispered, letting her lashes fall.

Jack's arm tightened about her; he swept her into the waltz.

Supper was provided in the booth, laid out on a narrow trestle table at the rear, along with a jug of lemonade and another of the famous Vauxhall punch. When they lifted the linen cloths from the dishes, they found delicate cucumber sandwiches, a selection of pastries and a large platter of the fabled wafer-thin ham.

"Exactly as I recall," Lucilla declared, holding up one near-transparent slice. She looked at Sophie. "When your mother and I were debs, we were always famished after a night at Vauxhall." Nibbling the ham, she added, "I told Cook to lay out a cold collation for when we get back."

Jack, Ned and Toby looked relieved.

Somewhere in the gardens, a gong clanged. The music had stopped some minutes before and the heavy note vibrated through the twilight.

"Time to view the Grand Spectacle!"

Jeremy's shout was echoed from all around. There was a surge of bodies as people left their booths to join the throng flocking to where a looming mountain, now brilliantly lit, rose craggily from amidst the otherwise unremarkable landscape. Fifteen minutes were spent in oohing and aahing at the various elements, some mechanical, others purely decorative, artfully placed within the alpine scene. Then the lights were doused. Chattering and exclaiming, the patrons returned to the walks, the booths and the dancing.

The last of their company to return to their booth, Sophie and Jack strolled through the twilight, her hand on his arm. She could feel the tension that gripped him, lending steel to the muscles beneath her fingertips.

"Sophie?"

Wreathed in shadows, Sophie looked up.

Jack stared at the pale oval of her face, the wide eyes

and slightly parted lips. For a moment, he was still, then, concealed by the shadows, he bent his head and swiftly kissed her.

Sophie's lips met his, her heart leaping at the brief caress. Her hands fluttered; her arms ached to hold him.

Jack caught her hands. "Not yet, sweetheart." His smile was decidedly crooked. "Just pray your uncle's carriage doesn't break an axle."

Sophie sighed feelingly and allowed him to resettle her hand on his sleeve.

Covering her hand with his, Jack gently squeezed her fingers. "We'd better get back to the booth." As they strolled out of the shadows, he added, "The fireworks come later."

Puzzled, Sophie looked up. "I hadn't imagined fireworks to be one of your abiding interests."

Jack glanced down at her, then his slow, rake's smile curved his lips. "There are many kinds of fireworks, my dear."

For an instant, Sophie glimpsed the dark, powerful passions behind his blue eyes. A distinctly delicious sensation slithered down her spine. But further discovery was denied her; they were caught up in the dancers and dragged into the heart of the revels once more.

The orchestra was now accompanied by a vocalist, a tenor whose pure notes drifted high over the booths to disappear into the increasing darkness. Stars speckled the sky as night slowly enfolded the scene. The Chinese lanterns came into their own, shedding their rosy glow over dancers and musicians alike. Laughter and the mellow murmur of conversation, softer now, muted by the effects of good food and fine wines, rippled through the shadows.

Throughout the evening, again and again, Sophie's eyes met Jack's. A magical web held them bound; neither was aware of those about them. And what passed between them was magical, too, carried in the weight of shared glances and the lingering touch of lovers' hands.

Their surroundings were part of the magic. At the conclusion of the musical interlude, the tenor embarked on a solo performance. Breathless, conversing softly, the dancers headed back to their booths. As she strolled on Jack's arm, Sophie noticed Belle Chessington on the arm of Mr. Somercote—surely a most unlikely Vauxhall patron. Belle waved and smiled hugely, her eyes sparkling. Mr. Somercote, too, smiled broadly, clearly both pleased and proud.

"Well, well," Jack murmured. "You'll have to tell your aunt she's achieved a minor miracle. Somercote's silence has been tripping the matchmakers up for years. It looks as if he's finally found his tongue."

Sophie laughed. "Indeed, you have to admit he won't need many words, not with Belle on his arm."

Jack smiled, then looked ahead.

And tensed. Sophie felt it, and followed his gaze to see the rotund figure of her uncle clearly visible in their booth.

"Just in time." Jack quickened his pace.

As they entered the booth, Lucilla beckoned to Sophie. "Mrs. Chessington just stopped by. Wonder of wonders!"

From the corner of her eye, Sophie saw Jack greet

Horatio. They exchanged a few words, Jack very serious, then both turned and left the booth.

Subsiding onto the chair beside her aunt, Sophie forced herself to concentrate enough to follow Lucilla's discourse. It proved a supremely difficult task. Her hands clasping and unclasping in her lap, she was acutely conscious of every little sound, every movement in the booth.

She jumped when the gong rang again.

"The fireworks!"

Once more, the patrons poured from the booths and from the shadowy walks, heading for a small arena surrounded by lawns. Smiling indulgently, Lucilla allowed Jeremy and George to tug her to her feet. Sophie rose uncertainly, glancing about. Ned offered Clarissa his arm; together with Toby they joined the exodus. Jack was nowhere to be seen.

"There you are, m'dear." Horatio materialized outside the booth. "Come along now or you'll miss the fun."

Sophie stared at him, her heart sinking all the way to her slippers. Hadn't Jack asked? Why wasn't he here? Did that mean..? Forcing her shaking limbs to function, she picked up her half-cape. Swinging it about her shoulders, she left the booth.

Horatio offered her his arm. They started to stroll slowly in the wake of the others, now far ahead. But instead of joining his family, Horatio stopped in the shadows, well to the rear of the crowd.

"Now, my dear Sophie, I understand you have had some reservations about Jack's financial situation."

Slowly, Sophie turned to face her uncle, her heart thudding in her throat. She held herself proudly, a silent prayer on her lips.

Apparently oblivious, Horatio rattled on. "It really was quite remiss of him, I agree. He should have told you much earlier. But you'll have to excuse him—not but what, with his experience, you might have expected a little more than the usual impulsive rush. But men in love, you know, tend to forget such minor matters as money." Smiling genially, he patted Sophie's hand.

Sophie drew in a slow, deep breath. "Uncle, are you telling me that Jack is truly wealthy? That he doesn't need to marry a rich bride?"

Horatio's grey eyes twinkled. "Let's just say that for him, expectations alone will be a more than sufficient dower."

A golden rocket burst in a flurry of brilliant stars, gilding Sophie's face. Her eyes shone, reflecting the glory.

"Oh, Uncle!" Sophie flung her arms about Horatio's neck.

Horatio chuckled and reciprocated her, then gently turned her. "Come, let's join the festivities."

Sophie was only too ready to do so. She peered into the darkness, eagerly searching the crowd every time another rocket lit up the scene. They found Lucilla and the boys in the front ranks. The boys pounced on Horatio, bombarding him with questions.

Then a large wheel lit up the night, hissing and spitting as the force of the rockets tied to its spokes whirled it round.

In the midst of the crowd, Sophie stood very still, her face slowly draining of expression. The steadier illumination confirmed beyond doubt that Jack, Ned and Toby were not present. Neither was Clarissa.

The memory of Gurnard's plan rushed into Sophie's mind, thrusting all other considerations aside. This was the time Toby was to have taken Clarissa to meet the dastardly captain. Yet Ned had been with them—he wouldn't let any harm come to Clarissa. But where were they? If Jack, Ned and Toby had gone to warn off the captain, where was Clarissa?

Sophie blinked in the glare of a set of coloured flares; elation, guilt and sheer frustration poured through her in a dizzying wave.

Horatio would know. She looked to where her uncle stood, Lucilla beside him, George's hand in his. Jeremy was throwing questions at his father in a never-ending stream. There was no possibility of speaking to Horatio without alerting Lucilla and, potentially worse, the boys.

Everything was probably all right; Jack would surely have the matter in hand.

But maybe Jack was elsewhere, ignorant of Gurnard's threat? Perhaps Toby and Ned had decided to handle it on their own? And Clarissa had followed?

Sophie turned and quietly made her way back through the crowd.

The majority of the patrons were viewing the fireworks, leaving the walks sparsely populated. Here and there, a couple or a small group still wandered, having seen the fireworks too many times. But the crush of revellers that had filled the walks earlier had given way to empty shadows.

Just beyond the booths, Sophie slowed. The Dark Walk, with the Temple of Diana, lay furthest afield, the narrowest and most heavily shaded of the Gardens' promenades. And the most secluded.

Grimacing, Sophie halted. It would be the height of folly to risk the length of the Dark Walk at night, alone. But if she went back up the Grand Wall, wide and well lit, she could take a side path across to the Dark Walk, emerging just a little above the Temple. It was longer, but she was far more certain to reach her goal by that route.

Clutching her cape about her, she turned and hurried up the Grand Walk.

At the Temple of Diana, deep in the shadows of the Dark Walk, Jack waited with Toby, concealed in thick bushes by the temple's side. A small structure in the Ionic style, the temple was little more than a decorative gazebo. The surrounding bushes had grown close over the years, filling the side arches until the space within resembled a room with green walls.

Jack peered through the shadows. Toby had delivered Clarissa to the temple at the appointed time. Ned had earlier hidden himself on the other side of the main archway, awaiting his moment of glory. Gurnard, however, was late.

The scrunch of heavy footsteps on gravel brought Jack's head up. Out on the path, the figure of a man came into view,

heading purposefully towards the temple. He made no attempt to conceal his approach;
a guardsman's red cape was thrown over one shoulder.

"Here he comes," hissed Toby.

They waited, frozen in the shadows, as Gurnard climbed the short flight of steps and disappeared into the temple.

"So far so good," Jack whispered.

Inside the temple, however, all was not going as either they, or Captain Gurnard, had planned.

Clarissa, delivered by a strangely serious Toby to the dim temple with a promise that her most ardent suitor—Ned, of course—would shortly join her, had entered the shadowy hall with high hopes. It was clear that Sophie would shortly receive the offer she desired; Clarissa, having expended considerable effort in encouraging Ned, expected that he would, tonight, at least take a more definite step in his wooing of her. With any luck, he might kiss her. Why else had he asked her here?

As the minutes ticked by, she had fallen to pacing, hands clasped behind her, her brow furrowed as she wondered how fast she could urge things along. A marriage in September, assuming Sophie did not opt for a long betrothal, seemed a distinct possibility.

She had reached this point in her cogitations when firm footsteps approached and ascended to the temple.

Starry-eyed, Clarissa turned.

And beheld the unmistakable outline of Captain Gurnard.

"What are you doing here?" she demanded, not the least

bit pleased at the prospect of having her tryst with Ned interrupted or—even worse—postponed.

Terrance Gurnard blinked. "Why, I'm here to meet you, my dear."

"I'm afraid, sir, that my time this evening is spoken for." If nothing else, Clarissa was Lucilla's daughter. She delivered the captain's dismissal with an affronted dignity that would have done justice to royalty.

For a moment, Gurnard was bewildered. Where was the youthful, wide-eyed innocent he had arranged to meet? Then he shook himself. The hoity young miss was just playing hard to get. "Nonsense, my dear," he purred, advancing on Clarissa. "We all know you're besotted with me. But fear not, for I'm equally besotted with you."

Even in the dimness, Gurnard could not misinterpret the icy rigidity that laid hold of Clarissa's slim frame. She drew herself up and, somehow, succeeded in looking down her nose at him. "My dear Captain, I believe you have lost your wits." The cool incisiveness in her tone bit deep. "If you will but consider, the notion that I, with suitors such as Mr. Ascombe, could consider you, who have nought but your uniform to commend you, is highly insulting, sir!"

Rocked by the strident vehemence in her tone, Gurnard blinked. Then he sneered. "You were ready enough to encourage me to dangle after you—do you deny it?" Abruptly, he closed the gap between them. He did not have all night to accomplish what he must.

"That was because you were being useful." Clarissa, her

own considerable temper in orbit, continued with undisguised relish, "Useful in ensuring that *Mr. Ascombe's* attention did not wander."

"Useful, was I?" Gurnard ground out. "In that case, my dear, you'll have to pay the piper." Roughly, he grasped her arms, intending to pull her to him.

Used to wrestling with her brothers, Clarissa anticipated the move enough to wrench one arm free. "Let me *go,* sir!"

Her furious shriek jolted Ned from the dazed stupor into which he had fallen. He shot up the steps, only just remembering their plan in time to change his automatic. "Unhand her, you fiend!" to a relatively normal, if slightly strangled, "Clarissa?"

He saw her immediately, one arm held by Gurnard. With an heroic effort, assisted by the calming effects of the cold rage that poured through him, Ned strolled lazily forward. "There you are, m'dear. I apologize for my tardiness, but I was held up." Commandingly, he held out his hand to Clarissa, his gaze, coldly challenging, fixed on Gurnard's face.

In order to take her hand, Clarissa chose to use the arm Gurnard was holding. She did so without in any way acknowledging Gurnard's grasp, much less his presence.

The action snapped Gurnard's patience. He had no time to play games, nor to brook interference of any sort. He waited until, as Clarissa's fingers slipped into Ned's palm, Ned glanced at her. Then he attacked.

And was immediately sent to grass—or marble, as was the case—by a punishing left jab.

In the bushes to the side, Jack allowed the battle-ready tension that had instantly gripped him to fade. "He said his left jab was coming along."

Inside the temple, Ned frowned, attempting to shield Clarissa from the sight of the captain stretched out on the marble floor. "I'm sorry, Clary. Not the sort of thing one should do in front of a lady, I know. You aren't feeling faint or anything, are you?"

"Good heavens, no!" Clarissa, eyes alight, both hands clutching one of Ned's forearms, peered around him at the captain's prone form. Satisfied that the captain was, at last temporarily, beyond further punishment, she turned her glowing eyes on Ned. "That was *marvellous,* Ned! How *thrillingly* heroic. You rescued me!"

And with that, Clarissa promptly hurled herself into her knight errant's arms.

The watchers in the bushes heard Ned mutter something that sounded like a weak disclaimer but his heart was clearly not in it. Then came silence.

Jack sighed and relaxed, looking up into the night sky, considering, with a certain rakish satisfaction, the prospect of the immediate future. Beside him, Toby shifted restlessly.

Then they heard Ned's voice, and Clarissa's replying; the pair turned, still hand in hand, Clarissa's head against Ned's shoulder, and made slowly for the steps.

"We'll follow," Jack said. "They may be almost betrothed but they're not betrothed yet."

They followed Clarissa and Ned at a distance; it was questionable whether either was aware of their presence.

When they reached the booth, it was to find Horatio beaming benevolently, and Ned standing, proud but a trifle hesitant, as Clarissa poured the details of her rescue into her mother's ear. Jeremy's and George's eyes were wide as they drank it all in. Seeing Jack, Lucilla smiled and asked, "Where's Sophie?"

Ned and Clarissa looked blank.

Toby blinked.

Jack froze—and looked at Horatio.

Suddenly serious, Horatio frowned. "I spoke with her, then we joined Lucilla and the boys. At the end of the fireworks display, Sophie had disappeared. I thought she was with you."

"She must have gone to the temple," Toby said, genuinely horrified.

"Gurnard's still there," Ned pointed out.

"I'll find her." Jack kept his expression impassive, despite the emotions roiling within. He exchanged a look with Horatio, who nodded. Striding to the door, Jack spared a glance for Lucilla. "Don't worry," he said. The smile that accompanied the words held a certain grim resolution.

Somewhat subdued, the rest of the party settled to listen to the last of the music.

"You know," Lucilla murmured as Horatio took the seat beside her. "I'm really not sure we've done the right thing."

"How so?"

"Well, I'm quite sure Sophie can handle Captain Gurnard. But can she handle Jack Lester?"

Horatio smiled and patted her hand. "I'm sure she'll contrive."

ON GAINING the Dark Walk, Sophie paused to catch her breath. Peering through the shadows, she could just make out the distant glimmer of the temple's white pillars, set back in a small grove. The path leading to the water-gate lay nearby; somewhere beyond the temple lay one of the less-used street gates.

Dragging in a deep breath, Sophie quit the shadows. There was no one about. Her soft slippers made little sound on the gravel as she neared the temple steps. Standing at the bottom, she peered in but could see nothing but shadows. Surely Clarissa could not be inside?

For a full minute, she vacillated, then, holding her cape close about her, Sophie mounted the steps. If there was no one inside, it couldn't hurt to look.

The shadows within enveloped her. Sophie glanced about, then stifled a shriek as a dark shape loomed beside her.

"Well, well, well. Come to look for your cousin, I take it?"

As the shape resolved itself into Captain Gurnard, Sophie gave an almost imperceptible gasp. Straightening, she nodded. "But as she isn't here—"

"You'll do just as well."

The captain wrapped one hand about Sophie's arm.

Instinctively, she tried to pull away. "Unhand me, sir! What on earth do you believe can come of this?"

"Money, my dear Miss Winterton. Lots of money."

Sophie remembered his scheme. "You appear to have overlooked something, Captain. I am not an heiress."

"No," Gurnard acknowledged. "You're something even better. You're the woman Lester's got his eye on."

"What's that supposed to mean?" Sophie carefully tested the captain's hold.

"It means," Gurnard sneered, convincing her his grip was unbreakable by shaking her, "that Lester will pay and pay handsomely to have you returned to him. And he'll pay even more to ensure you're…unharmed, shall we say?"

Sophie recoiled as Gurnard thrust his face close to hers. "It seems Lester's windfall is to be *my* gain." With an abrupt laugh, he turned and dragged her towards the door. "Come on."

Dredging up every ounce of her courage, Sophie went rigid and pulled back. Her full weight served only to slow the captain, but it was enough to make him turn with a snarl.

Sophie lifted her chin, refusing to be cowed. "There is, as I said, something you appear to have overlooked, Captain. I am *not* going to marry Mr. Lester."

"Gammon," said Gurnard, and tugged her on.

"But I'm *not!*" Sophie placed her free hand over her heart. "I swear on my mother's grave that Mr. Lester has not asked for my hand."

"It's not my fault if he's backward." They had almost reached the top of the steps.

Sophie lost her temper. "You imbecile! I'm trying to make it plain to you that I am *not going to marry Jack Lester!*"

Gurnard stopped and turned to her, fury in every line of his large frame. "You," he began, pointing a finger at her.

"Should learn to accept Fate graciously."

There was a split second of silence, then Gurnard turned.

Only to meet a left jab that had a great deal more power behind it than the one he'd met earlier.

The result was the same. The captain's head hit the marble with a resounding thump.

Sophie glared down at him, prostrate at her feet. "Of all the unmitigated scoundrels," she began.

Jack shook his head and sighed. "Are you and your cousin so lost to all sensibility that you can't even swoon at the sight of violence?"

Sophie blinked at him, then humphed. "If you must know, I'm feeling quite violent myself. Did you know he intended to—"

"I heard." Jack reached for her and drew her to him. "But you don't need to worry about him any more."

Sophie readily went into his arms. "But shouldn't we—"

"It's already taken care of." Jack looked down at Gurnard, then prodded him with the toe of his boot. His victim groaned. "I sincerely hope you're listening, Gurnard, for I'm only going to say this once. I've had a word with an acquaintance of mine, the Earl of Melcham. He was most upset to hear of the method you'd selected to raise the wind.

He doesn't approve—not at all. And I'm sure you know what happens to those of whom Melcham disapproves."

There was a stunned silence, then Gurnard groaned again.

Grimly satisfied, Jack turned Sophie towards the steps. "And now, my dear, I think it's time we left." Tucking her hand in his arm, he led her down onto the gravelled walk.

Sophie went readily, her mind seething with questions. "What happened to Clarissa? Did she go to the temple?"

Jack glanced down at her. "She did."

Sophie glared at him. "What happened?"

Jack smiled and told her, adding that Horatio had approved their scheme. "If Clarissa had simply not shown up, Gurnard would have assumed she'd been prevented from doing so, not that she wouldn't go to meet him. He'd have tried again to get her alone, and perhaps we wouldn't have learned of his intentions in time to foil him. It was best to make the situation as clear as possible."

"But what if he turns to some other young lady?"

"He won't have time. As of tomorrow, courtesy of Melcham, to whom Gurnard is deeply in debt, the captain will have entirely too much on his mind to think of persuading any other young lady to his rescue."

Sophie pondered his revelations, her feet following his lead. "So Ned floored the captain?"

"He seems to have floored Clarissa as well." Jack's lips curved in fond reminiscence. He slanted a glance at Sophie. "We all thought the opportunity too good to miss to advance Ned's standing with your cousin."

For an instant, Sophie stared into his smugly satisfied face. Then she burst out laughing. "Oh, dear. Was that supposed to be Ned's great scene—so that Clarissa would think him her hero and respond suitably?"

Frowning, Jack nodded.

"Oh, poor Ned." Sophie could not stop smiling. She glanced confidently up at Jack. "Just for your information, Clarissa settled on Ned some weeks ago, not all that long after we'd come up to town. She's been trying to nudge him along for the past two weeks at least. I'm not at all surprised to hear she flung herself into his arms. After all, what better opportunity she could hope for?"

Jack looked down at her through narrowed eyes. "Remind me," he said, "to tell Ned just what he's getting into, marrying a Webb female."

Sophie pressed her lips tightly together. When she was sure her voice was under control, she said, "I'm related to the Webbs; does that make me a 'Webb female', too?"

Jack's glance was supercilious. "I haven't yet decided."

It was then, when he stood back to usher her through the watergate, that Sophie realized that they had been walking in the wrong direction. A leafy lane stretched before them. Not far ahead, the lane ended by the banks of the Thames. Sophie halted. "Ah…Jack…?"

Jack looked down at her and held out his hand. "Your uncle's returned. He spoke to you, didn't he?"

"Yes." Eyes wide, Sophie studied his face. "He told me there's no reason we can't marry."

"Precisely." Jack smiled, closing his hand about the fingers she had automatically surrendered. He drew her closer and tucked her hand into the crook of his arm. "Which is to say that by common consent, general agreement and the blessing of Fate, my wait is, at long last, over."

"But shouldn't we..?" Sophie glanced back at the dark shrubbery of the Gardens, slowly receding in their wake.

Jack cast her a reproving glance. "Really, my dear. You don't seriously imagine that *I,* such as I am, could consider Vauxhall a suitable venue for a proposal, do you?"

There seemed no sensible answer to that.

But Sophie had no time to ponder the implications. They had reached the water's edge. She glanced about, somewhat surprised at the bustling scene. A stone wharf lined the river and extended out in a jetty where a small flotilla of pleasure craft bobbed gently at their moorings.

"If habits linger, he'll be at the end."

A most peculiar sensation started to creep along Sophie's nerves. She clung to Jack's arm as they wended their way between Garden patrons haggling with the boatmen, and others embarking for a slow ride home. The craft were of a variety of sizes, some holding no more than a couple, while others could comfortably carry a small party. Still others had canopies erected over their bows under which lovers could pursue their acquaintance in privacy, screened by drapes which let down about the sides.

It was towards one of these last that Jack led her.

"Rollinson?"

Sophie suddenly felt quite light-headed.

The beefy boatman in charge of the largest and most opulent craft turned from desultory conversation with his crew to peer up at Jack. "There you be, Mr. Lester!" He grinned, displaying a row of decidedly haphazard teeth, and tipped his felt hat to Sophie. "Got your message. We're here and ready, sir."

"Very good," Jack replied.

Sophie found it hard to follow the rest of their conversation, at least half of which was conducted in boatman's cant. She glanced about, trying to interest herself in the scene, rather than dwell on what their presence here probably meant. If she thought of that, she might feel obliged to protest.

As it was, she was not to escape making some part of the decision on her fate. Their itinerary agreed upon, Jack leapt down to the wooden planking of the boat's hull, which floated a good yard below the jetty.

He then turned to study Sophie, one brow rising. "Well, my dear?" With a graceful gesture, he indicated the boat and the curtain cutting off the bow. His slow, slightly crooked smile twisted his lips. "Will you trust yourself to me tonight?"

For an instant, Sophie stared down at him, oblivious of those about them, of the sly yet careful glances cast her by the boatmen. All she could see was Jack, waiting for her, a very definite glint in his eyes. For an instant, she closed her own. What he was suggesting was perfectly scandalous. Drawing in a deep breath, she opened her eyes and, with a soft smile, stepped to the edge of the jetty.

The familiar feel of Jack's hands about her waist was reassuring, soothing the peculiar jitteriness that, all of a sudden, had afflicted her. He set her down beside him, one arm slipping about her to steady her as he helped her across the rowing benches. Parting the heavy damask curtain that screened the bow, he ushered her through.

Sophie entered a private and very luxurious world of moonlight glinting on water. The curtain fell closed behind them, sealing them in. With a slight lurch, the boat got under way. Jack's arm came to urge her to a seat as the boat nosed out onto the river. Once clear of the craft by the jetty, the boat pulled smoothly, powerfully, upstream.

As her eyes adjusted to the deep shadows beneath the canopy, Sophie, fascinated, gazed about. She was seated amid a pile of huge silk cushions spread over a satin-draped platform, heavily padded, that was constructed to fit snugly across the bow. The platform all but filled the area behind the curtain, leaving barely enough room for a wine cooler, which, she noticed, contained a bottle, already open and chilling, and a small fixed buffet holding glasses and small dishes of unidentifiable delicacies. Jack turned from examining the buffet's offerings to look down at her.

"I think we'll leave the caviar for second course."

Sophie's eyes widened. She didn't need to ask what he fancied for the first. His eyes, even in the shadows, gleamed as they rested on her. Clearing her throat, suddenly dry, she asked, a trifle unsteadily, "You planned this?"

His smile was smugly triumphant. "To the last detail,"

Jack averred, coming to lounge on the cushions beside her. "It's customary, you know."

"Is it?" Sophie stared at him.

"Mmm-hmm." Jack leaned back, gazing upward to where the canopy overhead was drawn partially back, revealing the black velvet of the sky sprinkled with jewelled stars. "Seductions are never so satisfying as when they're well-planned."

Sophie bit her lip and eyed him warily.

His gaze on her face, Jack laughed and, reaching up, drew her down to lie among the cushions beside him. Sophie hesitated, then yielded to his gentle strength. Propped on one elbow, Jack smiled down into her wide eyes. Then he bent his head and kissed her, long and lingeringly, before whispering against her lips, "I'm not teasing, Sophie."

A thrill of desire raced through Sophie, all the way down to her toes. She opened her lips on a feeble protest—and Jack kissed her again. And kept kissing her until she had no breath left to speak.

"No, Sophie." Jack dropped soft kisses on her eyelids as his fingers deftly unbuttoned her gown. "I've had more than enough of wooing you, my love. You're mine, and I'm yours. And nothing else matters." His voice deepened at the last as he looked down at her breast, the firm ivory flesh filling his palm.

Sophie arched lightly as his thumb circled the rosy peak. Unable to speak, barely able to breathe, she watched him from beneath heavy lids as he caressed her. Then he lowered his head and she stopped breathing altogether, her fingers sinking into his shoulders as his tongue lightly teased, knowingly tantalized.

"Besides," Jack murmured against her soft skin. "We've only one thing left to discuss."

"Discuss?" The word came out weakly on a slow exhalation, the best Sophie could manage, her mind struggling against the drugging haze of his caresses.

"Hmm. We have to discuss what I'll accept as suitable recompense for my torture."

"Torture?" Sophie knew about torture. She was being tortured now, his hands touching her so skilfully she was gripped by an urgent longing. "What torture?"

"The torture of having to woo you, sweet Sophie."

Sophie stirred, consumed by the sweetest ache. "Was it torture?"

"Torture and worse," Jack vowed, his voice deep and raspy.

Sophie sighed. "What do you consider suitable recompense?" She just managed to get the words out before he stole her breath again with a caress so artful she thought she could faint. She didn't, but the sensations didn't stop, darting through her like lightning, spreading like warm fire beneath her skin.

Aeons filled with pleasure seemed to have passed before she heard his soft murmur.

"I know what I want as my reward for wooing you. Will you give it me?"

"Yes." Her voice was a soft whisper on the breeze.

Jack raised his head, a smile twisting his lips. "I haven't yet told you what I want."

Sophie returned his smile with one of her own. "It had better be me—for that's all I have to give you."

For the first time in his rakish career, Jack was lost for words. He looked down into her eyes, passion-filled and mysterious. "Sophie." His voice was hoarse, dark with his turbulent passions. "You're all I'll ever want."

"Then take me," Sophie murmured, wondering, very distantly, how she dared. She reached up and drew his lips to hers before her sane self could resurface and disturb the glorious moment.

Thereafter, her sanity or otherwise was not in question; desire caught her and held her until she glowed with its flame. Jack fed her fires, never letting her cool, until she ached for him to join her. When he did, it was as if the sun shone brightly out of the night-dark sky. Sophie surrendered to joy and delight and rapturous, delirious pleasure. For one timeless moment, she felt that she had flown so high she could touch the stars gleaming in the firmament. Then she softly drifted back to earth, safe, forever, in Jack's strong arms.

The gentle rocking of the boat, and Jack's heavy weight, drew her slowly back to reality.

Surprisingly, Sophie found her mind oddly clear, as if the sensations that had held her body in thrall had proved so overpowering that her wits had disengaged and retreated to a safe distance. She could feel the cool caress of the river breeze on her naked skin and her lover's touch as, propped now beside her, he gently stroked her hair from her face. She opened her eyes and looked up. He was a dark shadow as he hung over her, solid and comforting in the moonlight. Sophie listened for the shush of the water under the hull— and made a discovery. "We're not moving."

Jack's smile gleamed in the moonlight. "We're moored. Off a private park. The men left us nearly an hour ago." He reached up to spread out her curling hair, released from its moorings. "They'll come back later and take us home. My carriage will be waiting at the steps."

Sophie blinked. "You really did think of everything."

His smile grew broader. "I always aim to please." He shifted slightly, drawing her more comfortably into his arms and tucking a silk shawl tenderly about her. "And now that I've pleased you, how soon can we be wed?"

Still slightly dazed, Sophie stared up at him, marshalling her wandering wits.

"Not that I'm trying to rush you, my love, but there are any number of reasons why an early, if not immediate, wedding would suit us best."

As he turned her hand over to press a kiss into her palm, and the touch of his lips stirred the embers that were only now dying within her, Sophie abruptly nodded. "I see your point." She stopped to clear her throat, amazed she could think at all. "My father's due back for a quick visit next month—can we wait until then?"

Jack raised his head to look down at her. "It might be

hard." He smiled, his usual crooked smile. "But I suspect we can wait until then."

Sophie sighed, deeply content. She put up a hand to brush back the dark locks from his forehead. "You'll have to marry me; you've thoroughly compromised me. We've been away for far too long."

"I always intended to marry you. From the moment I first saw you in Lady Asfordby's ballroom."

Sophie studied his face in the moonlight. "Did you really?"

"From the moment I saw you dancing with that upstart Marston," Jack admitted. "I was smitten then and there."

"Oh, Jack!"

After the necessary exchange of affection brought on by that revelation, Sophie was the first to return to reality. "Dear Heaven," she exclaimed weakly. "We've been gone for hours."

Jack caught the hint of concern dawning in her voice. "Don't worry. Horatio knows you're with me."

Fascinated, Sophie stared at him. "Did you tell my aunt, too?"

"Good God." Jack shuddered. "What a horrible thought. If I had, I'd lay odds she'd have given me instructions. I don't think my pride could have stood it." Jack dropped a soft kiss on one delectable rosy peak. "Your aunt, my love, is just plain dangerous."

Privately, Sophie agreed but was far too distracted to find words to say so. Sometime later, her mind drifting in dazed consideration of the future he had spread before her, the home, the family—everything she had ever wanted—with him by her side, she returned to his point. "Speaking of marriage, sir, you have not yet asked me to marry you."

"I have—you quibbled and refused."

Sophie smiled into the night. "But you're supposed to ask me again, now that my uncle has given me permission to receive your addresses."

Jack sighed lustily, then shifted to move over her, one elbow planted on either side, his expression arrogantly commanding. His eyes, deep dark pools within which passion still smouldered, transfixed her.

"Very well, Miss Winterton. For the *very last time—will* you marry me? I realize, of course, that you are only a lady of expectations and not an heiress. However, as it transpires, I neither need nor want a wealthy bride. You, my beautiful, desirable Sophie—" Jack bent his head to do homage to her lips "—will do just wonderfully. You, my love, fulfil all *my* expectations." Another kiss stole her breath. "Every last one."

A soft smile curving her lips, her gaze misty with happiness, Sophie reached up to slide her arms about his neck. Her acceptance was delivered, not in words but in those actions which, to her mind, and Jack's spoke best.

AS THE WEBB CARRIAGE rocked into motion, leaving the shadows of Vauxhall behind, Lucilla sank back against the squabs. On the opposite seat, Jeremy and George yawned and closed their eyes, their faces wreathed in seraphic smiles. Behind, in the smaller carriage, Toby, Ned and Clarissa were doubtless still exclaiming over their exciting evening. Lucilla, however, was not impressed.

She had just been informed that Jack would be returning Sophie to Mount Street by a different route.

It was several long moments before she trusted herself to speak.

"And you told *me* not to meddle." With an audible humph, she cast a disgusted glance at her spouse.

Horatio was too wise to answer. He smiled serenely, glancing upriver as the carriage rattled over the bridge.

* * * * *

Find out what happens next with
the Lester family and turn the page to read an excerpt
from *An Unwilling Conquest*.

CHAPTER ONE

"IS IT THE DEVIL we're running from, then?"

The question, uttered in the mildest of tones, made Harry Lester wince. "Worse," he threw over his shoulder at his groom and general henchman, Dawlish. "The matchmaking mamas—in league with the dragons of the *ton*." Harry edged back on the reins, feathering a curve at speed. He saw no reason to ease the wicked pace. His match greys, sleek and powerful, were quite content to keep the bits between their teeth. His curricle rushed along in their wake; Newmarket lay ahead. "And we're not running—it's called a strategic retreat."

"Is that so? Well, can't say I blame you," came in Dawlish's dour accents. "Who'd ever have thought to see Master Jack landed—and without much of a fight, if Pinkerton's on the up. Right taken aback, is Pinkerton." When this information elicited no response, Dawlish added, "Considering his position, he is."

Harry snorted. "Nothing will part Pinkerton from Jack—not even a wife. He'll swallow the pill when the time comes."

"Aye—p'raps. Still, can't say I'd relish the prospect of answering to a missus—not after all these years."

Harry's lips quirked. Realising that Dawlish, riding on the box behind him, couldn't see it, he gave into the urge to smile. Dawlish had been with him forever, having, as a fifteen-yearold groom, attached himself to the second son of the Lester household the instant said son had been put atop a pony. Their old cook had maintained it was a clear case of like to like; Dawlish's life was horses—he had recognised a master in the making and had followed doggedly in his wake. "You needn't worry, you old curmudgeon. I can assure you I've no intention, willingly or otherwise, of succumbing to any siren's lures."

"All very well to say so," Dawlish grumbled. "But when these things happen, seems like there's no gainsaying them. Just look at Master Jack."

"I'd rather not," Harry curtly replied. Dwelling on his elder brother's rapid descent into matrimony was an exercise guaranteed to shake his confidence. With only two years separating them, he and Jack had led much the same lives. They'd come on the town together more than ten years ago. Admittedly, Jack had less reason than he to question love's worth, nevertheless, his brother had been, as Dawlish had observed, a most willing conquest. The fact made him edgy.

"You planning on keeping from London for the rest of yore life?"

"I sincerely hope it won't come to that." Harry checked the greys for a slight descent. The heath lay before them, a haven free of matchmakers and dragons alike. "Doubtless my uninterest will be duly noted. With any luck, if I lay low, they'll have forgotten me by next Season."

"Wouldn't have thought, with all the energy you've put into raising a reputation like you have, that they'd be so keen."

Harry's lip curled. "Money, Dawlish, will serve to excuse any number of sins."

He waited, expecting Dawlish to cap the comment with some gloomy pronouncement to the effect that if the madams of society could overlook his transgressions then no one was safe. But no comment came; his gaze fixed unseeing on his leader's ears, Harry grudgingly reflected that the wealth with which he and his brothers, Gerald as well as Jack, had recently been blessed, was indeed sufficient to excuse a lifetime of social sins.

His illusions were few—he knew who and what he was— a rake, one of the wolves of the *ton*, a hellion, a Corinthian, a superlative rider and exceptional breeder of quality horseflesh, an amateur boxer of note, an excellent shot, a keen and successful huntsman on the field and off. For the past ten and more years, Society had been his playing field. Capitalising on natural talents, and the position his birth had bestowed, he had spent the years in hedonistic pleasure, sampling women much as he had the wines. There'd been none to gainsay him, none to stand in his path and challenge his profligate ways.

Now, of course, with a positively disgusting fortune at his back, they'd be lining up to do so.

Harry snorted and refocused on the road. The sweet

damsels of the *ton* could offer until they were blue in the face—he wasn't about to buy.

The junction with the road to Cambridge loomed ahead. Harry checked his team, still sprightly despite their dash from London. He'd nursed them along the main road, only letting them have their heads once they'd passed Great Chesterford and picked up the less-frequented Newmarket road. They'd passed a few slower-moving carriages; most of the gentlemen intent on the week's racing would already be in Newmarket.

About them, the heath lay flat and largely featureless, with only a few stands of trees, windbreaks and the odd coppice to lend relief. There were no carriages approaching on the Cambridge road; Harry swung his team onto the hard surface and flicked the leader's ear. Newmarket—and the comfort of his regular rooms at the Barbican Arms—lay but a few miles on.

"To y'r left."

Dawlish's warning growl came over his shoulder in the same instant Harry glimpsed movement in the stand of trees bordering the road ahead. He flicked both horses' withers; as the lash softly swooshed back up the whip-handle, he slackened the reins, transferring them to his left hand. With his right, he reached for the loaded pistol he kept under the seat, just behind his right boot.

As his fingers closed about the chased butt, he registered the incongruity of the scene.

Dawlish put it into words, a heavy horse pistol in his

hands. "On the king's highway in broad daylight—never-you-mind! What's the world a-coming to, I asks you?"

The curricle sped on.

Harry wasn't entirely surprised when the men milling in the trees made no attempt to halt them. They were mounted but, even so, would have had the devil of a time hauling in the flying greys. He counted at least five as they flashed past, all in frieze and heavily muffled. The sound of stifled cursing dwindled behind them.

Dawlish muttered darkly, rummaging about re-stowing his pistols. "Stap me, but they even had a wagon backed up in them trees. Right confident of their haul the must be." Harry frowned.

The road curved ahead; he regathered the slack reins and checked the greys fractionally.

They rounded the curve—Harry's eyes flew wide.

He hauled back on the reins with all his strength, slewing the greys across the road. They came to a snorting, stamping halt, their noses all but in the low hedge. The curricle rocked perilously, then settled back on its springs.

Curses turned the air about his ears blue.

Harry paid no attention; Dawlish was still up behind him, not in the ditch. Before him, on the other hand, was a scene of disaster.

A travelling carriage lay on its side, not in the ditch but blocking most of the road. It looked as if one of the back wheels had disintegrated; the ponderous contraption, top-heavy with luggage, had toppled sideways. The accident had only just occurred—the upper wheels of the carriage were still slowly rotating. Harry blinked. A young lad, a groom presumably, was struggling to haul a hysterical girl from the ditch. An older man, the coachman from his attire, was hovering anxiously over a thin grey-haired woman, laid out on the ground.

The coach team was in a flat panic.

Without a word, Harry and Dawlish leapt to the ground and ran to calm the horses.

It took a good five minutes to soothe the brutes, good, strong coach horses with the full stubbornness and dim wits of their breed. With the traces finally untangled, Harry left the team in Dawlish's hands; the young groom was still helplessly pleading with the tearful girl while the coachman dithered over the older woman, clearly caught between duty and a wish to lend succour, if he only knew how.

The woman groaned as Harry walked up. Her eyes were closed; she lay straight and rigid on the ground, her hands crossed over her flat chest.

"My ankle—!" A spasm of pain twisted her angular features, tight under an iron-grey bun. "Damn you, Joshua—when I get back on my feet I'll have your hide for a footstool, I will." She drew her breath in in a painful hiss. "*If* I ever get back on my feet."

Harry blinked; the woman's tones were startlingly reminiscent of Dawlish in complaining mode. He raised his brows as the coachman lumbered to his feet and touched his forehead. "Is there anyone in the carriage?"

The coachman's face blanked in shock.

"Oh my God!" Her eyes snapping open, the woman sat bolt upright. "The mistress and Miss Heather!" Her startled gaze fell on the carriage. "Damn you, Joshua—what are you *doing,* mooning over me when the mistress is likely lying in a heap?" Frantically, she hit at the coachman's legs, pushing him towards the carriage.

"Don't panic."

The injunction floated up out of the carriage, calm and assured.

"We're perfectly all right—just a bit shaken." The clear, very feminine voice paused before adding, a touch hesitantly, "But we can't get out."

With a muttered curse, Harry strode to the carriage, pausing only to shrug out of his greatcoat and fling it into the curricle. Reaching up to the back wheel, he hauled himself onto the body. Standing on the coach's now horizontal side, he bent and, grasping the handle, hauled the door open.

Planting one booted foot on either side of the coach step, he looked down into the dimness within. And blinked.

The sight that met his eyes was momentarily dazzling. A woman stood in the shaft of sunshine pouring through the doorway. Her face, upturned, was heart-shaped; a broad forehead was set beneath dark hair pulled severely back. Her features were well defined; a straight nose and full, well-curved lips above a delicate but determined chin.

Her skin was the palest ivory, the colour of priceless

pearls; beyond his control, Harry's gaze skimmed her cheeks and the graceful curve of her slender neck before coming to rest on the ripe swell of her breasts. Standing over her as he was, they were amply exposed to his sight even though her modish carriage dress was in no way indecorous.

Harry's palms tingled.

Large blue eyes fringed with long black lashes blinked up at him.

For an instant, Lucinda Babbacombe was not entirely sure she hadn't sustained a blow on the head—what else could excuse this vision, conjured from her deepest dreams?

Tall and lean, broad-shouldered, slim-hipped, he towered above her, long, sleekly muscled legs braced on either side of the door. Sunlight haloed his golden locks; with the light behind him she could not make out his features yet she sensed the tension that held him.

Lucinda blinked rapidly. A light blush tinged her cheeks; she looked away—but not before she registered the subdued elegance of his garments—the tightly-fitting grey coat, superbly cut, style in every line, worn over clinging ivory inexpressibles, which clearly revealed the long muscles of his thighs. His calves were encased in gleaming Hessians; his linen was crisp and white. There were, she noted, no fobs or seals hanging at his waist, only a single gold pin in his cravat.

Prevailing opinion suggested such severe attire should render a gentleman uninteresting. Unremarkable. Prevailing opinion was wrong.

He shifted—and a large, long-fingered, extremely elegant hand reached down to her.

"Take my hand—I'll pull you up. One of the wheels is shattered—it's impossible to right the carriage."

His voice was deep, drawling, an undercurrent Lucinda couldn't identify sliding beneath the silken tones. She glanced up through her lashes. He had moved to the side of the door and had gone down on one knee. The light now reached his face, illuminating features that seemed to harden as her gaze touched them. His hand moved impatiently; a black sapphire set in a gold signet glimmered darkly. He would need to be very strong to lift her out with one arm. Subduing the thought that her rescue might well prove a greater threat than her plight, Lucinda reached for his hand.

Their palms met; long fingers curled about her wrist. Lucinda brought her other hand up and clasped it about his—and she was airborne.

She drew in a swift breath—an arm of steel wrapped about her waist; her diaphragm seized. She blinked—and found herself on her knees, held fast in his embrace, locked breast to chest with her unnerving rescuer.

Her eyes were on a level with his lips. They were as severe as his clothes, chiselled and firm. His jaw was distinctly squared, the patrician line of his nose a testimony to his antecedents. The planes of his face were hard, as hard as the body steadying hers, holding her balanced on the edge of the carriage doorframe. He had released her hands;

they had fallen to lie against his chest. One of her hips was pressed against his, the other against his muscled thigh. Lucinda forgot about breathing.

Cautiously, she lifted her eyes to his—and saw the sea, calm and clear, a cool, crystalline pale green.

Their gazes locked.

Mesmerised, Lucinda drowned in the green sea, her skin lapped by waves of warmth, her mind suborned to sensation. She felt her lips soften, felt herself lean into him—and blinked wildly.

A tremor shook her. The muscles surrounding her twitched, then stilled.

She felt him draw breath.

"Careful," was all he said as he slowly rose, drawing her up with him, holding her steady until her feet could find purchase on the carriage.

Lucinda wondered just what danger he was warning her against.

Forcing his arms from her, Harry struggled to shackle his impulses, straining at their leash. "I'll have to lower you to the ground."

Peering over the carriage side, Lucinda could only nod. The drop was six feet and more. She felt him shift behind her; she jumped as his hands slipped beneath her arms.

"Don't wriggle or try to jump. I'll let go when your coachman has hold of you."

Joshua was waiting below. Lucinda nodded; speech was beyond her.

Harry gripped her firmly and swung her over the edge. The coachman quickly grasped her legs; Harry let go—but could not prevent his fingers from brushing the soft sides of her breasts. He clenched his jaw and tried to eradicate the memory but his fingertips burned.

Once on *terra firma,* Lucinda was pleased to discover her wits once more at her command. Whatever curious influence had befuddled her faculties was, thank Heaven, purely transitory.

A quick glance upwards confirmed that her rescuer had turned back to render a like service to her stepdaughter. Reflecting that at barely seventeen Heather's susceptibility to his particular brand of wizardry was probably a good deal less than her own, Lucinda left him to it.

After one comprehensive glance about the scene, she marched across to the ditch, leaned over and dealt Amy, the tweeny, a sharp slap. "Enough," she declared, as if she was speaking of nothing more than kneading dough. "Now come and help with Agatha."

Amy's tear-drenched eyes opened wide, then blinked. "Yes, mum." She sniffed—then shot a watery smile at Sim, the groom, and struggled up out of the thankfully dry ditch.

Lucinda was already on her way to Agatha, prone in the road. "Sim—help with the horses. Oh—and do get these stones out of the road." She pointed a toe at the collection of large, jagged rocks littering the highway. "I dare say it was one of these that caused our wheel to break. And I expect you'd better start unloading the carriage."

"Aye, mum."

Halting by Agatha's side, Lucinda bent to look down at her. "What is it and how bad?"

Lips compressed, Agatha opened iron-grey eyes and squinted up at her. "It's just my ankle—it'll be better directly."

"Indeed," Lucinda remarked, getting down on her knees to examine the injured limb. "That's no doubt why you're white as a sheet."

"Nonsense—oooh!" Agatha sucked in a quick breath and closed her eyes.

"Stop fussing and let me bind it."

Lucinda bade Amy tear strips from her petticoat, then proceeded to bind Agatha's ankle, ignoring the maid's grumbles. All the while, Agatha shot suspicious glances past her.

"You'd best stay by me, mistress. And keep the young miss by you. That gentleman may be a gentleman, but he's a one to watch, I don't doubt."

Lucinda didn't doubt either but she refused to hide behind her maid's skirts. "Nonsense. He rescued us in a positively gentlemanly manner—I'll thank him appropriately. Stop fussing."

"Fussing!" Agatha hissed as Lucinda drew her skirts down to her ankles. "You didn't see him move."

"Move?" Frowning, Lucinda stood and dusted her hands, then her gown. She turned to discover Heather hurrying up, hazel eyes bright with excitement, clearly none the worse for their ordeal.

Behind her came their rescuer. All six feet and more of him, with a lean and graceful stride that conjured the immediate image of a hunting cat.

A big, powerful predator.

Agatha's comment was instantly explained. Lucinda concentrated on resisting the urge to flee. He reached for her hand— she must have extended it—and bowed elegantly.

"Permit me to introduce myself, ma'am. Harry Lester— at your service."